Isle of Broken Dreams

Mike Farris

ISBN 978-1-941071-96-0
eBook ISBN 978-1-941071-97-7

Other books by Mike Farris
The Bequest

STAIRWAY≡PRESS

The Armchair Adventurer

An Armchair Adventurer book
STAIRWAY PRESS—SEATTLE

www.stairwaypress.com
1500A East College Way #554
Mount Vernon, WA 98273

Cover Design by Chris Benson, BensonCreative www.BensonCreative.com

Acknowledgements

MY FRIEND KAREN Hamilton is the one who, knowing of my love for all things Hawaiian, first directed my attention to the world of Hotel Street during World War II. *Isle of Broken Dreams* seemed to naturally flow from my research, so many thanks to Karen for the "heads up." I want to thank my agents, Donna Eastman and Gloria Koehler, for their untiring efforts on my behalf in getting my books published. And I also want to thank the great people at Stairway Press—Ken Coffman, Stacey Benson, and Chris Benson. *Isle of Broken Dreams* is my second book with Stairway and hopefully not my last. Thanks, Ken, Stacey, and Chris, for all your hard work.

Dedication

To Susan, with *aloha nui loa.*[1]

---

[1] *Aloha nui loa*: all my love.

PART ONE

ARRIVAL AT HOTEL STREET

Chapter One
November 30, 1941

EARLY ON SUNDAY morning, at the first second of the first minute of the first hour of the first day of the eighteenth year of his life, Private First Class Tommy Tucker from the east Texas town of Lufkin woke up in his bunk at Schofield Barracks, on the island of Oahu, with two things on his mind: an erection and a determination to end his virginity. He believed that accomplishing the latter would resolve the former, and he knew that Hotel Street was the ideal place for both.

The brothels in Hotel Street didn't open until 9 a.m., but lines formed early on weekends and paydays. He had heard that men sometimes stood in line as long as two or three hours on particularly busy days. He had never been much of a whiz at arithmetic, indeed he had dropped out of high school before even learning basic algebra, but it didn't take Albert Einstein to know that the sporting girls would service dozens of men during the busy times, and he'd be damned if he wanted his girl to be worn out by the time she got to him.

He didn't sleep a wink the rest of the night, eager to join his buddies before dawn in the first taxi headed for Honolulu. He tossed and turned, his hand occasionally drifting inside the front of his skivvies. He tried to get his mind off of his engorged parts by mentally reciting lines from his favorite movies. At 2:30 a.m., he switched to reciting *Bible* verses. He hoped his Southern Baptist upbringing, where boys and girls were segregated socially and lustful activities such as dancing were forbidden, might help tame the fires. He soon switched to poetry, though, concerned that the image of his grandmother, chin hairs and all, reading the Good Book to him at the kitchen table might undermine his plans enough to make the trip to Hotel Street nothing more than a dry run.

The night seemed to last forever, but before daybreak, he and half the barracks were dressed and headed to the nearby taxi stand for the half-hour trip to town. By 8:00, he was on the brink of Nirvana, standing in line on the sidewalk leading to the Polynesian Rooms on Beretania Street in Honolulu. At least fifty men dressed in service uniforms—khaki-colored soldiers from Schofield and the Army Air Corps base at Hickam Field, and white-suited sailors from the ships at Pearl Harbor—were already in line ahead of him. He considered going to one of the other houses, but lines had already formed outside of them, as well. He would spend more time unsuccessfully searching for a shorter line than he would spend standing in this one.

He'd been to Honolulu before, even been to the section known as Hotel Street before, but never to "climb the stairs," as the boys put it. Rather than being a single street, it encompassed several blocks in a corner of Chinatown, bounded by Hotel, River, Beretania, and Nu'uanu Streets. Colorful in a way that Tommy had known only from pulp novels, the area was marked by fish markets, penny arcades, tattoo parlors, bars, and street concessionaires selling everything from jewelry and popcorn to post cards. Jabbering native shoeshine boys hawked their services for a quarter while teenaged girls sold flower leis and posed in grass skirts for pictures in front of fake palm trees. Bars bore names like Trade Winds, Two Jacks, and Just Step In, most with a four drink minimum, all four of which were often served at once, while burly bouncers encouraged customers to quickly drink up and move out, to make room for the next customer.

But the real attraction of Hotel Street was the fifteen "houses of entertainment," with names such as New Senator Hotel, Palace Hotel, Rainbow Hotel, and The Bronx Rooms. Heavyset Polynesian women regularly stood at the entrances to each, like Sumo wrestlers, with folded arms and stern visage, as if eager to kick some unruly ass, should the need arise. These "houses of entertainment" featured one form of entertainment and one form only: sex. And you could call them "sporting girls" all you wanted. Everyone knew what they really were: whores.

Hotel Street was where you came to get screwed, stewed, and tattooed.

And that was Tommy's plan for the day. Once he'd climbed the stairs at the Polynesian Rooms and paid his three dollars for three minutes, he planned to get drunk and then get tattooed. It would be a birthday he'd never forget.

Tommy clutched three one-dollar bills in his right hand as he whiled away the time talking with other men in line and fending off shoeshine boys who were insistent that his already polished shoes needed their attention. Anticipation mounted with each passing minute, but so did fear. Tommy didn't want to admit it, but he was petrified. He had been seventeen when he joined the Army after dropping out of high school during his junior year. The closest he had come to what was about to transpire was copping a feel on a local girl back home in Lufkin who, for a dollar, took off her shirt behind the tool shed at her grandfather's house, which was next door to where Tommy lived, and a dance hall girl in San Francisco while he was waiting to ship out to Oahu, who took him to a hotel, stripped him, then drugged him and absconded with his wallet while he was passed out.

At exactly nine a.m., a roar went up from men ahead of him. Tommy stepped into the street and strained to look to the front of the line. The Polynesian Rooms' doors were open and men were starting to funnel inside. Blood roared in his ears and raced to his groin, which surged. The smell of perspiration blended with odors of fish from the markets and urine and stale vomit from the alleys. He wondered if there were any other first-timers, but most of the men near him looked older, and none wore the same look of wide-eyed innocence that likely betrayed his secret. Maybe it was just his imagination, but he was sure they were all experienced in the ways of sex, ready to laugh at the virgin as he climbed the stairs for the first time. Embarrassed, he held his hands clasped together in front of him, hoping to hide the tell-tale clues of his excitement. But when he looked more closely at the others, he saw that *every last one of them was doing the same damn thing.*

The line moved quickly, almost too fast. He'd had all night and most of the morning to anticipate, but now it seemed as if the awaited climax might arrive before he could prepare himself for it. For a man who had never "known" a woman, in the Biblical sense, the real danger didn't lie in not being able to finish; it lay in finishing too soon.

The buzz of voices grew silent the closer they got to the door, almost as if the men were entering a church—where they all should have been on a Sunday morning. Tommy realized that everyone was nervous. Some, like himself, more than others, but no one was immune. He kept his hands in front and shuffled in the door, past the surly-looking bouncer woman who must have weighed two-hundred-fifty pounds. She was dark-skinned and dark-haired and dark-eyed, and Tommy thought he detected a hint of a smile on her face as he passed by. He felt his face redden, so he turned away to escape her bemused stare. Yep, she knew he was a virgin.

The line extended up a narrow stairwell next to a hall leading deeper into the hotel. A light clicked on in Tommy's head. "Climb the stairs." That was the phrase the boys used when they talked about going to Hotel Street. He never knew where most of the slang expressions he heard in the Army had come from, but this one suddenly made perfect sense. Next time someone said, "Let's go climb the stairs," he'd know exactly what they were talking about. It might even be a term that, merely hearing or speaking it, would spark an erection.

A caged booth waited at the top of the stairs where the boys paid their three dollars. A hand-stenciled sign was affixed to the front of the cage, just above the transaction counter: MEN ARE VERY FICKLE AND UNTIL A MAN IS IN THE TRICK ROOM HE HAS A RIGHT TO CHANGE HIS MIND. Tommy supposed that meant something, but damned if he knew what it was.

The woman inside the cage appeared to be in her forties, but who knew, really, what a woman's age was? The one thing Tommy did know was that you never asked a woman how old she was. She was attractive in a hardened sort of way, but her face was an emotionless mask. Was she one of the girls? No, probably not. They wouldn't let the girls handle the money. He figured she was most likely the house's madam. He hoped the girls were friendlier. And younger.

A hallway extended behind the cage, with rooms on either side and chairs outside of each. Young, scantily-clad women flitted from room to room. And by scantily-clad, he meant damn near naked. They wore flimsy robes or housecoats, unbuttoned in front, flashing glimpses as they ducked into open doorways. He worried, again, that he might reach his climax before he laid his money down.

He hesitated at the top of the stairs, money clutched in his sweaty hand. Was it too late to back out now? To just turn around and bolt down the stairs? He hadn't seen any of his buddies since they emptied the taxi, so no one would know if he chickened out. He could simply go back to Schofield and brag how he had serviced the girls, instead of being serviced, and no one would be the wiser.

"Come on, son," the caged woman said. She spoke sharply, her tone businesslike. "Step on up. Don't be shy."

A sailor pushed him forward. He staggered to the booth, aware that he was now the subject of everyone's attention, with a crimson letter "V," for virgin, on his back.

"First time?" the woman asked.

Tommy thought he detected a softer tone to her voice, almost motherly. His mind flashed back to Lufkin, Texas, and his own mother. A flush of shame colored his cheeks, which the woman apparently took as embarrassment.

"Yes, ma'am."

"Well, she won't bite you."

"No, ma'am."

"Three dollars."

He handed over the money, clutched in a ball. She uncrumpled it and handed him a red poker chip. He wondered if there was any significance to the red color. Why didn't she hand him one of the blue chips? Were those reserved for the more experienced men?

"Wait in the chair outside bullpen number three," she said. "Give this to her and she'll take care of the rest."

"Yes, ma'am. Thank you, ma'am."

He took the chip and tucked it in his pocket. As he started down the hallway, she called after him. "Don't lose your load before she's ready. No refunds, junior."

Cheeks burning, he hustled to the wooden chair designated for bullpen number three, as the men in line laughed. Thank God none of his buddies were with him. He would never live this down.

His butt barely touched the wooden seat when a very young Chinese woman came out of number three, a bundle of wadded linens clutched in her arms.

"You go inside," she said. "First one." Then she scurried away.

Tommy stepped inside the doorway. The room had been divided into three cubicles by flimsy wooden partitions that failed to reach the ceiling. He interpreted the Chinese woman's cryptic instructions to mean he was to stay in the first cubicle, which contained a single low cot, a table with a wash bowl and an alarm clock, and a wastebasket. A soiled towel lay on the floor.

He stood next to the cot, confused as to what to do next. From the other side of the partition, he heard the unmistakable sounds of the obvious—squeaks of a cot, and human grunts and moans. The sounds were distinctly male, with no female accompaniment. The only person having fun—or having anything, for that matter—was the man, not the woman. The bulge in his trousers throbbed.

The Chinese woman came in and scooped up the wadded towel from the floor. "Take clothes off," she said.

He stared at her, uncomprehending. Was she the girl? Surely not. He wanted a white woman.

She put a folded towel next to the wash bowl then hurriedly threw a threadbare sheet over the cot and tucked the edges in. When she turned back around, he was still standing there.

"Take clothes off now," she said, a command in her tone. "No waste time."

Then she was gone. Tommy unbuttoned his shirt and pulled it off as the sounds next door crescendoed. He sensed he had little time to get ready. He unbuckled his pants and pulled them down just as the male voice next door groaned, followed by a loud exhale of satisfaction, then a sigh.

There was a shuffling sound. A female voice said, "Come see me again, darlin'."

Then footsteps.

Tommy stripped off his pants and underwear and sat on the edge of the cot, his shoes and socks still on.

A woman came around the partition and considered him closely. He felt his erection wilt under her scrutiny, but then it kicked into high gear as her flimsy robe gapped open. He took her to be in her thirties. She didn't wear much make-up, just a light dusting on her cheeks and red lipstick. She was tall, maybe five-six or -seven, full-breasted, thin-waisted, and red-haired. He tried to keep his eyes off her bust and her silky triangle, which was also red. She might be a whore, but he was a gentleman and didn't want to offend her by staring.

She smiled and held out her hand. He stood and shyly shook it.

"No, son, I need your chip."

"Oh."

He grabbed his pants from the floor, extracted the chip from the pocket, and handed it to her. She dropped it into the pocket of her robe, where it clinked against others. He wondered how many were in there. What number was he that morning?

She took the folded towel and dipped a corner into the wash bowl to wet it, then knelt in front of him. His cheeks heated up again.

"Let's just check out your equipment," she said.

She reached for him. He flinched, drew in his pelvis, and pulled away. If she touched him now, it might be all over in an embarrassing and messy instant.

"Now come on," she said. "I'm not gonna hurt you."

"It's not that. It's just that——" He stopped. How do you explain to a woman like this that you're a virgin? How long since she was a virgin? Could she even understand what this was like for him?

"First time?" she asked.

He thought he detected a tone of tenderness. He found that Hotel Street was making him an expert in reading and interpreting female tones.

"Yes, ma'am."

"Well, it's not mine. I'll go easy with you, and maybe we can stretch this out at least a minute or two. But I've still got to check you out and clean you. Those are the rules."

He nodded and turned his head away. He didn't want to watch as she handled his most private part. She gently washed him with the dampened towel then dropped the cloth on the floor.

"Okay, you're good."

She took off her robe and let it drop. Although she lived in Hawaii, it was as if she had never been in the sun. Her skin was white as alabaster and smooth as silk. Tommy had never seen anyone so beautiful.

She sat on the edge of the cot, then swung her feet on top as she lay back and nestled her head in a small feather pillow. She parted her knees and spread her legs. He stared at her, as if he had never seen such a sight before. In fact, he never had.

"Come on, boy, we're on the clock here. You got three minutes."

"Yes, ma'am."

"And don't call me ma'am. You call your mama ma'am, and I don't think you'd do this with your mama, would you?"

"No, ma'am," he said, leaving the "hell, no" unspoken.

"Get on top, and I'll take it from there. You just enjoy the ride."

"Yes, ma'am."

She reached out and took him by the hand. Very gently.

"Come on, boy, I haven't killed anyone yet." But he figured he might just be the first.

He climbed on top of her and positioned himself, while she guided him in. She grabbed the clock from the bedside table and set the alarm for three minutes.

Then she began to buck and grind, lifting her hips and thrusting with a frenzied rhythm. Tommy hung on like a cowboy at the rodeo, content to let her do the work. After a few seconds, heat rose in his groin. He began to moan as an imminent explosion readied itself inside him.

While Norma Staunton was taking Private Tommy Tucker to the pinnacle of ecstasy at Madam Francis O'Brian's Polynesian Rooms, the *Kido Butai*—a Japanese aircraft carrier strike force under the command of Vice-Admiral Chuichi Nagumo—pushed its way across the north Pacific. Featuring the carriers *Akagi*, *Kaga*, *Soryu*, *Hiryu*, *Shokaku*, and *Zuikaku*, with more than four hundred attack aircraft onboard, the *Kido Butai* had departed four days earlier from Hittokapu Bay, in the Kurile Islands north of Hokkaido, under the utmost secrecy. Its target?

Pearl Harbor.

Chapter Two
December 2

STANDING AT THE rail of the *S.S. Lurline*, the crown jewel of the Matson Lines' luxury liners—the "White Ships"—nineteen-year-old Sadie MacKenzie realized that she had come an awfully long way from home. She remembered very little about Oklahoma, other than never having enough to eat, blowing dust, and then Daddy loading up the truck with all their belongings, Mama tucking her and her little brother Billy in the middle between herself and Daddy, and driving all the way to California in search of a new life. What she knew of California was being called an Okie, never having enough to eat, Daddy leaving one day and never coming home, Mama getting sick and taking Billy to an orphanage before she died, and then being on her own. And now here she was, heading west again, looking to start another new life.

She closed her eyes, turned her face skyward, and allowed the sun to heat her skin while the breeze cooled it at the same time. It rustled her auburn hair that she had unpinned and allowed to cascade around her shoulders. A few loose strands blew across her cheek, tickling her. If she opened her mouth, she could taste the salt, much as she used to swallow mouthfuls of dust back in Oklahoma. Even though she was alone now, she knew that things were going to be better once she arrived in Hawaii. Someday she might even be able to send for Billy and bring him over to live with her. The thought made her smile.

When she opened her eyes again, she sensed someone looking at her. Turning her head slightly, so as to utilize her peripheral vision, she saw nearby a handsome gentleman, at least fifty years of age, wearing a dapper straw hat over his graying hair and a lightweight white linen suit with a bow tie. She had seen him onboard over the past few sailing days, always in a group with others, always smiling, always in control. As far as she knew, he had taken no prior notice of her until then, the day before they were to arrive in Honolulu. He, too, was leaning on the rails and gazing seaward, though she noted that his glance repeatedly drifted her way. She was not a conventional beauty by any means, standing nearly five feet eight inches, but precariously thin, at least in her own estimation. Her eyes were green, but she felt they had been dulled by the hard life she had lived. What was there to see in her by a man of any age?

The next time he glanced her way, she turned and met his gaze. "How are you today, sir?" she asked.

He did not seem at all flustered that she had caught him staring at her. "I'm doing quite well, young lady," he said. "And you?"

"Just enjoying the sun and the sea breezes."

"First time to the Islands?"

"First time anywhere," she said, "if you don't count Oklahoma."

"Yes, I've been there a time or two, and I always considered myself quite fortunate to get on the gone side of leaving. Still, I believe that, in all fairness, it must count."

She laughed, and he smiled at the sound of her voice.

"Mighty young to be traveling by yourself, aren't you?" he asked.

"I'll have you know I'm nigh on to twenty-years-old," she said, trying to fill her voice with righteous indignation, half-hearted though it was. She was not insulted, merely disappointed that she didn't appear older to him. "Some would wonder why I've waited this long to travel by myself."

He chuckled and took off his hat. "I meant no offense by it. Youthfulness is a virtue." He moved closer and extended his hand. "The name's Joshua Sinclair, ma'am."

She took the fingers of his hand with hers and nodded slightly. "I am Sadie MacKenzie, of San Francisco."

"I'm pleased to make your acquaintance, Sadie MacKenzie of San Francisco."

She removed her hand and clutched it with the other, then turned and leaned on the rail again. "Do you live in Honolulu, Mr. Sinclair?"

"I have a home and an office there, but I spend a good deal of time on the mainland."

"Is Hawaii as beautiful as they say? I've only seen it in travel brochures."

He turned to face the ocean, leaning on the rail next to her. "Indeed it is. I've traveled many places in this world, but I prefer the Islands to all of them."

"I just know I'm going to love it there. I can't wait until we arrive tomorrow."

"What is the purpose of your trip? Going to visit relatives?"

"Oh, no. I'm going to live there. I'm on my way to a job. I'm going to be an entertainer."

A broad smile lit up Joshua's face. "Is that right? Well, maybe I'll catch your show. Where will you be performing?"

"It's a place called the Polynesian Room."

The smile froze on Joshua's face. "Polynesian Room? Or 'Rooms'?"

She sensed a shift in his tone. "I suppose you're right. It is 'Rooms.' It's on Hotel Street. Do you know where that is?"

He nodded, almost as if unable to verbalize a response. She turned to face him, concerned that perhaps he wasn't feeling well. "Mr. Sinclair, are you all right?"

"Yes, yes, I'm fine, dear."

"Is it pretty? The Polynesian Rooms, I mean?"

"I don't know. I've never been there."

She turned seaward again. "I wonder if there will be a crowd when I perform."

"I'm given to understand that there is always a crowd for the entertainers. I have, myself, seen lines outside the doors on occasion."

"Oh, that's wonderful."

He stared at her while she gazed at the water. She felt his eyes on her, as she had earlier, so she again turned to face him. "Is something the matter, Mr. Sinclair?"

"Miss MacKenzie, how much do you know about Hotel Street?"

"Oh, not much, really. I just know that they need entertainers to perform for our boys in uniform. And that's what I'm going to do. Miss Francis O'Brian has paid for my passage, and I'm going to work for her." She paused then added, "I'm going to be a star."

Joshua appeared to be a man at a loss for words. "Miss MacKenzie—" He stopped abruptly.

"Yes, Mr. Sinclair?"

He reached into his vest pocket and extracted a business card, then handed it to her. "Miss MacKenzie, should I ever be able to be of assistance to you while you're in Honolulu, please let me know. Any time, day or night."

She held up the card and read the words aloud. "'Joshua L. Sinclair, Esquire. Attorney-at-law.'" She put the card in the pocket of her dress and smiled at him. "Why, thank you, Mr. Sinclair. I don't believe I've ever met a lawyer before."

"Lawyers are a dime a dozen, Miss MacKenzie."

"Well, I'm mighty proud to make your acquaintance. And should you ever wish to see me perform, you let me know, as well. You can be my guest."

With a broad smile, she turned seaward again as Joshua walked away without looking back.

Joshua returned below deck to his *lanai* suite with a heavy heart. Even the luxury accommodations, with a separate dressing room, bathroom, and sitting room with a floor-to-ceiling window overlooking the Pacific, could not distract him from his concern. The young lady he had spoken to on deck had an innocence about her that clashed with his understanding of Hotel Street. She seemed naïve, yet spoke with the surety of one who was certain of her path. She said she was to be an entertainer on Hotel Street, and everyone knew what "entertainer" meant on Hotel Street. Indeed, the sporting girls, as they were also called, obtained "entertainment" licenses from the police department for the grand sum of one dollar per year.

And she spoke of having her passage paid by Francis O'Brian, whom Joshua knew, by reputation, as madam of the Polynesian Rooms. Madams routinely paid agents on the mainland anywhere from five hundred to a thousand dollars to procure women in places such as San Francisco, then paid their way to Honolulu. Most of the women, however, were experienced prostitutes, and Miss Sadie MacKenzie did not seem to fit that bill. Not by a long shot.

But it was none of Joshua's affair, really, what the young woman chose to do with her life. If Juanita were here, she would tell him to keep his nose where it belonged. "Don't involve yourself in the troubles of others without invitation." That was often her suggestion to him, which he considered damn good advice, and which he sometimes dispensed himself. As an attorney, he often involved himself in the troubles of others, but for a handsome fee and, as Juanita suggested, only at their invitation. The young woman on deck had not extended such an invitation, nor had she sought an advisory opinion. Nor, in fact, did she seem to be troubled about her destination despite her apparent knowledge. If she needed him, she had his card. If she extended an invitation, he would accept. But until then, he would mind his own business.

He removed his coat and hat, slipped out of his trousers and hung them in the closet, then lay on the bed to take a nap before dinner. He could not get the image of Sadie MacKenzie, with her angelic smile, out of his mind. He couldn't quite put his finger on it, but he knew in his heart—he *knew*—that she was sailing blindly toward an abyss that would destroy her soul if someone didn't warn her. He didn't know why he cared about a woman he had just recently met. Maybe it was because she was the age his own daughter would have been had she not fallen victim to tuberculosis just as the stock market was crashing. He had planned well and adequately protected his meager wealth at the time, but his obsession with doing so had resulted in neglect of his wife and child. Although Angela had not fallen victim to malnutrition, as had so many during the Great Depression, she was surely just as dead, as if she had.

Somehow Sadie MacKenzie had avoided a similar fate. Somehow she had survived the demise of the American economy. How had she done so? Had it been by trading sexual favors for money? Was that the path that now led her to Hotel Street? That didn't seem possible, as she had no markings of a prostitute in either her appearance or manner. Had her survival been insured by caring, loving parents who, unlike him, had nurtured their child through difficult times? If so, where were those parents now, sending their daughter alone to a strange place to "entertain" men in uniform?

Joshua's heart was burdened for Sadie MacKenzie. And so, sleep did not come.

The main dining salon, its walls lined with framed paintings of tropical scenes and ocean-going vessels, was filled with finely-dressed passengers for the Aloha Dinner, with a choice of sirloin steak, baked lobster, or chicken breast for the main course, followed by Baked Alaska or *petits fours* for dessert. A band played on a small stage at the end of the salon, and light from the chandeliers glinted off the brass of the instruments. Men wore tuxedoes and dinner jackets, and women wore satin and silk. The atmosphere was light, and sounds of laughter were occasionally heard over the murmur of voices engaged in dinner-time conversation.

This was Sadie's favorite time of the five-day trip from San Francisco to Honolulu. Although her cotton dress was the best her wardrobe had to offer, no one seemed to notice or care. She dined with wealthy passengers, listening raptly to stories of travel to worlds she hoped someday to visit. For a brief moment each day, she shared a table and broke bread with people who would not have deigned to give her a second glance on the streets of San Francisco, an experience that offered her the faintest glimmer of hope for a better tomorrow.

"Would you care to dance?"

Sadie broke out of her daydream to seek the source of the voice. Joshua Sinclair, dressed to the nines in a black tuxedo with tails and a white bow tie. She had seen him dining at the captain's table in the salon, seated adjacent to the *Lurline*'s commander, Charles A. Berndton, who was commodore of the entire Matson fleet.

"Mr. Sinclair, don't you look handsome tonight?" she said.

"And you, my dear, are quite lovely."

She knew he was just saying it. In a room filled with beautiful women, she was plain of countenance and drab in apparel. Mr. Sinclair was charming, handsome, and old enough to be her father. What was his interest in her? She had been warned of strange men who would seek to steer her into strange and perverse worlds, but nothing about this man triggered any alarm bells in her mind. He seemed to have plenty of friends aboard the *Lurline*, people above her station in life who treated him with great admiration and respect. She could see that as she stole glances his way throughout dinner. His dinner companions listened intently when he spoke, laughing at his jokes, and others flocked to his table to speak, as if there were value in merely being associated with him. Captain Berndton even appeared to defer to him just as others aboard ship deferred to the captain. And she had seen the wedding band on Mr. Sinclair's left hand. No, this man had nothing sinister in mind. She was sure of it.

"Mr. Sinclair, I would be honored to dance with you."

Joshua grasped the back of her chair and held it as she stood. As the band began playing "The Anniversary Waltz," he escorted her to the dance floor. He took her hand in his, placed his other lightly on her back, and glided her across the floor. Almost instantly, she felt at ease, enjoying the music and feeling important to be dancing with this man who commanded such respect.

"Where is your family, if I may ask?" Joshua asked.

"I have no family." She hated the question, and she felt sadness in her own tone that clashed with the air of cheeriness in the room. "I suppose that's not entirely true," she added. "I do have a little brother, Billy, but I haven't seen him in quite some time."

"Where is Billy?"

"He was taken to an orphanage, but I was old enough to be left on my own."

And by left on her own, she meant she was needed to nurse Mama through her sickness and then, once Mama had passed, she was too old to be taken in by an orphanage, not that anyone cared enough to even raise the question. She was simply left on her own by fate, with nothing to her name but the clothes on her back and her singing voice. The voice she had used to sing lullabies to Billy in Oklahoma when he was too hungry to sleep. And the same voice that she used to sing love ballads, and later lullabies, to Mama in her darkest moments. It was one morning in the wee hours, in the second verse of Billie Holiday's "God Bless the Child," that Mama closed her eyes for the last time. Shortly after she was buried in a pauper's grave, Sadie saw the notice seeking entertainers in Honolulu. She located the manager who posted the handbill notice, and he booked her passage on the *Lurline*, bound for a singing career. And now here she was.

"How about you, Mr. Sinclair? Is your family in Hawaii?"

"My wife is."

"What is her name?"

"Juanita."

"You must miss her."

"Terribly."

"I suppose she will be glad to see you upon your return home. Will she be at the dock tomorrow to greet you? I think I would like to meet her."

"No," he said.

Sadie expected more, but she noted a tone of sadness in his voice that seemed to match hers. They danced without talking further until the end of the song. Sadie felt as if she had dampened the mood by her insensitive question, though she didn't understand how her question was any more insensitive than his.

After the music ended, Joshua escorted her back to her table and pulled out the chair for her. "Miss MacKenzie," he said, "thank you for the dance. It was delightful." Then he left the dining room.

Later that night, after she returned to her cabin with its Pullman bed folded into the wall, Sadie packed her meager belongings into a battered leather valise. The same valise she had filled with her rags before the MacKenzie family fled the Dust Bowl of Oklahoma in search of elusive better times. Better times that they had never found. Would she find those better times in Honolulu?

She dressed for bed then crawled under the covers, her mind filled with thoughts of gourmet dinners and chandeliers and women in gowns and men in dinner jackets and captains and bands and dancing with lawyers and the unknown wonders that tomorrow surely would bring when she disembarked in paradise.

Chapter Three
December 3

SADIE WAS ON deck early the morning of December 3, not wanting to miss the first glimpse of Honolulu. She slid her handbag over her forearm and staked out a place among the throngs of passengers that included two college football teams from the mainland. The once-defeated Bearcats from Willamette University in North Carolina, and the San Jose State College Spartans, with its record of five wins, three losses, and three ties, were scheduled to play a series of games against each other and against the University of Hawaii Rainbow Warriors. Others lining the rails included Walter Dillingham from a prominent Honolulu family; several Hollywood cameramen, whose assignment was to film footage for a historical drama called *To the Shores of Tripoli*, starring John Payne, Maureen O'Hara, and Randolph Scott; and European war correspondent Joseph C. Harsch.

Sadie watched, almost giddy with excitement, as the *Lurline* steamed past the Big Island of Hawaii and Maui, then across the Moloka'i Channel. More passengers gathered on deck as they rounded Oahu's Makapu'u Point, where translucent green mountains rose up to Koko Head, which stood guard over white sandy beaches and Hanauma Bay. Along the southern coast of Oahu, Diamond Head loomed on the starboard side. Sadie stood and held her breath at the beauty she beheld.

Then they cruised past the most famous beach in the world, Waikiki, its white sand already spotted with sunbathers, while surfers rode their boards on the water and waited for just the right wave. The two elegant ladies of Waikiki, the Royal Hawaiian Hotel, also known as the Pink Palace, and the Moana-Seaside Hotel, looked just as Sadie had pictured them from travel brochures she devoured before boarding the *Lurline*. She couldn't keep the smile from her face, convinced that she would be taken for a simpleton if anyone were to notice.

"It's a lovely view, isn't it, Miss MacKenzie?"

Joshua Sinclair nestled into the crowd and claimed a spot on the rail next to her. He looked quite handsome in the morning sun, hatless but again wearing a linen suit. His silver hair seemed to sparkle in the sunlight.

"Oh, yes, Mr. Sinclair. I do believe it's the most beautiful sight I've ever seen. I can't wait until I visit the beach."

Sinclair frowned momentarily then made his face a blank. But Sadie noticed it.

"Did I say something wrong, Mr. Sinclair?" she asked.

"Nothing of the sort. I just wondered if you had your heart set on visiting Waikiki."

"Wild horses couldn't keep me away."

He nodded. "How will you get to your destination once you arrive?"

"I am to be met at the pier by a driver who will transport me to meet Miss O'Brian at the Polynesian Rooms. You must promise you will come to see me once I begin performing."

Sinclair said nothing, but merely gazed at the shoreline. In the distance, a formation of airplanes appeared on the horizon. A murmur swept through the crowd when the formation flew directly at the *Lurline*. They buzzed low overhead, a magnificent sight, the likes of which Sadie had never seen before.

"Oh, my, that was so exciting," Sadie said. "Mr. Sinclair, does this happen every time a ship arrives?"

Sinclair laughed then pointed down the way to a man standing ramrod stiff in full military uniform.

"That's Brigadier General Howard Davidson. He's the commander of Wheeler Field's Fourteenth Pursuit Wing. They're assigned to intercept any possible air attack on Oahu. I assume that fly-by was more in his honor than for our entertainment."

They eased past the Royal Hawaiian Hotel and neared Honolulu Harbor, guarded closely by the Aloha Tower lighthouse at Pier 9. Smaller vessels approached the *Lurline*, laden with friends and family of passengers.

Muscular young men, their bronze skin glistening, led the way in outrigger canoes, spreading flower *leis* on the water. Some of the passengers lining the railings tossed coins overboard, and young men and boys dove from the piers and canoes to retrieve them from the Harbor's bottom.

"Do you still have my card?" Sinclair asked.

"I put it in my handbag."

"Then you must make me a promise as well, Miss MacKenzie."

"Why, certainly, Mr. Sinclair."

"Promise me that you will not lose that card. Memorize the information on it to guard against that. And should you encounter any troubles while in Hawaii, promise that you will come to see me, or that you will send for me if you are unable to come yourself."

"Why ever would I not be able to come myself?"

"Just promise me, Miss MacKenzie. Make an old man happy."

Something in his tone captured her attention. She faced him, surprised to see tears glistening in his eyes. She saw something else in his eyes, as well. She saw compassion. Something stirred within her, and she felt tears fill her own eyes, though she didn't know why.

"Mr. Sinclair, you have my solemn vow."

Then she did something that surprised both him and herself: She kissed him on the cheek.

The *Lurline* docked at the Matson Pier, where a hustle-bustle of activity marked the area filled with families awaiting loved ones returning from the mainland. Dark-skinned natives stood by to tie off the steamer when she docked and to secure the gangplank. Greeters milled about, their arms full of plumeria and orchid *leis* to drape around the necks of disembarking passengers.

Among the waiting throng was Honolulu Police Department officer Sergeant Delbert Mooney. At thirty-seven years of age, Mooney had spent his entire adult life as a policeman, though his ascent through the ranks stalled years ago at sergeant. He believed the reason for the stall was his *haole*, or white, skin, as numerous Hawaiians, Filipinos, Japanese, and even Chinese had passed him by. Others, however, suggested that the real culprit was Mooney, himself. He carried an I-bow-to-no-man attitude like a hundred pound sack of cement on his shoulders, and possessed a mean streak that often crossed into cruelty, filling his personnel file with complaints from citizens and fellow officers alike.

He had recently, however, found a transfer that was to his liking and for which his mean streak served a purpose, even if it was not an official policy of the police department. As a member of the department's vice squad, it was his job to serve as liaison with the madams of Hotel Street and to see to it that the whores stayed in their place. That suited him just fine, and paid him quite well under the table.

Handsome, in a rugged sort of way, with a beard that required that he shave twice a day, and a thick, muscular build, he wore a linen suit and puffed on a cigar as he waited. There was nothing about his outward appearance to suggest he was a law enforcement official, other than, perhaps, the intense scrutiny with which he observed passengers exiting the *Lurline*. His seasoned eyes fell on a young, almost waifishly-thin, woman in a cotton dress, clutching a handbag and a small, battered valise.

He smiled, but the smile stopped well short of his eyes. It was more akin to that of a jackal than of a person. He stepped forward as the woman descended the gangplank to the pier.

Sadie had no idea who was to greet her, nor how they were to make connection. A native girl approached and extended a plumeria *lei* toward her.

"*Aloha*," the girl said.

"*Aloha*," Sadie replied. She leaned her head forward as she had seen others do, and the girl slipped the *lei* over it, then moved on to the next passenger.

"You Sadie MacKenzie?" a gruff voice asked.

Turning, she saw a man in need of a shave, wearing a brown suit and with a cigar clenched in his teeth.

"Why, yes I am."

"I'm Mooney. I'm to take you to Francis."

"Oh, Mr. Mooney, I'm so pleased to meet you."

She extended her valise to him, but he ignored it as he turned away from her. "This way," he said.

Sadie found herself taken aback. A gentleman always offered to carry a bag for a lady. Even in Oklahoma they did that. What a strange place these Hawaiian Islands must be where the normal courtesies and conventions of polite society were pushed aside. Oh, well, no matter. She was not going to let a rude driver spoil her mood. She had arrived in Honolulu, safe and sound, and her new life was starting. And what a grand life it would be. She could scarcely wait to get started.

She followed Mooney as he shouldered his way through the crowds, with nary an "excuse me" that she could hear. Even his rudeness could not dampen her spirits. Light breezes tickled her cheeks and swirled her hair about her face. As they got farther from the harbor, with its smells of oil and diesel, she caught her first whiff of paradise, a light, almost sugary, aroma from the brightly-colored flowers that seemed to grow at will, and maybe even from the ones around her neck. Someday she would task herself with learning the names of each, perhaps tending to her own garden in a house on the beach. The world was her oyster for Sadie MacKenzie.

Mooney led the way to a royal blue Ford Deluxe coupe convertible with its canvas top up. What a beautiful automobile! If it were hers, Sadie would lower the top for driving about town. She wondered why Mooney did not.

Mooney opened the driver's side door and got behind the wheel. Sadie opened the passenger side, pushed the seat forward, and deposited her bags in the rear. Then she returned the seat back to its original position and started to get in.

"In the back," Mooney said.

"Oh, Mr. Mooney, you don't need to chauffeur me."

He laughed, the sound more of a snort than an actual laugh. "In the back."

"But Mr. Mooney, it's awkward in my dress to—"

"In the back."

He spoke with a sharpness that frightened her. She'd have to tell Miss O'Brian that her driver was sadly lacking in manners. But not wanting to make an issue of it now, and not wanting to spoil a beautiful day, she climbed into the back. Before she could settle in, Mooney put the car in gear and drove off. The motion of the car slammed the door.

As they pulled out of the parking area, Sadie noticed Mooney staring at her in the car's rearview mirror. It was a disconcerting stare, not one of admiration or even curiosity, but more one of appraisal and judgment. She couldn't tell the results of his analysis, though, as his face bore no emotion. There was something cold and calculated about it that caused a shiver to course down her spine, even in the eighty degree heat. She was not normally one for forming instant likes and dislikes of people, but she had formed two within the past forty-eight hours: She liked Mr. Joshua Sinclair, Esquire, a great deal, and she detested Mooney the driver an equal amount.

"Mr. Mooney, how far is it to the hotel?" she asked.

"It's close enough."

"Will we drive past Waikiki Beach? I'd love to see it up close."

He glanced at her in the mirror again, an eyebrow raised, as if she had offended him. Mr. Mooney was a man whose path she hoped she did not cross with any frequency while she was in the Islands.

"We might as well go through the rules right now," Mooney said. "Listen, learn, and abide."

"Rules? What rules?" And who was this Mooney to think that he, a mere driver, was in any position to lay down rules for her?

Mooney lapsed into a clipped, staccato tone, as if he were an adolescent reciting a poem in a grade school class. It was obviously a speech he had given many times before.

"You may not visit Waikiki Beach or any other beach except Kailua Beach. You may not patronize bars or any better class cafes. You may not own property or an automobile. You may not have a steady boyfriend or be seen on the streets in the company of men. You may not marry service personnel, attend dances, or visit golf courses."

Sadie had a hard time grasping what Mooney was saying. Clearly some mistake had been made, but she didn't know exactly what it was. All she knew was that she had gotten in a vehicle with someone she shouldn't have. Was he really going to take her to Miss O'Brian, or did he have something else in mind? Something more sinister. Shock mixed with her confusion, and slowly transformed into horror as Mooney continued.

"You may not ride in the front seat of taxicabs or in the back seat with men. You may not wire money to the mainland without the permission of your madam. You may not—"

"My 'madam'!" Her normally soft voice filled the car with righteous indignation. She knew what a madam was. There were plenty of them in San Francisco. The enormity of the mistake that had been made began to settle in on her consciousness. "What do you mean by that?"

"You may not telephone the mainland without permission of your madam. You may not change from the house you are assigned to. You may not be out of the house after 10:30 at night."

He stopped speaking, turned, and looked at her. "Do you understand these rules?"

Sadie was rendered mute by the unsettling reality that Mooney had mistaken her for a common prostitute. She must speak up now, to point out his error. He clearly intended to pick up some other young woman at the harbor, not her. But he had known her by name. He had known he was to deliver her to Miss O'Brian. She began to realize that the error had been hers, not his. And she had made that error nearly two-thousand-five-hundred miles to the east, before she boarded the *Lurline*.

"I said do you understand these rules?" Mooney repeated.

Whatever mistakes she had made, there was no mistaking the harshness of his tone or his countenance. He was not a man to be trifled with.

"But why are there rules like that?" she asked. "I'm just a singer. I—"

"Abide by these rules and we'll get along just fine. Break them and there will be hell to pay."

Sadie leaned back in her seat and fought to comprehend the situation in which she found herself. She felt an urge to leap out of the car and run back to the harbor, but then realized the cunning of a delivery vehicle that essentially trapped you in the back seat of a coupe automobile, making it impossible to swing open a door and escape. And where would she go, even if she did escape? She knew no one in Honolulu and knew of no place to turn.

Well, she did know one person, and he had specifically instructed her to contact him should she ever be in need. Little did she know when he said it that the moment of her need would arise so soon after disembarking from the *Lurline*, but it surely had arrived. She opened her handbag and extracted the business card. She stared at it and memorized the address and phone number. Then she tucked the card inside the top of her brassiere. If Mooney were to search her handbag and find it, he would likely tear it up. She just hoped he would not search her undergarments, at least until she could find some other place to secure the card.

A short while later, Mooney reached a three-story building on Merchant Street, between Bethel Street and Nu'uanu Avenue, that was constructed of sandstone in the Spanish Mission Revival style, with massive front doors made of Philippine mahogany and adorned with terra cotta columns. But Sadie was too stunned to take notice of its architecture. What got her attention were the words HONOLULU POLICE STATION stenciled over the front doorway and the sign that marked the space in which he parked at the rear of the building: RESERVED FOR VICE.

After getting out, Mooney opened the passenger door and grabbed Sadie by the arm. He pulled her out then led her to the door and inside. She took barely a step as her feet dragged the ground, her legs unable to move for themselves. She clutched her handbag tightly with both hands, not even aware she held it.

Inside, Mooney dragged her across ceramic tile floors to a counter where a young dark-skinned officer waited. Sadie blinked and tried to get some sense of her surroundings, but all she could see was the face of the Hawaiian officer as he stared at her with disapproving eyes.

"Got another one, Sergeant Mooney?" he asked.

Sergeant Mooney! So this man was a police officer. She felt as if things were starting to make a bit of sense, though it was all still a jumble in her mind. But at least she understood the source of the mistake: She had been mistaken for a prostitute. She assumed prostitution was illegal in Honolulu, as it was in San Francisco, and she was about to be arrested on her very first day in Hawaii. But perhaps now that she understood the nature of the mix-up, she could clear things up. If, that is, she could convince the police that a mistake had been made.

But what were all those strange rules that Mooney had recited to her? If she was being arrested or, worse, was to be put on a boat back to the mainland, then why such rules as those she had been told? There was still a gap in her understanding that needed clarification.

The Hawaiian officer took an inkpad from beneath the counter, set it on top, and positioned a rectangular card next to it. Mooney yanked the handbag from Sadie and dropped it on the floor. He forced each of her fingers onto the inkpad one at a time, and then recorded her prints on the card. As Mooney worked, the officer took out a small notepad, akin to a ticket book, and pencil.

"Name?" he asked.

Sadie remained silent as she watched her prints reveal themselves on the card.

"Name?" the officer asked again.

"Sadie MacKenzie," Mooney said. "She's going to the Polynesian."

While the officer wrote, Mooney took a handkerchief from his pocket and scrubbed as much ink from Sadie's hands as he could, then wadded up the handkerchief and put it back in the same pocket.

The officer tore off the top page on which he had been writing and said, "That'll be one dollar."

Sadie rubbed at the ink on her fingers, her tips blue and dirty. They looked like fingers she had never seen before, as if they belonged to somebody else. Maybe to a criminal. Or to a whore.

"I said that'll be one dollar," the officer repeated.

"Oh for pity's sake," Mooney said. He grabbed her handbag from the floor and fumbled around inside before coming up with a small fold of money. He peeled off a dollar bill and handed it to the officer, who gave the page to Mooney. Mooney shoved it into her handbag then thrust the bag into her hands.

"Francis will need to see your license when you arrive," he said. "Don't lose it."

Sadie clutched the handbag with both hands, unconcerned that she soiled it with ink. Right then, it and her valise were her only lifelines to the world she left behind in San Francisco. As Mooney grabbed her by the arm and dragged her to the door, the first of many tears to come trickled down her cheek.

Chapter Four

ARMY MILITARY POLICE Sergeant Robert Sandford, in his mid-twenties, drove his Jeep in a gentle loop around Hotel Street: east on North Beretania Street to Nu'uanu Avenue, right to North Hotel Street, right again to River Street, and right again, along Nu'uanu Stream. Before he reached North Beretania again, he turned up North Pauahi Street, paused at the intersection of Pauahi and Maunakea before he turned on Smith Street, then back to Beretania and started over again. It was monotonous, but Rob liked it that way. Because it was a weekday, the lines were short and orderly at the hotels, in contrast to weekends and paydays, when the khaki and white lines snaked down the sidewalks and rounded corners, spilling over into the streets and ultimately into the Army and Navy stockades.

Rob had come a long way from the ghettoes of Brooklyn, New York, to the shores of Oahu, but the United States Army was an equal opportunity employer, and he was proud to be a man of color in a position of authority. He had never climbed the stairs on Hotel Street, and he vowed that he never would. Aside from the moral sensitivity instilled in him as a child by a grandmother who raised him in the church, he also had a philosophical issue with Hotel Street's two-door policy, with the front doors of the brothels reserved for white men, while servicemen of color, along with plantation laborers of various races, were relegated to back doors or to unregulated brothels across Nu'uanu Stream. He had even heard that there were two standards inside the houses, as well, with the lesser sporting girls servicing men of color. Apparently the whites objected to having their private parts embedded where those of what they considered lower races had also been.

Up ahead, he saw Mooney's brand new Ford Deluxe ease to the curb in front of the Polynesian Rooms. That damn Mooney! How could he afford that car on a police officer's salary? Rob couldn't prove it, but he knew that Mooney and other vice cops were taking payola from the madams to enforce the unwritten rules and even to run errands for the madams, such as picking up the newly arrived girls and depositing them at their assigned hotels. Though prostitution was illegal, it was unofficially sanctioned by the police so long as it stayed confined to the four corners of Hotel Street and didn't spill out to where it could offend the decent citizens of Honolulu. It fell to Mooney and others of his ilk to keep the activity confined.

Rob couldn't feel too self-righteous, though. After all, the military had turned the same blind eye as the police, even though the brothels clearly violated the May Act, passed just this past summer, which prohibited bawdy houses within a reasonable distance of any military base. Of course, he guessed that "reasonable distance" was subject to interpretation and, so long as the girls kept up the men's morale and the sanitary rules kept the disease rates low, no one was going to break out a dictionary or a law book anytime soon.

Rob pulled his Jeep to a stop directly across from Mooney's car and watched as the vice cop got out, circled his vehicle, and opened the passenger door. From inside, he heard a woman's voice cry out, "No, I won't go in there. I won't!"

Rob shifted upright in his seat, fully vigilant. He understood that girls brought over from the mainland came voluntarily, their eyes wide open as to the life they were entering, but something about this woman's cry bespoke otherwise. Startled looks from the men standing in line indicated they felt the same as he, as did the disapproving frown of Leinani, a two-hundred-fifty pound Polynesian woman standing guard at the door.

Mooney leaned inside the car and roughly pulled a thin young woman out of the back seat. She sprawled onto the street, clutching a handbag with both hands, but Mooney maintained his grip on her arm and jerked her to her feet. She was young, awfully young. And petrified, with tears streaming down her cheeks. Something was definitely amiss here.

The woman tried to dig her heels into the concrete, but Mooney grabbed both arms and shook her violently. Her head rocked back and forth, and an anguished sob filled the air, which was suddenly still and silent as death except for her cries. Mooney glared at the men who watched his antics, and the intensity of his stare forced them to avert their eyes.

"I won't go," the young woman sobbed, and Rob's heart broke in two.

Mooney pulled back his right arm and delivered a sharp blow to her cheek with his closed fist. She went silent and limp. Mooney forced her to remain upright, though she was clearly stunned.

Rob climbed out of his Jeep, his own fists clenched. "Mooney!" he called.

Mooney looked around, and Rob locked eyes with him. After a brief moment, Mooney seemed to wilt under the intensity of the stare.

"You mind your own business, soldier boy," Mooney said.

"It seems the lady is being brought here against her will," Rob said.

"She's bought and paid for. You got a problem with it, you take it up with Francis."

With that, he yanked the woman toward the door. She struggled to stay on her feet as he brushed past the line of men, ignored the disapproval of Leinani, and disappeared inside. The young woman looked back over her shoulder at Rob as Mooney dragged her through the door.

The two halves of Rob's broken heart shattered into pieces.

When Mooney lashed out at her face, it was all Sadie could do to avoid sinking into blackness. The events of the past half-hour were totally incomprehensible, but she knew that unless she maintained her wits, she would be lost. She vaguely thought she heard a male voice call to Mooney, followed by Mooney's indecipherable response. Something about being "bought and paid for." Then Mooney pulled her toward the door of the Polynesian Rooms. She knew that, once she was inside, all hope was gone.

Just as Mooney yanked her across the threshold, she looked back and saw a young soldier, a black man, standing in the street with clenched fists at his side. His nostrils flared and even at the distance, she recognized intensity in his gaze as he looked at Mooney. Sadie had seen that look before, and she knew it for what it was: hate.

Then the soldier's eyes shifted to hers, and they softened immediately, as if a switch had been flipped. Just as he disappeared from her sight, she could swear she saw a tear glisten on his cheek.

Sadie looked forward again, to appraise her new surroundings. Mooney led her down a hallway that flanked a set of stairs on which a number of uniformed men stood, all staring at her. Halfway down, he pulled her into a large parlor on the right, furnished with an array of couches, chairs, and even a *chaise longue* with a footstool, in the style she learned in San Francisco was called *duchesse brisee*. Red was the predominant color of the room, and velvet the leading material. It looked to her like what she had always thought a San Francisco brothel would look like. Then again, she supposed that was exactly where she had landed: in a whorehouse.

Mooney pushed her down on a fainting couch. "Wait there."

He left the room, and Sadie struggled to her feet. She wavered unsteadily, the pain in her cheek turning to numbness. A cloud settled on her consciousness, and she fought to chase it away. Her vision had turned double, her eyes blinded by tears. She wiped them dry and looked for an escape route. Her glance fell on the open doorway just as she heard Mooney say, "Get Francis. I've brought new meat." Then he returned and blocked the door with his broad frame.

New meat? Again, his words made no sense. Mooney was a police officer, not a butcher. Then her thoughts clarified. *New meat!* He meant her. Whatever disbelief she might have fostered, whatever hope she maintained that this was all still just a big mistake, disappeared and reality crystallized.

She wiped away tears and dried her hands on her dress. She stood straight and tall, chin held high, determined to maintain her composure and her dignity. A wave of dizziness passed, and her legs melted beneath her. She sat on the edge of the couch to keep from fainting, handbag in her lap, but her head still high. She would not let these people break her.

She heard a scuffle of footsteps descend the stairs, accompanied by a raspy woman's voice. "Excuse me, boys. Gotta inspect the talent fresh off the boat."

A moment later, a woman entered the parlor, with Mooney hard on her heels. "There she be, Francis," Mooney said.

As in control as Mooney had been when he picked her up, Sadie instantly sensed a shift of power. The real force in the room was this hard-looking woman, wearing a silk bathrobe with the initials "FOB" monogrammed on the left side. Her breasts, full and generous, swayed beneath the robe with each step, unfettered by undergarments. Sadie guessed that this was Francis O'Brian, who had hired her and provided her passage from San Francisco, a trip Sadie would gladly have taken in reverse at that moment.

The woman stopped directly in front of her. "Stand up, girl," the woman said.

Sadie gathered her legs beneath her, her handbag still tightly clutched in her hands, and stood. Francis squinted and looked her over, from feet to head, then back to her feet again. She squeezed Sadie's left breast. Sadie jerked away, which drew only a smile and a nod.

"A bit on the small side, but firm," Francis said. "A little thin, too."

"You can fatten her up a bit," Mooney said. "The boys won't mind so long as she spreads 'em."

The words were like additional blows of a hammer, driving Sadie's new reality into her soul. Francis grasped Sadie's chin, turned her head, and ran her fingers across Sadie's swollen, and already bruising, cheek.

"Mooney, how many times—"

"She fell against the car while she was getting in. I guess she hadn't regained her land legs after five days at sea." He shrugged. "It happens."

Francis leaned closer and studied Sadie's cheek. "Funny how the car seems to have knuckles."

Francis twisted Sadie's head again, pulling her face forward. "Are you Sadie?"

"There's been a mistake," Sadie said. "I'm a singer. I'm just a singer."

"Do you have your license?"

Sadie remained mute, unsure of the meaning of the question.

"From the police station, girl." She looked over her shoulder. "Mooney, you took her for her license, didn't you?"

Mooney grabbed the handbag from Sadie, rummaged inside and extracted the slip of paper Sadie had been given at the station. He handed it to Francis, who examined it approvingly. She turned it around for Sadie to see and traced the top line with a red-polished fingernail.

"In case you can't read, girl, that says 'Entertainer's License.'"

"I can read."

"Then tell me, do you see the word 'singer' anywhere on there?"

Sadie focused on the paper, although she already knew the answer. "But this is a bawdy house. I came to Hawaii to entertain the boys."

"Girl, if you think the boys aren't entertained when they come here, just ask them."

Mooney blurted a laugh, a bray like a donkey. "And they do *come* here."

"Miss O'Brian, there's been a terrible mistake," Sadie said.

"There's been no mistake, girl. I paid five hundred dollars for you and I booked your passage on the *Lurline*, and I aim to get my money's worth."

A young Chinese woman—girl, really; she couldn't have been so much as Sadie's age—entered the parlor. She was tiny, barely five feet tall, and would likely blow away in a strong wind. She kept her head bowed slightly, eyes barely glancing at Francis. The pecking order in the room was clearly established. Francis was at the top, followed by Mooney. Next came the Chinese girl. And Sadie would have to move up just to be at the bottom.

"Doctah Kalakaua here," the Chinese girl said.

"Tell him we'll be right there, Lum Yee."

"Yes, ma'am."

Lum Yee bowed at the waist but as she straightened, she lifted her head and looked directly at Sadie. As their eyes met, Sadie saw strength that she hadn't noticed upon her first entry. There was a presence within this wisp of a girl that Sadie felt sure no one in the room recognized but her.

As Lum Yee backed out of the room, Francis took Sadie by the arm, far more gently than had Mooney, yet with a firm grip.

"Let's get you examined, girl," Francis said.

"Examined?"

"Doc Kalakaua will check you over and give you your Wasserman. Can't have you giving our boys syphilis, can we?"

"That'd entertain 'em though, wouldn't it?" Mooney said.

Francis snatched the handbag from Mooney and gave it to Sadie. As she ushered Sadie to the door, Mooney cleared his throat.

"You forget something, Francis?"

Francis pulled a small fold of money from her robe pocket and handed it to him. "I ought to deduct for damaged goods," she said.

He grabbed Sadie by the chin and leaned his head back, looking down his nose at her. "It's just a bruise. It'll clear up. Besides, no one's gonna care about her face once she's lubed and primed."

Sadie jerked her head from Mooney's hand and glared at him, wishing him dead.

"Your work is finished for now," Francis said.

Mooney nodded. He stepped back and bowed at the waist. "At your service, m'lady." Then he looked at Sadie. "I'll see you again."

Francis pulled Sadie out of the parlor and down the hall to a small room beneath the stairway, starkly furnished with a chair, a cot with stirrups at one end, a diamond-shaped mirror, and a low hanging light with a naked bulb. An elderly Hawaiian man, clad in white pants and a flower-print aloha shirt, stood beside the cot. A black medical bag lay on the floor at his feet. From directly overhead, a cacophony of sounds vibrated through the ceiling: squeaking bedsprings and male moans and groans. The heart and soul of a bawdy house.

"Here she is, Doc," Francis said. She released her grip on Sadie's arm and left the room, closing the door behind her.

"You must be Sadie," the man said. "I am Dr. Kalakaua."

Except for the fact that Sadie knew this man was about to strip her of both her clothes and dignity, and invade every inch of her privacy, she might say the man sounded kind, even tender. Her façade of composure, carefully constructed to show defiance in the parlor, crumbled, and she burst into sobs.

"Please, my dear, there is nothing to be frightened of," Kalakaua said. "I am not going to hurt you. But I do need to examine you. So please, take off your clothes and lie down. Place your feet in the stirrups."

Sadie backed into the corner and her sobbing continued unabated. She held her handbag in front, as if it were a shield.

"Sadie, please. Do not make it necessary for me to seek assistance."

"From Mooney?" The words were barely understandable through her sobs.

Dr. Kalakaua pointed to her cheek. "He did that to you?"

She nodded.

"I must examine you, and Miss O'Brian will send someone to assist if I am unable to do so. I cannot guarantee that she will not send Mooney. So, please..."

Sadie stood rigidly in the corner, her eyes blurred with tears. Then she dropped her handbag on the floor and began to unbutton her dress.

Francis lounged on the fainting couch in the parlor and reflected back on a career that, growing up on a farm in Nebraska, she never dreamed she would enter. But times were hard and, when her brother returned from the war in Europe—the war to end all wars, they called it, which was fine if you decided that what was currently happening in Europe with the Nazis was not a war—he was shell-shocked from spending months dug into a trench while cannon shells exploded around him and looking for a substitute for the whores he had discovered while in Paris before going to "No Man's Land." He decided that, since she had the same thing between her legs as they, she would make a fine substitute. And when he started paying her to keep her mouth shut—and legs open—she discovered that she possessed all the equipment and training she needed to be an entrepreneur.

She honed her craft in the big cities of the Midwest, starting in Kansas City before migrating to Cleveland and then Chicago, where she heard that the Territory of Hawaii offered new opportunities, not to mention better climate. So she headed for San Francisco, where she boarded a ship for Honolulu. She got her start in the Polynesian Rooms, working for Irene O'Shaughnessy, a fiery Irish madam who taught Francis the business side of running a brothel. When Irene decided it was time to retire, she turned the girls and the hotel over to Francis, and then sailed off into the sunset. Every now and then, Francis still received a post card, postmarked from Tahiti. She dreamed of retirement, herself, some day, but her dream was of a second chapter in the same book, this time running a whorehouse in Paris—after the war, of course. If you wanted to be a movie star, the best of the best, you went to Hollywood. But if you wanted to be known as the best madam of the best, you went to France.

Doc Kalakaua interrupted her thoughts as he entered, wiping his hands on a towel. His face was grim, a look Francis knew didn't bode well.

"So, what is it?" she asked. "Syphilis? Gonorrhea?"

"As far as I can tell, she is disease free."

"Then what is it? You look like someone just stole your ice cream cone."

Kalakaua tossed the towel on a chair, then went to the bar and poured himself a small glass of a local whiskey called *okolehao*, or sometimes simply *o'ke*. He sat on the end of the *chaise longue* and took a deep drink, then looked at Francis.

"How much do you know about this girl?" he asked.

"Same as usual. I know her name and where she's from, but that's about it. They don't exactly fill out job applications and sit for interviews. I don't give a damn about her typing skills."

"And you know nothing of her background?"

"You know how it works. My agents let me know if they've found someone, then I wire the money for the agent's fee and the girl's passage. I rely on them to get me what I want, and I don't know any more than that. So spit it out, Doc. What are you getting at?"

"I do not think this girl is what you want. She is different."

"Different, how? What are you getting at?"

"Well, her hymen is still intact and—"

"Sweet lord! She's a goddamn virgin!"

She felt as if Doc had just slapped her in the face. Hell, no, she didn't want a virgin. That brought a whole new set of problems she hadn't bargained for. It would mean getting Mooney involved again, and the less she had to do with Mooney, the better she liked it.

"Yes," Kalakaua said. "She is a virgin."

"That means she'll need to be broken in."

Kalakaua shot to his feet. "Broken in? This girl does not belong here. Have you no decency?"

"What did you expect, Doc? I'm a whore."

Francis's laughter rang in Kalakaua's ears as he stormed out of the room.

Her tears dried, Sadie pulled her dress over her head and buttoned up the front. Then she sat on the edge of the cot, her mind a blur. She opened her handbag and took out a handkerchief. Something fluttered to the floor as she removed it. She reached down and picked up the card she had hidden from Mooney by putting it in her brassiere, and then had hidden from the doctor by wrapping it in her handkerchief when he turned his back.

At the sound of a rattling doorknob, she tucked the card back inside her brassiere, just completing the mission when the door opened. Francis O'Brian entered, followed by a young woman in a flimsy robe, whom Sadie at first took to be about her own age. She was pretty, with brown hair that reached her shoulders, but there was hardness about her round face that made her seem much older than she first appeared. Sadie knew, with a thought that struck like a dagger at her heart, that this woman was her future.

"Stand up, girl," Francis said.

Sadie stood, while Francis scrutinized her the same way she had done before, but with a hint of a smile on her face this time. Not a smile of joy, but more like the smile of a small boy focusing sunlight on an insect through a magnifying glass.

"Well, well, well," she said. "What have we here? A virgin, is it? Kelly, you ever seen a virgin before?"

Kelly giggled. She seemed embarrassed. "Not since before I was a teenager."

"What are we going to do with you, Sadie MacKenzie?"

"I don't belong here," Sadie said. "I just want to sing."

"Oh, we'll have you singing soon enough. Humming, too."

Kelly giggled again.

"I want to go home," Sadie said.

"This is your home now. You need to make the best of it. Kelly will show you around and get you settled in. Then the two of us will talk business."

"I—"

Francis cut off Sadie's words with a look. "You were about to say 'yes, ma'am,' weren't you?"

"Yes, ma'am."

Francis nodded. "Good. Now wash your face and Kelly will show you around. I'll be upstairs."

At the word "upstairs," Sadie unconsciously glanced at the ceiling, where the banging and squeaking still reverberated, as it had non-stop since she first entered the room. Francis spun on her heels and left. Kelly and Sadie looked at each other, but there were no giggles from Kelly now. Sadie felt that she understood, at least a little bit, what was going through Sadie's mind, and almost understood her pain. Almost, but not quite. No one could possibly understand her pain.

"I'll get you a damp cloth so you can wash your face," Kelly said, "then we'll get started."

She left, closing the door most of the way behind her, but open just a crack. Sadie sat on the cot again. She reached into the bosom of her dress, extracted the card from her brassiere, and studied it. She moved her lips, as if memorizing the words: JOSHUA L. SINCLAIR, ESQUIRE.

Then she spoke softly, "Oh, Mr. Sinclair, I need you."

Chapter Five

RICHARD CLEMENTS, CHAIRMAN of Pacific Navigation, sat behind his desk and listened impatiently to his agitated young visitor, Miles Cary, leader of the Social Protection Committee that was incessantly lobbying the Honolulu Police Commission, of which Clements was a member, to close down the brothels of Hotel Street. What these liberals didn't seem to understand was that the Police Commission, made up entirely of private businessmen, maintained a goal of protecting business interests in the Territory and not following radical social agendas.

He looked out the window of his third-story office in the Judd Building, named for missionary Gerritt P. Judd, who had been an advisor to King Kamehameha III in the nineteenth century. The office overlooked Merchant Street, just a few blocks away from the Honolulu Police Station, and a scant distance from Hotel Street. If they ever shut down the hotels, the whores would be free to infiltrate the better parts of the city. The last thing he ever wanted to see when he looked out of his window was prostitutes walking the streets below.

He spun back around and watched Cary pace. Cary's arm-waving was at least amusing to Clements. But that red face—he hoped Cary didn't drop dead of a heart attack in his office. Still relatively young, Cary couldn't understand what it was like to build a business and a life for yourself and your family. Those struggles had given Clements his gray hairs, though he liked to think of himself as distinguished-looking as opposed to gray-headed.

"You say you want statehood," Cary said. "You say you want recognition in the eyes of the United States, yet you turn your head while these...these..."

"I think the word you are looking for is whores," Clements said. "It's all right, Mr. Cary. You can say the word."

"Yes, whores. That's what they are, you know. Not entertainers, not sporting girls. They don't entertain. They don't play sports. They're whores."

"I understand that some of them are quite entertaining."

"This is not a discussion in which humor has a place, sir." Cary's voice shook with indignation. "As a member of the Honolulu Police Commission, I should think you would concern yourself with the law. Yet these whores flaunt the law. It's nothing more than public disrespect."

"Do you have any direct evidence?"

"Are you familiar with the May Act?" Cary asked.

"I read the newspapers. I seem to have some recollection of it."

With great ceremony, Cary extracted a folded page from his coat pocket, unfolded it, and held it at arm's length. "Permit me to refresh your recollection."

Clements leaned back in his chair, propped and crossed his feet on his desk, and clasped his hands behind his head. "By all means do. My mother used to read to me when I was a boy. Perhaps it will make me nostalgic for my childhood."

"Sarcasm does not become you, sir."

"Nevertheless, please read."

Cary cleared his throat and then began. "'Until May 15, 1945, it shall be unlawful, within such reasonable distance of any military or naval camp, station, fort, post, yard, base, cantonment, training or mobilization place to keep or set up a house of ill fame, brothel, or bawdy house—'"

"You left out a part," Clements said.

Cary peered over the top of the page in his outstretched arm. "What?"

"I said you left out a part. If you're going to lecture me on the law, son, at least be honest about it. Read the preamble to the Act."

Cary's eyes scanned upward on the page and came to rest on the preamble. "'An Act to prohibit prostitution within such reasonable distance of military and/or naval establishments as the Secretaries of War and/or Navy shall determine—'"

"So you see the problem."

Cary dropped his arm to the side. "No, sir, I don't. But I suppose you will enlighten me."

Clements took his feet from his desk, stood, and leaned forward on his knuckles. "It's a military issue. The Honolulu Police Commission is composed solely of businessmen. Private businessmen. Neither the Secretary of the Army nor of the Navy is a member. I am powerless—no, *we* are powerless to 'determine' anything that falls under the Army and the Navy's jurisdiction. Our hands are tied."

"But you have influence, do you not? Particularly your chairman, Mr. Sumner. Who, by the way, refused to see me."

"I'm starting to think he has the right idea."

"Again, I don't appreciate your sarcasm."

Clements sat back down. "Tell me the name of your organization again?"

"We are the Social Protection Committee of the Honolulu Council of Social Agendas."

"It just rolls off the tongue. Pithy, isn't it?"

"I don't care for your tone, sir."

"Nor I, yours. You have come to my office to dictate to me regarding something that is none of your concern."

"It is every decent citizen's concern," Cary said.

"But the conduct of the Honolulu Police Commission is none of your concern. We make our own decisions, and are able to do so quite nicely without the guidance of know-it-alls and busybodies such as you and your ilk."

Cary struggled to maintain his temper, which appeared on the verge of erupting. He carefully folded the page, ensuring perfect edges, and returned it to his coat pocket. When he spoke again, he did so with deliberate precision.

"Mr. Clements, we will see those houses closed if it's the last thing we do. It is the decent thing to do, and it is the duty of every decent citizen to see it done."

Clements stood again to make himself at eye level with Cary. "Mr.

Cary, there are hundreds of men to every woman in these islands. Many of those men—dark-skinned plantation workers and peckerwood soldiers and sailors—are just like animals on the prowl, looking for places to indulge their animal lusts. We owe it to our wives and daughters to keep them safe from the like. It is Hotel Street that provides a place to satisfy those animal urges. Hotel Street keeps our wives and daughters safe. We dare not even *think* about closing down Hotel Street, much less say it aloud."

Cary blinked, as if unable to believe what he had been told, by no less a person than a member of the Honolulu Police Commission. "That's madness. Pure madness."

Clements sat down again, pulled an article of correspondence in front of him, and lowered his head, pretending to read. "Thank you for your concern, Mr. Cary, but now if you'll excuse me, I have real business to tend to."

Chapter Six

SADIE STARED INTO a room through an open door from the hallway. She had seen a similar room once before, when she went with her mother to deposit Billy at the orphanage. It was rectangular in shape and filled with beds—more like cots, really—with their heads butted up against opposite walls, set up dormitory style. Each had a small bedside table, on which personal items were arranged with precision, designed to reflect the personality of the owner. There were photographs over some of the beds, some framed, some not, most of Hollywood movie stars, such as Gary Cooper, Clark Gable, Robert Taylor, and Humphrey Bogart. Strangely, over one bed hung a photo of Dorothy Lamour in a beaded gown.

Kelly stood in the row between the beds, with Lum Yee next to her holding Sadie's valise. "You can have the one at the end," Kelly said. She pointed to one over which no photographs hung, nor knick-knacks dotted the top of the bedside table. Lum Yee deposited the valise on the floor next to the bed, while Kelly chattered on.

"That one used to be Eleanor's, but she went back to the mainland. She was about your age. She didn't say much, but she was quite nice. You would have liked her. She was a singer, too. She used to sing at night when we went to sleep. It was like listening to lullabies. She knew all of Billie Holiday's songs by heart."

But Sadie's mind was stalled on the words "went back to the mainland."

"She went back?"

"Yes, about a month ago. That's why Francis sent for you."

"But she went back."

"Yes. She didn't want to, but Sergeant Mooney said she knew too much."

"What do you mean?"

"That's just what I heard, but I don't know what Sergeant Mooney was talking about."

"How long was she here?"

"Almost a year. But that's not for you to worry about."

Their conversation was interrupted by the sound of loud, angry voices outside. Kelly giggled then hurried out of the room. She stopped outside the doorway and looked at Sadie. "Come on. This will be fun."

Sadie and Lum Yee followed Kelly to the landing at the base of the stairs, where they watched the drama unfolding outside the front door.

MP Sergeant Rob Sandford continued cruising Hotel Street, eyes peeled for signs of trouble, but it had been a good day so far. He knew that the real trouble would come once the sun went down. By then, the men would have had a full day of drinking, often downing their four drink minimums in short order before rolling on to the next saloon for four more. By nightfall, inhibitions would be non-existent and drunks would do what drunks do, which inevitably led to fights. It wasn't uncommon for the stockades at various bases to put out figurative "no vacancy" signs as his counterparts in the Navy—the Shore Patrol, with gold lettering of SP on the sleeves of their pea-coats—joined him and his comrades patrolling Hotel Street and Waikiki, seeking out unruly service personnel.

But Rob was troubled by the girl he had seen earlier, the waifish one whom Mooney had assaulted with his fist and forced into the Polynesian Rooms. He had seen the comings and goings of many of the sporting girls, most of whom either wore the hardened looks of experienced whores or glassy-eyed stares induced by smoking opium or shooting morphine. The drugs were usually pushed on them by their madams, and the girls gladly indulged. It was the only way they could cope mentally with serving as the play-toys of dozens of men a day. Rob also knew that the madams often withheld drugs as punishment to ensure that the girls complied with the rules or whims of the hotels.

But this girl was neither hardened nor drug-addled. She was fully in control of her faculties, albeit on the verge of hysterics, until struck by Mooney. He was sure that, until the blow, she was not only cognizant of her surroundings, she was also dead-set against entering the doors. It was only by the raw strength and brutality of Mooney that she was forced inside. What Rob didn't know was whether she was simply being returned after breaking the rules or if something more sinister was at play. He knew it was none of his concern, though, and certainly outside of his jurisdiction. Nevertheless, he was unable to get her off of his mind.

Now he cruised down Beretania Street, toward the Polynesian Rooms, where he saw business at hand. A soldier in front of the hotel rushed the doorway, only to be body-blocked by the massive bouncer who guarded the doors. He had seen Leinani at work before, and he marveled at her speed and agility in blocking out intruders, arms folded across her generous bosom, never touching the men with her hands or fists while keeping them at bay with a skill that would make any professional football lineman proud. The others in line had turned into a cheering section, and he suspected wagers were being made, though the smart money was on Leinani. The smart money was always on Leinani.

He stopped his Jeep as close to the side of the street as he could. He got out and forced his way through the crowd as the drunken solder screamed, "I've got money. You have to let me in."

Leinani's voice offered a calm reply, "You too drunk. You no can make business."

Rob stepped onto the sidewalk just as the soldier made a run, then bounced off Leinani and staggered almost into Rob. Just as he gathered himself for another run, Rob grabbed him by the back of his collar and yanked him off his feet.

"Hold on there, soldier," Rob said.

The soldier struggled upright, his collar still firmly in Rob's grasp. He twisted around, nearly strangling himself, as he sought out the source of the restraint. Rob gave him a brisk shake, enough to rattle his teeth. The soldier broke free. He weaved for a second, teetering on the brink of balance, then regained it with a wave of both arms. He focused on the MP armband on Rob's sleeve and sobered almost immediately.

"They won't take my money, Sarge."

"Another time, soldier."

"But I'm horny."

"And you're drunk. You probably can't even get it up. Now either move along or I'll haul you into the stockade. It's your choice."

The soldier weaved a moment, weighing his options. Then he stormed off down the sidewalk, with a last farewell yell at Leinani. "You think this is the only whorehouse in Honolulu? My three dollars'll spend down the street."

"You go, *haole*," she said. "You *pupule*."

"Let me know if he comes back," Rob said to Leinani.

As she nodded, he got a glimpse inside past her wide body, and there she was—the girl who didn't belong. They made eye contact briefly then she followed another girl up the stairs.

Kelly giggled as the drunken soldier disappeared from view and Leinani called after him.

"What's pu...pu..." Sadie stopped, unable to say the word.

"*Pupule*? It means he's crazy. But now that the fun's over, let's go upstairs and I'll show you how we do things around here."

Kelly pushed past the line of men on the stairs and headed up. Sadie started to follow, pausing long enough for one fleeting glimpse outside, past Leinani's body. Freedom was just that close, mere feet away, but she knew she had no better chance of getting past Leinani than did the soldier. But still, was it worth a try?

Then her eyes fell on the black man from before, who stared straight at her. Was he in cahoots with Mooney? She didn't think so, not based on their prior encounter, but he was still in a position of authority, and she had seen that authority blessed this operation and her imprisonment there.

She ducked her head and went up the stairs. Kelly waited at the top, next to a caged booth in which Francis sat, collecting money and dispensing poker chips. Francis ignored them, intent on her business.

"Follow me," Kelly said.

She led Sadie past the booth to the hallway, lined with doors on both sides. There were benches for waiting customers, while maids scampered from room to room carrying soiled linens. The sounds that escaped from the rooms provided stereophonic obscenity to Sadie. An occasional soldier or sailor brushed past and disappeared into doorways. Others departed rooms, still buckling belts or tucking shirts into trousers.

"It's three dollars for three minutes," Kelly said. "It gets pretty hectic on the weekends and on paydays, so stick to the schedule. Some of the girls use alarm clocks. I do. Middle of the week's not so bad, and that gives you some breathing time. Hours are nine a.m. to two p.m., no days off."

Tears welled in Sadie's eyes. She suspected they would be constant companions until she could find a way to escape. But Kelly seemed oblivious to her distress, chattering on.

"The house keeps one dollar," Kelly said, "and you get to keep two. Room and board is one hundred dollars a month, and you have to tip the maids. If you don't, they won't take care of you. Doc Kalakaua comes by every week for the exams. That's another ten dollars a week, unless you test positive for VD. Then you have to go to the hospital, and that costs more, so make sure you don't get VD. And make damn sure you don't get pregnant."

Sadie was having a hard time processing the information, which seemed to come at her like a flash flood in a thunderstorm. VD? Pregnant? Hospital?

"The Army and Navy have pro stations set up for free, so the men have to go there and—"

"Pro stations?"

"Prophylaxis stations. That helps with the VD. And try to make them wear rubbers. That helps with the other."

The distress on Sadie's face finally kicked in for Kelly. "You'll get used to it soon enough," Kelly said. "Until then, there are things you can do to help."

"Like what?"

"Opium. Morphine. Plus, just keep thinking about how much money you're making. If you're careful with your spending, you can make twenty or twenty-five thousand dollars in a year. If you want to go back to the mainland then, maybe you can."

"A year? There's no way to go sooner?"

"Not a chance in hell. At least not until Francis makes back her investment."

"How much is that?"

"It varies. She probably paid five hundred dollars to the agent for you. Then there's the ticket for your passage on the *Lurline* and the payola to Mooney. She's probably got upward of a thousand dollars invested in you so far. So, if she gets one dollar for each trick, that's—"

"One thousand men."

The words came out in a whisper. As the enormity of it all sank in, a tidal wave of despair rolled across Sadie. She opened her mouth as if to speak.

All that came out was an agonizing wail.

Francis and Kelly sat silently in the parlor, waiting for Doc Kalakaua. The experience with Sadie had unnerved Kelly, who still heard Sadie's wail echo in her head. A high-pitched, animal-like cry as she dropped to her knees and rocked back and forth. Keening, Kelly had heard it called when she attended a funeral as a little girl of a distant relative from Scotland. She also knew of the legend of banshees, fairy women who wailed as an omen of impending death. Was Sadie a banshee? If so, who was going to die?

Francis seemed to take it all in stride, as if she had been through this before. Not in Kelly's tenure in the house, though, which reached back nearly three years. There was something different about Sadie that Kelly had not seen in any of the girls, either at the Polynesian Rooms or in the other hotels. She had a child-like innocence that Kelly had not known since she was eleven and had been visited in her bed by a drunken uncle.

Many of the other sporting girls had similar experiences to Kelly's, and nearly all had their first sexual encounters in their early teens. A lot of the girls seemed to have buyer's remorse upon disembarking in Honolulu, but Sadie's resistance seemed more than that. Doc Kalakaua said that Sadie was a virgin, and Kelly began to sense that Sadie had, indeed, been brought here against her will.

Doc Kalakaua entered, his black bag in hand. "I have given her a sedative, so she should sleep for several hours."

"What's wrong with her?" Francis asked.

"She is obviously in distress. I would even say she is in shock."

Francis shook her head in disgust. "I can't tell you how many customers she chased off with her yowling. The boys have a lot of choices, and they damn sure don't want to be haunted by the insane while they're doing their business."

"She is not insane. She is—"

"And Kelly here, she's missing work, too."

"I don't mind, Francis," Kelly said. "I'll make it up later."

"Doc, this girl is costing me money," Francis said. "I need to get her up and working, and soon." She paused, laughed, then added, "Or down and working."

Kalakaua exhaled in disgust. "She is just a girl, Francis. Have some compassion."

"To you, she's just a girl. To me, she's a liability. My compassion is in short supply."

Sadie slept in the bed Kelly had delegated to her in the dormitory. Lum Yee sat in a chair by her side and watched. Sadie's face, eased by the doctor's sedative, was at peace, a far cry from the reddened, tear-streaked countenance Lum Yee had found when she rushed to Sadie on the floor next to a dumbfounded Kelly, who seemed panicked at the condition of her charge. Lum Yee reached out and gently caressed Sadie's face. She brushed aside a stray hair.

"You sleep, Missy," she said in a near whisper. "Lum Yee take care."

"Lum Yee, upstairs now!" Francis's voice jolted her. "*Wicki-wicki!*"

Lum Yee looked over her shoulder at Francis, who stood in the doorway.

"Doc said she'll be asleep for a long time, so she has no need of you now," Francis said. "Now get upstairs and go back to work."

Lum Yee stood, bowed almost imperceptibly—just a dip, disrespect fully intended—and scurried out of the room.

Francis approached the bed and looked at Sadie. For a brief instant, a look crossed her face that could have been interpreted as compassion. But as soon as it arrived, it disappeared, replaced by the hardened stare of a businesswoman who trafficked in human flesh.

Then she left, while Sadie slept.

Chapter Seven

CLAD IN HIS golf togs, Army Major General Walter Short leaned over his ball on the putting green at Fort Shafter's golf course. Sixty-one years old, Short had been appointed head of the Hawaiian command in February, and he and his wife took up residence at Quarters 5 at Fort Shafter, about midway between downtown Honolulu and Pearl Harbor. One of the things he liked most about the command was the convenience of a golf course right there on base where he honed his skills with regular weekend games against Navy Admiral Husband Kimmel, Commander-in-Chief of the U.S. Pacific Fleet at Pearl Harbor.

Major Frank Steer, who commanded the military police on the island, approached silently, then stopped a respectful distance away and awaited the putt. Now forty years of age, the Oklahoman had seen action as a teenager during World War I, in the Meus Argonne Offensive. After returning stateside, he received a commission to West Point then spent time in service in the Philippines before his transfer to Hawaii in 1940.

Short pulled back his club a short distance, then brought his arms forward. The head of the club gently *thwacked* against the ball, which jumped forward, rolled softly, then arced away from the cup. Short pulled another ball over and repeated the process, right down to the arc away from the cup.

"Can you see what I'm doing wrong, Major?" Short asked.

Steer marveled at Short's ability to not only sense that someone was behind him, but also to know who that somebody was. Steer had thought his approach was stealthy enough as to disguise his presence, but apparently not.

"I'm not a golf instructor, sir," Steer said. "I wouldn't presume to know."

"Watch me and see if you can spot anything out of line. If I don't straighten this out, Admiral Kimmel will eat my lunch Sunday morning."

Another putt, another miss. As far as Steer could tell, the only thing wrong was Short's decision to play golf in the first place.

Short continued to putt and miss as he talked. "Major, how closely are you following what's going on in Asia?"

"I read the papers, but that's about it. I'm just a cop. I'll leave diplomacy to others better suited for the task."

"The Japanese are continuing their hostilities in China, and they're moving forward in Indochina. They have practically encircled the Philippines and are in striking distance of our trade routes."

"What about our embargo on oil and gas? Is that having any effect?"

"As a matter of fact it is," Short said. "The effect is to royally piss the Japanese off."

"But the alternative—"

"The alternative is worse. We can't let them have unfettered access to fuel to drive their invasions forward. Their belligerence is just a necessary by-product. But it's troubling, nevertheless."

At last, a putt found the cup. "I think I've figured it out," Short said. "I was rolling my wrists just slightly on the follow-through." He lined up another putt and again found his target.

"And let's not underestimate the impact of their alliance with Germany and Italy."

"I don't understand, sir," Steer said. "What does Europe have to do with the Pacific?"

"The Japanese are emboldened by their allies' success in Europe. They think the war there will be over quickly and that now is their time to strike, to duplicate the success of their partners."

Another putt, another miss. "Damn! I thought I had it figured out." He dropped his putter and turned to face Steer. "In short, Major, I don't see how we can avoid war with Japan. Their likely first target will be the Philippines. Or Guam."

"Not Hawaii?"

"Not likely. Even if they tried, we have five mobile radar stations that would alert us before they could get into striking distance. No, Major, our biggest concern here is sabotage, not attack."

"Sabotage?'

Short looked up from his putting. "Look around you, Major. This island is overrun with Japs. Any one of them could sneak out at night and plant explosives on our aircraft. That's my biggest concern. War is coming, but not here if we can stop it in the Pacific first."

"Yes, sir."

"The point I'm getting at, Major—and I assure you that there is a point to all this—is that you and your MPs can expect a dramatic increase in the number of troops that will soon be stationed on Oahu. We will be the number one way-station for our boys on their way to the Philippines and Guam. I need to be sure you can handle that."

"My men are quite capable, sir."

"We need to keep them occupied and out of trouble, ready to ship out on a moment's notice if conditions worsen. Entertainment is vital, Major. There are forces in Honolulu coming to bear, but the boys need an outlet, a release, if you will." He paused then added, "Are you getting my drift?"

"I think so, sir." Steer knew exactly what he was getting at: Keep Hotel Street open, no matter the efforts of citizens' groups such as the Social Protection Committee of the Honolulu Council of Social Agendas. And notwithstanding the May Act.

Short picked up his putter and lined up his next putt. "Thank you, Major. That will be all."

Chapter Eight

THE GIRLS SAT around a long dinner table in the dining room, enjoying their evening meal of fish and fresh fruit. Francis sat at one end, the matriarch of the table. At the other end sat Norma Staunton, the clear leader of the girls, who just that morning had serviced another young soldier from Lufkin, Texas, for his very first time. When she arrived at the Polynesian Rooms a few years earlier, working her way westward from Chicago, she was already a hardened veteran of the sex trade, having serviced thousands of men. She sometimes spoke of her vagina interchangeably as a tollway or a turnpike, and claimed it had made enough to finance highways from Illinois to the Pacific Coast.

There was one empty chair, wedged in between Kelly and Dolly Mumford, another veteran, originally from Los Angeles. Lum Yee waited on the girls, refilling their drink glasses and fetching seconds as plates emptied. The girls paid her no mind, as if she was merely an extension of the furniture. But while she maintained a poker face, Lum Yee listened carefully to the dinnertime conversation.

Norma glanced at the empty chair. "Where's our new girl?"

"She's having a little…adjustment problem right now," Francis said.

"I believe I heard that," Norma said. She laughed. "I think we all did. The poor boy I was with pissed himself while I was checking his equipment. Maybe we can offer that as a new service."

The other girls giggled. All except for Kelly. "That's not fair," she said. "She's just—"

"A spoiled brat," Francis said.

"That's not fair, Francis."

"Oh, really?"

"Really. She's very sweet. She's just not—"

"Not what?" Francis said, her voice rising. "A whore like the rest of us?"

"She's a virgin."

Norma stopped with her fork halfway to her mouth. The other girls watched for her reaction, as if they knew, or expected, something funny to come from her mouth.

"Excuse me, did you say she was a virgin?"

"Yes. That's what Doc Kalakaua said."

"What's a virgin?"

Again the table erupted with laughter, some of the girls laughing too hard, trying to earn Norma's approval by laughing the loudest.

"Did you know they cancelled the virgins march in San Francisco this year?" Norma asked. "One of them was sick, and the other one didn't want to march alone."

More laughter from the girls, as Norma added, "Or maybe she just decided to sail to Hawaii." She turned to Francis. "Well, Francis, this is an interesting kettle of fish. Did this girl not read the fine print in your handbill?"

"I didn't include 'no virgins allowed' in the advertisement," Francis said. "I wasn't aware that there were any left in San Francisco."

"I dare say there aren't, now that she's here. Do you suppose she even knows what power she possesses between her legs?"

"I suspect not," Francis said. "But we'll make a whore out of her, soon enough."

"You may need to have her start with the fellows with the small ones until she's ready for the big boys." Norma took a bite then asked, "What else do we know about her?"

"She's a singer," Kelly said.

The table erupted with laughter again. Most of the girls, except for Norma, fancied themselves actresses or singers or dancers—some form of entertainer. Whoring was just a way to pay the bills until their true talents were discovered. Kelly once dreamed of being a stage actress, though that dream was dashed years ago. But Norma, on the other hand—well,

Norma was an unabashed whore. She made no pretense of aspiration and held nothing but contempt for any girl in the hotel who did.

"A singer, is she?" said Norma. "I hope she sings better than we heard today."

Lum Yee clucked her tongue and refilled Norma's glass with water, then resumed her station by the door. Her face remained expressionless, except for an occasional twitch of her right eye.

The sounds of laughter reached Sadie's ears. It sounded as if it came from far away, at the end of a tunnel. The voices were light and gay. She longed to join with them and to be happy again. It had been a long time since she had been happy.

She opened her eyes, surprised at the darkness in the room. She wondered how long she had slept, wondered, even, if it was the same day on which she had disembarked the *Lurline* and plunged headlong into a nightmare. She felt an aching between her eyes. She stared at the ceiling then at the chandelier, which seemed to sway, a blurry vision of crystal and glass. She felt numb, as if she had been in a deep sleep. A very deep sleep. She wondered if the events of the day had all just been, in fact, a true nightmare.

She sat up, swung her legs over the side of the bed, and shook her head to throw off the shackles of dullness that clouded her senses. She looked around and realized, with despair, that if it had been a dream, she was still in the middle of it. She remembered this dormitory-style room, remembered the doctor giving her a drug, remembering that her future consisted of sleeping with a thousand men before she could be free.

She got to her feet and swayed unsteadily. She was wearing a thin linen nightgown that she had never seen before, and that hung loosely around her bosom. The true owner was obviously more well-endowed than she. She slid her feet into a pair of slippers at the foot of the bed then sought out the source of the laughter. She moved by shuffling her feet and feeling with her hands for bedrails to support herself upright. When she reached the door, she gripped the door jamb on both sides with her hands. The laughter was closer now, the fog lifting, her senses clearing.

She moved slowly down the hallway that ran alongside the stairs, toward a door that opened to a dining room. Lum Yee, the Chinese maid who had helped her earlier, stood just inside. She glanced at Sadie and shook her head.

From inside the room, Sadie heard a loud voice.

"What kind of singer is she?" the voice said. "Like Billie Holiday?"

"More like Dinah Shore," Sadie said as she stepped into the room.

All chatter and clatter of silverware stopped as the entire table turned its attention to Sadie. Her eyes were puffy from tears and still glassy from the drugs, but her attitude was defiant, at least on the surface. Inside, though, she cowered like a frightened child.

"So," Norma said, "this is…"

"Sadie MacKenzie."

"Well, Sadie MacKenzie, I'm Norma. We were just talking about you. So you're a singer, are you?"

"Yes."

"And you're not a whore?"

"I am not."

"Then why don't you sing for your supper? Let us decide whether you're a singer or a whore."

Sadie remained still, her chin up, hoping it projected an aura of confidence that she didn't feel. Nobody spoke for a long minute as the girls watched her expectantly. She didn't know if she was really meant to sing or if she was being made fun of.

Kelly pushed back the empty chair next to her and patted the seat. "Come on, honey. Sit down and eat."

Sadie dropped her chin and headed for the chair. Norma halted her with a sharp tone.

"No!"

Sadie met Norma's gaze evenly. If this was to be a war of wills, the victor was preordained, but Sadie was determined to hold out as long as she could. All eyes were on the two women, facing off with each other. All eyes, that is, except Lum Yee's. She glared at Francis, as if willing her to put an end to this torture, but Francis seemed content to see how things would play out. As if there was any doubt.

"You can eat after you sing," Norma said, "but you will sing. Now, Sadie MacKenzie, regale us with a song."

"What do you want me to sing?"

"You're the singer; you choose."

Sadie stood silently, her mind awhirl. She had sung for audiences before, small family gatherings and at church, but never for such a hostile crowd. In her drug-addled state, she was able to convince herself that, if she sang well, she would somehow be reprieved from a life of sex. Maybe they would actually let her sing to entertain the troops instead of spreading her legs for them. The stakes were high, and the consequences of failure disastrous. What should she sing that offered the best chance of success? She thought for a moment on all her favorites, searching the most obscure reaches of her memory, made all the more obscure by the sedative she still had not completely shaken.

Finally she settled on a number. She cleared her throat and started on Dinah Shore's hit from the year before, "Yes, My Darling Daughter." Her soprano voice sounded soft and shaky in her own ears as she sang the first words, and she knew she was somewhat off-key, but it was important that she sing. Sing as if her soul depended upon it. And it very well might.

There were titters and giggles from the girls at the table, all except Kelly.

Norma's face was stone. "Louder," she said.

Sadie upped the volume.

"Louder," Norma said again.

And Sadie upped the volume again, the quiver in her voice more pronounced the louder she sang. It also became more disturbing. The girls still giggled, now not at her, but embarrassed *for* her. Kelly bit her lower lip and ducked her head.

Suddenly Norma slammed her open hand down on the table. The slapping sound echoed, startling everyone. Silver and dishes danced and clattered. Sadie stopped in mid-verse. Tears glistened in her eyes as she looked at Norma, unable to understand exactly what kind of monster this woman was.

"Well, Sadie MacKenzie, I've made up my mind," Norma said.

Sadie held her breath. The moment of truth had arrived.

"You're a whore, Sadie MacKenzie," Norma said, "just like the rest of us. Today, you sang for your supper. But tomorrow, you'll fuck for it. Just like the rest of us."

Sadie burst into tears and ran from the room. Lum Yee ran after her.

The girls sat silently for a moment, as if afraid to speak. Norma broke the silence. "Well, that was just about the worst singing I've ever heard. I hope she's better flat on her back than she is on her feet."

The tension broke and the girls laughed. Again, except for Kelly.

"You didn't have to be so mean to her," Kelly said.

Norma stared her down. When she spoke, her tone left no room for disagreement. "I damn sure did. We all had our first time, and it was hard for all of us. I had my cherry popped before I was out of junior high school. I know about yours. An uncle, wasn't it? When you were what, ten or eleven?"

Kelly glared at Norma, hate in her eyes.

"Like I said, the first time was hard for all of us, and she's no better than the rest. She's gotta be tough, or she'll never make it. You can't baby her. That's the worst thing you can do. The sooner she learns the real facts of life, the better."

Sadie flung herself on the bed and buried her face in a flimsy feather pillow to drown out her sobs. She could live with the humiliation—she had been embarrassed before—but the pronouncement by Norma of her sentence to serve as a whore was more than she could take. Whatever flicker of hope had existed was now snuffed out completely.

She felt movement in the bed as someone sat next to her. A gentle hand rested on her shoulder. "Missy?"

It was Lum Yee.

"Go away," Sadie said, her voice muffled in the pillow.

"Missy Sadie?"

Sadie rolled over and angrily slapped away Lum Yee's hand.

"I said go away."

Lum Yee leaned forward and spoke in a whisper. "Missy, you no belong here. You not sleep tonight. Lum Yee come get."

Of course she didn't belong there, and the odds of her being able to sleep were already non-existent. But what was that bit about "Lum Yee come get"?

"You pretend sleep tonight. Lum Yee come get."

"I don't understand what you're saying."

From the dining room, Francis's stern voice blared. "Lum Yee! Get your ass back in here. We're ready for dessert."

Lum Yee stood and looked at the door, then back at Sadie. She leaned close and whispered in Sadie's ear. "Tonight. After midnight. Lum Yee come get. You no sleep."

Then she shuffled out of the room, leaving a very puzzled Sadie behind.

Chapter Nine

SERGEANT ROB SANDFORD returned that night to Schofield Barracks, located on 18,000 acres in central Oahu, about 17 miles from his patrol area in Honolulu. Schofield, the largest Army post in Hawaii, was home base for the Military Police Platoon, 25th Infantry Division, sometimes called "Tropic Lightning" after the lightning insignia the men wore on their shoulders. When he joined the Army, Rob wanted to see the world and defend his country from its enemies. Instead, the only world he had seen was the saloons and whorehouses of Chinatown, the only enemy he had confronted had been drunken soldiers wearing the same uniform as he, and the only combat he had encountered was breaking up fights between soldiers and sailors and, on days like today, fights between drunken soldiers and female Polynesian bouncers. He didn't recall hearing about any of that during the recruiting pitch he listened to when he dropped out of high school.

He slipped his MP armband from his sleeve and peeled off his sweat-soaked uniform. As much as he enjoyed the tropical weather—the thing he liked most about Hawaii—it always left his uniform drenched by the end of his shift. He wrapped a towel around his waist, stepped into his rubber thong slippers—or *slippahs*, as the Hawaiians called them—and headed for the showers.

He thought again about the girl at the Polynesian Rooms. He had seen a lot of sporting girls in Hotel Street, some young, some not so young, some pretty, some on the back side of pretty, some thin, some plump. There were all manner of girls, but they all shared at least one common characteristic: they all had a hardened, glassy look about them. Even the youngest of them, often drug-addled, draped blasé auras about themselves like shields against the moral decay that surely must be rotting them from the inside out. But not this girl. Anyone could see that she was frightened. Anyone could see that she was a fish out of water. If there was one word to attribute to her, it would be "innocent." And innocence did not belong in Hotel Street.

Rob stood under the hot water and scrubbed his face and chest with a bar of Ivory soap, but no matter how hard he scrubbed, he could not wash away the image of the tear-streaked face bearing the brunt of Mooney's fist.

Mooney pulled his Deluxe into the driveway that ran beside a tidy bungalow in a neighborhood full of tidy bungalows in lower Manoa, nestled in the mountains north of downtown Honolulu, where he had lived with his mother and stepfather ever since he was a child. He parked behind his mother's 1938 black Buick Roadmaster and went inside.

"That you, Delbert?" Mother called from the den.

He could tell from the throaty slur that she had started early with her whiskey. That also likely meant that she had male company. He entered the den and found her sitting on a padded wicker sofa. The room stunk of cheap perfume, old person body odor, and cigarette smoke. Mother wore a blue housecoat thrown open, beneath which she had on a brassiere and a silky slip. Rolls of white fat overlapped the waistband. Next to her sat a balding man with a five o'clock shadow of whiskers on his cheeks, a blue-striped seersucker suit, and an unzipped fly. Mooney had no doubt that the offending member had been tucked back inside at the sound of the back door opening.

Cigarettes smoldered in an overflowing ash tray, one of the culprits for Mother's leathery skin and the mask of wrinkles that branched from her dull eyes. Her faded blonde hair, mixed with ash gray strands, hung limply on her shoulders. The pink on her cheeks and rich red lipstick applied without regard for staying within the lines gave her a clownish appearance. How could any man not be repulsed by that? Then again, he knew it wasn't her face that interested them.

"How was your day, Delbert?" she asked. It was an obligatory question designed to deflect any substantive response from Mooney and speed him on his way to his bedroom and then back out into the night so that she could complete ungodly acts with the dickless wonder next to her.

"It was fine," he said.

The man seemed uncomfortable at his presence, which made Mooney want to stay longer, to turn up the heat. Or maybe to lower the heat. He suspected his appearance had already wilted the man's desire and, at his age, it might be difficult to incite resurgence in his flaccid instrument. At the same time, Delbert had no desire to spend any more time in Mother's company than necessary. If the "gentleman caller" beside her was now unable to function as she hoped, he knew she would come knocking later, as she had when he was a boy and she first realized he had entered puberty. At least now she begged instead of commanded.

He cleared the room and entered the hallway to the bedrooms. As he left, he heard her laugh, as if she were a twenty-year-old coquette, then say, "Now, where did that thing go?"

He sought out the closed door at the end of the hall. He leaned against the wood and listened. The radio was on and a phlegmy cough informed him that Pop was listening to his shows. Sounded maybe like *The Great Gildersleeve*, a character voiced by actor Harold Peary that had first been introduced on *Fibber McGee and Molly*. Or maybe it was an episode of *The Inner Sanctum*, another of Pop's favorites.

Confined to his bed by what was already starting to be known as Lou Gehrig's Disease, named for the ballplayer who had passed away just that summer after his career was cut short by amyotrophic lateral sclerosis, Pop spent his waking hours listening to the radio with the door closed in order to shut out the sounds of his unfaithful wife cavorting with the likes of the man in the seersucker suit. At least the visitors usually left a ten spot on the coffee table when they departed. They weren't three-minute men, like those on Hotel Street, and the higher price was due to a longer tenure with his mother's sagging body than they could buy from the girls at the hotels. Mooney was surprised anyone ever left her more than a dollar.

Mooney tapped gently on the door, then opened it and stepped inside. A foul odor immediately assaulted his senses. The only light came from a naked bulb in a candlestick lamp on a low table beside the narrow bed. There were no other furnishings except for a Philco radio on a dressing table next to the side wall, barely within arm's reach of the bed, and a wicker frame wheelchair. The bed linens were dingy, something Mooney knew more than saw, due to the dim lighting and the fact that they were always dingy. The radio was broadcasting *Gildersleeve*.

A frail figure lay in the center of the bed, head propped up on a feather pillow, a sheet and threadbare blanket pulled to his chest. Thin arms, muscles long since atrophied, extended from the covers, hands clasped at his waist. His eyes were closed, his face aged decades beyond his years. Were it not for an occasional gasp for air and pronounced swallowing, the figure might be mistaken for a corpse.

"Pop, you awake?" Mooney asked.

The old man opened his eyes and, without moving his head, looked at Mooney.

Mooney closed the door behind him and crossed the room to the window, which was barely ajar. He pushed it as far open as it would go. A sultry breeze swept in and lightly mussed the old man's hair.

Mooney pulled the covers back to reveal the source of the stench: Pop's pajamas were soaked at the crotch and the sheets beneath him stained brown by watery stool from a bowel movement that probably occurred hours earlier.

"Okay, Pop, let's get you cleaned up," Mooney said.

He took off his shoulder holster and laid it on the dressing table, then left the room and returned moments later carrying a pan filled with warm water, a wash cloth, and a towel. Working efficiently, as if well-practiced at the routine, he stood Pop up beside the bed and gently removed his pajamas. He placed Pop's hands on his shoulders, and Pop shifted his weight, leaning on Mooney. He, too, knew the routine.

Mooney cleaned Pop thoroughly, helped him don clean pajamas, and lowered him into the wheelchair. Then he set about stripping the bed and cleaning the mattress as best he could with bleach. As he worked, the old man's eyes followed his every movement, but his head remained rigid.

"Okay, Pop, you wait right there."

Mooney lifted the thin mattress with ease and carried it from the room. He dragged it down the hall and through the living area, where Mother knelt in front of the balding man, her head buried in his lap. The man had his head back, his eyes closed, and his mouth opened in an "O" shape. Neither of them noticed Mooney as he carried the mattress through the kitchen and out to the back yard. He dropped it on the grass, next to another mattress of similar size, stained brown and yellow, but at least dry. He grabbed the dry mattress and took it back to Pop's room, where he positioned it on the bed frame, then covered it with a set of fresh sheets.

"Okay, Pop, all cleaned up now. You eaten yet?"

Pop's eyes locked onto Mooney's, and Mooney knew the old man had probably not eaten since Mooney fed him breakfast that morning before leaving for the day. He went to the kitchen, catching the sounds of the balding man's climax while he heated a watery stew that sat cold in an uncovered pan on the stove. He returned to Pop's room with a bowl and spoon, then sat on the edge of the bed. He tucked a napkin into the front of Pop's pajama top and fed him one spoonful at a time. He waited patiently for him to gum the vegetables, and each swallow seemed an endless exercise, with success or failure undecided until the final moment.

When the bowl was empty, he wiped Pop's mouth with the napkin then eased him from the wheelchair back into the bed. He pulled the covers up to his chest and positioned his arms as they were earlier, hands folded at his waist.

"Okay, Pop, I gotta go."

He leaned over and kissed the old man on the forehead, grabbed his holster, and left without another word. He entered the room adjacent to Pop's and closed the door. Thirty-seven years of age and still living with his parents. But somebody had to look out for Pop; God knows Mother wouldn't.

He dropped his holster on the floor, sat on the small bed, and swung his feet up, boots and all. He surveyed the meager furnishings of his cell, which is how he thought of it. Yet, as tiny as it was, it was better than the cell in which Pop resided, whose iron bars were a frail body that locked up an alert mind, able to hear and understand his wife's infidelity under the same roof, yet without the freedom of movement to get up, walk down the hall, and put a bullet in her brain.

Besides the bed and small bedside table, Mooney's room contained a dresser, a low secretary, and a rocking chair. He wondered where all his money had gone. Not his salary, which was hardly worthy of consideration, but there had been enough cash from the madams on Hotel Street to afford him a more luxurious lifestyle than this tiny cell. Then he remembered where it had gone—his Ford Deluxe, drink, and sex. The kind of sex he wanted—the kind of sex he *needed*—was hard to come by, and it cost more than the three dollars the whores in Chinatown charged.

He leaned his head against the wall and closed his eyes. He removed his Smith & Wesson .38 revolver from the holster and took out all the bullets save one. He spun the cylinder and placed the barrel in his mouth with his right hand. He clenched his lips around the cold metal. With his left hand, he unzipped his fly, reached inside, and freed himself.

He sat there for a moment, eyes closed, both hands tightly clenched around their respective handles. He slowly stroked with his left, as he began pulling the trigger with the index finger of his right. He squeezed his eyes tightly shut. Would this be the time? Would it happen tonight?

He felt movement in the trigger. Then—

Click.

He opened his mouth and exhaled, but left the gun where it was. He was barely aware of the tears in the corners of his eyes as he clenched the barrel again with his lips and pressed his finger against the trigger. A cough from Pop's room freed him from his trance. What would happen to Pop? How long after Pop died before Mother would even notice? Before anyone would notice? He would lie there and rot for days, and no one would be able to detect the fetid smell of decay because it would blend with the stink of urine and feces that were already a constant.

He removed the gun from his mouth and, unfinished, zipped himself back up. The ritual was complete, and he had survived again. This time he actually pulled the trigger, something he did only half the time. No need to press his luck.

He stood, reached into his pants pocket, and pulled out the cash Francis had given him for delivering the new whore. Thirty minutes later, he cruised the darker streets of Chinatown in Mother's black Buick, with a fedora pulled low across his brow and sunglasses despite the darkness of the hour. He stayed away from Hotel Street, where he was widely known, but chose instead an area known for its opium dens and gambling houses, called Blood Town. This area had once been patrolled by police officer Chang Apana before he rose in the ranks of the Honolulu Police Department and became the inspiration for novelist Earl Derr Biggers' fictional detective Charlie Chan. Honolulu's red light district seemed glitzy and glamorous compared to the narrow streets and alleys, bars, and storefronts of this section. It was a Wednesday night and the sidewalks were not crowded. A few stragglers roamed from bar to bar, while others disappeared into alleys to back entrances of living quarters. Here, Mooney could be anonymous as he sought what he needed.

He drove slowly, checking out those who walked alone, looking for familiar faces. Most people barely glanced his way when he idled beside them, checked them out, and moved on down the street. At last, up ahead, in the wide glare of his headlights, he saw a likely target, walking alone. Hard to tell from the back, but probably Hawaiian, or maybe Japanese or Chinese, medium height and slim build. He pulled up beside the figure and rolled down his window for a better look. Hawaiian. Thirteen years old, maybe; maybe younger.

Mooney pulled abreast and stopped, catching the walker's attention. Their eyes met, and he guessed maybe as young as eleven or twelve. He held up a fistful of cash.

The boy opened the passenger door and got in.

Chapter Ten

DARKNESS BLANKETED HOTEL Street, the moon partly obscured by clouds that promised rain. The bars had shut down hours ago, leaving only a few drunks staggering around in search of taxis or who resolved to walk to their homes. The servicemen had long since abandoned the hotels, which were now locked up tight, and their prime customers were fast asleep in bunks at Pearl, Schofield, Hickam, and Wheeler. The sporting girls were also fast asleep, some with the aid of opium or morphine, others simply spent from the rigors of all-day sex that were more mental than physical. The money was good, with the women in charge, but the self-degradation and disillusionment that came with that power were demanding mistresses, and their prices were steep.

A slight figure, dressed in black from head to toe, moved furtively down the darkened alley that paralleled Beretania Street. It stayed close to the buildings in order to remain in the deepest of shadows without cutting a silhouette in the splays of moonlight that forced their way through the clouds. The figure stopped at the rear entrance to the Polynesian Rooms, extracted a key from a pocket, inserted it in the lock, and slowly turned. The sound of the latch being displaced from the jamb seemed like an explosion in the figure's ears, but in reality was barely more than a soft *thunk*.

The figure pushed the door open and stepped inside, leaving it ajar. The intruder wore soft-soled shoes that barely registered on the hardwood floors, tiptoeing down the hallway to the dormitory room where the girls slept, most lying on their sides, as if unconsciously avoiding their work positions. The intruder stood in the doorway for a moment, and then moved inside.

◊ ◊ ◊

Sadie lay in her bed, covers pulled to her chin. Her tears had dried, crusting her eyelashes, but there would be plenty of time for more tears the next day. Something moved in the doorway, and Sadie caught her breath. Looking that way, she saw someone gesture to her in a "come hither" motion. Squinting, she recognized the Asian features of Lum Yee.

Sadie slid from beneath the covers. She wore the same dress she had worn all day and clutched her handbag in one fist. Wood creaked beneath her bare feet as she put them on the floor and stood. She froze, afraid to breathe. In the next bed, Kelly rolled to her other side, snorted softly, then stilled.

Sadie moved quickly to the doorway, where Lum Yee waited with a finger pressed to her lips in the universal "shhh" signal. They exited the room and moved down the hallway toward the back. Just as they reached the kitchen, Sadie heard sounds of footsteps overhead. She caught her breath again. Blood roared in her ears, and her knees buckled. Lum Yee grabbed her by the arm and helped her stay on her feet.

"Come, Missy, we hurry," Lum Yee whispered.

Abandoning silence for speed, the two women raced across the kitchen and outside. Sadie closed the door behind her, but it swung open as they turned and ran down the alley. Lum Yee led the way, moving surprisingly fast for such a small stride, with Sadie hard behind, looking over her shoulder to spy their pursuer. But none appeared.

At the end of the alley, a Ford Standard Touring Car waited on Maunakea Street, its engine running. Lum Yee opened the rear door and ushered Sadie inside, then she followed.

"*Wicki-wicki*," Lum Yee said to the Chinese driver.

The man behind the wheel pressed on the gas, and the car lurched forward. Sadie and Lum Yee both turned and peered out the rear window, toward the mouth of the alley.

Nothing.

Sadie handed Joshua Sinclair's business card to the driver. "Please take me to this address."

◊ ◊ ◊

Clad in red silk pajamas, Francis descended the stairs, a half-drunk glass of *o'ke* in her hand. An insomniac, her usual night-time routine consisted of touring her house in the dark with a stiff drink, topped off by a snack, then back upstairs to lie on her back, stare at the ceiling, and count dollars. She reached the kitchen, where she downed the remainder of her *o'ke*, then rinsed the glass and set it on the counter.

She had just turned back toward the hallway when a creaking sound, followed by a soft bang, caught her attention. She turned and looked in the direction of the sound.

The back door swung inward, bumped into the counter, bounced back, then swung and bumped again. She went to the door and looked both ways down the alley. Nothing but stillness, a welcome change from the activity of the day. She closed and locked the door that she was sure she had locked earlier. How could it possibly have opened? That would take a key.

Then it hit her. She hurried to the girls' bedroom and flipped the switch. The sudden attack of light roused the girls, who awoke muttering and complaining. Francis scanned the room. All the beds were occupied except the one she knew wouldn't be.

All the girls, except Norma, gathered in the parlor, looking disheveled, as if they had just spilled out of bed—which they had. No one noticed that Sadie was missing except Kelly, but she kept her mouth shut. None of them were accustomed to the new arrival, but since Kelly's bed was next to the one assigned to Sadie, she saw in an instant that Sadie was gone. Her valise was still there, but her handbag was not. Kelly wasn't sure what it meant, but she had her suspicions.

Francis stood in the doorway, her visage much like that of Leinani's standing guard at the front door during business hours. She scanned her charges, saving Kelly for last, where she locked gazes. Kelly shrank back under the intensity. This was not going to be good. For what seemed like an eternity, no one spoke, but the whole time Francis stared at Kelly. One by one, the other girls looked Kelly's way, also.

"Where is Sadie?" Francis asked.

"I don't know," Kelly said.

"It was your job to look after her."

"I can't look when I sleep."

"Her bed is next to yours. Are you telling me you didn't hear anything?"

"That's what I'm telling you."

"Are you sure you didn't just turn your head the other way while she slipped out the door?"

"I'm positive. I was asleep."

Francis broke her eyes away from Kelly and scanned the room again. "And none of you heard anything? Not a blessed thing?"

There were shakes of heads, but no one spoke for fear of being singled out for Francis's wrath, which was legend among the hotels in Chinatown. And they all knew that her bite was worse than her bark.

"She had to walk right past every one of your beds. Am I supposed to believe you were all just so worn out from fucking that you slept right through it?"

No response. Francis turned her glare back on Kelly. "Where would she go?"

"I don't know."

"Well, damn it, she didn't just vanish into thin air. If you know anything—*anything*—about where she might have gone, you better tell me now."

A quiver crept into Kelly's voice. "Francis, I swear it. I don't know."

Norma sauntered in, silk robe cinched at the waist, make-up on and every hair in place. As the senior whore, and the main attraction of the Polynesian Rooms, she commanded her own separate bedroom upstairs, next to Francis's room.

One of the girls moved to a couch, freeing up the *chaise longue* for Norma, who said, "Well, well, well, did our little crooner fly the coop?"

"It's because you were mean to her," Kelly said.

"Is it, now?"

72

"Yes. You were such a bitch."

"Listen, girlie, why don't you crawl back into your opium pipe and let the grown-ups deal with this?"

Kelly bit back a reply and stuck out her bottom lip in a pout. She craved just one puff on that pipe, to make all this go away, at least for a little while.

"How do you suppose she's going to get by out there?" Francis asked. She looked at Kelly again, as if no one else were in the room. "Huh? She got any money? No. Any friends? No. Where's she going to go? I can guarantee you she won't make any money singing."

"That's for damn sure," Norma said. "She'll be back any day, begging for us to let her in. You'll see."

The interrogation was interrupted by a loud knock on the front door. More of a banging than a knock. Francis disappeared out the doorway then returned in a moment with Mooney at her side. He looked as if he had been dragged out of bed and hurriedly dressed. His thick beard was overshadowed only by the darkness of his eyes. The air seemed to be sucked out of the room as soon as he entered. Francis's bite had arrived.

"You want to tell me what happened?" he asked.

He stood next to Francis and ostensibly asked the question of her, but his glare, like hers, was reserved for Kelly. The siren song of Kelly's opium called to her.

"No one seems to know," Francis said. "We're all just a bunch of see-no-evil, hear-no-evil, speak-no-evil whores."

Mooney snorted. "Kelly, Francis tells me you got pretty close to this girl today."

"I just showed her around, that's all."

Mooney walked toward Kelly until he loomed over her. His shadow clouded her features as she looked up at him. Frightened though she was, she tried her best to put a look of defiance on her face. She had been on the receiving end of Mooney before.

"I better not find out you're lying to me," Mooney said. "If I do…"

He let the unfinished sentence hang in the air.

Kelly rubbed her cheek. Her fingers rolled over a lump that was the result of a break that had healed unevenly just over a year ago.

Yes, Francis's bite was far worse than her bark.

Chapter Eleven
December 4

THE MORNING SUN peeked down an alley on Kuhio Avenue and stretched its way toward the shadows where Sadie sat behind a row of trash cans with her back to the wall and her head resting on her drawn-up knees. Sleep had not come easy for her. She had shivered for hours in the tropical warmth until at last, overcome with exhaustion, she cried herself to sleep. But now the city was coming to life and street noises mixed with the sunlight to rouse her. She raised her head and wiped at dried tears that crusted her eyelids shut. When she was finally able to open her eyes, she looked around at her surroundings, to confirm that, although she might be tossed out with the trash in an alley, she was at least not captive in a whorehouse.

A police car passed by on the street, and she shrank back, making herself small. She held her breath, convinced the next sounds she heard would be the squeal of brakes then the purr of an engine in reverse. Would it be Mooney or another policeman in cahoots with him? She sat and waited, but heard nothing more. She slowly let out her breath, only to catch it again as she heard another vehicle. She had not seen this one go by, yet she heard the unmistakable sound of a door opening, followed by shoes scuffling on concrete. Then the jangling of keys, as if being fitted into a lock.

She moved cautiously to the edge of the alley, careful not to kick any of the trash cans. At the edge, she hugged the building and peeked around the corner. She felt warmth at seeing Joshua Sinclair, Esquire, unlocking the door to his office.

"Mr. Sinclair," she said. Her voice came out in a hoarse whisper.

Joshua stopped, key in the door, and looked around. Apparently seeing nothing, he extracted the key, turned the knob, and pushed open the door.

"Mr. Sinclair." Louder this time.

Joshua looked her way then walked to the corner. His eyes widened in surprise at the sight of Sadie shivering in the alley.

"Miss MacKenzie? What on earth are you doing here, child?"

"I've run away from Hotel Street. You said if you could ever be of assistance—" Her voice faltered. She cleared her throat then tried again. "I need your assistance, sir. You have no obligation to help me, but—"

She spied a police car approaching. She gasped, then scuttled to the end of the row of trash cans and squatted down.

Joshua turned to see what had frightened her. He waited until the police car passed, then gestured to Sadie. "Come, child. Quickly. Quickly."

Sadie ran to Joshua, who ushered her inside his office and closed the door.

Mooney pulled into his reserved spot in back of the police station and went inside. He was exhausted, having cruised the streets of Honolulu for hours throughout the night, but to no avail. He thought he knew every inch of this city, but last night he saw areas he never knew existed as he systematically drove, and walked if the area called for it, a grid starting at the bull's eye of Hotel Street, and steadily working his way outward in an ever-widening circuit. But somehow, this little virgin had disappeared into thin air. Fitting in a way, as a virgin on Hotel Street was surely a mythical creature.

He went directly to the office of Honolulu Police Chief William Gabrielson, who had summoned him by radio after receiving a call from Francis that morning about the missing whore. Gabrielson walked a fine line on Hotel Street, between enforcing the laws to keep decent society off of his back and pacifying the military, who used the whores of the red-light district to babysit its boys. It was a delicate balance that depended upon compliance by the whores with the rules—the "You may nots"—and enforcement by men like Mooney. If the officers took a dollar or two from the madams, that was fine with him as long as this particular vice stayed bottled up in Hotel Street.

The stern-faced chief didn't look up when Mooney entered, but instead kept his face buried in a report. Mooney stood at attention in front of his desk and waited until Gabrielson was ready. He had learned that the chief had his own timetable for doing things. He had also learned that the longer the chief made you wait before turning his attention to you, the angrier he was and, thus, the more trouble you were in.

Gabrielson kept Mooney waiting a full ten minutes; he must have read the same report at least half a dozen times. At last, he shuffled the report aside and looked at Mooney.

"Have you found the whore?" he asked.

"It's just a matter of time."

"I'll take that as a 'no.' This will go much better if you simply answer the questions I ask."

"Yes, sir."

"How long has she been gone?"

"Francis isn't quite sure. It's been about seven hours since she called me. The girl obviously left some time before that."

"If she's on foot, she can't have gone far."

"My men are still searching, sir. They'll find her soon enough."

"Maybe not. Not if someone is helping her hide."

"There is no one, sir," Mooney said. "She has no family and she has no friends here."

"Did she arrive on the *Lurline* yesterday?"

"Yes, sir. I met her at the pier."

"Then perhaps she met someone on board. Someone who has opened his or her doors for her. Get the passenger manifest from yesterday's arrival and see if there are any likely candidates, then send your men door to door."

Mooney couldn't understand why the chief was so insistent on finding this girl. He also couldn't understand the lengths to which he wanted Mooney's men to go as part of the search. Gabrielson must have read the question on his face, because he said, "This is not a good time to have whores on the loose, Mooney. I'm getting pressure from the good citizens of Honolulu, some horseshit group called the Social Protection Committee, to shut the houses down."

Gabrielson stood and leveled his index finger at Mooney. "Find this girl, Mooney, and take her back where she belongs."

Ahhh, but there's the rub, Mooney thought. This girl didn't belong there.

Sadie sat on a sofa and sipped tea. Joshua first sat in a Queen Anne chair across from her as she started her tale, but soon took to his feet and paced. By now, she figured he must have covered a mile and worn a layer of thread from the silk Oriental rug that graced the hardwood floors. Every few laps, he banged his fist on the partner's desk behind him, its top cluttered with papers.

"I kept your card, Mr. Sinclair, as you told me to," she said. "I didn't know where else to turn."

"You did the right thing by coming here." He banged the desk again. "Damn! And you had no idea what you were getting into?"

"None whatsoever, sir. I wanted to be a singer. I was told I could perform for the boys in uniform if I came to Honolulu. I had no idea even when Officer Mooney met me at the pier. In fact, I had no idea Officer Mooney was a police officer. I thought he was simply a hired hand to bring me to the place where I would perform. It wasn't until..."

Her voice trailed off, and she took another sip of tea to hide her sniffle.

Sinclair stood over her, took her chin in his hand, and turned her head. She winced and closed her eyes as he inspected her bruised cheek.

"Did Mooney do this to you?" he asked.

"Yes, sir."

He snorted. "He's an evil man, that one is. Damnably evil."

"Do you know him?"

"Only what I hear. Rumors."

"What kind of rumors?"

"Rumors of things not fit for your ears."

He resumed his pacing. "I must apologize to you, Miss MacKenzie. I could have prevented this."

"That's nonsense, Mr. Sinclair."

"No, it's true. I was aware of the things that happen on Hotel Street. I should have spoken up; I should have questioned you when you said that was your destination. But I didn't. I'm just a foolish old man." He banged his fist on the desk again.

"You are not a foolish old man, Mr. Sinclair. You're a kind, gentle soul. You spoke to me when you didn't have to. Even when you thought I was a...a whore, you were kind to me. Most people would have shunned me, like the woman at the well in the *Bible* story. But you didn't. You were kind and you offered your assistance. It was your kindness that led me here now."

"Thank you, Miss MacKenzie, for your generous words."

"And please do call me Sadie, Mr. Sinclair."

"Only if you'll call me Joshua."

"All right, then. Joshua it is."

"Would you care for more tea?"

"No, thank you. I shouldn't stay. I'm afraid I may already have gotten you in trouble if Officer Mooney learns that I'm here. I know it's against the law to be away from the Polynesian Rooms."

"It's not against the law."

"But Officer Mooney said—"

Joshua banged his fist on the desk again. "Mooney is a liar. A liar and a sadist. There are rules for Hotel Street, but not laws. You have broken no laws."

They both fell silent. Joshua resumed his position in the Queen Anne.

"Mr. Sinclair—Joshua, I want to go home. Will you help me?"

"Of course I'll help you. I'll book you passage on the *Lurline*, which is leaving tomorrow to return to San Francisco."

"I have no money to pay you."

"Seeing you on board a ship bound for home will be payment enough."

"What will I do until tomorrow?"

"You'll come home with me. We'll get some food in you and get you cleaned up. Some of Juanita's things may fit you. And Nani, my housekeeper, will stay with you while I go to the Matson Lines to book your passage to San Francisco. Mooney will most likely check the passenger manifests on all ships, so we'll determine a suitable name for you to travel under. He'll also have eyes and ears on the pier, so we'll have to determine a way to get you on board the *Lurline* without Mooney or his men discovering you. And then you'll be headed miles away from Hotel Street."

"Oh, Joshua, that would be wonderful. Do you think we can succeed?"

"We will, or I'll die trying."

Mooney assembled a room full of vice and uniformed police officers and passed out passenger manifests from the *Lurline*. Once each man had his copy, Mooney addressed the group.

"These are passengers who arrived yesterday on the *Lurline*. I have narrowed it down to the most likely one hundred."

"Most likely what, sir?" a uniformed officer asked.

"Most likely persons that Sadie MacKenzie might have associated with on the ship. These are the people whose staterooms were in proximity to hers, who shared dinner times with her, or who are close to her in age. She has no friends, no money, no visible means of support in Honolulu. She expressed a desire to return to San Francisco, so that means she may be looking for a way to board the next ship out. That's the *Lurline* again, tomorrow. But until then, she has to find a place to hide, and that means somebody is harboring her. If she was on the streets, we would have found her by now. So we'll go door to door and talk to these people and see if any of them knows the whereabouts of our young runaway."

A young officer entered with another handful of pages. Mooney directed him to pass them out, after first taking one for himself.

"Gentlemen, we will find this woman. If not today, then tomorrow at the pier. Or the next sailing, or the next or the next. We will watch all gangways, all dinghies, all means to stow away on a ship. We will find her, gentlemen, or I'll know the reason why. And there's a bonus in it for the man who finds her."

He held up the page for all to see—a hand-drawn sketch of a young woman who looked strikingly like Sadie MacKenzie.

"She's a looker, boys," he said. "And she's a virgin. I'll give you one of my turns at her."

The room broke into applause.

Chapter Twelve

WEARING A FLOWER-PRINT dress about two sizes too large, Sadie sat alone at the dining room table in Joshua's house and ate heartily of *opakapaka*—Hawaiian pink snapper—steamed Chinese style, along with fresh vegetables, yeast rolls, and a side dish of pineapple. Joshua's housekeeper, a heavyset Hawaiian woman named Nani, kept her glass filled with ice water and watched with approval as Sadie ate.

"Nani, this fish is delicious," Sadie said.

"Glad you like it, sistah. After you finish, we work on that dress, make it fit you fine."

"Are you sure Mr. Sinclair won't mind my wearing it?"

"He say to fit you in it. Ever since Miss Juanita pass away las' year, he no can bring hisself to empty her closet. He happy it put to good use."

"Have you been working for Mr. Sinclair long?"

"Mo' than ten year."

"Tell me about his wife."

"She *da kine ono*." Sadie wrinkled her brow in confusion. "She a good woman," Nani said. "Just like Mistah Joshua."

Sadie cleaned her plate then washed down the last mouthful with water. She leaned back and sighed, full and optimistic for the first time since her arrival. Nani began clearing the dishes.

"How did she die?" Sadie asked.

"I don' know doctor words, but clot? That how you say?"

"Yes, blood clot. Where?"

"*Po'o*." Another wrinkle of Sadie's brow. "Her head."

Ahh, a blood clot in her brain. Sadie had heard of that happening before, and she knew it to invariably be fatal.

"Mistah Joshua on mainland when it happen. By time we get word to him and he return, Miss Juanita already bury. Mistah Joshua *kaumaha* since that day. *Kaumaha* mean sad."

Sadie had noticed sadness about Joshua. She recalled their conversation aboard the *Lurline* when she asked about his family. He said his wife was in Hawaii, but that she would not be at the pier to meet him. And that he missed her terribly. Now she knew why.

She heard the door open, followed by footsteps. Joshua entered the room and whispered something to Nani, then removed his hat and sat at the other end of the table as Nani brought his meal, the same as she had served Sadie. He pulled a ticket from his pocket and laid it on the table.

"There you are, Miss MacKenzie, one first class passage to San Francisco. You'll be traveling under the name of Ruth Sinclair. You'll be my niece for the trip."

"Oh, Joshua, first class? I'll never be able to repay you."

"I'm a regular on the Matson ships so I sometimes am entitled to special dispensation on price and accommodations." He took a bite of his *opakapaka* and nodded at Nani, as if to signify his approval. "Knowing that you are safe and in comfort will be sufficient repayment. And you must promise me that you'll be my dinner companion on my next visit to San Francisco."

"I promise."

A loud rapping noise at the front door interrupted their conversation. Joshua looked sharply at Nani, who hurried to Sadie and pulled her chair back.

"Come, child," Nani said. "To the back of the house."

Sadie did as she was told, a puzzled look on her face. She went down a narrow hallway to the guest bedroom that had been prepared for her, entered, and closed the door. Then she pressed her ear against the wood and tried to hear what was transpiring in the front part of the house.

Joshua continued eating as if there had been no interruption, while Nani went to answer the door after first quickly clearing away Sadie's place setting. A moment later, she returned with a rough-looking man in tow.

"Mistah Sinclair, this *maka'i* wish to speak to you."

As Joshua suspected, and feared—a police officer. He had been told that the police obtained a copy of the passenger manifest from the Matson Lines for the *Lurline*. He also thought he knew why. He put his fork down, took a sip of water, and wiped his mouth with a napkin.

"Can I help you, officer?"

"I'm Sergeant Mooney. Honolulu vice."

"I repeat, Sergeant, can I help you?"

"You sailed on the *Lurline* from San Francisco and arrived yesterday." Mooney paused, as if he had primed the pump and now it was Joshua's turn to talk.

"You're providing me with information that I already possess, Sergeant, but you're not answering my question."

"I understand from other passengers that you spoke with a young lady on board."

"I spoke with a lot of young ladies on board. And elderly ladies. Even a gentleman or two."

Joshua sensed frustration mounting in Mooney, and he suppressed a smile. It took him back to his younger days as a trial lawyer, frustrating his opponent's witnesses as he questioned them in court.

Mooney reached into his inside coat pocket and extracted a folded page, then opened it and showed it to Joshua. Joshua looked at an uncanny likeness of Sadie and silently complimented the artist.

"This young lady, Mr. Sinclair," Mooney said. An accusatory tone crept into his voice.

"Yes," Joshua said. "I saw a young woman on board who resembles that sketch. I believe I may even have spoken to her."

"You may even have danced with her."

"Perhaps. Is it a crime to dance onboard ocean liners with young ladies? If so, it's news to me. And if so, I believe you're a little out of your jurisdiction, Sergeant."

Mooney folded the page and slipped it back into his pocket. While Joshua felt that he had put the officer off balance a moment earlier, the man seemed to be regaining his stride. He realized that he was being too defensive and that it was setting off alarm bells for Mooney.

"No, it's not a crime to dance with young ladies on a ship," Mooney said.

"Then what seems to be the problem?"

"This woman is a whore."

Joshua struggled to control his temper. To let Mooney know that he was offended would raise the question of *why* he was offended.

"So is it a crime to dance with whores on a ship?" Joshua asked. "Not that I was aware that I traveled with any."

Mooney smiled. "No sir, it's not. But whoring is against the law in Hawaii, and it's a crime to help a whore evade arrest."

"Oh, it's a crime, is it? Then I wonder why Hotel Street operates night and day with the cooperation of the Honolulu Police Department. I have even heard tell that police officers, vice officers, receive money from the madams on Hotel Street. But I don't suppose you'd know anything about that, would you, Sergeant?"

Mooney's smile shortened into a tight grimace. "No, I wouldn't."

"No, I was sure a man of your obvious integrity would be ignorant of such matters." Joshua turned back to his meal.

"So you're saying you haven't seen this woman?"

Joshua set his fork down and leaned back in his chair. "No, Sergeant. Your listening skills are in decay. I'm saying I have seen that woman—on board the *Lurline*. I spoke with her, and I may even have danced with her. But I assure you I am not aiding any whores in evading arrest."

A truthful statement if ever he had spoken one. After all, Sadie MacKenzie was not a whore.

"All right, sir," Mooney said. "I apologize for interrupting your supper. Good night, sir." He turned to leave as Nani approached. "I can see myself out."

Joshua ignored his exit, calmly eating his fish. Calm on the outside, that is. But on the inside, his fears roamed his heart at will. They would not be calmed until Sadie MacKenzie was safely aboard the *Lurline* and outside of Hawaii's territorial waters. The question was whether he could get her there before Mooney found her.

Chapter Thirteen
December 5

NANI WRAPPED A scarf over Sadie's head and slipped a pair of sunglasses onto her face, and the transformation was complete. Wearing a frilly white dress, heavy on the ruffles and lace, with pancake make-up covering her bruised cheek, and a pile of hair lying on the floor where it fell after Nani snipped it, Sadie didn't even recognize herself when she looked in the mirror.

"I swear, Nani, you're a miracle worker," she said.

"Now your own mother not recognize you." She brought a pair of low-heeled shoes and set them on the floor. "Put these on, Miss Sadie."

Sadie slipped her feet in and smiled. They were snug, but comfortable enough.

"Mistah Joshua waitin'," Nani said.

She picked up a valise that Joshua had filled with his wife's clothes, while Sadie clutched her handbag with both hands. Nani led the way to the parlor. Joshua looked up from the sofa, where he was reading the newspaper. He raised his eyebrows and laughed.

"Miss MacKenzie, if I didn't know who you are, I wouldn't know who you are."

He stood and checked his pocket watch. "I understand the *Lurline*'s departure has been delayed, but we'll go ahead and get you on board."

Sadie gasped. "Delayed?"

"Don't fret, my dear. It has nothing to do with you. There is a particularly large contingent of passengers for the voyage, and it has caused some scheduling difficulties. But that will work to our favor, as it will provide added protection to be lost in such crowds. Once you're on board, I'll find you in your stateroom. Then, if the police search the boat, which is highly unlikely, I'll be the one they find in the stateroom. I'll make my departure when last call is made to go ashore. After the *Lurline* leaves the dock, you'll be safe and sound."

He grabbed a thick envelope from a coffee table and handed it to her. "Put this in your handbag. This will help you to make a start once you reach port in San Francisco."

"Mr. Sinclair—"

"I thought we settled that. It's Joshua."

"Joshua, I can't take your money. I've already taken enough of your kindness."

"Now you shush. Make an old man happy and take it with you."

Sadie dropped her handbag and threw her arms around Joshua. He squeezed her tightly for a moment and then held her at arm's length.

"All right, we must go. Remember, stay close to Nani. I don't think Sergeant Mooney got a close look at her last night. And she'll wear her floppy hat, which will offer plenty of disguise in any event. Besides, men like Mooney think all *kanakas* look alike."

"Kanakas?"

"That means natives. But I'm sure he'll remember me after our conversation. I'll provide the diversion you and Nani need to ascend the gangplank."

Sadie nodded.

"Good. Let's go."

Throngs had gathered at the pier for "boat day," some to see off family and friends among the 800 passengers, while others simply sought any excuse for a party. The color of the day was white: white cotton dresses, white linen suits, white hats, white parasols, white, white, white. Beachboys serenaded young ladies, hula dancers posed with young men, Hawaiian women sold leis, streamers fluttered, and the Royal Hawaiian Band played the music of the Islands. All in all, Sadie thought the scene resembled a Hollywood extravaganza.

She and Nani worked their way through the crowd, blending with other passengers. As they drew closer to the ship, Sadie saw Mooney positioned at the gangplank. He freely moved his head as he scrutinized every passenger that passed by. Other officers were scattered throughout the crowd and at different entry points to the *Lurline*. Sadie clutched her handbag and cast her eyes downward, afraid to make eye contact with anyone.

Glancing up again, she saw Mooney looking her way. She stopped, her feet frozen to the ground. Nani took her by the arm, valise in the other hand, and whispered, "Come on, child. Don't attract attention."

"He'll know me."

She raised her head again and saw that Mooney had looked away. She saw Joshua near the gangplank, who looked back at her, smiled, and nodded. Then he approached Mooney.

Mooney shifted from one foot to the other, tired of standing. He had been there for hours, since long before the scheduled boarding time. With the repeated delays, his feet were starting to scream and his back ached. He was starting to wonder if the girl would even show up. Surely not at the gangplank. She would need a ticket, and she certainly couldn't afford that, not even for steerage. No, if anything, she would stow away, like the little beggar she was.

He was just about to summon one of his men to take his position by the gangplank so he could survey the length of the ship when he heard a familiar voice.

"Any luck, Sergeant?"

Turning, he saw the lawyer with whom he had spoken the night before. Sinclair, wasn't it?

"What are you doing here, counselor?" Mooney asked. "I thought you just returned from the mainland?"

"Seeing a business associate off. It's always a grand celebration when the *Lurline* leaves port, don't you think?"

Sinclair walked in a narrow semi-circle, and Mooney shifted so that he continued to face him. Sinclair looked up at the passengers lining the decks and waved. Mooney glanced over his shoulder. High up, a man in a light-colored suit tipped his hat and waved back at Sinclair. Or at least so it seemed.

"I'm curious about something, Sergeant," Sinclair said.

"Yeah? What?"

"Do you think we'll be attacked by the Japanese?"

"What the hell kind of question is that?"

"You're a police officer. I wondered if maybe you heard things or had access to news that others of us might not. Much of my business involves the shipping of goods, so I wondered if you could help ease my mind."

Sadie and Nani watched as Joshua engaged Mooney in conversation. Each time Joshua moved away from the gangplank a bit, Mooney shifted his body to face him. They appeared to be deep in conversation, and Mooney no longer had his eye on the passengers.

"Okay, Missy," Nani said. "We go now."

Nani positioned herself between Sadie and where Mooney would be when they got to the gangplank, and the two women drifted to the far side of the flow of passengers going aboard. Sadie's feet still felt frozen, but Nani grabbed an arm and nudged her forward, one agonizing step at a time. Sadie didn't know how he did it, but Joshua seemed to have fully captured Mooney's attention.

Mooney turned his head suddenly, as if aware that he had fallen down on the job. His gaze swept over the approaching passengers, paused momentarily on Sadie, who cringed behind Nani's bulk, and then passed on to next passenger. He didn't recognize her! Joshua must have said something because Mooney turned back to him, again taking his eyes off of the crowd.

She breathed a sigh of relief. Just a few more steps.

Then they were at the gangplank. She felt the incline as she took her first step upward. Deliverance was at hand.

"So you don't worry about it at all?" Sinclair asked.

"Pearl is too well protected. If they hit anywhere at all, it'll be where they think we're vulnerable. I assure you, it will not be Honolulu."

"I certainly hope you're right."

Sinclair shuffled further to his right, and Mooney shifted with him. Suddenly it hit him what Sinclair was doing: He was diverting his attention from the passengers.

He looked up the gangplank, now only able to see backs. But one passenger turned and looked over her shoulder at him. A thin woman wearing a scarf, walking next to a large Polynesian woman. The Polynesian woman seemed familiar, though didn't they all look alike, really? He glanced down and saw a valise in the Polynesian woman's hand. A valise he thought he had seen before, scuffed and scarred. Or was he just imagining things? A valise was a valise was a valise, wasn't it? Didn't they all look pretty much alike, just like those damned *kanakas*?

But the woman with the scarf—there was something distinctive about her. Maybe it was the frail frame or the hesitation in her step, but alarm bells rang in his head. He raced the few steps up the gangplank and grabbed the scarfed woman's arm, which flung around, holding a handbag. And he damn sure had seen that handbag before. In fact, he had even searched it.

The woman tried to jerk her arm away. He slapped the sunglasses from her face and looked her in the eyes.

It was her. Goddamnit, it was the virgin whore!

Sadie jerked away and swung her handbag as hard as she could. It landed squarely on Mooney's nose, yet he was able to grab her arm before she could withdraw it. He squeezed her elbow, his hand a vise on the soft tissue on either side, pressing into nerves. Electric pain shot up her arm. She opened her mouth to scream just as Joshua yanked Mooney around.

"Unhand her!"

Mooney released his grip on Sadie, set his legs, and delivered a roundhouse blow to Joshua's jaw. The lawyer dropped to the gangplank, flat on his back. The other passengers scattered, fear in their eyes, as if they had just walked into a war.

While Mooney had his back turned, Nani put her arm around Sadie and they bolted up the gangplank. Mooney gave chase, overtaking them quickly. He grabbed Sadie by the hair, clutching it and the scarf in one meaty grip, and yanked. Sadie leaned backward, but was held on her feet by Nani pulling in the opposite direction. A second police officer joined the fray. He stepped over Joshua's prone body, lowered his shoulder, and bull-rushed Nani from behind. She released her hold on Sadie as she was driven forward by the man's momentum. When she let go, Sadie's feet came out from under her and she landed on her backside, her upper body held aloft by Mooney's grip on her hair.

Mooney grabbed her by the hand and pulled her down the gangplank toward the dock. She wriggled to free herself, but to no avail. As she was dragged past Joshua, he rolled to his side and struggled to focus on her. He got unsteadily to his feet and charged Mooney. His shoulder caught Mooney in the ribcage and sent him staggering. Mooney released Sadie and sprawled face first on the rough wooden gangplank.

Unable to regain his own balance, Joshua fell in a heap next to Mooney. Sadie reached to help him just as Mooney returned to his feet. Sadie swung her handbag again, and it caught Mooney in the side of the face. He staggered to his right, his foot caught the edge of the gangplank, and he tumbled off the side. The drop to the dock was about five feet, where he hit with a dull thud, then rolled once. He stopped, teetering precariously at the edge of the water.

Joshua stood with Sadie's assistance, still unsteady on his feet. "Miss MacKenzie, a dollar. Give me a dollar."

She stared at him in confusion.

"A dollar, Sadie. Now."

Still confused, she reached into her handbag and pulled out a dollar bill. Just as she handed it to him, Mooney grabbed her from behind and jerked her away. He threw her to the dock, where another officer captured her. The dollar fluttered from her hand to the gangplank, just out of Joshua's reach. As Joshua bent to pick it up, Mooney removed a weighed sap from his pocket and swung upward. It slammed into Joshua's face. Joshua dropped on his back. Blood gushed from a rip on his forehead. He pressed his hand to his face to staunch the flow of blood, which was already streaming into his eyes, blinding him. He wiped it clear and watched helplessly as the other officer dragged a screaming Sadie away.

Joshua rolled over and got to his knees. Mooney delivered a roundhouse kick to Joshua's face. He flopped onto his back. The dollar bill blew off the gangplank, toward the water's edge.

Sadie wrestled free from the officer and swung her handbag at him, but he ducked under it. She had just drawn back her hand to swing again when Mooney grabbed her arm and spun her around. He struck with the sap again, and it smashed into her forehead. She dropped unconscious to the dock. Mooney and the other officer each grabbed her by an arm and dragged her through the crowd.

Nani, her nose bleeding, tried to help Joshua to his feet. His face was covered in blood and he looked wildly about, as if searching for something. Then he spied the dollar bill on the dock, on the verge of blowing into the water. He pulled away from Nani, rolled off the gangplank, and dropped several feet to the dock.

"Mistah Joshua," Nani yelped.

He got to his hands and knees and crawled, with agonizing slowness, to the edge of the dock.

"Mistah Joshua, what you do?" She waddled down the gangplank. "Mistah Joshua!"

Just as a gust of wind lifted the dollar bill, Joshua caught it and let out a triumphant "ah, hah!" He clutched the bill in his bloody hand and held it up for all to see. "You're my witnesses. You all saw it."

An elderly man helped him to his feet. "Yes, we all saw it. They beat you and took the girl."

Joshua clenched the bill tightly and held it in the man's face. "No, this. This!"

"What, sir?"

"She paid my retainer. I'm her lawyer now."

Then he collapsed lifeless on the pier.

Chapter Fourteen

SERGEANT ROB SANDFORD sat in his Jeep across Beretania Street from the Polynesian Rooms and watched the lines of servicemen to the hotels wind down as closing time approached, but his mind wasn't on his job, which thus far had included breaking up three fights and making four arrests for public drunkenness. No, he was still thinking about the frightened young girl he had seen two days earlier. The one Mooney punched in the face. The one who met his gaze with sad, frightened eyes. The one who had occupied his thoughts nearly non-stop for the past 48 hours. He didn't know why, but he couldn't get her out of his mind.

Mooney's Ford Deluxe squealed to a halt outside the Polynesian Rooms, scattering some of the men who feared it was going to jump the curb and plow into them. Mooney got out of the driver's seat while another cop got out of the passenger's side. Mooney opened the rear door and dragged out the young woman who haunted his thoughts. She dropped to the street, lifeless. Rob bolted from his Jeep and ran toward her as Mooney and the other cop each grabbed an arm and jerked her upright.

"Ma'am, are you all right?" Rob asked.

He ran straight into Mooney's outstretched stiff-arm that shoved him away.

"Leave her be, soldier boy," Mooney said. "This is none of your concern."

The girl's eyes were open, but as far as Rob could tell, unseeing. She seemed dazed. Blood streamed from her forehead and crusted on her face, around her nose and mouth. She blinked, as if fighting for consciousness, then looked at Rob, clearly unfocused. But for just a moment, he believed she recognized him.

Rob clenched his fists and ramped into fight mode. Some of the servicemen started to gather around, itching to see a fight.

"What did you do to her?" Rob asked.

"She had a little accident, that's all. Whores are notoriously clumsy."

"I'm not a whore," the girl said.

"Shut up," Mooney replied.

Rob took the girl by the chin and inspected the damage to her face. A bruise on her cheek revealed itself beneath melting make-up, but a new bruise decorated her entire forehead, which was still bleeding from a deep gash. Her lower lip had been split and both eyes were blackened.

"Big tough man, huh?" Rob said. "Is this how you get off, beating up girls?"

"Go back and get in your Jeep where you can watch all your little soldier boys line up to dip their biscuits in the gravy. Is that how you get off? Huh? Maybe Francis will offer you a special price to lurk in the corner and watch."

"Kick his ass, Sarge," one of the onlookers shouted. "Sic 'em, Sarge," another said.

Reality seemed to set in on Mooney as he realized he was challenging a soldier while surrounded by servicemen. Soldiers might dislike MPs, but they hated cops. Rob could almost read Mooney's face as he sought a strategic retreat.

"I'm acting on Chief Gabrielson's orders," Mooney said. "If you've got a problem with that, take it up with him."

Mooney nodded to the other cop, and the two of them roughly dragged the girl to the front door. Leinani stepped aside and allowed them to enter.

Rob stood in the street, aware that his heart was racing. Blood pounded in his head. He had never felt so helpless.

Mooney and the cop dragged Sadie into the parlor and threw her onto the fainting couch. She still couldn't see or think straight. Something had happened outside, but she couldn't grasp exactly what. It seemed to have involved that young black soldier she had seen before. If she didn't know better, she'd think he had tried to come to her aid.

Mooney nodded to the other cop. "You're through here."

The cop nodded, glanced at Sadie with a look that might have been described as pity, and left.

A thoroughly furious Francis strode into the parlor. She looked at Sadie, bleeding on the couch. Sadie squinted, the narrowing of her eyes sufficient to condense two Francises into a blurry one.

"Lum Yee!" she yelled. "Lum Yee, get down here now, goddamnit! And bring some towels."

She went to Sadie and inspected her face, just as the young black soldier had done outside. Then she spun on Mooney.

"What the hell did you do to her?" she asked.

He shrugged. "You wanted her back; I brought her back."

"You didn't have to do that to her face."

He shrugged again. "She fell."

"How many times?"

Another shrug, as if it had become a nervous tic. "I lost count."

"I'm sure she had some help."

"Who she had help from was some damn lawyer trying to sneak her onto the *Lurline*," he said. "I suppose it would be expecting too much to hope for some gratitude from you. I'm not the one who let her fly the coop in the first place."

Lum Yee arrived, holding an armful of towels. She gasped when she saw Sadie but said nothing.

"I also need water," Francis said. "Then go get Doc Kalakaua."

Lum Yee brought the towels to Francis, but her eyes never left Sadie. Sadie watched Lum Yee and nodded, a signal not to antagonize Francis.

Francis yanked the towels from her arms. "Oh, for heaven's sake, girl, give me the towels. Get Doc Kalakaua."

"You want water?" Lum Yee said.

"I'll get the water. You fetch Doc. Now. *Wicki-wicki!*"

As Lum Yee backed out of the room, Francis tilted Sadie's face up and blotted the blood with a towel. She spit into the towel and wiped away the blood on her forehead, to get a better look at the gash.

"That's gonna need stitches."

"I'm still waiting on my 'thank you, Mooney.'"

"You'll wait 'til hell freezes over. She's going to have a scar, thanks to you."

"She shouldn't have run away."

"But the face, Mooney. The face. How many times do I have to tell you: Not the face. My customers want pretty girls."

"Your customers don't care what they look like as long as they spread their legs."

"When they're face-to-face, believe me, they care." She continued to wipe at Sadie's forehead. "Make yourself useful and get me some water."

Mooney left and returned a moment later with a shallow basin of cold water. Francis dipped a towel in it then turned back to Sadie.

"When do I get my money?" Mooney asked.

"You'll have it before you leave."

"I've promised to share my bonus with some of my men. When can they collect?"

Francis turned to look at Mooney. "I need to hear what Doc Kalakaua has to say first. He's going to need to stitch that up before anything happens. And I need to know if there are any other injuries that might affect her ability to perform. After that, then maybe you'll get your bonus."

Sadie tried to focus on the words they were saying. She understood that Mooney was being paid to retrieve her, but what was that about a bonus? And sharing it with Mooney's men?

"Maybe then you can tell me whether a scar matters," Francis said.

"We'll just close our eyes," Mooney said.

It cleared up for Sadie: She was the bonus.

As Doc Kalakaua stitched the cut on her forehead, Sadie sat on the edge of the cot in the same examination room where this same doctor had examined her just two days earlier to determine if she was hygienic and disease-free enough to be a whore. She wore nothing but a thin cotton gown. Now, as then, sounds of the unthinkable resonated through the ceiling directly overhead. Unless a miracle happened, she would soon be up in those cubicles earning her room and board and repaying Francis for her passage on the *Lurline*. The price would be a little piece of her soul each time.

"Will it leave a scar, Doctor?" she asked.

"I'm afraid so, miss."

He kept working, his lips pursed as he pinched the skin with one hand and pushed a needle through with the other, then nodded as he tied off the last stitch. "There, that should do it." He put the needle and thread back into his bag, and leaned back to appraise the stitches. "I'll have some headache powder sent over a little later. Don't do anything strenuous for at least the next twenty-four hours."

"What do you mean by strenuous?"

He looked at her for a long moment, and then he left wordlessly.

Francis and Mooney descended the stairs as Kalakaua exited the examination room. He frowned at Mooney, who ignored him, then gestured for Francis to follow him into the parlor.

"Alone," he said.

Mooney turned up the hallway and stopped outside of the examination room, then grabbed the door knob and pushed it open. Sadie stood in front of the mirror, inspecting her wounds as Mooney stepped inside. Her eyes widened in panic.

"Get out!" she shrieked.

Mooney closed the door behind him and turned the key to lock it. Sadie backed into a corner, her arms crossed in front.

Mooney stepped closer until he was within arm's reach. He put his hand in his coat pocket, pulled out something, and held it toward her. She kept her arms crossed, as if to ward off evil spirits. And truly, she had never seen a more evil spirit than this man before her.

Mooney opened his hand, and a red poker chip dropped to the floor. It bounced up on its edge and rolled under the cot. Mooney pulled out another poker chip and dropped it.

And another. And another.

◊ ◊ ◊

Like Sadie, Francis also had her arms folded, not in a protective manner but a defiant one. She raised her voice as she spoke to Kalakaua.

"Don't you try to tell me how to run my business."

"I do not mean to do so," Doc Kalakaua said, "but—"

"But, my ass. She'll work when I tell her to, and not you or anyone else will tell me different."

"At least twenty-four hours, Francis. Forty-eight or seventy-two would be better, but at least one day."

A commotion from the front of the hotel interrupted their conversation. Loud, angry voices.

"Goddamn drunken sailors," Francis muttered.

"Miss Francis!" Leinani called. "You needed here now."

Kalakaua followed her to the entryway where Leinani blocked the door. She glanced over her shoulder at Francis and moved aside. Francis stepped into the doorway to confront a very angry man with gray hair and a bandage across his nose and cheek and wearing a blood-spattered white linen suit.

"What's the meaning of this?" she asked.

"Madam, I'll thank you to show me to my client," the man said.

He extracted a business card from his vest pocket and handed it to Francis, who glanced at it quickly, then back at the man.

"And just who the hell is your client, Mr. Joshua L. Sinclair, Esquire, attorney-at-law?" She spoke the words as if spitting out a vile epithet.

"Miss Sadie MacKenzie," he said.

An ear-splitting scream emanated from the bowels of the house.

Chapter Fifteen
December 7

ALL WAS STILL and peaceful in the early morning hours on the Pacific, 230 miles north of Honolulu. The moon cast its light on the inky black waters, with an occasional whitecap to break the monotony as waves crashed against each other. A sound called from the distance, over the ocean's roar, like the angry buzz of a hive of bees. Something slowly appeared on the horizon, silhouetted against the darkness: Aircraft carriers, with the Rising Sun flag waving above each of them. The *Kido Butai*—the Japanese strike force.

On the decks of each of the ships, row after row of warplanes were lined up, their engines racing and propellers spinning. Over four hundred in all. Two reconnaissance planes had already launched and were on their way to Oahu. Another four scout planes patrolled the area between the *Kido Butai* and the privately-owned Hawaiian island of Ni'ihau. Pilots who were to make up the second attack wave lined the flight decks. As the first wave taxied into position, the waiting pilots raised their arms in rhythm.

"Banzai! Banzai! Banzai!"

Plane after plane after plane raced down the runways and off into the night sky. Airborne, they hooked up in tight formation and flew low on the horizon.

PART TWO

LIFE ON HOTEL STREET

Chapter Sixteen

LIFE CHANGED IN the blink of an eye throughout the Hawaiian Islands. Within an hour of the attack, territorial governor Joseph Poindexter, acting under authority of the Hawaiian M-Day Bill, found that "a state of affairs exists arising out of an attack upon the Territory of Hawaii and that all of the circumstances make it advisable to protect the Territory of Hawaii and its inhabitants," and he declared "a defense period to exist" throughout the territory. That same afternoon, Poindexter issued a second proclamation suspending the writ of *habeas corpus* and placing the territory under martial law.

That second proclamation turned over all governing authority to the United States military under the control of Lieutenant General Walter Short, who assumed the position of military governor and issued a proclamation of his own under authority of the Hawaiian Organic Act of 1900, a federal law that established a government for the Territory of Hawaii. General Short's proclamation told the Hawaiian people: "The imminence of attack by the enemy and the possibility of invasion make necessary a stricter control of your actions than would be necessary or proper at other times. I shall therefore shortly publish ordinances governing the conduct of the people of the Territory with respect to the showing of lights, circulation, meetings, censorship, possession of arms, ammunitions, and explosives, the sale of intoxicating liquors and other subjects."

Short's proclamation concluded with an admonition that divided the population into categories of "good citizens" and "others": "In order to assist in repelling the threatened invasion of our island home, good citizens will cheerfully obey this proclamation and the ordinances to be published; others will be required to do so. Offenders will be severely punished by military tribunal or will be held in custody until such time as the civil courts are able to function."

The ordinances promised by General Short did, in fact, follow, placing nearly every aspect of daily life in the entire Territory under the iron-fisted control of the United States military. Rumors abounded that the arrival of Japanese paratroopers was imminent, who would then kill citizens in their sleep. A fifth column was supposedly already at work, poisoning water supplies and signaling to the Japanese fleet that was rumored to still be nearby in the Pacific. Radios were silenced, barbed wire was strung on beaches, including Waikiki, trenches were dug in public areas, public parks were converted to storage depots, and gas masks were issued to citizens. A sundown to sunup curfew was implemented, clearing the streets at 6:30 p.m. Terrified citizens bought out grocery stores and markets during the day, then huddled inside darkened houses after curfew, with gas masks close at hand and tarpaper or black paint blotting out windows lest Japanese warplanes, which surely were on constant patrol overhead, spot a target for their bombs.

But worst, as far as many were concerned, was that the brothels of Hotel Street were shut down. Many were converted to makeshift hospitals and clinics for wounded servicemen, whose numbers overwhelmed the city's hospitals. To the surprise of "decent society," the sporting girls spent their spare time, created by the shutdown, caring for the wounded. It was no surprise on Hotel Street, though, as the girls had developed bonds with the military personnel that went deeper than three dollars for three minutes. No one mistook sex-for-pay for love, but for at least three minutes, a homesick young man could feel as if, to someone, he was the most important person in the world. And, conversely, if they closed their eyes and let their imaginations free, the girls could feel as if they were someone special to each man they laid. So when these same young men turned up in their beds, injured and dying, the girls didn't hesitate to sit by their sides, comfort their pain, clean their wounds, and hold their hands while they cried.

Sadie's own nightmare continued unabated. Now, afraid for her very life, she was relegated to sleeping on the hard wooden floors and missing meals while tending to the wounds of young men whose skin had been peeled away by burning oil in the harbor or limbs obliterated by explosives, their eyes often blinded by chemicals, unseeing but releasing tears that tracked the dirt on their faces. She had not formed the same bond with the men as had the other girls, and she viewed each of them as simply a future rapist. It was anathema for her to nurse a man to health who might someday return to assault her, but she followed orders from Francis lest Mooney be summoned to exact payment for the pile of poker chips he had dropped at her feet.

She hustled up the stairs carrying a bundle of towels. The same cubicles that were usually full of young men intent on three minutes of passion were now filled with the wounded, their cries and groans filling the air. She ducked into the first cubicle, its narrow bed occupied by a young man, surely no more than twenty-five years old. Bandages covered his eyes and hands and a thick swath of gauze encircled his abdomen. Blood seeped through the gossamer material and oozed down his side onto the cotton ticking that served as a mattress. His skin had been burned black. How long would he survive?

She set the bundle on the floor, then knelt by his side and dipped the corner of a towel in a pan of water on the nightstand and dabbed at the grease on his arms and side. He twitched at her touch.

"It's all right," she said. "I'm just cleaning you up a bit."

"Thank you, miss," he said. His voice was low and phlegmy, the words slurred as if his mouth were full of cotton.

She looked at his face, but he was unable to see back. Something about him seemed familiar, but she couldn't place it. Surely just one of the dozens of men she had seen on the stairs while she was led around in a daze that first day.

"Are you in any pain?" she asked.

"I can't feel my hands," he said. "But my chest hurts. I'm one of the lucky ones, though. At least I'm still alive. I thank the good Lord for that. But my buddies…"

His voice trailed off.

Sadie continued to dab at the grease. As it cleared away, she realized that his skin was not burned; it was naturally back. He was a Negro. Now she thought she knew why he seemed familiar.

"Were you on one of the ships?" she asked.

"No. I was at Schofield Barracks."

"You're a military policeman."

"That's right. How did you know?"

"I saw you the day I first arrived."

He sat up, grimacing at the pain, and swiveled his head her way. "You're her." There was recognition in his tone.

"Yes."

"You don't belong here."

"No."

"Then why are you here?"

"I'm here to take care of you."

He lay back down. "Then it must be God's will."

God's will! God's will? How could it possibly be God's will that she be in a whorehouse, her virginity lost to brutal rape by an animal like Mooney, with a future of degradation ahead? What kind of God had a will like that? But then she remembered a Bible verse her mother had taught her as they traveled from Oklahoma to California, driven out of their home by drought, famine, and dust that blew across the prairie with vengeance. "All things work together for good for those who are called according to his purpose." Mama had assured her that good comes from bad if you just have faith to see it through. But Sadie hadn't seen the good. Papa left, Mama died, and Billy had been taken away, and now here she was. Where was the good?

She fought back a tear. "I have to go now," she said.

She stood, but he grabbed her arm, his bandaged hand rough on her skin. "Please don't go," he said.

"I have others I must tend to."

His voice quivered when he spoke next. "I'm scared."

"I know you are. I'm scared, too."

"I don't want to be alone."

"I'll be back. But there are other boys I have to take care of, too."

"You promise you'll be back?"

"I promise."

He released his grip on her arm. She stepped back then picked up the bundle of towels and left the greasy, bloodied one behind in the corner. She turned for the door.

"What's your name?" he asked.

She stopped in the doorway, but didn't turn around. "My name is Sadie."

"God bless you, Sadie."

She stepped into the hallway and scurried to the next cubicle.

As the hour for curfew drew nigh, Mooney wheeled his Deluxe down Ala Moana Boulevard, headed toward Chinatown. Even his badge would not immunize him if he were caught out after hours, particularly if he was stopped with the crumpled package on the floorboard. The military had clamped down on the city, forcing its good citizens to hunker down behind locked doors and blackened windows. Everyone lived in fear of the next attack, which Mooney was convinced was inevitable. The Japs had caught them with their pants down, and the next wave of Zeroes would strip them of both their pants and drawers. The question wasn't whether that would happen, but when.

The panic in the aftermath had led to, in Mooney's opinion, a vast overreaction that stripped the civil authorities of all control over a city that had been his playground. Previously able to move about at will, terrorizing whores into submission and doing as he pleased, he and his whole department had been subjugated to the same military authorities whose slumber had resulted in the current crisis. Martial law had placed him and his brethren under the thumb of the negligent. Rage boiled inside him and filled every cell of his being. But contemptuous though he was, he also realized he was powerless to complain, at least for now.

The sidewalks were abandoned as he pulled to the curb on Beretania Street in front of the Polynesian Rooms, reached across and opened the passenger door, then pushed the package over the threshold. Without coming to a complete halt, he used his right foot to push it the rest of the way out the door onto the filthy street, then he accelerated away, the rising speed of the car forcing the door shut as he went.

As Sadie descended the stairs, she heard a vehicle slowing outside, a dull *thump*, then the roar of an engine and the screech of tires on cement. She tucked the bundle of towels beneath her arm and went to a window, pulled aside the tarpaper, and looked outside. It was not yet sunset, though the shadows were lengthening. She saw a distinguishable lump at the curb.

"Miss O'Brian!" she exclaimed.

"What is it?" Francis's voice revealed her annoyance. She emerged from the parlor, glass in hand. Well on her way to her evening drunkenness, following hard on the heels of her afternoon drunkenness, which followed her morning drunkenness, Francis stood in the doorway, her robe open and her breasts sagging toward her abdomen. She had gotten intoxicated in the aftermath of the attack then, as her business had been converted into a makeshift hospital and her beds filled with dying men, she crawled into an *o'ke* bottle and emerged only long enough to sleep at night.

"There's a boy," Sadie said.

"There are no boys," Francis said. "There won't be any more boys. They're all dead or useless."

"No, not a soldier. A boy. Outside. In the street."

Other girls gathered round Sadie and peered through the gap in the window created by the pulled-back tarpaper.

"She's right, Francis," Kelly said. "He's just a child."

Norma sauntered down the stairs. Sadie had been amazed at the transformation wrought in her nemesis, who had taken control of the house as Francis disappeared into a fog of intoxication. She flitted about as an angel of mercy, tending to the wounds of the injured. After their first meeting, Sadie believed that this woman had no concerns but for herself and no care except for her own welfare, but Norma had proven her wrong. Somewhere, deep inside, was a caring person with mothering instincts who had previously been hidden beneath a hard shell.

"What's going on here?" Norma asked.

Kelly pointed out the window. "Look."

Norma worked her way between Kelly and Sadie and looked outside. "Oh, my Lord," she said. She turned toward Francis. "Get the key and open the door."

Francis stared at Norma, as if uncomprehending. Her breasts hung like balloons filled with water, tugged downward by age and gravity. Her sex was exposed, the pubic hair wild and tangled.

"Put the glass down and get the key," Norma said. There was an edge to her voice that cut through the haze surrounding Francis. "Open the door."

Francis dropped her glass on the floor. It shattered on the hardwood, and shards of glass scattered among droplets of *o'ke*. She pulled her robe closed and tied it together, then turned and walked away. She returned moments later with a keyring in her right hand. She unlocked the door and stepped aside.

Sadie led the way out, followed by Kelly and Norma. She knelt beside the boy and cradled his head in her lap. He appeared to be no more than twelve or thirteen years old, the same age Billy had been the last time she saw him. He appeared dainty, almost feminine, his frame slender and willowy as he curled into the fetal position. His face was battered, both eyes swollen shut, lips cracked and bleeding. He wore only dingy underwear and a torn aloha shirt. The blood red hibiscus flowers on the shirt's pattern were sprinkled with real blood. And there was blood soaking the seat of his underwear.

"Get the boy inside," Norma said. "And someone go fetch Doc

Kalakaua."

"But Norma," Kelly said, "the curfew..."

"To hell with the curfew. Go fetch Doc Kalakaua."

The boy turned his head and looked up at Sadie. His black and puffy eyes were barely opened.

"Don't let him get me," he said.

"Don't worry," Sadie said. "You're safe now."

Chapter Seventeen

WHILE DOC KALAKAUA examined the boy, the girls gathered in the parlor and awaited his diagnosis. No one wanted the filthy, bloody ragamuffin in their bed. Although injured servicemen occupied many of them, battle wounds were different. Blood-filled underwear meant something else entirely.

"This is ridiculous," Norma said. "We've done our part for this city and for the boys, and all it's gotten us is hard floors to sleep on and bloody sheets in our beds."

"Sounds like you have a proposal to make," Francis said. Her voice was thick and her words slurred. The effects of alcohol were firmly in control of her speech, but not her brain.

"I'm saying it's time to move out," Norma said. "We'll still work here, if we ever get to reopen, but at least we'll have somewhere to live."

"Do you really think the police will let us?" Kelly asked. "The rules say—"

"Fuck the rules! In case you haven't noticed, people have a little bit more on their minds right now than keeping track of whores. And as long as the houses are closed for business, no one will even notice we're not here. By the time we reopen, as long as we're on our backs on time, no one will care."

"Where will we go?" Susie Overton asked.

"There are houses to rent all over this city," Norma said. "We've all got money saved." She turned her gaze toward Kelly. "At least those of us who don't spend it on opium."

"I have money," Kelly snapped, her eyes blazing. "I can pay my share of rent anywhere we find."

"So you're in?"

"I'm in."

Norma looked around the room at the other girls. She paused to make eye contact with each before moving on to the next, until she came to Sadie. Her eyes swept past her as if she were an empty chair. Sadie shrank back, reminded once more that she was nothing more than a liability in a money-making business for which she was ill-equipped, and even less inclined, to contribute.

"So, what say ye, girls?" Norma asked.

There were nods all around the room. Sadie looked at Kelly, who quickly looked away when she felt Sadie's gaze. Sadie's heart sank. Was she to be left alone in this hellhole? What if the girls didn't come back? When the house reopened, would she be expected to service all the men who slapped down their three dollars?

The sound of the examining room door opening and Doc Kalakaua's footsteps in the hallway distracted her. He appeared in the doorway, wiping his hands on a towel.

"What's the word, Doc?" Francis asked.

"The boy's been badly beaten," Doc said. "His cheek is fractured and he has several broken ribs. He may even have some internal bleeding. He needs to be in a hospital."

"This is the best hospital in town," Norma said. "Or haven't you noticed?"

"Who beat him, Doctor?" Sadie asked.

All sounds in the room ceased as if on cue; all eyes turned toward Sadie.

After a pregnant silence, Norma said, "Well, she speaks."

"He says it was a Japanese soldier," Doc said.

"Oh, my God," Kelly said. Her words came out in a whisper. "They're here."

Kelly had voiced the fear they all held, that Japanese forces had landed somewhere under cover of the assault on Pearl Harbor, waiting for the moment of surprise to fall on the citizens of Honolulu and murder them in their beds. Rumors had abounded over the past few days, but they had proven to be just that: rumors. But now there was proof!

"I should point out," Doc said, "that the boy was also sodomized."

Which explained the blood in the seat of his underwear. And, Sadie knew, proved another point, as well. "If it was a Japanese soldier," she said, "he would be here to kill, not to rape little boys."

"She's right," Norma said. "I'll be damned, but the singer is right. Raping's the job of our own soldiers, not the Japanese."

"It's not rape if they pay for it," Francis said.

"Now, Francis, please allow us to continue the illusion of our own virtue," Norma said. "If we've been raped, then we're not whores. Isn't that right, singer? Did Mooney pay you?"

"Who would do this to a child?" Kelly asked.

"It would take a monster," Sadie said.

She had already met such a monster.

Sadie slept more uneasily than she had in prior nights. The fear of another Japanese attack had been pushed to the back of her mind, replaced by the fear of another attack by Mooney. A monster. She wondered if she could survive another bout with him. He had nearly split her asunder as he thrust inside her, each move accompanied by a sound more akin to that of an animal than a man. She had opened her eyes only once. The sight that greeted them was the face of a feral creature, with eyes rolled upward showing only the whites, lips pulled back in a snarl, teeth bared and gritted. Not a face of pleasure, but a face of rage. He had not been making love, had not even been simply having sex. It had been an act of violence, an assault so brutal that it had drawn more blood even than what she experienced during her time of the month. And, hard as it was to comprehend, it appeared to be as distasteful to him as it had been to her.

She had heard of men who did not like women, but who liked other men. Even of men who liked little boys.

Quietly, she tiptoed to the examining room, opened the door, and slipped inside. A lamp glowed from the bedside table and lit the battered face of the boy, whose eyes had lost some of their swell. He appeared to sleep soundly under the sheet that had been pulled to his chin. The outline of his tiny body beneath the sheet was almost that of a large doll rather than a human being.

A faint cry escaped his lips.

She sat on the cot beside him and gently ran her fingers through his hair. He shifted from his side to his back then opened his eyes. He jerked back, startled, and scooted to a sitting position in the corner.

"It's okay," Sadie said. "I'm not going to hurt you."

Her soothing voice seemed to calm him, and she saw tension seep from his frame.

"What's your name, child?"

"Ricky."

"How old are you, Ricky?"

"Thirteen."

"I have a brother. Billy. He's just about your age."

"Does he live here?"

"No, he lives in California." Or did he? Sadie couldn't even say for sure that he still lived at all. "Do you have a family?"

"I have *makuahine*."

"What does that mean? *Makuahine?*" She sounded the word as best she could, but it felt silly in her ears.

As, apparently, it did in Ricky's. He smiled.

She smiled back. "Did I say it right? I'm not too good at talking Hawaiian."

"You said it good. *Makuahine* means mama."

"Do you have a daddy? How do you say that in Hawaiian?"

"*Makuakane*. I don't see him since I was born." He looked at his hands folded together in his lap, then back at Sadie. "Do you have *ohana?* Family?"

"Just Billy." She paused. "How do you say brother in Hawaiian?"

"*Kaikua'ana.*"

"I don't think I can say that one. I'll have to practice before I try. I wouldn't want you to make fun of me since I don't talk as good as you do."

He smiled again, followed by a giggle. He had a high-pitched voice, almost girlish. Soon his voice would be turning and, as he grew larger, masculine features would start to shape his body differently. Muscles would develop and he would grow in stature. Whiskers would dot his cheeks. Would he still be the target of monsters, or were they simply looking for children to take advantage of?

"Who hurt you, Ricky?"

He dropped his eyes to his hands. "It was a Japanese soldier. He came in an airplane."

She waited until he looked at her again, which took more than a minute. She knew that her gentleness had made an impact, and he regretted misleading her. But fear controlled.

"I'm going to ask you some questions," she said, "and you don't have to say anything. Just nod or shake your head. Okay?"

He looked at her and nodded, then dropped his eyes to his hands again.

"Was it really a Japanese soldier who did this?"

After a pause, he shook his head.

"Was it a white man?"

He nodded again.

"Was it a policeman?"

He suddenly looked up, his eyes wide with terror. He looked down again and shook his head violently from side to side.

And she had her answer.

Sadie scrambled eggs in a small pan and dropped two slices of Portuguese sausage into another. Kelly sat at the table and watched Sadie cook.

"I see you've gotten your appetite back," Kelly said. "I don't believe I've seen you eat two bites since…"

Sadie just stared as the words choked off in Kelly's throat. They both knew the ending of the sentence: Since Mooney raped you.

"It's for the boy."

"Poor thing," Kelly said. "Who do you suppose did that to him?"

"I can't imagine the kind of monster it would take to do that." But she could imagine—and she did. She had no proof other than the frantic denials of a traumatized young boy and her own hatred for Mooney. But she had seen the look on Ricky's face. She hadn't mentioned Mooney by name, but she knew the truth in her heart.

"I'm going house hunting today with Norma," Kelly said. "God, it will be so nice to see something other than the four walls of this place."

"Good."

"Want me to ask Norma if you can go?"

"That would be a useless exercise. I don't exist as far as she's concerned. And Francis would never let me out of the house."

Kelly looked at Sadie's face, but Sadie turned her back so that Kelly couldn't see the glisten of tears in her eyes.

"It won't be so bad," Kelly said. "We all got used to it. Just think of it as supporting the troops."

"I don't want to get used to it. I never want to get used to it. It's a sin."

"Everyone gets fucked, sweetie. At least we get paid for it, and it's more money than you could make doing anything else. Once you've made enough, you can leave and never look back."

"By then I'll be a ruined woman."

"Then you just go someplace where nobody knows you. You can be a woman of wealth and mystery. Nobody has to know anything about this."

Sadie scooped the eggs and sausage onto a plate, then poured a glass of milk. "I've got to feed Ricky."

"Is that his name? Ricky?"

"Yes."

"My advice to you is not to get too attached to him. He's not so innocent. I've seen him around. He gets paid just like we do. He's a lost soul."

"We're all lost souls," Sadie said. She grabbed the eggs and milk and went to the examining room.

"Here you go, Ricky," she said as she opened the door. "Breakfast."

But all that was left as proof that Ricky had even been there were blood-stained sheets.

◊ ◊ ◊

Upstairs at the Polynesian Rooms an Army medic sat next to Rob Sandford's cot and slowly unrolled the bandage from around his head. Rob kept his eyes closed. He was afraid to open them lest he see no light as each rotation was removed. He felt it best to be disappointed all at once rather than gradually.

When the last wrap was removed, the medic said, "Okay, any time you're ready, soldier."

Rob nodded, took a deep breath, and raised his lids. The medic stared at him, concerned. His blondish hair had been cropped military style, leaving large ears extending on both sides of his head like open car doors. His nose was enormous, casting a shadow over buck teeth. One eye seemed slightly askew, not quite making contact with both of Rob's. It was a face only a mother could love—and it was the most beautiful face Rob had ever seen.

"You are one ugly sonuvabitch," Rob said. Then he broke into a laugh, something he had not done since the pre-dawn hours of December 7.

"Soldier," the medic said, with a broad smile, "when they start insulting me, it's time to pronounce them hale and hearty." He looked at Rob's unwrapped hands, blistered and swollen, but skin apparently still intact. "You feel anything in those?"

"Just a tingle."

"That means feeling's coming back. We'll put some more ointment on 'em and wrap 'em back up, but as soon as we can, we'll get you out to Schofield."

"I'm ready any time."

After the medic left, Rob lay back and looked around the small cubicle, taking in every detail he saw. Though his vision was still slightly blurred, his eyes were actually working, something he had feared might never happen. Blindness would earn him a discharge from the Army and relegate him to a life of begging on the streets of Brooklyn. Better to be a slightly scarred MP in a war zone than a seller of pencils in the slums back east.

Movement in the doorway to the cubicle caught his attention. Turning, he saw the girl standing there, looking at him.

"Sadie," he said.

"You can see me?"

"Yes, I can see you."

"That's wonderful, soldier."

"My name is Rob."

"Is that short for Robert?"

"Yes."

"Then I shall call you Robert. Is that okay?"

"Yes, indeed. And I'll call you Sadie."

"Do you need anything?"

"I'd like a little company."

"We're closed for business," she said.

He detected a tremor in her voice, reinforcing what he had felt the first time he saw her: She did not belong there.

"I just want to talk," Rob said. "Nothing more."

She stood rigidly, as if debating with herself. At length, her shoulders slumped and she exhaled a deep breath. "Then I shall be delighted to keep you company, Robert."

Joshua stood in front of the territorial courts building, with a writ of injunction in hand. He had come each morning since the day of the attack, but each day the doors were locked. The same order, signed by Chief Justice Samuel Kemp of the Hawaii Supreme Court, that had been posted on the morning of Monday, December 8, remained on the front door, mocking him on his daily routine: "Under the direction of the commanding general, Hawaiian Department, all courts of the Territory of Hawaii will be closed until further notice. Without prejudice to the generality of the foregoing, all time for performing any act under the process of the Territory will be enlarged until after the courts are authorized to resume their normal functions."

How nice, Joshua thought. The statutes of limitations have been indefinitely extended, which was little comfort for those whose rights had been abrogated and for whom time was of the essence. It surely would be of little comfort to Sadie MacKenzie, held prisoner in a whorehouse.

Dejected, he turned toward home, resolved to return again the next day—and the next and the next—until the courthouse doors would again be open and justice served.

Chapter Eighteen

IN A SMALL sign of return to normalcy, the brothels of Hotel Street reopened for business a few weeks after the attack. On her first day on the job, Sadie waited in the cubicle that had once housed the young MP she knew as Robert. She remembered their conversations, the way he talked of home and his family that he had not seen in more than a year. By the time he left to return to his barracks to finish recuperating, she felt as if she had lost her only friend. Sure, there was Joshua, but she had had no contact with him since the day she had been recaptured and returned to the Polynesian Rooms. She trusted that he was endeavoring to secure her release through the legal system, but she had been told that the Army had assumed control over Hawaii and had shut down the courts. Not that she could blame them. After all, with the ever present threat of another sneak attack by the Japanese, the concerns of a whore on Hotel Street commanded very little attention.

And that was exactly how she had come to think of herself: a whore. Though she had not yet had her first encounter with a man for pay, she had come to accept the inevitable. She had been a whore-in-waiting, but today she would become a whore-in-fact. Kelly had schooled her in what to expect and tried to assure her that it was not as bad as it seemed, that it was just a job—and a well-paying job at that. "Some of the boys will finish before they even start," Kelly said. "First-timers and boys who haven't seen a woman for months are the easiest. You just have to be careful when you check their equipment that you don't get a face full."

"Why do you have to check their equipment?" Sadie asked.

"To make sure they don't have any diseases. Some of the boys will want you to use your mouth. They always come quick, too. If you get a lot of those, you might make thirty or forty dollars more in a day. But most of them will do it the regular way."

"What's the regular way?"

Kelly giggled. "You know, missionary style."

Sadie frowned, uncomprehending.

"The man on top," Kelly said. "Isn't that the way Mooney did it?"

It was. Right before he turned her face down and did it again in the other place. She prayed that was not on the agenda.

She now stood at the foot of the cot, wearing only a thin kimono Kelly had given her, and waited for her first customer. She listened to the footsteps of young men climbing the stairs.

The Polynesian Rooms were open for business once again.

Francis pushed her way past the eager line on the stairway. The murmurs grew hushed as she passed. They knew who she was, and they knew that once she reached the cage at the top of the stairs, their dreams would be just minutes away. She sensed their excitement at being back in Hotel Street for reasons other than hauling off the dead and injured. She entered the cage and opened the transaction window.

"All right, boys, step right up and put your money down."

A fuzzy-cheeked ensign approached the cage, dollar bills clutched in his fist. He dropped the money on the counter and awaited his poker chip.

Francis spread the three bills apart and lined them up. "I need two more dollars."

"But it's always been three," the ensign said.

"In case you hadn't noticed, there's a war on," Francis said. "Hard times mean higher prices. If you want to get laid, the price is five dollars."

"Five dollars!"

The words practically exploded out of his mouth, loud enough to reach the ears of those waiting in line. The ensign pressed his argument with Francis.

"But my pay is less than thirty dollars a month, and you're almost doubling the price. No whore is worth that."

"You're free to leave any time you like, son."

"I'll just take my money to one of the other hotels."

"You'll find the price is the same there. Of course, you can always take your dick across the river. There's whores over there who'll still fuck for three dollars, but I've got to warn you, they fuck Negroes and Filipinos and Chinamen, too. The clap's a high price to pay just to save two dollars."

Everyone knew about the whorehouses across the Nu'uanu Stream, the unregulated ones that competed with the regulated houses by offering lower prices but higher disease rates. With the rapid build-up of forces after the attack, many of whom were southern white boys, most of the reopened Hotel Street houses imposed a color line, leaving the unregulated houses across the river as the sole option for men of color.

The ensign heaved his shoulders in a sigh. He pulled his billfold from his pocket, extracted two more dollars, and dropped them on the counter.

Men came and went down the corridor outside Sadie's cubicle. A few stopped in the doorway but continued on to the next cubicle after taking one look at her. She couldn't blame them. Most of the girls were full-figured with hardened looks that suggested they knew what they were doing. Most of the men were young, some looking as frightened as she felt, and they all moved on in search of more experienced whores. They were not willing to risk their poker chips on a flat-chested waif such as Sadie, who looked as if she wouldn't know what part went where once her robe and their pants hit the floor.

Although she was relieved as each man passed her cubicle, soon she felt insulted. Who were they to say she didn't measure up? Was it the stitches on her forehead? She might be young and inexperienced and scarred, but she was just as much a woman as any other girl in the house. All she needed was a chance. She almost laughed out loud as she realized that her pride was at war with her virtue, and might even be winning. She also knew that she owed Francis one thousand dollars just for her initial outlay, not to mention room and board. If she ever wanted to buy her freedom, she needed customers.

A cleared throat broke into her thoughts. She looked at the doorway where a young soldier stood in his khaki uniform. He appeared to scarcely be seventeen or eighteen years old. His brown hair was close-cropped and his cheeks were rosy, as if he had been caught in a brisk wind—but there were no brisk winds in Hawaii. The boy was clearly embarrassed.

"Come on in," Sadie said. "Do you have your chip? I'm supposed to collect your chip."

"Yes, ma'am," the soldier said.

He handed it to her and she dropped it in the pocket of her kimono.

"You'll have to take your pants off. I'm supposed to examine you," Sadie said.

"Yes, ma'am." He turned his back to her as he shed his trousers and olive green boxers. Sadie caught a glimpse of alabaster white buttocks beneath the tail of his uniform shirt, which he left on.

When he turned back around, his rigid and circumcised penis poked out like a flagpole through a gap in the front of his still-buttoned shirt. It was the first she had ever seen other than when she used to bathe Billy as a small boy. She had not seen Mooney's, but had merely felt it as he impaled her body on it. She dampened a rag in the wash basin beside the bed and knelt in front of the soldier. She was as curious by what she examined as she was repulsed by the thought of what it would be used for.

She reached for it, but he flinched his hips and pulled away.

"They tell me I have to examine you and wash you," she said.

"I'm afraid if you touch me, I'll go."

"Is this your first time?"

"No, ma'am, but it's been a while. A long while."

"I'll be gentle."

"Okay."

He relaxed and closed his eyes. She carefully took him in her hand. It felt warm and firm, though spongy on the surface. A vein bulged on one side and she could feel his pulse as it throbbed in her hand. She didn't know what she was looking for, but quickly concluded that this boy was unlikely to harbor any disease, regardless of whether he was a virgin or not—and she had her doubts as to his truthfulness in response to her question.

She washed it gently with the damp cloth then set the cloth aside. "Are you ready?"

He nodded, unable to speak. She sensed that he was as nervous as she was. Somehow, that helped. She stood and stepped back until she felt the cot against the back of her knees. She untied the sash on the kimono and slid the robe off her shoulders.

As the kimono dropped to the floor, exposing her nakedness, the soldier moaned.

Then he ejaculated.

Chapter Nineteen

MAJOR FRANK STEER rode in the passenger seat of an Army Jeep, on his way to Hotel Street. It had been over a month since the attack, and there had been no new sightings of Japanese planes or submarines, but the sudden influx of service personnel and civilian defense workers had brought other problems. Many of the workers were rough-hewn, hard-edged men from the rural American South, who were there to drink, fight, work, and fuck. They were blue collar itinerants, used to manual labor and instability, their adult lives spent moving from job to job, which made them a perfect fit in post-Pearl Harbor Hawaii. A lot of them were Negroes, which was a relative oddity in the Islands. In an atmosphere already ripe with racial unrest between the *haole* interlopers and the native *kanakas*, the addition of yet another race of people into the Hawaiian caste system, that now included a solid cadre of Southern racists, was an additional ingredient in a recipe for disaster.

As if that wasn't enough, nearly all of them were male, inflating an already out-of-proportion male to female ratio. Steer had heard estimates ranging from as low as 150 to 1, to as high as 1,000 to 1. He generally accepted the compromise estimate of 500 to 1, but even that was a logistical nightmare for getting the men serviced. With the brothels of Hotel Street shut down for weeks following the attack, rumors of rape and sexual assault flitted about the Islands. Some were true, but others were simply the imaginations of frightened islanders run amuck as mothers and fathers feared for their daughters.

And so it was a welcome relief not only to the enlisted personnel, but to the officers, right up to and including Steer, that the brothels had reopened. But if the reports he had received were true, he had still another problem to deal with.

A Who's Who of Honolulu's prostitution industry gathered in the parlor of the Polynesian Rooms and awaited Steer's arrival. Among their number were Mrs. Hun Yee Yei, the lone non-*haole* madam, who ran as many as forty girls out of two brothels, the Ala Rooms and the Park Rooms; Darlene Foster, who ran twelve at the Service Hotel; Patricia De Corso, madam to ten girls at the Midway Hotel; Ruth Davis of the New Senator Hotel, with its fifteen girls; and Francis O'Brian with the host hotel's eighteen girls.

Rivals though they had been before the attack, the war brought an end to their competition, as tens of thousands of additional servicemen, not to mention war workers, arrived in Oahu. When their doors reopened, they found lines like they had never seen before. But while demand had risen, supply remained the same. The madams already had feelers out to the mainland for more girls, but with travel disrupted by the war, there were no immediate reinforcements on the horizon. Girls sometimes had to service as many as seventy-five to one hundred men a day. Masters of capitalism, the madams had decided to raise prices, leading to the summons from Major Steer that had brought them together this evening.

Sadie stood at the front door and peered out of the window through a pulled-back corner of tarpaper. She had lost track of the number of men who had climbed the stairs and mounted her, her mind as numbed as her private parts. Kelly and the others quickly packed up and left the house at the end of the work day, headed for their new residences in Honolulu. They would return tomorrow just before opening time, but they now had the luxury of normalcy in the evenings. Sadie was left alone overnight to assist Lum Yee in cleaning the house, and washing towels and sheets in preparation for the next day.

A Jeep pulled to the curb and a man with hawk-like features spryly hopped out. His driver, a black man, sat rigidly behind the wheel. She heard the first man say something to the driver, who looked his way and nodded. She recognized the driver instantly: Robert.

"Miss O'Brian," she said. "The major is here."

"Well, let him in, girl," Francis said.

Her tone reflected her irritation at all things Sadie, but at least her voice wasn't slurred. Sadie wasn't privy to the situation, so she had no idea what was at issue, but she did know that this man was important and that the meeting with him was crucial to the madams' business. Sadie opened the door before Steer could raise his hand to knock then stepped aside to allow him to enter.

He took off his hat and smiled at her. "Thank you, young lady," he said.

She dipped her head and cast her eyes down, ashamed to have a man of his stature see her in a whorehouse. When she raised her head again, she saw Robert looking at her from the Jeep. His hands were covered with white gloves, but had obviously healed enough to grip a steering wheel.

She quickly turned away and ushered the major into the parlor.

Rob sat at the wheel and stared at the door. This was the first time he had seen Sadie since the day he left to return to Schofield. He was still not fit for full duty, but once his hands were capable of gripping the steering wheel, Major Steer had selected him as his driver as a means to keep him active. When Major Steer said he wanted to be driven to Hotel Street, Rob hoped to catch a glimpse of Sadie. He would forever be indebted to her for her kindness to him in his darkest hours. She had not cared about the color of his skin, but had tended his wounds, comforted his fears, and had even sung him lullabies when he was unable to sleep. Even now, he called to mind her soothing tones when nightmares kept him awake as he lay in his bunk. What he wouldn't give to have her sit by his side and sing to him once again.

"Ladies," Major Steer said, "I appreciate your attendance at this hastily called meeting. And I'm sure you suspect the purpose of our little get-together."

"We're not lowering our prices," Francis said. "And that, I presume, brings our meeting to an end."

"I wish it were that simple," Steer said. "And, to a certain extent, it is. The long and the short of it is, the price of meat is still three dollars."

It seemed as if all the madams spoke at once in a babble of protest.

Steer held up his hands. "Ladies, ladies, one at a time please. I'm here to listen to your arguments, but unless you can provide me with a compelling argument why you should not honor your patriotic duty to keep our boys satisfied without gouging them, my mind is set."

Ruth Davis, madam of the New Senator Hotel, stood from the *chaise longue* where she had perched on its end. She wore a navy blue kimono festooned with birds-of-paradise, with its sash loosely tied just below her bosom. She brushed her dark hair from her brow, cleared her throat, and spoke with the elocution of a politician.

"Sir, you speak of our patriotic duty, but I believe we are honoring that duty. We are in a war being fought to maintain our freedoms, including the freedom to set our own prices. Supply and demand. The American way of business has long been built on that principle, and that principle is at play here. We honor America and her fighting men by embodying one of the very principles for which this war is being fought."

Sadie sat on the stairs that the soldiers and sailors climbed during the day. It didn't matter if the price was three dollars or five dollars or one hundred dollars, the result was still the same: three minutes that rotted her from the inside out with each tick of the clock. She had been a "sporting girl" for only a few active days, but had already engaged in over one hundred paid encounters—and had been chastised by Francis for underachieving. Even whores had their standards, she guessed, and according to Francis O'Brian, Sadie MacKenzie did not measure up.

As voices rose in the parlor, she stood to go to her room where she could lie on her bed, alone, and shut out the sounds of the debate over how much her virtue was worth. The front door opened behind her and Lum Yee entered.

"Missy Sadie," she said. "Soldier outside want talk."

"Miss O'Brian has forbidden me to leave the house."

"Go kitchen. Lum Yee bring soldier to back."

Before Sadie could protest, Lum Yee slipped back out the front door. Sadie tiptoed down the hallway and into the kitchen, where she waited by the rear door, which opened tentatively and Lum Yee slipped in.

"Soldier outside. You go, Lum Yee keep watch."

She took Sadie by the hand and pulled her toward the door, then pushed her outside. Robert stood in the alley's shadows. He smiled when she stepped onto the rear stoop and saw him.

"Hello, Sadie."

"Hello, Robert."

An awkward silence followed. After a moment, Sadie asked, "How are your injuries?"

"I'm on the mend."

"I'm pleased."

"I had a good nurse."

"And I had a good patient."

Yet another awkward silence. Sadie felt her heart pound in her chest, as if trying to beat its way out of her body. She had spent hours talking to this boy while he lay upstairs, and had wept when he left early one morning without saying good-bye, yet now she had no words to say. What a foolish girl he must think she was.

"I wondered if I would see you again," she said. "I thought perhaps you would be sent home."

"Only the seriously wounded are being sent home. Now that my vision has fully returned and the shrapnel injuries have healed, I still have a use to the Army." He paused then asked, "How have you been?"

Sadie averted her eyes. "If you know the houses are open for business, then you know how I've been. You know what I am."

The words came out harsher than she intended, but she felt no control over her emotions. And the emotion that reigned supreme, next to anger, was shame.

"Yes, I know what you are," he said. "And I know what you are not."

Major Steer believed that he had always been fair with these women and their girls. Left completely under the control of the Honolulu Police Department, whose vice officers were rumored to receive up to fifty dollars a month to look the other way, life would be very different in

Hotel Street. It was the need to keep up morale of the men that led to the benign dictatorship imposed by the United States military. He knew that these women trusted him and he believed that he had earned their trust. He also believed that they would honor his wishes now.

"Ladies," he said. "I don't wish to disrupt your business. But we're all making sacrifices. The Army appreciates your assistance in caring for our wounded. I realize that it was an inconvenience, and that it was a financial burden to close your doors for business. But now that business is up and running as usual, my number one concern is our troops. I understand the principles of supply and demand in a free enterprise system. I also understand that, with increased demand, income increases even if prices remain the same. I'm not asking that you sacrifice your profits. I'm simply asking that you be aware of the burdens a price increase will place on the already thin dollars of our boys for whom the next visit up the stairs at Hotel Street may well be their last."

The words had their desired effect. He saw instantly that countenances softened and firm-set lips relaxed.

"I've heard it said that a man who won't fuck, won't fight. Well, I'm here to tell you that our boys will willingly do both. But remember that they're fighting for you and your right to keep your doors open and earn your profits. I'm simply asking that you do something for them in return.

"I tell you again that the price of meat is still three dollars. I say that, but what you do within the confines of your hotels is exclusively within your control. I pray that you will do the right thing for our boys."

Prices stayed at three dollars.

Chapter Twenty
April 1942

POLICE CHIEF GABRIELSON gazed out the window of his office. The latest conversation with Richard Clements of the Civilian Honolulu Police Commission had put a damper on an already bad day. Truth be told, every day since December 7 had been a bad day, with his department now subject to the whims of generals, but today was a particularly bad day.

"Miles Cary paid me a visit," Clements had said. "He and his Social Protection Committee are outraged. It seems that whores have invaded our neighborhoods, right under the so-called watchful eye of your vice squad."

"What do you mean?" Gabrielson asked.

"They've used the war as a pretense to break the rules. They've bought and leased houses outside of Hotel Street. All over Honolulu, in fact. They've even been seen on the beaches. On Waikiki. They own property, drive automobiles, frequent cafes and bars. And I have it on good authority that whores in a house in Pacific Heights are even having wild parties after curfew. Drinking, gambling, and fornicating for money, I'm sure."

"Do you have the address?" Gabrielson asked.

Clements extracted a slip of paper from his coat pocket and laid it on the chief's desk before leaving. His words had shaken Gabrielson. It was not enough to worry about invading Japanese; now the whores were invading. And so he awaited the arrival of his secret weapon.

He spun around at the knock on his door. "Come in."

The door opened and in stepped Delbert Mooney.

128

◊ ◊ ◊

The house was modest enough by the standards of this exclusive neighborhood on a mountainside overlooking downtown Honolulu. Built bungalow style in traditional Hawaiian colors of green and red, with a wrap-around lanai, it had three bedrooms—one each for Norma and Kelly, and one to accommodate other girls who rotated through—and a picture window view of the city. Kelly knew that the neighbors were suspicious of two single women living together and a steady stream of other young women on a nightly basis. The occasional party they threw attended by servicemen and war workers that violated the curfew laws also probably raised eyebrows. Were it not for the windows blackened with tarpaper, the neighbors might really get an eyeful.

The house offered a welcome respite from a world that had ensnared Kelly years ago and from which she knew she would never escape. But up here on the mountainside, she felt on top of the world. It was a better feeling than even opium had brought the first time she took in a pipe full. The only question was whether the feeling would soon fade, as had the high of opium until she needed more and more just to feel normal.

She lounged on a wicker sofa in the living area, rereading an old movie star magazine, when movement from outside the front window attracted her attention. A dark sedan, followed by a police cruiser and a paddy wagon, pulled up in front of the bungalow. Out of the lead vehicle stepped the devil himself.

"Norma!"

"What is it?" Norma answered from the rear of the house.

"Mooney is here."

There was silence then Norma uttered an expletive. She joined Kelly, who now stood at the front door.

"What do we do?" Kelly asked.

"Just open up and see what he wants."

"I know what he wants. He wants us."

There was a heavy banging on the door. Kelly would know the sounds made by Mooney's fist anywhere. She opened the door about a foot and peered outside. Mooney raised his leg and slammed the bottom of his foot against the wood. The edge smashed into Kelly's forehead. She staggered backward a step then fell. The back of her head slammed against the tile floor and she lay still.

Norma dropped to her knees and cradled Kelly's head. Her fingers felt sticky. She held them up to see that they were coated with blood.

Mooney stepped inside and loomed over her. She looked at him with hate-filled eyes. He raised his sap high above his head.

"This is your eviction notice," he said. Then he brought the sap downward with all the force he could muster.

Chapter Twenty-One

IT FELT GOOD to Rob to be back on patrol. Full sensation had returned to his hands and the scar tissue was barely noticeable—so long as he wore gloves or kept his hands in his pockets. He knew that he should consider the prune-like skin a badge of honor, but the good-natured joking from his fellow MPs left him wondering: What woman would ever want to feel the touch of his hand on her skin? Even the sporting girls on Hotel Street would likely be repelled by the thought.

A vehicle careening wildly down Beretania Street grabbed his attention. He knew the automobile as the famous maroon Zephyr that belonged to Norma Staunton. Fortunately the streets were clear as curfew approached, but the wild gyrations of the automobile bouncing from curb to curb posed a danger to the buildings that closely lined the street. Norma was obviously intoxicated and hastening to reach the sanctuary of the Polynesian Rooms before curfew. He was no traffic cop, but he was nevertheless responsible, under martial law, for safety in Honolulu. The Zephyr roared past his Jeep. He was startled by its driver. He knew Norma Staunton on sight, but the driver of the vehicle was not Norma. A thief, perhaps? He fell in behind the car.

The automobile skidded to a stop in front of the Polynesian Rooms, its right front tire on the sidewalk. A dark-haired woman burst out of the car, wailing hysterically. Rob pulled to a stop behind the Zephyr and got out as she pounded on the front door.

"Francis! Francis! He's got them!" Her voice reached a high pitch, almost a shriek as she wailed the words.

She slumped to her knees, still pounding. Rob ran to her. With an arm around her waist, he helped her back to her feet.

"Miss, are you all right?"

The front door opened. Lum Yee and Francis stood in the doorway. Behind them, Rob saw the wide-eyed countenance of Sadie. All three women were clearly alarmed.

"Dolly, what the hell is the ruckus?" Francis asked.

"He's got them," Dolly Mumford said. Her words came in ragged gasps through her sobs. "Norma and Kelly. He's got them."

"Who's got them?"

"Mooney. I think they're dead."

Sadie gently washed Dolly's face with a damp cloth as she lay motionless on a davenport in the parlor. Lum Yee held a tray of tea, while Francis and Rob stood side-by-side and waited for the return of consciousness.

Dolly's eyelids fluttered.

"Miss O'Brian, I think she's waking up," Sadie said.

Lum Yee set the tray on a small end table and poured a cup full of green tea. She dissolved a lump of sugar while Dolly stirred, then opened her eyes.

"Step aside, Sadie," Francis said.

As Sadie moved over beside Rob, Francis sat on the edge of the davenport and caressed Dolly's cheek. It was a sight Sadie had never seen before: Francis treating one of her girls with the love and tenderness of a mother for her child. All Sadie had ever received from Francis had been ridicule and abuse. She might be one of Francis's whores, but she was not one of Francis's girls.

"Tell us what happened," Francis said. "Where are Norma and Kelly?"

"I was in the bathroom when Mooney came. When I peeked out, I saw him knock Kelly to the floor. Then he struck Norma in the face with his sap. I hid in the bathtub and waited my turn, but he never came. When I heard the front door close, I ran to the window and saw policemen dragging them by their feet toward a paddy wagon. They weren't moving. And there was so much blood."

Francis turned to Rob. "What do you know about this?"

"Nothing."

"I thought you boys at the Army were in charge of everything."

"We don't control the likes of Delbert Mooney."

"I want to know where my girls are," Francis said. "Hospital, jail, or morgue? Wherever they are, I want to know."

"Yes, ma'am," Rob said. "I'll find them for you."

He remained standing next to Sadie, as if awaiting further orders. Francis delivered them quickly.

"Go, boy. Now!"

Francis turned her attention to Sadie after Rob left. "This useless lawyer of yours who keeps trying to serve me with legal papers, do you know how to get in touch with him?"

"Yes."

"It's time for him to become useful."

Kelly awoke with an aching head. She last remembered lying on a sofa and reading a magazine, but now she found herself on a narrow cot with a thin cotton-filled ticking mattress. The floor was cement, as were the walls. Scarcely seven feet away were iron bars. She sat up and swung her feet onto the floor. The back of her head ached. She put a hand to it and felt a matted mass of hair. She looked at her fingers, sticky with blood.

Footsteps clicked down the cement passageway outside her cell. She held her breath in anticipation. A man came into view, smiling at her through the bars—but with no mirth in the smile. Teeth bared like a wild animal. He ran a billy club across the bars, creating an off-key tone.

"Well, well, well, Sleeping Beauty has awakened," Mooney said. He inserted a key in the lock and opened the door, then stepped into the doorway. "You slept for quite a while."

"Why am I here?" she asked. "I haven't done anything wrong."

"You mean besides whoring?"

"I paid for my license. And my check-ups are clean."

"Who let you out of Hotel Street?" he asked.

"Our house was full of wounded. We had no choice; we had no place to sleep."

"I don't recall authorizing it."

Things started to come back to her now. The pounding on the door. The sudden burst into the house that slammed the wooden edge of a door into her face. Then blackness.

Mooney patted the end of the billy club in the palm of his hand. "You know there are consequences for violating the rules."

"I'll go back to Hotel Street," she said. "Just let me out of here and I'll go straight back."

"There are penalties to be paid first."

He dangled the billy club at his side, the strap around his left wrist. With his right hand, he unbuttoned the fly on his trousers.

Sadie stood beside Francis on the sidewalk outside the police station on Merchant Street. The sun had set, so they were flaunting the law by being on the streets after curfew. Although the temperatures were still in the 80s, a chill rattled her body. She remembered the last time she had been at this building, scant months before, frightened and confused as Mooney dragged her here to take fingerprints and steal a dollar to obtain her whore license. If only that day could be undone and she were able to retrace her steps to the harbor, reboard the *Lurline*, and return to San Francisco and pretend she had never been here.

Headlights drew near, and Rob's Jeep pulled to a halt beside them. He hopped out and hustled around to the sidewalk.

"They're definitely being held in the jail here," he said. "More MPs are on the way."

"So they're not dead?" Francis asked.

"Not as far as I know. But they may be injured. If so, we'll see to it that they're taken to the hospital for treatment." He paused, as if delaying unpleasant news. "If not, they may have to stay in jail until they can be tried."

"Tried for what?" Francis asked.

"They've been arrested and been charged with prostitution. It's still a crime, believe it or not."

"I thought you soldiers had taken over the criminal law," Francis said. "What authority do the police have to keep my girls locked up?"

"I don't know the ins and outs of martial law," Rob said. "You'll need to talk to a lawyer about that."

"One is on the way." Another vehicle approached, its headlights cutting through the dark. "This may be him right here."

Sure enough, a dark blue Hudson parked behind Rob's Jeep and Joshua got out. His eyes widened when he saw Sadie. The jagged scar on her forehead brought back the nightmare of Mooney's sap delivered to her face on the pier and his failure to protect her. He headed straight for her, but Francis stepped between them.

"I'm your client, counselor," Francis said. "I'll be paying your fee."

"Mr. Sinclair," Sadie said. "It's all right. I'm fine. It's the other girls who need your help."

Joshua looked at her with an appraising eye. "Are you sure you're fine?"

"I'm sure. But we believe Kelly and Norma have been injured by the police. Robert says they've been locked up here."

"Who is Robert?"

Rob stepped toward him. "Sergeant Robert Sandford, sir. We understand that the two girls were beaten and then brought here."

"Do you expect the police to allow us to see them? If they refuse, I can't even get a writ of *habeas corpus* to have them produced."

"The military police have been assigned an office here. I placed a call to the night duty officer, and reinforcements are on the way," Rob said. "If the police resist, we'll storm this building by force, if necessary. But we will see those girls, mark my words."

Kelly curled in a ball in a corner of the cell as Mooney hiked up his trousers and buttoned his fly. He picked up his billy club from the floor and inspected it, then wiped blood on the mattress ticking. He had just reached the cell door when he heard multiple footsteps approaching. He opened the door and looked down the passageway at a veritable army—soldiers, whores, and what damn sure looked like that lawyer Sinclair. You could always tell a lawyer. They were the ones with constipated looks on their faces.

Mooney stepped into the passageway and planted himself, with arms akimbo. The billy club dangled from his wrist. A drop of blood slipped from its end and spattered on the cement floor.

"Well, Francis," he said. "Fancy meeting you here." He dipped his head in a sarcastic bow. "And little Miss MacKenzie."

The black MP, Sandford, stepped forward. His jaw clenched as he obviously tried to fight anger. The lawyer was angry, too, as reflected by a deepening of his apparent constipation. Mooney laughed. Make them angry, he knew, and they get careless. They always did.

"We've come for Kelly Foster and Norma Staunton," Sandford said.

"They're in my custody," Mooney said.

"I demand that you turn them over to me."

"By whose authority?"

"By authority of General Order Number Four issued by Lt. Colonel Green on December 7, 1941."

"Ah, yes. You soldier boys shit out general orders like normal people shit out turds," Mooney said. He turned to Sinclair. "Have you read all the general orders, counselor?"

"I have."

"Then you know that they may have closed the courts, but they don't say that I can't arrest and detain."

"But they do say any trial will be before a military tribunal," Sandford said. "So I'm taking custody of these two prisoners to ensure their appearance when one is convened. Now step aside."

Mooney complied with a mock bow and a sweep of his hand. "Be my guest, soldier boy."

Sandford brushed past Mooney and into the cell. The others remained in the passageway, facing off with Mooney, who smirked at Francis as if daring her to challenge him.

"Miss O'Brian," Sandford called from the cell. His voice sounded odd, as if he were short of breath. "We need you."

At the sound of Rob's voice, Sadie knew instantly what they would find when they entered the cell. She had experienced Mooney's brutality, and she had seen his handiwork on Ricky. Why should Kelly and Norma be any different?

She followed Francis and Joshua around Mooney, who stuck out his foot as she passed. She stumbled but quickly regained her balance. She felt his smile on her back but she didn't give him the satisfaction of looking at him. She came to an abrupt stop when she saw Kelly, curled on the floor.

The entire entourage halted, as if afraid to approach. Sadie pushed past Francis and Rob, and ran to Kelly, then knelt by her side. She pulled Kelly toward her and felt something wet on the back of her head. She rocked slowly as Kelly sobbed.

"Shh, shh, shh," she said. She gave Kelly a quick once over, looking for other visible signs of trauma. There was blood on the floor just behind Kelly's derriere. She knew that if she checked, she would also find blood in Kelly's underwear just as she had found in Ricky's.

Joshua placed his hand on Sadie's shoulder.

"Is she all right, child?" he asked.

"No, Mr. Sinclair, she's not. She'll never be all right again. None of us who have dealt with Mooney will ever be."

"Mooney!" Rob yelled. "Goddamnit, Mooney, what did you do to this girl?"

Sadie looked back as Mooney sauntered into the cell. Behind Mooney, two MPs entered and stood closely at his back, blocking his exit.

When Kelly saw Mooney, she snuggled more tightly into Sadie's arms, as if seeking the comfort of a womb. "Please don't let him hurt me anymore," she whispered.

"Shh, shh. You're safe now."

Rob faced off with Mooney, his fists clenched as they had been the first time Sadie saw him confront Mooney. Francis stood by Rob's side. Her shoulders appeared to quiver. Sadie wondered if she was crying.

"Where is the other one?" Rob asked.

Mooney shrugged. "I suppose she's here somewhere."

"Where?"

"Next cell over. She's resting, though. I wouldn't want to wake her. At her age, she needs her beauty sleep."

Rob leaned toward Francis, but kept his eyes on Mooney.

"Check it out, please, Miss O'Brian."

Francis skirted around Mooney, as if afraid to be too close to him. The two MPs stepped aside as she exited the cell. Rob and Mooney continued their staring contest.

From the next cell, they heard the sound of Francis collapsing to the floor.

Chapter Twenty-Two

FRANCIS GATHERED THE girls in the parlor in the morning, the doors shut to business. They knew something had gone terribly wrong the day before, but rumors ranged from the murders of Norma and Kelly to the murder, by Norma and Kelly, of Delbert Mooney. As each girl arrived to prepare for the day, Francis directed them to the parlor to await the arrival of all.

Sadie sat on the edge of Kelly's bed and bathed her brow with a damp cloth. Joshua paced restlessly, clearly embarrassed. Were it not for the horrible circumstances, Sadie might have been amused at his discomfort. He was a good man, a gentleman in all respects, who likely had never darkened the door of a whorehouse before. In fact, in his one prior appearance at the Polynesian Rooms, he and his court order had been denied entrance.

"Mr. Sinclair, please, you must rest. You've been up all night and your perpetual movement will exhaust you."

"I apologize, but I'm at my wit's end. I failed you, and now I feel as if I've failed these two girls."

"Oh, Mr. Sinclair, you haven't failed me. Not at all."

"My dear, I insist that you call me Joshua. And yes, I failed you. The scar on your forehead is testament to my failure. I've been unable to procure your freedom from this place. The reasons are of no consequence; what matters is simply that I failed. I pray every night that you'll forgive me."

"Joshua, I've read the general orders as they were published in the *Star-Bulletin*. Though I confess I haven't fully understood the legalities, I understand that you're forbidden by law from seeking the necessary writs in my behalf. No forgiveness is necessary."

"You're very kind to an old man. And I promise you that I shall renew my efforts to obtain your release."

Kelly moaned and rolled onto her side, her back to Sadie. Sadie saw blood on the sheets where Kelly's hips had been. She lifted the sheet and saw that the seat of her underwear was bloody.

"Good God," Joshua said.

Sadie put the sheet back down. She stroked Kelly's hair where it escaped from her bandage. It, too, showed the leakage of blood.

"I must ask a favor of you, Joshua."

"Anything, child."

She took a deep breath. "I must ask that you cease your efforts on my behalf."

At that, Joshua abruptly stopped his pacing. He strode toward her and stood close, his face a mask of puzzlement. "I'll never cease my efforts on your behalf."

"Then I must insist that your efforts take a change in direction. My place is here, now. Kelly needs me. She may never fully recover from this night, and it's my lot to care for her. She took me under her wing, and now I must take her under mine. I cannot leave her to the devices of Francis, who has sought refuge from the war in a bottle."

"Your sentiments are admirable but—"

"Are you a *Bible*-reading man, Joshua?"

"I am."

"I remember as a little girl my mother reading to me the story of Esther, in the *Old Testament*. I remember when Esther's uncle, Mordecai, pled with her, as the wife of the king, to intercede on behalf of the Children of Israel. Do you remember what he said to her?"

"He said that perhaps God had put her in a position of authority in the kingdom—"

"'For such a time as this.' They say that God works in mysterious ways. I've often wondered at those ways as I sought to understand how I came to be whoring in a house of ill-repute. But now perhaps I understand. Who can say but that I've been placed here—"

"For such a time as this." Joshua smiled. "You are a remarkable woman, Sadie MacKenzie."

"You flatter me, Joshua."

"I assume that you have given thought to how I might redirect my efforts."

"That, I have."

"But Dolly told us that both of them were dead," Gladys Strahan said.

"Beaten and left for dead, yes," Francis said. "But Kelly lies yonder in her very own bed, and Norma is under an army doctor's care in Tripler Hospital." She paused, took a drink from her glass, then refilled it. "I have been told that Norma may never awaken from her coma."

"They may as well be dead," Dolly said. "Now the police will force us all back into Hotel Street, or we, too, will feel the sting of Mooney's club. And there's not a damn thing we can do about it."

Sadie entered, followed closely by Joshua. "Perhaps there is," she said.

All eyes turned toward her. She suddenly found herself the center of attention, something that had not happened since the evening when Norma had forced her to sing. In the intervening months, she had kept silent unless alone with Kelly or Lum Yee, the only ones she counted as friends in this house. Some of the girls surely wondered whether she had lost her voice since that night, and their astonishment at now hearing her speak publicly was evident.

"What is your great plan, Sadie?" Francis asked.

"The civil courts have been reopened," Sadie said. "Although there are still restrictions, such as prohibitions against trials by jury, they are nevertheless open for actions at law. Mr. Sinclair has agreed to file a lawsuit in Kelly and Norma's names against Mooney and the Honolulu Police Department for assault and battery."

"What good will that do?" Francis asked.

"It will place Mooney and his actions under scrutiny. He may be a monster, but he's not stupid. He will, at least during the pendency of a lawsuit, likely be more circumspect in his actions. It won't stop him, but it may slow him down. And by suing the police department, putting it at risk for money damages, it may also engage the attention of his superiors."

"It will also embarrass the department in the eyes of Honolulu's citizens," Joshua said. "It may provoke some effort at atonement."

"And if not?" Gladys asked.

"We'll also approach the military police to ensure our protection," Sadie said.

"Why would they help?" Francis asked.

"The same reason why Major Steer would come here and speak to the madams," Sadie said. "We serve a function that's valuable to the military, and they have an interest in protecting that. I have no illusions that they would act out of some great altruistic or benevolent motive, but self-interest is a powerful motivator."

The room was silent. Not only did the girls appear shocked that Sadie could speak, they were double-shocked that she could be so well-thought in her words. She sensed an almost instant shift in the regard with which she was held by these women.

At length, Dolly asked, "Has Kelly agreed to this lawsuit?"

"I'll speak to Kelly and secure her agreement. As for Norma…"

Her voice trailed off as she thought about Norma, who lay lifeless in a hospital bed, almost unrecognizable due to the severity of the beating she had received at Mooney's hand.

"We'll petition the court to make me her guardian," Joshua said. "I can then file an action in that capacity."

"What do you need from us?" Gladys asked.

"I want your blessing—from all of you—to pursue this course," Joshua said. "The initial reaction from the police may be unpleasant, but I believe that will soon pass. Nevertheless, we must be prepared for the worst."

"I saw what Mooney did to Norma," Dolly said. "The worst has already happened."

"Who's going to foot the bill for all this lawsuiting?" Francis asked.

"I'm offering my services *pro bono*," Joshua said.

Francis raised her eyebrows, as if the notion of a free lawyer were foreign. "Why would you do that, counselor? You're all prim and proper and contemptuous of whores. I'm shocked you didn't pass out when you first set foot in this whorehouse."

"Because Sadie asked me to," Joshua said.

The girls looked at him expectantly, as if waiting for the stick. For women of their ilk, there was always a stick that followed the carrot.

He added, "And because maybe I have come to a whorehouse for such a time as this."

Chapter Twenty-Three

JOSHUA EXITED THE territorial courts building with copies of the filed lawsuit in hand and headed toward the police station to serve the defendants. It was intimidating enough to return to the days of his youth as a litigator, but more so when he had made a promise to Sadie, and he knew how important this was to her. He also knew that, notwithstanding the assurances he and Sadie had given the girls of the Polynesian Rooms, there was no guarantee that Mooney would not spread brutality in his wake. Sergeant Sandford assured him that the military police would protect the girls, and the *Honolulu Star-Bulletin* confirmed that the military had assumed control, but that did not give him total confidence in their safety.

He paused at the door of the police station, steeling himself for the task at hand. His phone call had determined that Mooney was present in the vice squad room. Soon he would hand Mooney a copy of the lawsuit naming him as a defendant and suing him for one hundred thousand dollars, plus punitive damages, for the horrendous attacks on Kelly Foster and Norma Staunton. He was about to declare his own private war on the Honolulu Police Department.

Kelly waited inside a cubicle at the end of the corridor, awaiting her first customer of the morning. She had assured Francis that she was fully recovered and ready to resume her duties, but in truth, she had no idea if she was ready or not. All that she knew for sure was that she had no choice. It was the only life she knew.

She untied the sash on her silk kimono and opened it. She hooked her thumbs under the waistband of her underwear then paused. What would she find? Images, sounds, and feelings flashed through her mind. Just snippets, not a full-blown portrait of events. Lying on a cement floor—Mooney—his limp penis —a rage-filled expression, teeth bared—pain, as a billy club violated her—face pressed hard against the cement floor—the barrel of a gun beside her head, visible only in her peripheral vision, its gunsight like a sea serpent's hump rising from the water—the gun removed from her sight—more pain, harsher, sharper—an awareness that surely her anus was being ripped apart—then the gun on the floor beside her head again, its barrel covered with blood.

She clenched her eyes to chase away the memory, afraid that one day it would fully flesh itself out. She waited for the effects of the opium to eject the montage of horror. She had smoked the last of her supply in the alley, but to no avail. The murmur of voices and scuffle of boots told her that men were starting to climb the stairs. She pulled down her underwear, stopping at her knees. She looked down, afraid of what she would find, but knowing full well what it would be.

Blood soaked the fabric.

She heard a gasp. Looking up, she saw Sadie at the doorway, her eyes wide in horror.

"Don't tell Francis," Kelly said.

With the lawsuit's pages torn in half and tucked in his pocket, Mooney parked his Deluxe at Tripler Hospital, got out, and went in the front door. At the head of the stairs on Norma's floor, Mooney glanced down the hallway. No medical personnel in sight, though he heard voices from the interiors of various rooms. He made his way to her ward and slipped inside. Rows of beds lined both sides of the room, most occupied by unconscious servicemen. At the far end, face wrapped in bandages, lay an obviously feminine figure. He moved quickly to the bed. Her entire face was swaddled in gauze with the exception of her nose and mouth, left uncovered so she could breathe.

He checked the chart at the foot of the bed: Norma Staunton.

After one last look behind him, Mooney covered her mouth with one hand; with the other, he pinched her nostrils tightly closed. When he removed his hands a minute later, he leaned close and put his ear next to her nose. No breath sounds, no soft exhale on his cheek. Confident that his goal had been accomplished, he quickly exited.

Chapter Twenty-Four

LUM YEE CARRIED a tray of green tea and chicken broth to the girls' bedroom. Kelly lay on her side, her face toward the wall. All the other girls, except Sadie, had left for the day, scattered to their leased houses or hotel rooms.

Lum Yee set the tray on the bed next to Kelly's. "You eat now, Missy Kelly. Make you feel better."

But Kelly made no move.

Lum Yee pulled back the sheet and exposed the spreading red stain on Kelly's nightshirt and the mattress at her hips. She raised the sheet to Kelly's shoulders and turned to leave. As she stepped, something crunched beneath her foot. She looked down at the broken glass of an opium pipe.

"No, Missy Kelly, no," she whispered.

"It's what she needed," Francis said from behind her. She lounged in the doorway, *o'ke* glass in hand.

"It no good for her," Lum Yee said. "You bad woman."

"Careful how you speak to me, or I'll chase your Chinese ass right out of here."

"Lum Yee get Doctah Kalakaua. Missy Kelly very very sick."

"She just needs to sleep it off. She's got a big day at work tomorrow."

"She no can work. She broken. Call Doctah Kalakaua to come fix."

"She can quit working when she hits the jackpot with her lawsuit. Until then, I'll decide if she can or can't work."

A pounding at the front door interrupted their argument. Lum Yee made a move toward the front, but Francis continued to block her way.

"Sadie!" Francis called. "Get the door."

"I get door," Lum Yee said.

"Not until you get your attitude straight." When the pounding continued, Francis yelled again, "Sadie, the door. Now!"

Sadie piled the sheets in a corner of the corridor that lined the cubicles then hurried to the stairs and down. The pounding on the door continued at a steady pace. She heard Joshua's voice.

"Miss O'Brian, it's Joshua Sinclair. I must see you."

Sadie raced to the door, turned the key, and opened it. Joshua stood outside, flustered and red-faced.

"Joshua, whatever is the matter?"

"It's Norma. She has passed."

"Oh, dear Lord. Come in, come in."

Sadie escorted Joshua to the parlor, where they were quickly joined by Francis and Lum Yee, who had overheard what Joshua said.

"What happened to Norma?" Francis asked.

"The doctors called and said that she had stopped breathing sometime during the day."

"Why would they call you?"

"I'm her lawyer. I gave the hospital explicit instructions that I was to be informed of any change in her condition. They told me that she was unconscious but breathing the last time she was checked, then simply stopped breathing. It was something we all knew could happen."

"What happens to her lawsuit now?" Francis asked.

"It likely will be dismissed unless she has heirs. Her estate could succeed to her cause of action, but if she has no heirs, there is no one left to prosecute the claim."

"It was Mooney."

The voice was so soft, it nearly went unheard. All turned to see its source. Kelly stood in the doorway, wearing a nightshirt. Blood trailed down her calves.

"He'll come for me next," she said.

"Joshua," Sadie said, "could it have been Mooney?"

"It's possible. I served him with the lawsuit today, and he was outraged. Had we not been in the police station, I would have feared for my safety."

"Would he know that murdering Norma might end her case?"

"It's a fine legal point because it depends upon the existence of heirs, but it would be a logical conclusion by a layman to assume that death would end a lawsuit. And even if he gave any thought to the question of a probate estate, it would be another logical conclusion that someone like Norma would not have heirs."

"It's Mooney, I tell you," Kelly said. "He'll come to finish what he started."

"You're safe here, Kelly," Francis said.

"Or she can come to my home," Joshua said. "Where I can keep a close eye on her."

"No offense, counselor, but I can take care of my girls in my own house."

Kelly turned abruptly and ran back to the bedroom. Sadie followed close behind. By the time she got there, Kelly was already in bed, knees pulled to her chest and sheet pulled to her chin. Sadie sat on the edge of the bed and gently wiped tears from her cheeks.

"We won't let Mooney get to you," Sadie said.

"He's already ruined me," Kelly said. Her voice was thick and throaty. "Just ask the boys who visited my bed today. No man wants blood on their private parts."

"Mooney does."

"Not even Mooney does. That's why he used his billy club. That's why he used the barrel of his gun."

The words shook Sadie to her soul. She knew Mooney was a sadist, had even suspected that he preferred little boys to women, but she assumed that he viewed both his fists and his penis as his weapons. Now she knew that he had other arrows in his quiver.

"Things tore inside me," Kelly said. "Both sides. I'm ruined."

"You can heal."

"Maybe my private parts can heal, but *I* can't. I've been a fallen woman since I was a child. Now I'm a broken woman. I have nothing to live for."

"You have everything to live for."

Kelly locked her eyes onto Sadie's with such intensity that Sadie felt uncomfortable under her stare.

"Tell me what I have to live for," Kelly said. "What use is a whore who can't fuck?"

"You don't have to do this forever. You can get out whenever you choose."

"And do what? Teach Sunday School?"

"I'm sure there are lots of things you can do. We just have to find them."

"You've been kind to me, Sadie, and I thank you for that kindness. But you don't know what you're talking about. Now, I'd like to talk to my lawyer."

Unable to offer a rejoinder, Sadie stood and left the room, returning a moment later with Joshua. Sadie stayed by his side as he approached Kelly's bed.

"What do you wish to speak to me about, Miss Foster?"

Kelly glanced at Sadie. "I need to speak to my lawyer alone."

Sadie hesitated, unwilling to move.

"Don't worry, Sadie. I'm not going to fuck him. I can't, remember?"

Joshua's face glowed red. Sadie glared at Kelly, angry that she would deliberately embarrass this man who had taken her under his wing.

"It's all right, my dear," Joshua said. His face still held a pinkish hue. "A privileged conversation between an attorney and his client really should be held in confidence."

"All right, then," Sadie said. "I'll be in the parlor."

Joshua waited until Sadie left the room, then he pushed aside the untouched tray of tea and broth, and sat on the bed across from Kelly.

"What do you wish to speak to me about, Miss Foster?"

"I want to make a will. Can you do that?"

"I can."

"I don't know all the fancy words, you know, about being of sound mind and all."

"I can write those words for you. Just tell me who you want to leave your property to."

"I want to leave my house to Sadie. Or at least my half of it. And all of my worldly goods, meager though they might be."

"Have you no family?"

"I have received more kindness from Sadie in a few short months than I received in my entire life from my family."

Joshua pulled a folded envelope and a pen from his inside breast pocket and made appropriate notes. "All right. Is there anything else?"

"You said before that a lawsuit dies when a party dies, unless there are heirs. Can I give my lawsuit to somebody so that it lives on when I'm gone?"

Joshua tried hard to recall his law school courses on probate. He remembered something about "choses in action" and their being intangible property rights that were, in fact, assignable to third parties and, he believed, could be willed to one's heirs. He would have to do a little research to confirm, but he felt relatively confident in venturing a guess.

"Yes, I believe so."

"So if Mooney does away with me, my lawsuit is not dismissed?"

"That would be my understanding."

Kelly appeared to think about that for a moment. "I leave my lawsuit to Sadie. And put something in there that says if Mooney does to me what he did to Norma, then Sadie will not stop the lawsuit until she drives Mooney to the poor house."

Mooney cruised the streets, looking for curfew violators. More specifically, looking for one curfew violator in particular. Kids didn't read newspapers or proclamations from the military governor. They did what kids do—they flaunted rules and thumbed their noses at authority, so he knew if he covered enough ground, he would find who he was looking for.

A cauldron of rage burned out of control inside him. Whores had sued him in court. Whores! As if they had the same rights as decent citizens. Surely the civil courts had not been reopened just so law enforcement authorities could be punished for doing their jobs. The rules were the rules, and every whore had them ingrained in her very core. You may not live outside of Hotel Street. You may not have a bank account. You may not own a car. You may not visit the beaches. Yet Norma Staunton and Kelly Foster, and who knows how many other whores, had bought houses and cars and had even been reported sunbathing behind barbed wire on Waikiki Beach.

And while the rules were the rules, so, too, the punishment was the punishment. Whores had to be kept in line, and the only thing they understood was brutality. You couldn't simply send them to bed without supper or make them stand in the corner. Short of stitching their pussies closed, there was no other way to enforce the rules without applying the rod. It was goddamn Biblical, after all. Spare the rod, spoil the child. He was simply the rod of the Almighty, ensuring that the whores of Hotel Street were not spoiled. For that, he had been summoned to court to answer for his righteousness.

But without complainants, there would be no lawsuit. One down, one to go. And now he needed sustenance for his own soul.

Sure enough, in an alleyway in the part of Honolulu known as Blood Town, he saw movement in the shadows. Sometimes the boy slept in these alleys, behind trash cans to stay out of sight. But if you knew which rocks to turn over, you could always find the bugs when you wanted to.

He eased his Deluxe to the curb and got out. The movement in the alley stilled. Mooney gripped his sap in one hand and entered the shadows.

"Ricky, I know you're in there."

Silence.

"If I have to come all the way in there to get you, you'll wish I hadn't."

He paused and listened. A bottle clattered across the hard-packed dirt alley.

"You'd never make a good player at hide-n-seek. Now don't make me have to come in there."

A figure popped up from behind a stack of crates. Mooney gauged the slender, willowy outline of the boy in the dimness. He reached in his pocket and pulled out a wad of one dollar bills. With his sap held at his hip in his right hand, he raised his left with the handful of cash.

"I've got money."

Ricky moved out of the shadows and into the middle of the alley. His dark skin blurred his features but wide eyes focused on Mooney's uplifted hand. Mooney nearly laughed. It was like extending a dab of peanut butter to a mouse. All the creature saw was the brown gooey dollop; its little brain never fully comprehended the metal trap, spring-loaded, ready to snap across its fragile neck as soon as it tasted the food.

"How much you got?" Ricky asked.

His voice was high pitched and singsong. Mooney knew that, as the boy grew older, his voice would drop in tone as whiskers sprouted on his cheeks. Would that revolt Mooney? He didn't know. He would worry about that later. For now, he simply enjoyed the boyish image with its tender openings.

"Enough," Mooney answered.

"You gonna hit me?"

"That's up to you. It's always up to you."

"Maybe I don't feel like it tonight."

"When's the last time you ate?" Mooney asked. He knew the weaknesses to exploit in order to get what he desired. And when those failed, well, there was always the rod.

Ricky approached and held out his hand. His face was now visible. The marks from their last encounter had faded and he was once again the same smooth-cheeked, androgynous visage that stirred Mooney's loins.

Just as they stirred now.

Chapter Twenty-Five

ON APRIL 18, 1942, sixteen American B-25 bombers did what most thought impossible as they took off from the deck of the carrier *USS Hornet* and delivered payloads of ordnance on military and industrial targets in the Japanese cities of Tokyo, Yokohama, Kobe, Osaka, Nagoya, and Yokosuka. The attack humiliated the Japanese military leaders while, at the same time, struck the same fear into the hearts of Japanese civilians that Hawaii's population had been living with for the past four-and-a-half months.

Determined to regain control of the war, the Japanese sought to take all of New Guinea and the Solomon Islands in the Pacific, and thereby seduce the American aircraft carriers into a hellstorm that would decimate them. Instead, the Americans achieved a strategic victory in early May in what became known as the Battle of the Coral Sea. The Japanese light carrier *Shoho* was sunk and the carrier *Shokaku*, which had been part of the *Kido Butai* at Pearl Harbor, was decimated. One month later, the Americans would achieve a dramatic victory at the Battle of Midway, which would see another member of the *Kido Butai*—the *Hiryu*—sent to the bottom of the ocean and three others—the *Soryu*, *Akagi*, and *Kaga*—reduced to flaming trash heaps. Scarcely six months since the Pearl Harbor attack and the tide in the Pacific would have turned. But on the streets of Honolulu, a different war was playing out that summer.

Police Chief Gabrielson slammed down the phone. How dare that bastard speak to him that way! He didn't give a good goddamn if Melvin Craig was a lieutenant colonel or if he was the second coming of the Messiah. Gabrielson was the police chief of Honolulu and, war or not, that ought to mean something. That ought to command some kind of respect.

"Next time you want to move out some whores," Craig had said, after reading him the riot act for the assaults on two girls from the Polynesian Rooms that had resulted in one death, "you let the MPs know. They'll look into it and then get back to you."

"Do you understand who I am, Colonel?" Gabrielson asked.

"I do. And I also understand where you fall in the pecking order. Like I said, you let my boys know if you've got a problem with any of the girls. As long as they're not turning tricks outside of Hotel Street, it's none of your concern where they live."

Gabrielson pulled a notepad in front of him, grabbed a dull pencil, and began writing. He titled the document Administrative Order No. 83. Short and sweet, he dashed off his memo in five minutes then summoned his secretary to type what he had written. While she typed, he dialed a number on his phone and waited for a pick-up on the other end.

"Mooney, I have something for you to deliver, discreetly, to the editor of the *Honolulu Star-Bulletin*."

Lt. General Delos G. Emmons, the military governor of the Territory of Hawaii, exploded as he hurled the May 7 edition of the *Star-Bulletin* across his office. A career military man, the fifty-three-year-old Emmons had succeeded Walter Short as commander-in-chief when Short was called back to Washington D.C. in disgrace by Army Chief of Staff George C. Marshall only ten days after the Pearl Harbor attack. The pages scattered and fluttered to the floor. The headline that aroused Emmons's ire stared at him mockingly: *Military Police to Handle Vice Cases*.

He summoned his secretary with her steno pad. "Take a letter to Police Chief William Gabrielson." As soon as she sat, he spoke in a harsh, clipped tone, hopeful the attitude would be reflected in the written document. "I desire to inform you that your understanding regarding the responsibility for vice conditions in the City and County of Honolulu is in error," he said as his secretary wrote. He ended his missive with the curt demand: "Cancel Administrative Order No. 83."

◊ ◊ ◊

Sadie sat on the edge of Kelly's bed and tended to her as she had every day since Mooney's assault, while the other girls gathered at the dinner table. Some had been run out of their homes, while others voluntarily returned to the Polynesian Rooms as vice officers spread across the neighborhoods and beaches of Honolulu to enforce the re-instituted "rules." Notwithstanding the military's public pronouncement that control over prostitution was still in the hands of the police, MPs routinely arrived at eviction scenes and halted the proceedings, often creating public spectacles, with the girls caught in the middle. But there simply weren't enough MPs to go around as the vice squad hopscotched across Honolulu's neighborhoods and chased them away.

"You'd best go have supper," Kelly said.

She seemed to diminish with each passing day. The only spark of life she had shown flared when Joshua returned a week ago with her Last Will and Testament. Using Lum Yee and Francis as witnesses, Joshua read it to Kelly, and then she scratched her signature onto the bottom of the page.

"This is the only legal document, besides my lawsuit, that's ever had my name in it," she had told Sadie. "When I'm gone, you carry on my lawsuit. This will prove to the world that I was here and that I left my mark."

The words chilled Sadie. It was as if Kelly had already given up, and Sadie had rarely deserted her side since, leaving only to tend to her duties upstairs during work hours.

"Are you hungry?" Sadie asked. "I can bring you something to eat."

"No, you go eat. I'll be fine."

"All right, then." Sadie rose to leave. "I'll bring you a slice of pie when I'm finished."

Just as Sadie reached the door, Kelly called to her. "Sadie?"

Sadie turned. "Yes?"

"Thank you for being good to me."

After Sadie left, Kelly reached under her bed and found the precious document. She held it before her and read the words aloud, as she had done every day since the lawyer brought it to her. "I, Kelly Foster, being of sound mind, make this my last will and testament."

She felt a sense of pride seeing her name in the midst of a flourish of legal language. Sadie's lawyer had done right by her. He had taken her seriously as a person, and he had taken care to write this will for her complete with five-dollar words. It made her feel as if she mattered and that, even with her misspent life, she would be missed.

She lifted the edge of her mattress and reached beneath, feeling for the small burlap package Dolly had brought when she arrived earlier. Opium had always been her drug of choice, and Francis kept her supplied in order to keep her whoring. The sense of euphoria it brought helped to wash away the degradation she felt each time she spread her legs. But now she needed something more.

With trembling fingers, she untied the string at the top of the small bag and took out a syringe. She clenched her fist on her left hand and, with her right, guided the needle into a vein at the crook of her elbow. There was just a tiny pinprick of pain, and then the needle slid in. She pressed the plunger and heroin rushed into her body.

She rested her head on her pillow. With the needle still in her arm and the will on her chest, she closed her eyes.

Sadie sat at the table, and Lum Yee served her a plate of rice and chicken. Ellen Elster, a brash blonde from Ohio who was now the senior girl with the demise of Norma, was holding court, exercising her newfound seniority. Sadie sat quietly and listened.

"It's just not right," Ellen said. "We did our part for the boys. We nursed them and even gave up our beds for them. Now they expect us to leave our homes and pretend none of that ever happened."

"The MPs are doing what they can," Dolly said. "There just aren't enough of them."

"They have other things to do besides babysitting whores," Francis said. "What do you expect?"

"There's got to be something we can do," Ellen said. "We provide a service to the soldiers. And if it weren't for us, they'd be going after the daughters of the so-called decent folks, so we provide them a service, too. We sacrifice our purity for the sake of theirs."

"You haven't been pure since you had your first period," Francis said, provoking gales of laughter, including from Ellen.

"We could strike," Sadie said. She spoke quietly, almost unheard amidst the laughter.

"What was that, Sadie-girl?" Ellen asked.

The others quieted. It was Sadie, after all, who had suggested the idea of a lawsuit against Mooney and the police. Might she have another idea?

"I said we could strike."

"Strike?" Ellen said. "What do you mean, 'strike'?"

"If we refuse to perform, the boys will surely protest to Major Steer. That will put pressure on the military. And if the citizens think the boys will be looking to others for their...services, they'll put pressure on the police. Then maybe the two will get together. Right now they're at cross-purposes with each other, but getting us back on the job would become a common purpose. If nothing else, we would get their attention. Then we'd have a chance to present our case."

There was complete silence at the table, not even the clatter of silverware, as the girls contemplated what, at first blush, seemed like a crazy notion. But the more they thought about it, the better it sounded.

"It will only work if all the girls do it," Sadie said. "From all the houses."

"I like it," Francis said. "If we all close our doors—well, I can just hear the howl that will set off. I'll talk to the other madams."

"We'll need to have a list of demands," Sadie said. "Things that we want in order to go back to work."

"Can your lawyer help with that?" Francis asked. "Make it all pretty and legal like?"

"I'm sure that he can."

"Then see him tomorrow. I'll make the rounds with the others and drum up support."

As the girls chatted excitedly about ideas for picket signs, Sadie left to see about Kelly. She carried a saucer with a slice of lilikoi pie, a light chiffon pastry made from passion fruit that had been a favorite of hers since setting foot on the island. She was also excited to tell Kelly about the plans the girls had come up with. If it worked, Kelly would be able to move back into her house in Pacific Heights without fear of additional visits from Mooney.

Or would she? As long as Kelly continued to press her lawsuit, Mooney would perceive her as a threat, in which case she would not be safe outside of the Polynesian Rooms. Unless Mooney were informed that Kelly's passing would not end the action, but that Sadie would pick up the banner. That might make Sadie a target, but she didn't care. If Mooney realized that there was no advantage to eliminating the plaintiffs in the lawsuit, perhaps—just perhaps—he might think twice about targeting Kelly.

Sadie entered the bedroom and called out, "I've brought pie. Your favorite."

She knew instantly that something was amiss. Kelly lay on her back, the pages of the will on her breast. Her eyes were closed. It was then that Sadie saw the syringe still attached to her arm. She set the pie on a bedside table and hurried to Kelly. There was no movement of the pages, no rise and fall of breath. Her face was calm, lips slightly upturned as if in a smile.

Sadie sat on the edge of the bed beside her. Gently, she removed the needle from Kelly's arm and dropped the syringe on the floor. She stretched out on the bed beside Kelly, her arm around her shoulder, and held her close as she softly sang her favorite Billie Holiday song: "God Bless the Child."

Chapter Twenty-Six

ON A MISTY Sunday morning, lines of soldiers and sailors formed outside the doors of Hotel Street's houses of entertainment. Grumbles went up from the masses as opening hour came and went, but no doors opened. This was not at all like the madams, businesswomen all, who counted every minute in terms of dollars: three minutes equals three dollars times the number of girls in each house. Oh, sure, they might delay opening for a few minutes on any given day, but this was clearly out of the ordinary. What were the odds of every house having a delayed opening on a Sunday, typically the busiest day?

At 9:30, the doors to all the houses opened simultaneously. The first man in line at each was greeted by the same instruction from the female bouncer: "Step aside. The girls are coming through."

Dressed in their finest, which ranged from modest cotton gingham to slinky cocktail dresses, the sporting girls filed out of their respective houses and marched down the streets, with the madams leading the way. It was a sight never before seen. They began meeting up with each other until they had formed an army over 200 strong. The throng of sporting girls made its way down Beretania Street until it reached the Polynesian Rooms, the only house that had not yet opened its doors. Servicemen in the lines had fanned out on both sides of the street as if they were bystanders watching a parade. They stood in silent awe at the mass of whores. What in the hell was going on?

At the Polynesian Rooms, Leinani, the massive bouncer, opened the front door, and the girls exited and joined their cohorts waiting in the street. Sadie stayed at the back and held the door open while Leinani, at one end, and another equally brawny bouncer at the other carried a plain wooden casket outside. Six bouncers then flanked the casket, three on a side, and lifted it onto their shoulders.

The procession, now swelled in number by dozens of curious servicemen, made its way slowly to Nu'uanu Avenue, turned north, and headed toward Oahu Cemetery, at the base of Nu'uanu Valley. It took nearly a half-hour to make the less than a mile-and-a-half trek. The crowd swelled along the way as word spread of a funeral procession of whores making its way through downtown Honolulu.

Joshua stood at the entry gate to Oahu Cemetery, the oldest public burial ground on the island, and looked southward. A light mist had begun to fall. He removed his spectacles and dried the lenses with a handkerchief, then put them back on as the procession slowly made its way toward him.

The slam of a car door distracted him. Turning, he saw Mooney striding his way.

"It's a sad day, isn't it, counselor?" Mooney said. "Any time a lawyer loses a client, it's like taking money out of his pocket."

"I hold you responsible for this, Mooney. This girl's blood is on your hands as surely as if you had personally snuffed out her breath."

Mooney laughed. It was a harsh tone that grated on Joshua's ears. "From what I hear, she was a dope fiend who finally did herself in. And save your crocodile tears. We both know that your outrage is over the loss of your lawsuit and not your client."

"What makes you think I've lost my lawsuit?" Joshua asked.

"The lawyers for the department tell me that a dead plaintiff without heirs means no more lawsuit."

"Who said there are no heirs?"

Mooney stiffened. His snarl faded to a blank look of shock. "You're bluffing."

"Since you're represented by counsel," Joshua said, "we shouldn't be speaking of the case. You're welcome to join me in mourning, but I'll leave any further discussion of the lawsuit to your lawyers."

Joshua walked forward to join the procession and fell in beside Sadie. He left a slack-jawed Mooney at the gate.

"What did he have to say?" Sadie asked.

"He thinks his lawsuit is over."

"I suppose you told him different?"

"I hinted, but I'll leave that up to his counsel." They walked silently for a few steps. "Your life may be in danger once he finds out," Joshua added.

"Then let this be my legacy."

The mist grew thicker, though still not actual raindrops. Joshua took off his spectacles again and dried them, but quickly gave up and slipped them into his coat pocket.

"You should know something else," Joshua said. "The deed on Kelly's house, which was fully paid for, was listed jointly in both her name and Norma's. When Norma died, title passed, by law, to Kelly. As Kelly's lawful heir, you are now the sole owner."

Sadie stutter-stepped, her foot catching on a stone as she looked up at Joshua. "But I paid nothing for it."

"It's the way of wills and devises. You're now a fee-simple property owner."

"In violation of the rules."

"Rules that may soon change," Joshua said. "In the meantime, I suggest we keep your new status as property owner a secret. There's no need to throw kindling on the fire of Mooney's rage."

The procession weaved its way through elaborate headstones to an excavated gravesite next to a freshly-filled one near the back of the cemetery. Two plain markers had been placed at the heads of the sites. One read *Norma Staunton*, with no birth or death dates, and a simple inscription: *"And there shall be no more death, neither sorrow nor crying. Revelation 21:4."* The marker on the open site said *"Kelly Foster, God bless the child."*

The burly Polynesian women removed the casket from their shoulders and set it onto straps across the opening. No preacher had been found to deliver a eulogy, as none had been willing to speak over the graves of whores. Apparently the ministers of Honolulu had long since forgotten the example of Jesus, who admonished those who sought to stone a woman caught in the act of adultery to "let he who is without sin cast the first stone."

As the casket was slowly lowered into the ground, Sadie stepped forward and, in a voice that others would later say sounded eerily similar to Billie Holiday, began to sing.

> *Them that's got shall get,*
> *Them that's not shall lose,*
> *So the Bible said and it still is news.*
> *Mama may have, Papa may have,*
> *But God bless the child that's got his own,*
> *That's got his own.*

Other girls joined as Sadie continued to sing, harmonizing.

> *Yes, the strong gets more*
> *While the weak ones fade.*
> *Empty pockets don't ever make the grade.*
> *Mama may have, Papa may have,*
> *But God bless the child that's got his own,*
> *That's got his own.*

Soldiers and sailors added their basses, baritones, and tenors. The heavens opened and rain fell in buckets.

> *Money, you've got lots of friends*
> *Crowding round the door.*
> *When you're gone, spending ends,*
> *They don't come no more.*
> *Rich relations give*
> *Crust of bread and such.*
> *You can help yourself*
> *But don't take too much.*
> *Mama may have, Papa may have,*

But God bless the child that's got his own,
That's got his own.

Chapter Twenty-Seven

THE DAY AFTER the funeral, the doors to the houses remained closed again. The customers understood yesterday's closing, but two days in a row was inexplicable. They stood in line and grumbled. Gratification delayed for twenty-four hours was acceptable; gratification delayed for forty-eight was a catastrophe.

At 9:30, the doors opened and the girls came out of all of the houses at once. Fully dressed again, although not in their funeral finery, they carried signs tacked onto posts and two-by-fours. One by one, they lifted the signs above their heads and began marching alongside the lines waiting to be serviced. Mouths dropped open in shock as the boys read the signs.

Some were diplomatic: "Whores on Strike!" "Whores Have Rights Too." "We Want a Life Outside of Hotel Street." "Whores are Not Slaves."

Others were catchy, unknowingly playing off of Mooney's favorite *Bible* verse: "Spare the rod, save a whore."

And some were downright obscene: "No more pussy" and "Do it yourself."

There was also a whole string of signs with "mays" instead of "may nots": "You may visit Waikiki." "You may own property." "You may have a boyfriend." "You may patronize bars." "You may have a bank account."

While most of the girls paraded the streets of Chinatown, Sadie joined a group that marched south on Nu'uanu Avenue, the opposite direction they had followed the day before, to the police station on Merchant Street. Business people looked out of their windows, aghast that the very disease they had tried for years to keep bottled up in Hotel Street had now exploded into the pure areas of town—pure, if you ignored things like greed, avarice, lying, and cheating in business.

The girls, thirty in number, formed a flattened circle and marched with signs held high. At first they walked silently, unused to the attention of unfriendly eyes. One of the girls shouted at the crowd, "What are you looking at?"

Another repeated the question. Soon it swept through the picket line and became a chant. "What—are you—looking—at? What—are you—looking—at?"

Then one of the girls changed the chant. It took a few moments for the new one to catch on and for the spectators to understand what was being said. When it finally soaked in, the women in the crowd turned their faces and walked away, but the men—the supposed respectable businessmen—merely laughed.

Sadie blushed and kept her mouth shut, but kept marching.

The front door to the station opened and Chief Gabrielson stepped out. He listened for a moment, unable to distinguish the words being chanted.

"What are they saying?" he asked an officer who stood on the curb.

The officer turned to see who had asked the question. His smile left when he saw that it was the police chief.

"I asked you what they're saying, son," Gabrielson repeated.

The officer lowered his head and mumbled an unintelligible response.

"I couldn't hear you. What was that?"

"They're saying—" He stopped, then continued. "'No rights, no pussy.'"

"Say that again, son."

"'No rights, no pussy.'"

Gabrielson clenched his jaw so tightly the muscles popped. This was exactly why the whores belonged confined to Hotel Street. Chanting obscenities on the streets of Honolulu, in front of the police station, was an affront to him and his entire department. He spun on his heel and re-entered the building. With determination in each step, he went in search of Major Steer, who had, along with his MPs, evicted some of his assistants and occupied their offices at the station.

"Steer!" he bellowed as his footsteps clicked in the hallway. "Steer!"

"Who's that walking on my bridge?" a voice called from an open door.

Steer and his damned sense of humor. As if Gabrielson were merely one of the billy goats gruff and Steer were the troll that controlled the bridge. On the other hand, maybe that wasn't so bad. In the fairy tale, the third billy goat had tossed the troll from the bridge and gained control over it. The day would come when Gabrielson would do the same thing and eject Steer and his damned MPs from this house.

He stormed into Steer's office. Steer remained sitting at his desk, nonchalant as he damn well pleased.

"Your whores are picketing in the streets," Gabrielson said.

Steer tossed his head in the direction of the window that overlooked Merchant Street. "So I see."

"What do you plan to do about it?"

"Not a damn thing. It's your problem, not mine."

"If you think that, then you haven't thought it through," Gabrielson said. "I dare say it will be your boys left standing on the sidewalks of Hotel Street with their peckers in their hands if the girls don't go back to work."

Steer pursed his lips and knitted his brow. Gabrielson knew he had delivered a direct hit.

"I suppose you've got a point," Steer said. "Seems to me it's both our problem."

"So what do we do?"

"That's above my pay grade. I need to take it up with General Emmons."

"I'd suggest you move quickly," Gabrielson said. "I'll have the Police Commission breathing down my neck as soon as word of this gets to them. And I'll warrant it won't take long to get to them. In the meantime, we need to keep this confined. If the newspapers get hold of this and run pictures of the pickets, Miles Cary and his Social Protection Committee will be clamoring once again to shut down Hotel Street, torch the houses, and ride the whores out of here on a rail. That will be an even bigger problem for both us."

Steer grabbed the phone and raised it to his ear. "I'll keep you posted," he said as he dialed.

At the end of the work day, the girls placed their placards over their shoulders and walked back to Hotel Street, just like normal workers who punched time clocks and left their factories to return home at the end of the day. As they turned north on Nu'uanu from Merchant Street, Sadie caught sight of Mooney standing on the corner. He sought her out with his eyes and beckoned with his finger. She ignored him and kept walking.

Mooney stepped off the curb and flanked the cadre of girls. They bunched tightly around Sadie, like a pack of dogs protecting their young. Mooney threw an elbow and caught a girl from the New Senator Hotel in the solar plexus. She bent involuntarily at the waist, retched, and vomited onto the street. As she straggled, Mooney infiltrated the group and moved directly beside Sadie. He gripped her by the wrist and marched in step with her. The other girls drifted away from them. It was subtle at first, but Sadie noted that a bubble of space had enveloped them. She didn't begrudge the girls the loosening of her protection. Self-preservation was a strong commodity, and Mooney struck fear into every heart.

He struck fear into hers, as well. It was easy to be brave while discussing a lawsuit in the parlor at the Polynesian Rooms or at the dinner table discussing a strike, but now, outside the sanctuary of Hotel Street, walking side-by-side with the devil himself, her courage betrayed her. How funny, she thought, that she once considered Hotel Street a prison but at this very moment, she sought it as a sanctuary.

"Well, well, well, Sadie MacKenzie," Mooney said, matching her step for step. "I understand you're to blame for all this."

"All we want is the right to live our lives as other people do."

"Other people don't spread their legs for money."

"What do you want, Sergeant Mooney?"

"I am given to understand that you have inherited a lawsuit. I think dismissal would be in your best interest."

"More likely it would be in *your* best interest."

"Or maybe in both our best interests. Isn't that what compromise is all about? After all, I am nothing if not a reasonable man."

"You are far from a reasonable man."

"Mighty brave little girl, aren't you? How brave will you be when you're not surrounded by other whores?"

The blocks to Hotel Street seemed as if they were miles long. Each step with Mooney was excruciating. Sadie wondered when he would suddenly strike like a rattlesnake with his sap. It would take only an instant, and no one would be able to prevent it.

"I'm watching you," Mooney said. "Do you remember what I told you when you first set foot on this island?"

She shook her head. That whole day was still a painful blur.

"I said obey the rules or there would be hell to pay. Well, hell has come to collect. Mark my words."

Sadie sensed movement in the ranks of the marchers ahead. As they parted, she saw, with great relief, Joshua walking her way with a determined stride. In one hand, he held a paper sack loosely at his side.

"Unhand her," Joshua said.

If Mooney doubted the steel in Joshua's voice, there was no mistaking the set of his jaw or the fierceness in his eyes. Though Mooney would be more than a match for Joshua on the streets of Honolulu, the battleground Joshua had selected was the courtroom. There, notwithstanding Joshua's protests to Sadie of rustiness, the advantage tipped decidedly his way.

"We were just having a nice little legal discussion," Mooney said. His tone was nonchalant, but he released his grip on Sadie's wrist.

"You are to have no discussions, of any topic, with my client. If you have something to say, your lawyers will say it for you."

"I prefer to speak for myself."

"Those days may soon be at an end," Joshua said. "I have already received settlement overtures from the police department, and they haven't completely closed the door on your termination."

Mooney came to a complete halt. Sadie took three more steps to Joshua's side then turned to face Mooney. She saw a look on his face she had never seen before: uncertainty that bordered on panic. She didn't know if Joshua was telling the truth or if it was merely a lawyer's bluff, but the remark had revealed a weakness in Mooney. His job as a vice squad officer was his license to brutalize. Take that away, and he was nothing but a helpless bully.

Joshua placed a hand on her elbow and steered her away from Mooney and toward the Polynesian Rooms.

"Is what you said true?" she asked.

"In a manner of speaking. Your strike has ruffled feathers. I have already received a telephone call from the police department's counsel. Though they won't say it, I sense that the sight of the girls picketing, hard on the heels of yesterday's very public funeral attended by hundreds of military personnel, have combined to soften the resolve to litigate. They fear that the good citizens of Honolulu will learn of these events and that sympathies may be transferred to Hotel Street unless all of the matters can be resolved quickly. It occurred to me that Mooney's job, if not his scalp, in exchange for other concessions might sweeten the pot."

Sadie took Joshua by the arm and pulled him close. "Joshua, you are a genius." She smiled. She couldn't be sure, but she thought it might be the first time she had smiled since stepping off the *Lurline* a lifetime ago. "I have the best lawyer in the world."

"A lawyer is only as good as his client."

"Even if his client is a whore?"

Joshua blushed. "You're not a whore, Sadie MacKenzie. That's something I'll never accept."

She squeezed his arm and leaned her head against his shoulder. "What are you doing here?" she asked.

"I wanted to see how the first day of the strike went." He held out the paper sack he still clutched in his other hand. "And I have something for you."

Chapter Twenty-Eight

"WHAT DO YOU suggest?" General Emmons asked as he and Major Steer sat at a corner table of the Officer's Club. Their cigars smoldered in ash trays and half-drunk mugs of beer sat on a scarred table top. "It's been a week and they're still marching."

"And the men are suffering." He laughed. "Well, I guess it depends on how you define suffering. Some of them are developing forearms like Popeye's."

Emmons snorted. "A silver lining behind every black cloud. But the real question is whether morale is suffering."

"Not so you can tell, but it's early yet. A few more weeks and it might be a different story."

"Is there a happy medium, Major? If we back the whores, we'll alienate the police, maybe for good. But if we back the police, we'll lose the cooperation of Hotel Street."

"It may seem odd, but these are honorable women," Steer said. "They've always honored the rules and never uttered a cross word. The only reason they broke out of their houses in the first place was because their beds were occupied by our wounded. And now that they've had a taste of freedom, is it really reasonable to expect them to go back to the old ways?"

Steer polished off his mug and took a puff on his cigar. "The problem is that the police have pressures of their own, coming from the likes of Miles Cary and his Social Protection Committee. The only reason we haven't felt their squeeze ourselves is that the police have been our buffer."

Emmons frowned. "I don't like the idea of civilians dictating policy."

"We don't have to let them dictate policy, but it will go a long way to smoothing things over if we at least lend our ears to their complaints."

"Are you suggesting we meet with Cary? Don't we legitimize him and his muckrakers by doing that?"

"My suggestion is that we meet with Chief Gabrielson, who will then meet with the Police Commission," Steer said. "Cary's group has the Commission's ear, so we'll hear indirectly what their demands are, but our negotiations won't be directly with them. But before we do that, we need to get the demands from Hotel Street."

Emmons shook his head. He signaled to the bartender for another beer, then leaned forward and whispered, almost conspiratorially. "As much as I don't want to meet with Miles Cary's group, I can't meet with the whores on Hotel Street."

"I've met with them."

"You're not the military governor."

"Then what do you suggest?"

"You meet with them again. At least with their leaders."

"Their leaders?"

Emmons nodded. "It's like trying to resolve any other labor dispute. When you win over the head, the body will follow."

Sadie lay on her bed reading the book that Joshua had given her. After she told him, while on the *Lurline*, of her family's flight from the Oklahoma panhandle during the Dust Bowl, he had purchased a first edition of Steinbeck's *The Grapes of Wrath* when he arrived home in Honolulu. He held on to it for months until he finally found an opportunity to give it to her on the first day of the strike. Mama had read books to Sadie when she was a girl, and later, when Mama was ill, Sadie read to her. But Sadie had never had a book of her own. Now, as she read the saga of the Joad family who fled Oklahoma just as the MacKenzie family had, she vowed that she would someday own more books than any whore in Hawaii, and maybe even in the United States.

Francis stepped inside and interrupted her reading. "I need to talk to you."

Sadie put Joshua's business card, which she had once clung to tightly as a lifeline, in the book to mark her place and closed the cover.

"Major Steer wants to meet to discuss our demands," Francis said. "He's asked that we assemble a team of girls to form a committee. An 'executive committee,' he calls it."

"Not the madams?" she asked.

"He said the madams are management." She laughed. "He wants to deal only with labor, and he wants to address the leaders."

"That means they're taking us seriously. Or at least the Army is."

"I've spoken with the other madams, and it's unanimous. We want you to be the spokesman of that team."

Sadie was stunned. This was the same woman who had once laughed at her, scoffed at her virginity, and thrown her to Mooney as if throwing a lamb to a wolf. And now she was asking Sadie to be a leader of the girls? That didn't make sense.

"Why me, Miss O'Brian? I've only been here six months."

"Everyone knows that the lawsuit against Mooney was your idea. And the strike was your idea. Maybe the fact that you haven't been here long works in your favor. We all think like whores, but you still think like a citizen."

"But how can I be the spokesman? I don't know anything."

"You know enough. And you have three things no other girl has: you're smart and you've earned the respect of Hotel Street."

"Including your respect?"

Francis hesitated. Sadie knew that for Francis to actually say the words would be to admit she had been wrong about Sadie.

"Yes, damn it. My respect, too."

"That's two things," Sadie said. "What's the third?"

"You have a lawyer who believes in you."

"Joshua, I'm terrified," Sadie said.

She wore the same drab cotton dress she had worn in the dining room of the *Lurline*, the best she had to offer, and had pulled back her hair and tied it with a ribbon. The dress blew in the steady trade wind that typified

Honolulu, cloth swirling around her ankles and billowing at her waist. Beside her, Joshua wore a white linen suit with a red silk handkerchief in the breast pocket. His gray hair tousled in the wind. They walked at the head of a group of ten girls who had been appointed by their madams as the "whore committee." They would never tell Major Steer that they referred to themselves that way, opting instead for his more diplomatic "executive committee."

"You'll be fine, Sadie."

"I still think that you should speak on our behalf."

Joshua shook his head. "A lawyer's words carry the taint of being bought and paid for, but your words will come from the heart."

The committee turned right on Merchant Street and headed toward the main entrance to the police station. Uniformed officers stood on the sidewalk, sneering and jeering, forcing the girls onto the streets. Closer to the door, plainclothes officers waited. Vice squad, with Mooney front and center. Sadie shivered at the sight. Joshua put his arm around her waist to steer her past him.

"Pay him no mind," he said. "He's powerless today and, if you're successful, may be so evermore."

Sadie averted her gaze, though she could feel Mooney's burning glare as they drew closer. Just as she came even with him, she looked him squarely in the face. For a brief moment their eyes locked. It took every fiber of her being to maintain her poise, her jaw set, lips pressed firmly together. Then at the last moment, just as she and Joshua passed, Mooney looked away. Sadie wasn't sure but thought perhaps she had seen, ever so briefly, fear in Mooney's eyes.

Two MPs waited just inside the doors, one of whom was Robert. He smiled reflexively at Sadie, then quickly erased it from his face and dipped his chin slightly in a subtle nod. Both were simple gestures, but filled Sadie with confidence. Between Joshua and Robert, she would have the support she needed for the task she was to fulfill.

The MPs led the committee up a flight of stairs to a conference room on the second floor. Chairs lined an oval table, the centerpiece of the room. Others were lined up behind them. Major Steer stood behind a chair on one side, flanked by two Army officers. Sadie had seen Steer only once before, the day of his meeting with the madams at the Polynesian Rooms. He was clearly the power in this room.

Robert pointed to the seat directly across from Steer. Joshua pulled out the chair and Sadie slipped in between it and the table. Joshua took the chair to her right. Other girls filled in empty seats at the table and in the chairs lined up behind them. The room was thick with tension. On the wall behind Steer, a smiling portrait of Franklin Roosevelt presided over the gathering.

"Let's get started," Steer said. He looked at Joshua. "Madam, I mean no offense when I tell you that you're the ugliest sporting girl I have ever seen."

The room erupted with laughter. All tension vanished, and Sadie was instantly put at ease. She knew that this was a man who, although he clearly took his duties seriously, did not take himself too seriously. This was a man she could talk to.

When the laughter subsided, Joshua said, "I'm simply an attorney-at-law, here to offer my support."

"You have an interesting clientele, counselor."

"A lawyer does not always find his clients; sometimes they find him."

Steer shifted his gaze from Joshua to Sadie. "And who might you be?"

"My name is Sadie MacKenzie." She spoke in a strong voice, a sound that was surprising even in her own ears. Joshua had encouraged her to speak firmly even if she didn't feel the confidence it would exude. No reason for the others to know that she was terrified on the inside.

"Well, Sadie MacKenzie, this little strike you girls have embarked on has caused quite a stir. So let's see what we can do about resolving it, shall we?"

"You have my agreement that we will do our part, sir. We just want to be sure that everyone else does their part, as well."

"I can assure you the United States military will."

"Which leaves the police."

Steer nodded sagely. "Indeed it does. But leave that to me."

Steer shifted forward in his chair and rested his elbows on the table.

"All right, Sadie MacKenzie, I'm all ears."

Sadie cleared her throat. The night before she had written down what she planned to say and had stayed up late into the night to memorize it. Before leaving the Polynesian Rooms, she folded her speech and tucked it into her dress pocket. Now, as her memory abandoned her, she reached for the paper, but it was not there. A shot of adrenaline disguised as panic rushed through her body. She felt her face flush. All she could think was that she had failed to tuck it deep enough, and the winds that had accompanied their walk to the police station had played the thief.

She remained silent for a long moment. The room seemed to lose its air in anticipation, and she felt short of breath. Joshua reached under the table and, unseen by others, grabbed her hand that was balled into a fist in her pocket. Gently he stroked the back of her wrist with his thumb until she relaxed her hand. Her fingers uncurled. Her breath returned.

She cleared her throat once again and began to speak.

"Major Steer, I realize that there are many in this city who believe that we're beneath them, that we're mere gutter trash who must be swept away from view. But you have honored us by agreeing to this meeting, and I'm humbled by your graciousness in hearing what we have to say. For that, I thank you."

"You're certainly welcome."

Sadie felt her confidence grow as she spoke, helped along by the kind eyes of Major Steer that seemed to encourage her as she went.

"I first came to these islands with dreams of being an entertainer. I arrived with wide eyes and anticipation, but the life I fell into was not what I could have imagined in a thousand years. I'll not belabor the details of how I found myself, mistakenly, in Hotel Street, providing a different form of entertainment than that which I envisioned when I first stepped on board the *Lurline* in San Francisco. At first, I was devastated by what I perceived as abandonment by God when I fell prey to the clutches of one who can only be called a monster, but I found myself surrounded by the most unlikely of companions. Many would call them whores, as did I at first. But now I know better. Now I call them friends."

Though there had been shifting and rustling at the start of her speech, every person in the room sat rigidly still.

"I dare say many of the young men who have climbed the steps of Hotel Street would say the same thing. When the Japanese planes came, it was the girls of Hotel Street who gave up their beds and took in the injured. It was the girls of Hotel Street who tended to their wounds, sat by their sides, and cried with them. Sometimes we even held them as they died, so they wouldn't be alone in their final moments.

"We may be whores in our profession, Major, but we're also caring human beings who gave of ourselves when so many in this city were huddling behind closed doors and tarpaper, afraid to step outside and see the suffering of our boys. Of your men. I believe we have proven ourselves worthy of a little freedom by the way we have given of ourselves in the crisis of war. But more than that, I believe we have proven ourselves worthy of your respect."

A tear trickled down Sadie's cheek. She couldn't be sure, but she thought she saw one glisten in Major Steer's eye, as well.

"Necessity forced us into the communities of Honolulu. And you know what? The world didn't come to an end. We walked the beaches at Waikiki, swam in the Pacific Ocean, ate in restaurants, shared drinks in saloons, rode in automobiles, bought houses and property, and opened bank accounts. I have it on good authority that some of us have even dated servicemen and accompanied them to dances and other socials. Yet despite the hysterical ravings of the Chicken Littles of this city who got conked on their heads by falling acorns, the sky has decidedly not fallen.

"But now there's a move afoot by some to shovel us up and force us back into the confines of Hotel Street, not out of some need, but simply out of a desire not to have to acknowledge our existence. Out of sight, out of mind. It's as simple as that for them, but for us it's life and death. We've tasted freedom, and we're not willing to go back."

She paused and looked around the room at her rapt listeners. "Is not freedom what this war is being fought for? Is not freedom what all American wars have been fought for? If that be so, then how can you possibly justify depriving us of the very freedoms our boys are giving their lives for?"

She stopped, aware that her voice had risen as passion for her message overtook her. She didn't know whether she had offended Major Steer, a man who surely was not used to being spoken to in such a harsh tone.

He clasped his hands in his lap and leaned back in his chair. "There is a little matter of the law, Miss MacKenzie."

"If you decide we're criminals, then lock us up and throw away the key, and burn Hotel Street to the ground. But if you decide that we're not criminals, and that we serve a function in the war effort, then all we ask is that we be treated with basic decency and fairness. That's not an unreasonable request, is it, Major, to be treated fairly and decently?"

Steer leaned forward again. "No, ma'am, it's not."

He looked at her for a long moment. She held his eyes, which did not seem to judge. At last, he smiled and nodded.

"Well done, Miss MacKenzie," he said. "Well done."

Chapter Twenty-Nine

JOSHUA SAT AT his office desk and reviewed his accounts. The war had initially taken its toll on his cash flow, but with the assistance of manufacturing colleagues on the mainland who shifted their focus to the war industry, his income had actually taken a turn for the better. He felt a sense of shame at profiting from the business of war, but assuaged his conscience with the knowledge that he served a legitimate end in facilitating the supply of goods to a territory under siege, coupled with his steadfast refusal to gouge either the military or the citizens on prices for the goods he imported.

His thoughts turned to Sadie, as they so often did these days. It had been more than a week since her remarkable appearance before Major Steer. He couldn't help but marvel at her defense of a profession into which she had been unwillingly drafted and from which she desired to escape. His own heart broke as he realized that she had accepted her lot as a sporting girl, determined now to earn her way out rather than simply flee. He didn't know how many dollars she had accumulated, but he had some investment ideas he wanted to share with her that might help to finance her way out of Hotel Street.

He heard the squeal of brakes on the street outside. Looking through the glass, he saw an Army Jeep parked at his door. He recognized the man who hopped out and entered the building.

"Major Steer, to what do I owe the pleasure?" he asked.

"Mr. Sinclair, I believe I've come with good news, but there's one last hurdle to overcome. I need your assistance."

Joshua beckoned to a chair across from his desk. "Please have a seat." He closed his ledger books and pushed them aside as Steer sat.

"I've had a series of meetings with Chief Gabrielson," Steer said, "who has had his own meetings with the Police Commission. Who, I might add, have met with the Social Protection Committee or the Social Decency Committee or whatever damn name Miles Cary's group has given itself. In any event, we're on the brink of an arrangement that would allow the girls of Hotel Street to live as normal citizens."

"Can you be more specific?"

"If we succeed, the girls will be able to live outside of Hotel Street and will be able to visit the beaches for their rest and relaxation. The military will take over inspections of the brothels for violations of the sanitary code and will also be responsible for ensuring that the girls get regular medical checkups. The police will be left with the responsibility of enforcing the law, but not their so-called rules. The rules will be a thing of the past."

"That's good news, indeed." Joshua opened the bottom desk drawer and pulled out a bottle of Scotch whisky and two glasses. "I'd say it calls for a drink."

"I welcome the drink, but let's not celebrate prematurely. There's one small hitch, and that's what brings me to your door."

Joshua held the bottle aloft over a glass, but didn't pour. "And what is that hitch?"

"Please pour, counselor. I think we deserve the drink, hitch or not."

Joshua poured into both glasses then slid one across the desk to Steer. The Major lifted the glass in a salute and downed it in one gulp. Joshua left his full glass on the desk, waiting for the other shoe to drop.

"There is the little matter of your lawsuit for damages against the police department," Steer said, "and its attack dog, Delbert Mooney." He gestured toward his empty glass and Joshua refilled it. "I read your papers filed with the court, and I know what Mooney did."

"You mean what we allege he did."

"I know of Mooney," Steer answered. "I have no doubt that he's done what he's accused of doing. I also assume he's the monster of whom Miss MacKenzie spoke in her most eloquent speech." He shook his head. "Remarkable young woman."

"He is, and she is."

"I understand, then, if your goal in the lawsuit is to destroy the monster. There are, however, bigger goals to be achieved."

"What could be a bigger goal than destroying a monster?"

Steer stopped with his glass at his lips and set it back on the desk. "I misspoke. What I mean to say is that there are broader goals. Your lawsuit is the sole impediment to a resolution that benefits all the girls of Hotel Street, and I'm here to plead my case."

"Your case needs to be pled to Sadie, not to me. She's the plaintiff; it's her decision to make."

"And you're her lawyer. I sense that she holds your counsel dear. I also sense, from the passion of her words, that she holds the welfare of her friends on Hotel Street dear. I believe she'll act in the best interests of the broader good, and I believe that she'll listen to you and will accept your recommendation. So I'm here to present an offer on behalf of the police department, and, in fact, from the military governor, General Emmons, that I hope you'll recommend to Miss MacKenzie."

"What's the offer?"

"Fifty thousand dollars," Joshua said.

Sadie sat at the dining table in the Polynesian Rooms and let the number sink in. She had learned to count her money three dollars at a time and quickly did the arithmetic in her head. Sixteen-thousand-six-hundred-sixty-six men. Plus two minutes of an additional man to account for the final two-thirds. It would take her nearly two years to earn that much on her back.

"I also have some ideas on how to invest that money, should you accept the offer," Joshua said.

"And the money I've already earned?"

"Yes. How much is that?"

"Wait here."

She left the room and returned a few minutes later with the same battered valise she had carried with her on the *Lurline*. She handed the valise to Joshua, who opened it and looked inside at bundles of one-dollar bills, carefully banded together.

"Fifteen thousand dollars," she said. She had already done that arithmetic in her head, as well. She paid Francis one dollar per man as her take, plus an additional fifty cents per man for room and board. That meant she cleared a dollar fifty per man.

Fifteen thousand dollars. Ten thousand men. In six months.

Joshua sat silently at the table, the valise in front of him. Sadie knew he had done the arithmetic, too. He looked at her with tears forming in his eyes.

"Take the offer, Sadie. Let me invest your money for you and get you out of this God-forsaken place."

"I have one more question first. If I settle the lawsuit, what becomes of Mooney?"

Mooney slammed his gun and badge down on Chief Gabrielson's desk with sufficient force to cause the other items on the desk to dance.

"I can't believe we're letting whores dictate the rules to this department," he said. "I've done my duty, and this is the thanks I get."

"Don't forget, Delbert, that you've cost this department fifty thousand dollars and have eaten away much of what's left of the goodwill we have with the Army."

"So I'm the scapegoat."

"If you choose to view it that way, then yes, you're the scapegoat." Gabrielson grabbed the gun and badge and put them in a drawer of the filing cabinet beside his desk. "But you'll get these back in thirty days."

"And my rank?"

"That, I'm sorry to say, is gone for good. When you return, you'll simply be a member of the vice squad, but not its leader."

"Goddamnit!"

Mooney spun and stormed out of the office, slamming the door behind him. No one dared speak to him as he marched through the station. This was all the handiwork of Sadie MacKenzie. He knew she would be trouble from the day he first laid eyes on her. Playing all coy and innocent when in reality she was a scheming, manipulating little bitch. The day would come soon enough when he would have his revenge. Maybe not today or tomorrow, but soon enough.

Chapter Thirty

SADIE OPENED THE front door of Norma and Kelly's house in Pacific Heights—make that *her* house—to greet Joshua, who stood on the *lanai* with a bottle of wine. He held it up and smiled.

"*Lafite Rothschild*, 1931," he said. "I've been saving this for a special occasion, and christening your new home seems to fit the bill."

She took the wine and kissed him on the cheek. "How thoughtful. Thank you."

Across the street, she saw a small gathering of people. All *haole*, all middle-aged, all very serious-faced. Joshua glanced back at them.

"Welcoming committee of neighbors?" he asked. "Will they come bearing gifts like hot apple pie and a casserole?"

"I don't know. I've not met any of them yet."

She ushered him inside and closed the door. When she turned back around, she saw him frozen, staring at the faint but still visible stains on the tile floor of the entryway. She had scrubbed and scrubbed, but to no avail. She would never be able to fully erase the blood.

She took Joshua by the arm and escorted him past the stains. "Let's go to the kitchen and you can help me with dinner. I must confess that I'm a terrible cook."

"Besides," he said, breaking out of his trance, "we need to open that wine and toast to your new life."

"You mean my new home."

"A man can dream, can't he?"

Yes, Sadie thought, so can a girl. But new lives take money and, although the settlement of the lawsuit was a big step forward, she did not yet have enough to break free. Besides, she had nowhere to go and no skills to peddle other than what she had been peddling for the past months, though that could hardly be called a skill. She had once thought of herself as a singer, but now she knew she was a whore. No, when she finally broke away from this life, it would be forever. And that meant she must earn as much as she could over the next few years. Then, and only then, could she safely make her break.

As Joshua struggled to open the wine, Sadie got out two glasses and set them on the counter. She wished she had crystal, but crystal was way down on her list of "must haves." She knew she was fortunate to own her own home, free and clear, but it had come at a very dear cost.

There was a knock at the front door.

"I'll see who that is," she said. "And I hope there will be wine in my glass when I return."

Joshua merely nodded, his face red from exertion as he fought with the bottle. Smiling, she returned to the door and opened it. The people who had been gathered across the street now stood on her lawn. A stern-faced woman of perhaps forty had apparently been selected as the spokeswoman of the group, though even she stood at the edge of the *lanai*, nearly six feet away.

"Can I help you?" Sadie asked.

"We live in this neighborhood," the woman said.

"How nice of you to stop by. My name is Sadie MacKenzie."

"We know who you are," the woman said. "And we know how you came to have this house." She took a deep breath and looked over her shoulder, as if summoning strength from her neighbors. But strength would not come from them. They were all cowards.

"We don't want whores in this neighborhood," she said.

"How neighborly of you."

"Make one thing clear: You may own this house, but we are not your neighbors. We will never be your neighbors. We have children to protect, and we will do what is necessary to protect them from the likes of you."

"But you don't even know me."

"A whore is a whore."

Sadie fought back tears that were determined to find their way out. In an instant, her pride at owning her own home had been trampled beneath the feet of the neighborhood hate committee.

"Who is it, Sadie?" Joshua called from behind her. He approached, drying his hands on a dish towel.

"It's a group of Honolulu's finest citizens," Sadie said, "come to chase away the whore."

Unable to control her emotions any longer, she burst into tears. She turned and ran for her bedroom, past a startled Joshua who continued to the door. She threw herself facedown on the bed and wept. Behind her she heard raised voices, one male—Joshua's—and one female—the neighborhood hangwoman. As long as she remained in this place, it didn't matter in which neighborhood, the taint of whoredom would always be a millstone around her neck. She redoubled her resolve to earn a sufficient fortune to sail away and never look back.

After a few moments, she realized the voices had subsided. She felt a sag of the mattress as Joshua sat on the bed and put his hand on her shoulder.

"Are you all right?" he asked.

She rolled over and looked up at his kind face. His mere presence warmed her heart. She realized that just one Joshua, or even one Robert, could almost overcome the contempt of the rest of the city. Almost, but not quite.

"I'm afraid I abandoned you to my welcoming committee before they could present me with an apple pie," she said.

"I don't think you'd want to eat it if they had."

Sadie laughed.

"They did come bearing gifts, though," he said. "They want to buy your house from you."

"I don't want to sell my house."

"If you accept their offer, you could buy two houses with the proceeds."

Sadie sat upright. "Two houses?"

"Yes, they're offering you quite a tidy profit over the market value of the house. These aren't people you want for your neighbors anyway, so if

I were you, I'd accept their offer, and then I'd buy two houses."

"But why would I want to buy two houses?" Sadie asked.

Joshua smiled broadly. "Because then you would have two houses to sell."

PART THREE

LEAVING HOTEL STREET

Chapter Thirty-One
August 1, 1944

MOONEY PULLED HIS Deluxe into the driveway of his house and turned off the engine. He sat motionless, eyes closed, and squeezed the steering wheel. Across the black screen of his eyelids, fireworks exploded and sparklers trailed back and forth. He clenched his teeth, and a knot bulged at his jaw. A band tightened across his chest, squeezing with each gasp of air he tried to gulp. For an instant, he wondered if he should back out and head straight for the hospital, but fears of a heart attack were soon replaced by thoughts of the culprit for his condition. Not alcohol; not cigars. No, it was a goddamn whore who had started his decline two years ago. But he had been patient and, when the time was right, he would have his revenge, even if it killed him. And he knew that it well might.

He opened his eyes and stared at his reflection in the rearview mirror. He barely recognized the face that stared back at him. Gone was the steely-eyed man of confidence who once controlled a squad of vice officers and the daily lives of dozens of whores on Hotel Street. The man whose appearance once struck fear into hearts, whose very name commanded respect. But the Mooney of old did not stare back at him from the mirror. In his place sat a frightened boy, stripped of his rank and ever fearful for his job, fearful for his health, and fearful for his continued existence. He had been reduced to insignificance.

When he opened the car door and slid out, he noticed a ragged blue coupe parked in front of the house. He had paid it no mind as he drove past and turned into the driveway, but now it appeared as another plague in his life. Another gentleman caller for Mother. She had likely serviced as many gentleman callers as any whore on Hotel Street, yet she did not abide by any of the rules. At least the whores got regular medical check-ups, but Mother was a cancer run amuck.

As he stepped inside the kitchen, he heard a raspy smoker's voice in the den.

"Awfully dusty down there."

Dry, maybe, Delbert thought, but certainly well-traveled.

"It's been a while since anyone visited," Mother said. Then she giggled. A coquette and her admirer.

He heard a blowing sound, a sort of *whoof whoof*, then, "Plenty of room, though. You've been a busy girl."

Mister, you have no idea. You'll be lucky to make contact unless you're hung like a racehorse.

"Just getting ready for you," Mother said, followed by another giggle.

Mooney opened the icebox door. He rustled around, rattling wax paper and clanking beer bottles against each other. He grabbed a beer and popped the top with an opener.

"Is someone here?" the gentleman caller said.

Mother called out, "Delbert, that you?" which was followed by a panicky male voice: "Good God!"

Mooney sauntered into the den, beer in hand. The sight that greeted him turned his stomach: A greasy-haired man, thin and gawky, had obviously just rolled off of Mother. He wore his trousers at his knees, his tool wilting rapidly as he reached for a pair of glasses on the coffee table with one hand and tried to cover his crotch with the other. Within seconds, he was successful in providing complete cover. Mother sat shamelessly on the couch, leaning back, legs splayed, slip hiked above her dusty triangle, underwear tangled around one ankle.

"You could march an army through there, buddy," Mooney said. "It'd be like fucking a big old hole in the ground."

The man slid his glasses on. His eyes widened in recognition. He struggled to pull his pants up with one hand, while covering himself with the other. "I'm sorry, Officer Mooney. I didn't know she was—"

"She was what? My mother? You just thought she was an old whore?"

"No. I mean—"

Mooney felt as if someone had flipped a switch in his mind. In an instant, he went from beleaguered to fully enraged. He threw the beer bottle against the wall directly above the gentleman caller's head. Glass and liquid splashed over the man as he ducked, then buckled his pants and bolted for the door.

"Yeah, you get your skinny ass out of here before I cut your dick off and shove it down your throat."

Mooney swung a foot at the man as he passed but merely grazed him. The door slammed as the frightened man scurried out into the dark night, a sultry breeze slipping in before it closed. Mooney turned to face Mother, her legs still splayed, her womanhood obscenely exposed. She grabbed a pack of cigarettes from the coffee table and lit one.

"He had money," she said. She brushed a hand across her graying pubic hair. "And I was ready."

"You're always ready." Mooney glared at her. "Cover up."

"What am I supposed to do now?"

Mooney reached into his pocket, grasped a wad of bills, and threw it in her face.

"You want money? There's money."

"That's not what I'm talking about." She sat up straight, cigarette dangling from the corner of her mouth. She brushed her hand across the front of Mooney's trousers and gripped his bulge.

He pulled away. She smiled.

She reached for the buckle on his belt. "Looks like mama's little boy needs her."

He slapped her hand away.

"Oh, come on now, honey. You used to like this when you were little."

"I never liked it." Mooney's voice came out as a growl, the menacing tone he reserved for whores who ignored the rules. The tone that turned defiant whores into whimpering children, begging for mercy. The tone that backed down the upstarts, intimidated the madams, and had once made him the cock of the walk on Hotel Street.

The tone that had no impact whatsoever on his mother.

She grasped his belt with both hands and started to unbuckle it. "Come on, sweetie. Mama will make it all better."

His groin tingled and his phallus throbbed. Goddamnit! This was his mother. His mother, for God's sake. The woman who birthed him. The woman who fed him. The woman who bathed him. The woman who visited him in his bedroom at night and taught him things no boy his age should know. He couldn't remember the first time it grew, but he remembered being scared by it, convinced something was wrong with him. At first he had been ashamed, but finally he broke his silence. He couldn't remember where Pop was, but somehow it seemed like the thing you asked your mother. After all, she was the one who took care of him when he was sick, and if the enlargement was related to illness, Mother was the one to ask.

"It's perfectly natural," she had said. "It happens to all boys. Sometimes your age, but sometimes older. It's a good thing."

"What's good about it?"

"Let mama show you."

Then she took him to his bedroom and removed his clothes. He lay down and she grasped him in her hand. He quickly became engorged. Then she took off her own clothes, straddled him, and guided him inside. She did all the work as he lay on his back, eleven years old, frightened and fascinated at the same time.

When they were finished, she said, "This will just be our little secret."

He had kept that secret ever since. But the secrets soon started to pile up as she paid regular visits. And tonight she wanted to create another secret for him to keep. Only now he knew what it all meant. He wasn't eleven years old anymore. He was a grown man, and his fascination with the wonders of his mother's body had ended many years ago. In fact, his fascination with women's bodies in general had vanished as well, driven into exile by a relentless mother who refused to let him rest in peace. It had been replaced by a fascination with the bodies of boys.

"Enough," he said. He grasped her wrists, halting her efforts with his belt buckle.

"Mama knows what you want," she said. "Let mama take care of you."

"You have no idea what I want." He squeezed her wrists, hard.

A small cry escaped her lips. "You're hurting me."

"And you've hurt me for years."

"I never hurt you, Delbert. Now please, let me go."

"You're disgusting."

He roughly pushed her away, and she sprawled on the sofa. She took the cigarette out of her mouth and flicked the lengthening ash in a saucer on the coffee table. Then she leaned back with her eyes closed. With her left hand, she manipulated the cigarette, blowing smoke out of the side of her mouth. She slid her right hand beneath her slip, her underwear still around her ankle.

"If you're not going to help, then go away and I'll take care of myself," she said.

She opened one eye and looked at him. When he turned and stormed down the hallway, she smiled, then opened her mouth and moaned. As Mooney neared his bedroom, he heard the sounds of the radio behind Pop's closed door. Sounded like *Gildersleeve*. Behind him, Mother moaned again, the sounds obviously exaggerated to show him what he was missing. But he didn't miss it one goddamn bit!

He entered his room and slammed the door. He removed his shoulder holster and weapon and tossed them on the bed, then finished unbuckling his belt. As the belt dropped to the floor, he stripped off his shirt and sat on the edge of the bed. He unbuttoned his trousers, unzipped his fly, and extracted his erect phallus. He took his gun from its holster and emptied the cylinder of all the bullets save one. He spun the cylinder and lay back, gripping the gun with one hand, himself with the other. He began stroking.

He squeezed his eyes shut, put the barrel in his mouth, and pulled the trigger.

Click.

No spin, but another pull of the trigger.

Click.

Mooney felt warmth well up in his groin. He clenched his teeth on the gun barrel, squeezed his finger on the trigger.

Then three things happened at once: From the front room, Mother screamed "Oh, my God! Yes, yes!"; Mooney ejaculated; and the gun exploded as he pulled the trigger. He had removed it from his mouth and pointed it at the ceiling just as he climaxed. Shards of plaster sprinkled on him from the hole in the ceiling.

He put the gun on the bed and cleaned himself with his wadded shirt. When his ears quit ringing, he could again hear the muted sound of *Gildersleeve* from Pop's room.

Pop. Had he been able to hear, again, the infidelity of his feckless wife while she relegated him to the status of furniture—stationary, lifeless, and unfeeling? He wondered what it was like to be imprisoned in your own body, aware of your surroundings but unable to communicate the thoughts that surely must torture you every waking second. Did he fantasize about such things as mundane as feeding himself or combing his hair or even wiping his own ass?

Or murdering his wife? Surely Pop's thoughts must take that dark path on occasion. Just as the Biblical Samson, shorn of his strength-giving hair by Delilah, had prayed for one last blessing from God—the strength to pull down the temple on his tormentors—surely Pop had asked God for strength to rise from his bed so he could walk down the hall and permanently dispatch his wife. Mooney thought that, if Pop didn't pray that prayer, then Mooney could never truly respect him anymore.

He left his bedroom, stepped across the hall to Pop's room, and rapped gently on the warped wooden door.

"Pop, you awake?"

No response other than the voices of characters on the radio. But a familiar odor crawled under the door and assaulted Mooney's nostrils.

"Goddamnit!"

He opened the door and instantly the stench slammed into his face. He waved his arms as if the filth had manifested itself into a cloud obscuring his vision. Anger welled inside his gut and marched its way to his brain. It had to have been hours—hours!—since Mother had last checked on him. Hours lying in his own waste, unable to clean himself, or even to protect his own nostrils from the vile odor.

Mooney's eyes watered. He held his hand over his nose as he stared at the lifeless figure in the bed. Pop lay still, eyes closed, head back on a thin pillow. Urine and watery stool saturated the thin sheet, painting most of the bed a yellowish brown. Mooney pulled the sheet to the foot of the bed, then onto the floor. Pop's waste had seeped into the mattress and spread, like a sponge soaking up fluid. Never had Mooney seen it so bad. It looked as if someone had fully opened the spigot on Pop's bowels and then simply left it open all day.

"Pop, we've got to get you cleaned up."

No response.

"Pop? You hear me?"

Mooney gently grasped the old man's shoulder and shook. Pop's torso slid sideways, and his head slumped forward. The sudden movement frightened Mooney. He let go and jumped back. He stared at Pop as realization sank in. He reached out his hand, unaware that it trembled, placed his first two fingers gently on the side of Pop's neck, and felt for a pulse.

Nothing.

He walked around the bed, turned off the radio, and sat in the rocking chair. He took Pop's limp hand in his as he rocked. Softly, almost inaudibly, he sang the words of an old hymn Pop had sung to him as a boy, soothing him to sleep.

"No, never alone. No, never alone. He promised never to leave me, never to leave me alone."

Sadie sat at Joshua's dinner table, her food untouched on the plate. Her hands began to shake as she held the bulletin entitled *Prostitution in*

Honolulu. Joshua watched silently while she read the document issued that day by the Social Protection Committee. When she finished reading, she put it on the table and stared at Joshua.

"Why would they do that?" she asked.

"They've never been happy with the settlement of the strike. As far as Miles Cary was concerned back then, the strike should have continued on to infinity."

"What right does he have to tell the world where we all live? He includes a map, for goodness sake." She took the map from behind the bulletin and held it up, her finger jabbing at a point. "There is my home. Right there. For all my neighbors to know."

"That was the point. To let people know who lives in their neighborhoods."

"They want us put back in Hotel Street."

"They want you banished from the Islands, but Hotel Street will do for their purposes for now."

She pushed her plate away, her appetite non-existent. "How much money do I have?"

Joshua reached to the buffet behind him and grabbed a ledger. "I knew you would ask that, so I've gone over your books. Not everything is liquid, of course, particularly your real estate holdings, although I suspect your current residence will be highly marketable once your neighbors review Cary's map. But you have no debt, and the value of all of your assets approaches four-hundred-fifty-thousand dollars. That's enough to live quite comfortably on for the rest of your life."

She mulled the number in her mind. She had come to Hawaii nearly three years earlier with nothing but the clothes on her back and less than fifty dollars in her handbag. Now she was among the wealthiest of the Territory's citizens. But at what price?

It was time to get out.

"Help me make a plan, Joshua," she said. "I won't go back to Hotel Street. I'll never go back."

Chapter Thirty-Two

MOONEY STOOD AT the doorway to the kitchen. He held Pop's filthy sheet wadded in his hands and watched as Mother sat at the kitchen table, her back to him, and ate a meal of sticky rice, pan-fried mahi-mahi, and pineapple. On the stove, a slab of fish smoldered in a cast iron pan; a serrated knife and an uncooked half of fish on a cutting board sat beside it on the counter. A cigarette smoldered in an overflowing ashtray. On the table before Mother, an open movie star magazine held her attention; she was oblivious to his presence, just as she had been oblivious to Pop's as his body lay rotting in the bed all day.

Mother must have finally sensed him behind her. Or maybe she merely smelled Pop's shit. It was certainly the kind of thing that might ruin an appetite. Still, she never turned her attention away from the magazine as she spoke.

"There's rice on the stove," she said. "And mahi."

Mooney tossed the feces-laden sheet over her head, like a fisherman throwing out his *hukilau* net in a cove.

"Shit, Delbert!"

He stood in the doorway and watched as she thrashed about, like a dog fighting out from beneath a towel that a child might have thrown over it to amuse himself. He was tempted to grab a corner of the sheet and re-wrap her as she worked her way out, but instead he remained frozen in the doorway.

At length she freed herself.

"Shit, Delbert, what'd you do that for?"

She stood, but Mooney pushed her back down. He grabbed the chair and turned it around so that she faced him, then he leaned over her, fists resting on the table on either side. Pop's waste trickled down her cheek and spackled her hair. It seemed fitting, he thought; after all, she was a piece of shit.

"When did he go, Mother?"

She tried to duck under his arms. He forced her back into the chair and this time leaned with his fists against her. He pushed hard, digging his knuckles into her meaty shoulders, and spoke in an even, steady voice. The look in Mother's eye revealed that she knew it for what it was: calm before a storm.

"Delbert, I've got to get cleaned up," she said.

"When did he go?"

"I don't know what you're talking about. When did who go?"

"Pop. When did he go?"

"He's not gone anywhere. He's in his room. Now I've got to get cleaned up. I'm covered in shit."

"Sit there and stew in it. Just like you made Pop do."

"That's not my fault. If he's going to shit the bed, then it serves him right."

Mooney retreated to a dark place within, where he went from time to time when unpleasant things had to be done and he had to be the one to do them.

"He's gone," Mooney said, his tone now flat and cold, his eyes dark.

She stared at him for a long moment, after which she nodded. "Well, then he's gone to a better place. Dust to dust. God rest his soul."

"He's gone to heaven," Mooney said.

"We'll see him again in Glory."

"No, we won't."

"What do you mean?"

"Because we'll be in hell. And you're going first."

He turned and looked at the counter. Mother didn't see what he was looking for, but she took advantage of the brief moment of inattention to push his hands away and get to her feet.

"I've got to get cleaned up," she said.

In one smooth motion, he grabbed the serrated knife, pushed her back into the chair with his free hand, and plunged the blade deep into her torso, perfectly centered between her breasts.

She screamed. Blood spurted onto Mooney's face.

He pulled the blade out, accompanied by a grating sound as metal scraped bone. Then he raised his fist high and drove the blade down again.

And again and again. Her screams stopped on the fourth blow. Her mouth contorted, but no sound escaped. Her eyes rolled back in her head, leaving nothing but white.

Exhausted, Mooney stepped away and beheld what he had done. Mother sat upright in the kitchen chair, her head tilted backward. Blood pooled on the floor.

And he saw that it was good.

He spun the chair around, grasping her hair in his fingers to hold her head upright as he pushed the chair under the table. From behind, she appeared simply to be an old woman enjoying her dinner. He set the knife on the counter then took a bar of soap from the window sill over the sink and scrubbed his hands, taking care to clean blood from beneath his fingernails.

He grabbed a bottle of whiskey and sat at the table across from Mother. He pulled her plate, sprinkled with blood, toward himself, picked up the mahi with his fingers, and took a bite.

"So, Mother, how was your day?"

He grabbed a handful of bloody rice and shoved it into his mouth. He cocked his head, as if listening, while he stared at her across the table.

"Sounds like a busy day," he said after he swallowed.

He paused then, "Mine was good, thanks for asking. I beat a whore today. Then I raped a teen-age boy. You would have been proud."

He uncorked the whiskey and downed a big swallow in one chug. He set the bottle down with a clank that jarred the table. He wiped his mouth and leaned forward on his elbows.

"Something happened today while you were whoring around that I think you should know about."

He paused, as if listening to her response.

"Yes, I'm afraid it's bad news." Another pause, then, "Pop died."

Mother's head shifted forward and her eyes rolled back into place. For a brief second, it was as if she made direct eye contact with Mooney—cold, lifeless eyes staring into cold, lifeless eyes—then her chin slapped against her chest and her eyelids closed.

After dragging the feces-sodden mattress to the back yard and replacing it with the dry back-up, Mooney meticulously cleaned Pop, dressed him in fresh pajamas, and laid him in the bed, close to the edge on the far side. He pulled the sheets to Pop's chest then tuned the radio to clear up static and settled on *Fibber McGee and Molly* for Pop's farewell broadcast.

He walked to the kitchen, where Mother sat at the table with her head resting on her chest. He scooped her up in his arms and returned to Pop's room. He lowered her bloody body onto the bed next to Pop. The red fluid soaked into the sheets and spread beneath her as he positioned her body.

He stepped back and stood silently for a moment, hands at his sides. He couldn't remember the last time his parents had shared a bedroom, much less a bed, but this was how it was supposed to be. Husbands and wives—fathers and mothers—forsaking all others, to honor and cherish, in sickness and in health, 'til death do they part. Mother had gotten it backwards. Forsaking Pop for a parade of men, to scorn and deride, in health and especially in sickness, but now, in death, no longer to part.

He bowed his head and said the only prayer he knew, one he had learned as a boy. "Our Father, who art in Heaven, hallowed be thy name. Thy kingdom come, thy will be done, on earth as it is in Heaven. Give us this day our daily bread, and forgive us our trespasses as we forgive those who trespass against us. And lead us not into temptation, but deliver us from evil. For thine is the kingdom, and the power, and the glory forever. Amen."

He retrieved his gun and holster from his bedroom, went outside, and slid behind the wheel of Mother's Buick Roadmaster. He cruised the darkened streets of Honolulu—along Waikiki, the moon glittering on the surf that washed ashore on the white sand, through the business district, around the perimeter of Chinatown, toward Pearl, then into the mountains toward a neighborhood of tidy houses and well-kept lawns, rich with tropical flora. These were the people who looked upon Mooney and his fellow officers with contempt, as if they were no better than those they policed. But let the police go off duty for even a day, and these same contemptuous citizens would raise a hue and cry as the line would blur between polite society and the unwashed who would amass at the boundaries to their beautiful neighborhoods like Huns at the gate, waiting to invade.

Many of these people didn't know it, but the Huns had already invaded. There was already a whore living in their midst, but disguised in respectable clothing and with feigned social graces, a façade carefully created and maintained by a shyster lawyer. Once a whore, always a whore, and he was about to pull back the curtain and expose her to the world for what she was.

Mooney drove past Sadie's darkened house at slightly more than idle speed. He carefully regarded the structure and the neighborhood in which it resided. Maybe crime didn't pay, but whoring sure did. A fire of anger burned in the pit of his stomach, fueled by the kindling of jealousy. Here he was, an officer of the law, doing God's work among the heathen and living in squalor with mommy and daddy while this whore spread her legs for money and dwelt in the lap of luxury.

He thought back to that first morning when he had picked her up at the pier. A different time in a different world. Before the Japs and their sneak attack. He remembered how haughty she had been, thinking he was her servant to carry her luggage and chauffeur her around. He had set her straight soon enough. He proved to her that her place was at the bottom of the pecking order. She was just a whore, and she would always be a whore.

But the Japs had changed everything. As if the attack at Pearl wasn't enough, then the Army decided that whores ranked higher than the police. They opened the door to Hotel Street and, for the first time in his memory, it swung outward instead of inward. Sadie MacKenzie marched right through it, stomping on his authority with each step. That just wasn't right.

And it was about to change.

The windows and shutters on the house were open, but no lights burned inside. The sun had set nearly two hours ago. If she were home, the lights would be on, as they were in the houses of her neighbors, no longer fearful of sneak attacks from the Japs. She was probably dining at some fancy restaurant, spending her sin money on a sumptuous meal. He cruised to the end of the block, then around the corner and parked. From beneath the seat, he pulled out the kitchen knife, traces of Mother's blood still soiling its blade. He held it at his side as he walked back to Sadie's house, eyes flicking side to side, searching out observers in yards or peering out of windows. Nothing and no one. All was still and silent.

He reached her house unseen. With one quick glance around, he scampered across the yard to the side. Sheer curtains on a large picture window waved in the night breezes, fluttering outside of the open shutters like dancing ghosts. With a nimbleness that belied his size, Mooney clambered over the sill and dropped to the floor beside a flower-print divan.

It was darker inside the house than out, with shadows cast by walls and corners. He stood without moving for a full minute and allowed his pupils to enlarge. Faint shapes took on distinction as his eyes adjusted. He swiveled his head to view the furnishings of a whore's house. Would the walls be ripe with photographs of men and women engaged in hedonistic rituals and unchaste sex? Would the furniture be gaudy and loud?

He felt his way to a small lamp on a writing desk in a corner and turned it on. He rotated in a full three-hundred-sixty degree circle as he surveyed his surroundings. Rattan furniture on pine floors gave the room a homey look. Instead of sex pictures, tasteful Hawaiian scenes decorated the walls, including water color prints in pastels.

And on the far wall, there were bookshelves filled with books. Lots of books. Lots and lots of books. Classics, such as *The Mayor of Casterbridge* by Thomas Hardy, *A Tale of Two Cities* by Charles Dickens, *The Brothers Karamazov* by Teodor Dostoyevski, *Kidnapped* by Robert Louis Stevenson, and a row of Mark Twain: *The Adventures of Huckleberry Finn*, *A Connecticut Yankee in King Arthur's Court*, *The Tragedy of Pudd'nhead Wilson*, and *The*

Innocents Abroad. A Hemingway section, with *For Whom the Bell Tolls*, *The Sun Also Rises*, and *A Farewell to Arms.* Recent bestsellers, like Steinbeck's *The Grapes of Wrath*, Betty Smith's *A Tree Grows in Brooklyn*, Daphne du Maurier's *Hungry Hill*, and *Dragon's Teeth* by Upton Sinclair; mysteries like Ellery Queen's *There Was an Old Woman* and Raymond Chandler's *The Lady in the Lake.* Even books on theology, like C.S. Lewis's *The Screwtape Letters.*

Mooney could scarcely believe what he saw. Could it be true? A well-read whore? He was sure Sadie MacKenzie was not a college graduate, maybe not even a high school graduate. So where did the interest in reading find its origin? Surely not lying on her back and servicing America's fighting boys three dollars at a time. Probably from the lawyer. He was Henry Higgins turning Eliza Doolittle from a Cockney flower girl into a duchess.

He tore himself away from the bookshelves and found his way down a darkened hallway, leaving droplets of blood from the knife behind him on the pine floor like a trail of bread crumbs. He stood in the doorway to her bedroom, illuminated by moonlight shining through an open window on the far wall. A light breeze sent cheesecloth curtains fluttering inward.

He took a deep breath, as if trying to inhale her essence. A faint tickle of plumeria tickled his nostrils. The perfume she wore as a trademark. The bedroom was as tastefully furnished and decorated as the living room, including pastel water colors of hibiscus, torch ginger, and birds-of-paradise framed on the walls. The bed was made and stacked with stuffed animals. Did she entertain men here? Mooney didn't think so. She wouldn't want to sully her home with the stench of Hotel Street.

He moved quickly to a closet door, opened it, and stepped back to examine her wardrobe. A closet full of dresses in quality fabrics and bright colors. He took a white garment by the hem and held it to his nose. He inhaled deeply, again drinking in the aromas and tell-tale signs of Sadie. He wiped the blade of his knife on the dress and dragged blood stains across the cloth.

On impulse, he went to a dresser on the far wall, laid the knife on its surface, and opened the top drawer. As he expected, it was filled with lacy, frilly things. Bright colors and dark colors, with red and black predominating. He rummaged through them until he came to a pair of black silk panties, sheer with stripes and beige lace trim, the kind he had seen on pin-up models. But Sadie was no model; she was no movie star— she was a whore. And these were meant to tantalize and tease.

He held the panties to his nose and inhaled. A clean, fresh aroma. He closed his eyes and rubbed the silk across his cheek. With his free hand, he stroked his groin as he thought of Sadie MacKenzie.

But nothing happened. Not a twinge, not even a shudder.

He thought of Mother's oversized cotton underwear flapping on the clothesline. His penis twitched. Then he pictured them tangled around her ankles as she sprawled on the couch. More movement, then sudden growth.

Goddamnit! Sick, twisted. How could a man be aroused by his own mother? Clearly there was something wrong with him. She was a disgusting, flabby, wrinkled old woman. She was his mother, the woman who gave him life. And whose life he took. He pictured the expression on her face as he raised the kitchen knife and plunged it into her chest. Blood rushed to his groin. Fully erect now.

He opened the fly on his pants, took himself in a hand stained with blood, and wrapped the black silk around his member. He stroked in rhythm to the raising and plunging of the knife in his mind's eye as he drove it again and again into Mother's breast. Her screams echoed in his mind. Within seconds, he ejaculated into the underwear. He used the silk, sodden with his seed, to wipe off the handle of the knife. He wrapped the panties around it and placed it in the lingerie drawer where it nestled in her most intimate clothing. He pushed the drawer in, leaving it ajar about an inch.

Then he grabbed a black pearl necklace from a jewelry box on top of the dresser, tucked it in his pocket, and left the bedroom.

Sadie maneuvered her maroon Zephyr, the same color and model of automobile that Norma had owned, into the driveway beside her house and turned off its engine. She had long since moved past her own disapproval of herself, but now that she had made the decision to disappear forever from Hotel Street, the only question was whether her soul had already been mortally wounded. Joshua didn't think so, but she wasn't so sure.

As soon as she stepped foot inside her home, she knew that it had been invaded. There was a scent that was out of place. A male scent—lingering hints of cigar or maybe of cologne. Or maybe of sweat.

The smell of Mooney.

She moved through the house, turning on lights as she went. It was only as she paused at the mouth of the hallway that she first saw it: a trail of tiny droplets on the floor. She glanced over her shoulder and saw that it originated in front of the large window behind the divan, led to the bookcase, then to the hallway and toward her bedroom. She knelt and examined the droplets, dark red in color. She knew blood when she saw it.

Her pulse quickened. She felt a flush of heat in her cheeks, and a shortness of breath overtook her. She grabbed an umbrella from a stand by the front door and held it in front of her, like a swordsman. She listened closely, but heard no sounds. The scent of Mooney was stale. He was no longer there, but the mere fact that he had been stoked the fire of her emotions, which ran the gamut from fear to outrage. In the early days, fear had predominated, but she soon realized that Mooney was nothing more than a bully. And with that knowledge, she gained courage.

Moving one hesitant step at a time, umbrella-sword held at the ready, Sadie followed the droplet trail to her bedroom door. It was open, just as she always left it, the lights dormant and the room in shadows. She stood in the doorway and scrutinized her boudoir. At first glance, all looked as it should be, but when she turned on the light, she saw that her closet door was open. She knew it had been closed when she left. She crossed the room quickly and jabbed at her dresses with the umbrella. She poked and prodded the length of the closet but met no resistance. Satisfied, she stepped back and caught her breath. It was as if her heart had stopped and only now had restarted. A wave of heat washed over her; her hand carrying the umbrella trembled.

She turned to survey the room again when something caught the corner of her eye. Something out of place. She looked back at her dresses. There it was, a swipe of red on a white dress. She dropped the umbrella and grabbed the fabric with both hands. She pulled the dress into the light and the redness glistened. Whose blood was it? One of the girls? Was Mooney sending her a message?

Then came a more practical question: To whom did she report this? If her home had been violated, then this was a police matter. But if indeed the intruder had been Mooney, then reporting to the police would be a meaningless gesture. Perhaps she should tell Robert. He seemed to have the ear of Major Steer, although the military would likely hold a home break-in to be the province of the civilian authorities. Or perhaps Joshua. He would know what to do. He always did, even though she often failed to heed his advice.

As she turned back toward the doorway, she saw that her lingerie drawer was partly ajar. She rushed to the dresser and yanked the drawer fully open. And gasped. There lay the exposed blade of a knife, small swaths of blood streaked on the metal, the handle wrapped in her underwear. A message from Mooney, no doubt about it now. But what was the message? What was Mooney up to? What had he done?

Her mind was atwitter with apprehension. Whatever his deed, whomever he had injured—or worse—he was trying to put the blame on her. Would he, himself, make an anonymous report to the Honolulu Police and then personally respond to the report to discover a murder weapon and a victim's blood in her house? Would he then haul her off in handcuffs to stand trial for the murder of some unknown victim that he would find a way to connect to her? She wouldn't put it past him. She knew him to be capable of exactly such evil.

She returned to the closet and pulled a small stepstool from behind her dresses. She positioned it in the center then stepped atop it. High on the closet shelf, in the far corner, she felt for a small wooden box. When it rested in her hands, she stepped down and opened its top.

She took out a derringer and dropped it in the pocket of her dress.

Chapter Thirty-Three

MOONEY SAT AT the kitchen table and smoked one of Mother's cigarettes. A small gasoline can was on the floor by his feet. He had acted impulsively in killing her, though it was impulse built upon a solid foundation of hate. He had known for decades that it was just a matter of time until he butchered her. He suspected, even, that Pop's death—whenever that might be—would be the catalyst. A good prosecuting attorney could make a compelling argument that the act was premeditated, planned over a course of years. That is, if he knew Mooney's heart and mind. But no one did. Mooney wasn't even sure he knew his own heart.

With the knife now safely planted at the home of a whore who had openly and notoriously feuded with Mooney for years, his cover story was in place. Now all he had to do was put the final touches on it. He extracted the necklace from his pocket and hefted it in his hand, as if weighing the pearls. They were real, of that much he was sure, from the South Seas. Valuable and easy to sell on the black market. He had no idea how much the necklace was worth, but whatever it was, the financial sacrifice he was about to make would pay off tenfold when Sadie MacKenzie was lined up in front of a firing squad. He planned to be there. Hell, he might even volunteer to put on the blindfold and light her final cigarette.

He set his own cigarette in the ashtray, took the necklace between his teeth, and yanked hard, breaking the string. Pearls cascaded to the floor. They bounced and rolled to the nether reaches of the kitchen, though some bogged down in the viscous blood pooled around Mother's chair. One more piece in the puzzle that would seal Sadie's fate.

He put the cigarette back between his lips, picked up the gasoline can, and trudged to Pop's bedroom. Part of him hoped that he would find Pop's eyes open as he listened to his radio programs. But he was gone and the shrew who killed him lay dead by his side. Oh, maybe she had not killed him directly, but she had certainly stolen life from him. In reality, Pop had been dead for years. Heartbeats, alone, did not a life make.

He approached the side where Mother lay and took a deep puff on the cigarette. The ashes glowed red on the end. With both hands, he lifted the can and sprinkled gasoline on her midsection. Not much, just a few drops. He set the can on the floor and extended the cigarette over her. He lightly tapped it, and tiny embers fluttered onto her body. They smoldered for a moment and then flickered to life.

He took the cigarette, positioned it between her fingers, and draped her hand across her waist. It would be a slow, smoldering fire, hopefully with plenty of smoke. He trusted that it would be discovered before the house reached a full blaze, and the clues he had planted would be discovered.

He went to the far side of the bed, knelt, and gently stroked Pop's face. Then he leaned forward and kissed him softly on the forehead.

He went to his bedroom and retrieved the valise he had packed. It didn't contain all his worldly belongings, but only those that were of the most value to him. Questions would be raised if he somehow managed to escape with all his possessions, especially since he was not supposed to be home when the fire broke out. He had learned enough from his years in law enforcement to set up answers to questions before they could be asked.

He slipped out of the house and down the street to where he had parked Mother's Roadmaster. He got behind the wheel, started the engine, and pulled away.

Sadie pulled her Zephyr to a stop directly in front of Mooney's modest home. The interior lights were ablaze, and Mooney's Deluxe was parked by its side. She was shocked by the house's shabbiness as well as its smallness. Hiding assets could have been part of Mooney's grand scheme, disguising thousands of ill-gotten gains obtained from raping and beating the girls by appearing to live within the means of his police wages, but that would have been out of character for him. Mooney's personality screamed for attention. He wanted you to know who he was, how powerful he was—and how affluent he was. The latter he revealed with his fancy car and dandy attire. Payoffs to Mooney and others of his ilk were the worst kept secret in Honolulu, so there was no reason for him to conceal anything. The only conclusion to be drawn was that Mooney's money was spent elsewhere.

She confirmed that the knife was still beneath the car seat. She touched the derringer in her pocket to ensure that it was within easy reach, and then exited the car with deliberate purpose. She strode to the door and pounded on it with the side of her fist.

"Mooney! Mooney, I know you're in there."

A light clicked on over a porch next door.

Sadie kept pounding.

"Mooney, I know you're in there."

A voice called to her from the neighbor's back door. "Hey, sistah, what you doing?" An elderly *kanaka*, clad in a hibiscus-print *mu'umu'u*, stepped onto her porch. She peered at Sadie over thick glasses. "People sleeping heah."

"I'm looking for Delbert Mooney," Sadie said. "Is he home?"

"Das his car, but I don't see him tonight."

Sadie turned back to the door and pounded again. "Mooney, open up. I'm not leaving until you let me in."

The neighbor lady clucked her tongue and muttered, "You *pupule*, *wahine*." She disappeared back inside, but her face remained pressed to the window, watching the crazy white woman banging on Mooney's door.

Sadie stopped knocking, stepped back, and surveyed her surroundings. That was, indeed, Mooney's car, and where Mooney's car was, Mooney was never far away. It was almost as if his identity was inextricably intertwined with the vehicle. But why wasn't he answering the door? She knew for certain it wasn't from fear of confrontation. Mooney was a man who thrived on that, particularly when he held the upper hand—and he nearly always held that hand. Even tonight, notwithstanding Sadie's righteous indignation at the invasion of her home and the derringer in her pocket, the moral abyss of Mooney's conscience would give him that same advantage.

So why was he not answering?

She grabbed the doorknob and turned it. Unlocked. She pushed the door open and stepped inside, where she found herself in a tiny living area that was as remarkable for its poverty as it was for its size.

"Mooney!"

No response.

She thought she smelled smoke. She inhaled deeply. The odor was not that of Mooney's cigar, nor of the man, himself. Then she saw faint wisps floating lazily in the air, though the source was unclear.

The kitchen! Something must be burning on the stove, unattended. She crossed the living area to a room on the far side where she saw an icebox just inside the doorway, but pulled up short, stunned at the sight. A pool of blood sparkled beneath a chair pulled out from a table. But it was far more blood than could possibly be expected from a mere kitchen accident. Sadie thought immediately of the blood on the knife.

She turned to leave, but something froze her in place. Tiny orbs sprinkled throughout the pool. She stepped forward and, bending at the waist, gingerly plucked one of the spheres from the fluid. She wiped away the blood and held it close to examine.

A pearl. Not just any pearl, but a black pearl, identical to those on her necklace.

And Mooney had been in her house. She had not checked her jewelry box, but the scheme began to clarify itself in her mind. Mooney had stolen the necklace and salted this blood with clues linking her to whatever had occurred here. A link that would lead back to a bloody knife at her house.

A half-eaten meal of mahi-mahi and sticky rice sat atop the table, sprinkled with blood. Then she remembered why she had entered the kitchen in the first place. She glanced at the stove, but nothing smoldered there and the smell of smoke was weaker. It must be emanating from the other side of the house.

She went back to the living area and glanced around, seeking clues to Mooney's psyche. The room was filled with photos, mostly family pictures, many of them featuring Mooney with an older woman. Mooney at all ages, even as a young boy, always with the same woman.

Mama's boy. That explained a lot.

She entered the hallway, where the air was thick with haze. At the end of the narrow passage, she saw smoke escaping from beneath a closed door. She hurried to it and placed the palm of her hand flat against the wood. No heat. Whatever lay on the other side may have been smoldering, but it was not yet blazing. She gingerly grasped the knob and opened the door just a crack. Smoke assaulted her face, driving her back a step, but still no unusual heat. No flames, no crackling of fire.

She slowly swung the door open all the way then stepped back as smoke billowed out. She swatted at it with both hands. Her eyes watered and tears rolled down her cheeks. When at last the haze had cleared somewhat, she stepped to the doorway and searched for the source. Her eyes were drawn to two figures reposed on a small bed, lying side-by-side. The one on the near side was an elderly woman, the apparent source of the fire. Her shabby clothing smoldered and smoked. Blood covered her breast and spilled onto the mattress and even to the floor. Peaceful in death, her features matched those of the woman in the photographs with Mooney.

Beside her lay a frail man with snow white hair that matched his skin coloring. Even though there was no resemblance to Mooney, Sadie guessed that this was his father, but there were no hints of the man in the family photographs. To judge from the living room, Mooney didn't have a father. And the shriveled body almost suggested a man who had been starved, like photographs she had seen in the Honolulu papers of prisoners-of-war. His form was unmarked by trauma, however; no blood, no wounds, no signs of death at the hands of another. If this man was dead, and by all appearances he was, it had been a natural death.

As the smoke continued to clear, something else revealed itself to Sadie that she had not noticed at first. The woman's dress had been hiked to her hips, and her underwear had been pulled to her ankles. Sadie continued to put clues together in her head. The tale they told was as sordid as it was sad. Mooney's mother had dishonored her husband and son with infidelity. Perhaps Mooney had caught her in the act, or perhaps he merely knew of it. In any event, something had triggered a violent outburst—maybe the death of his father—and Mooney had engaged in an act as time-honored as the traditions of the Greeks: matricide.

She rushed back to the kitchen, fell to her knees, and began plucking pearls from the bloody pool. The rest of the story had not yet been written, but she could read it as clearly as if the words had already been etched. The police would respond to a report of fire and arrive at Mooney's house to find the bodies and the pearls. Someone, perhaps even Mooney himself, crying crocodile tears that would have made Shakespeare proud, would speak the words to target her: "Sadie MacKenzie has a necklace with pearls such as that."

The next stop would be her house, where the authorities would find her streaked white dress in her closet and the bloody knife in her lingerie drawer. Her battles with Mooney were legend in Honolulu, and the old neighbor woman had seen her banging on the door. The puzzle would be pieced together in mere moments, and then Mooney would have his revenge.

She heard a knock at the door, followed by a woman's voice.

"Hello? Mrs. Mooney? Hello? Is everything all right?"

Sadie frantically fished pearls from the pool and dropped them in the pocket of her dress without wiping off the blood. Just when she thought she was finished, she caught sight of one at the lip of the icebox. She shuffled over on her knees, painting bloody streaks on the floor, grabbed the pearl, and put it in her pocket.

The knocking escalated in volume and urgency. "Mrs. Mooney? Hello?"

Then the front door opened, the voice closer and clearer. "Mrs. Mooney? It's Ellen from next door."

Sadie took one last look around. Seeing no other pearls, she bolted for the rear door, leaving bloody shoeprints behind. They would be clues for the police that, even without the pearls, might very well lead to her doorstep. After all, the dainty prints clearly belonged to a woman, and only one woman had been bold enough to publicly do battle with Mooney. She would see to it that the shoes and her bloody dress would never be found, nor the knife, but she couldn't guarantee that pearls wouldn't be found under the icebox or in a corner. And the neighbor had seen her upon her arrival, pounding on the door and screaming Mooney's name. Mooney's plan would not be foiled forever.

She snuck around the corner of the house. It would be just a matter of seconds before the woman found the blood and, inevitably, the bodies. She ran to her car and climbed behind the wheel. If Mooney was on a rampage, others were also at risk. She knew only too well that an enraged Mooney was a dangerous Mooney. He had already set her up, and she thought she knew whom he would target next. She went in search of Ricky.

Chapter Thirty-Four

AS ANGER RAGED in his mind and blood lust boiled in his heart, Mooney cruised the shabby streets of Blood Town. Its atmosphere was as sordid and seamy as his soul. A life spent feeding his dark side had led him to this crisis point. Even as a boy, he had always given in to the urges that beckoned him. The *Bible* that Pop used to read to him preached that he should "flee from youthful lusts and seek righteousness," but his practice had always been to flee from righteousness and seek youthful lusts. He always knew that the inevitable result would be a headlong rush into hell.

He struggled to control his breathing, which escaped in ragged gasps. Coiled springs ratcheted up the pressure in his brain and threatened to explode at any moment. He wondered if he had a tumor in his head, or if this was simply what a long dormant, but now awakened, conscience felt like. Having done the deed, he hoped for peace. Mother was out of his life forever, and she would not be missed by anyone, including her "gentlemen callers," who would simply find other outlets for their seed. Even Pop's death should have brought some relief, knowing that his tortured soul had finally been released from the earthly bonds that had shackled him to a bed at the mercy of a malevolent caretaker.

But Mooney felt no peace, no calm, no release. Only a dark urge he was compelled to satisfy.

And so he prowled, a predator seeking his prey.

His eyes alert, he scanned darkened alleyways behind saloons, opium dens, and the unregulated whorehouses that made Hotel Street look like a silk-stocking district. Figures lurked in shadows and scuttled out of his headlights' beam like cockroaches scattering. A loud voice drew his attention to an open doorway from which an inebriated sailor staggered.

The serviceman was far from the safe confines of Hotel Street, even farther from the sanctuary of his ship at Pearl. If it hadn't already happened, he would soon be relieved of his wallet and watch, maybe even of his life, with his body dumped in a garbage can or in the vile Nu'uanu Stream, or perhaps hauled up the *pali* and left in the rain forest.

Mooney cast his eyes forward again—and there he was, standing on a corner, leaning over the passenger window of a tattered Ford coupe. Mooney admired the still boyish form, slender and nimble. He flashed back to a similar boyish form he had seen nearly three years ago as Sadie MacKenzie disembarked from the *Lurline*. She had since blossomed, a late bloomer as the saying went, into a woman with all the physical attributes that drew sailors and soldiers to Hotel Street like a Siren's song. And yet Mooney still found himself drawn to boyish figures.

He pulled up behind the coupe and flashed his high beams. He watched through the rear windshield as the driver glanced in his rearview mirror, then put his vehicle in gear and drove off. Ricky swiveled his head toward Mooney. He approached and leaned into the passenger window.

"Howzit, Mooney?"

"Who you talking to?"

"What? You jealous, brah?"

"I'm a cop. Just need to know who the lawbreakers are in town."

"You the lawbreaker, Mooney."

"You ever read *Great Expectations*?" Mooney asked.

"I never read anything."

"Read it sometime; then you'll see." Mooney held up a thick fold of money. "You're Pip, and I'm your benefactor."

Ricky's face curled up like a question mark, the literary reference escaping the boundaries of his limited education.

"Get in," Mooney said.

"That for me?" Ricky reached for the money.

Mooney pulled the money back and tucked it into his shirt pocket. "I never pay first; you know that."

Ricky looked at him for a moment then opened the door.

◊ ◊ ◊

Sadie watched as Ricky got in an unfamiliar Buick Roadmaster and it pulled away. She took her foot off the brake and fell in behind the car, keeping a safe distance so as not to be noticed. The Buick headed east, passed through downtown on King Street, then turned *makai*, or oceanward, on Kalakaua Avenue. It appeared to be going toward Waikiki. Maybe the driver had nothing more sinister in mind than a late night stroll. But late night pickups in Blood Town of young hustlers like Ricky were not acts of innocence. And they rarely, if ever, climaxed in public places.

After crossing the Ala Wai Canal, the Roadmaster turned once more, on John Ena Road, just west of Fort DeRussy, a military reservation built for Honolulu's protection during World War I. The car turned again on Ala Moana Boulevard, and a knot tightened in Sadie's stomach. She had learned Hawaiian history since being there, both ancient and recent. And she knew of terrible events that had happened in this place scarcely more than a decade earlier.

Known simply as the Massie affair, in 1931, a young naval lieutenant's wife had accused five local boys of beating and raping her. Thalia Massie, her allegations most likely concocted to explain an extra-marital encounter to her enraged husband, Lieutenant Tommie Massie, wove a tale of horror of having been abducted on John Ena Road, driven to the abandoned animal quarantine grounds at the end of Ala Moana Boulevard, and assaulted over and over by Henry Chang, Horace Ida, Ben Ahakuelo, David Takai, and Joseph Kahahawai. The accused came to be known as the Ala Moana Boys. When a mixed race jury was unable to reach a verdict in the face of evidence that established that the boys had been on the other side of town during the critical time, Lieutenant Massie and his mother-in-law, New York socialite Grace Fortescue, along with sailors Edward Lord and Albert "Deacon" Jones, concocted a scheme to kidnap one of the boys and coerce a confession. Their brilliant plan resulted in the murder of Joseph Kahahawai.

Following their arrest while seeking to dispose of Kahahawai's body at the Halona Blowhole, the four were charged with his murder in a case that brought the famous Clarence Darrow out of retirement to provide their defense. The trial resulted in one of the greatest miscarriages of justice in American history when, after they were convicted of second degree murder and sentenced to ten years of hard labor, territorial governor Lawrence Judd, caving to public pressure from the military and Washington, commuted their sentences to one hour in the custody of the sheriff.

A horrible thing had once happened here, Sadie knew; would it again?

She turned off her headlights so as to become invisible, but kept her eyes on the tail-lights of the Roadmaster. Ala Moana Boulevard narrowed, the dirt path rutted and rough, as it followed the coastline to the old animal quarantine grounds at the end of the road. This was the infamous place where Thalia Massie had been beaten and raped. *Supposedly* been beaten and raped.

The Roadmaster pulled to the side of the road just past the quarantine station. Sadie stopped and waited. The passenger door of the Roadmaster opened and someone got out. It was a slight, almost girlish silhouette: Ricky. Then the driver's door opened and a man got out. A large man, his features indistinguishable in the darkness, but, like Ricky's, a familiar shape. Even if the car was unfamiliar, Sadie would know that shape anywhere.

She watched as Mooney circled the vehicle. He looked her way, and Sadie held her breath. The night was dark, as was her vehicle, but she could swear Mooney was staring directly at her. He cocked his head, as if listening. Sadie had not killed her car's engine, confident the night breezes and the faint murmur of the ocean provided ample cover. Now she didn't dare do so lest the sudden absence of the motor's purr betray her presence.

After a moment, Mooney looked away. Had he seen her? She couldn't be sure, but she didn't think so.

Ricky disappeared into the trees, with Mooney right behind him.

Sadie turned off the ignition. She reached under the seat, grasped the knife, and got out. She quietly closed the door and hurried down the road, hugging the shadows of the trees, until she reached the Roadmaster. She made a quick search of the vehicle's interior but found nothing alarming or even of interest. Then she followed the path Mooney and Ricky had taken into the trees.

Mooney's musky scent soured the night air; Sadie's stomach roiled at the stench. Palm fronds rustled overhead, the steady *whapita-whapita-whapita-whapita* obscuring the sounds of her footsteps as she picked her way over downed leaves that crinkled underfoot. There was just enough moonlight filtering through for her to see her quarry ahead, a large shadow following a smaller one. After a few moments, she heard voices. First the lilt of Ricky's high-pitched tenor, which was followed by Mooney's growl. She couldn't make out what they were saying, but the tone didn't suggest disagreement, just conversation. Wherever they were going, whatever they were about to do, Ricky was a willing participant.

Then it seemed as if the shadows stopped. Sadie halted and hid behind a tree trunk. She felt light-headed, and her breath caught in her lungs. She opened her mouth wide and exhaled from deep in her diaphragm, forcing stale air out and then sucking in fresh. What was she doing there? Mooney had already left two bodies in his wake, one perhaps the victim of natural causes but another whose life had clearly been ended by a human hand. Common sense dictated that she immediately retrace her steps to her car and drive away, but there was Ricky to consider. Her mothering instincts said to stay. Had she followed those instincts three years ago and stayed close to Billy, she would not be in her current predicament. She would not abandon those instincts again. She would not leave Ricky to fend for himself with Mooney.

She took a deep breath then approached. As she drew closer, she could faintly make out their shapes. Ricky led Mooney by the hand to the center of a clearing, lit by a moonbeam. It was as if he were seeking a spotlight on a stage to perform. Sadie crouched behind a thick bush, watched, and listened.

Mooney faced Ricky, who lightly ran his hand across Mooney's cheek. Mooney touched him back. Sadie flinched at the sight, which picked at the scab of her own memories of Mooney's touch. She could barely hear the words being spoken.

"Is this private enough for you?" Ricky asked.

Mooney said nothing.

"Show me your money," Ricky said.

Mooney reached in his pocket and pulled out a fold of bills. Ricky reached for it; Mooney snatched it back.

"Come on, bruddah," Ricky said.

"You know the rules," Mooney said. "Play first; pay later."

"You don't trust me?"

"I don't trust anybody."

Ricky knelt directly in front of Mooney. Mercifully, Mooney's broad back blocked Sadie's view of what she knew was happening.

"Mooney, there's blood on it!" Ricky said. He stood and stepped back, but Mooney grabbed him by the shoulder with his free hand and forced him back to his knees.

"Just do it," Mooney said.

"You gotta disease?"

"Do it."

"I nevah saw blood on one before."

Mooney held the money above Ricky's head. When Ricky snatched at it, Mooney yanked it away then dropped it on the ground beside him.

"It's all yours," Mooney said. "Just forget about the blood."

Then Mooney leaned his head back, his face toward heaven. Sadie clenched her eyes shut and prayed that God would strike him dead.

When she opened them again, she saw that Mooney was still alive, his face skyward. He held his arms to the side, palms outward, as if he had been impaled on a cross. But Sadie knew that Mooney was no savior. She had to get Ricky out of there. But how? He was obviously there of his own accord and, other than the sordid sex act he was currently engaged in with Mooney, he had not done anything to raise alarm, nor had Mooney made any overt threatening moves. If she revealed her presence now, catching Mooney in the act and uncovering his secret might be exactly the trigger to set him off. If that happened, she and Ricky would both be in danger.

Mooney raised his hands skyward, until both arms extended straight up. A sound emanated from his mouth. It seemed to start deep in his soul, and then it escaped in a high-pitched sound. It was a visceral, animal-like screech that chilled her spine. Both of Mooney's hands clenched into fists.

Ricky rocked back on his heels. He looked up at Mooney, his expression a mix of fear and anger.

Mooney's right fist came down like a sledgehammer. The knuckles crushed Ricky's cheek. Ricky slumped to the ground, motionless. Mooney straddled his body.

Sadie sprang from her hiding place and screamed. "Mooney!"

Chapter Thirty-Five

PATROL OFFICERS FRANK Haniali'i and Ralph Sterling arrived at the shabby house to find a hysterical woman waving her arms on the front porch. She ran to the passenger side as Frank killed the engine and got out.

"Dey dead. Both of dem. Dead!"

She crowded the car, babbling the same words over and over, trapping Ralph inside.

"Ma'am," Frank said. "Please back away from the car."

He took her by the arm and led her far enough away that Ralph could open his door.

"Ma'am, what is your name?" Frank asked.

"Ellen. Dey both dead."

"Who is dead?"

"Mrs. Mooney and her husband. De girl did it. Plenny *koko*. Plenny *uahi*." Lots of blood. Lots of smoke.

"What girl? Do they have a daughter?"

"No, just a son. Delbert. He's police, just like you."

Frank looked at Ralph, who muttered under his breath, "God damn."

"Who's the girl?" Frank asked.

"I don't know. I nevah see her befo'."

"What did she look like?"

"Skinny *haole wahine*. She drive a big fancy car."

"A Zephyr?"

The woman shook her head. "I don't know cars. It was dark red. Maroon, I tink. She come driving up, looking like a bigshot. Den she bang on de door, plenny *huhu*, yelling for Delbert. Den she went inside. I nevah see her before. Das when I come ovah to see if Mrs. Mooney all right. The *wahine* was gone, but I see dem in the bedroom. Both dead. Plenny *koko*."

Frank shared another look with Ralph. Skinny *haole* girl in a big maroon car, angry and looking for Mooney. Could only be one person.

"Ma'am," Frank said, "here's what we need you to do. Go inside your house and wait there. Understand? Wait there and don't come out."

"She dangerous?"

"I need you to go inside and wait. You understand?" Frank asked.

"I understand," she said.

"Repeat it back to me."

"I go inside, wait dere."

"Yes, ma'am. That's right. We'll take care of things here."

He nodded at Ralph, who escorted the woman to her door and waited as she went inside, then returned to Frank.

"Let's check it out," Frank said.

Both cops unholstered their guns and entered the house, with Frank in the lead. The first thing he noticed was the lingering smell of smoke. They followed the wisps down a narrow hallway to an open bedroom door. Lying side-by-side were the bodies just like the hysterical neighbor had said. Plenny *koko*. But only one of them—the woman—was covered in blood; the other, an emaciated old man, seemed peaceful in death.

"That Mooney's mama and papa?" Ralph asked.

"I don't know."

Ralph pointed at the woman. "That look like something you think Sadie would do?" The tone of his question suggested an answer in the negative.

Frank shook his head, his eyes fixated on the underwear twisted around the woman's ankles. "But that damn sure looks like something Mooney would do."

Ralph pointed to a trail of blood that led back down the hallway. "Missed that when we came in."

The officers followed the trail back to the front of the house, through the living area, and into the kitchen, where a pool of blood glistened. Smears of red streaked away from the edge of the pool toward the icebox, and small footprints led out the back door.

"It was either a woman," Ralph said, "or a *menehune*."

"You believe in the little people?"

"Nope."

"That leaves us with a woman."

"And she was looking for something under the icebox," Ralph said. He followed the smears toward the appliance, then got on his knees and looked underneath it. He placed his gun on the floor and unhooked the flashlight from his belt. Following its beam, he saw something at the far side.

He stood. "Help me move this."

The two men slid the icebox forward enough that Ralph could squeeze behind it. He squatted and plucked something from beside the baseboard.

"What is it?" Frank asked.

Ralph held up his hand. Pinched between his forefinger and thumb was a single, black pearl. "You know someone who wears pearls like that?" he asked.

Frank nodded. Then both of them looked again at the woman's footprints leading to the back door.

"Go call it in," Frank said. "We need an APB on Sadie MacKenzie."

Rob sat behind the wheel of his Jeep on Hotel Street and watched drunken servicemen stagger out of saloons in twos and threes. Was this really what his life had become? There was a war being fought out there and here he was babysitting grown men who didn't have the sense God gave a kindergartner. On the other hand, a part of him could understand the futility of it all. Already places with strange-sounding names like Guadalcanal, Corregidor, and Tarawa had filtered their way into American consciousness where thousands of men—boys, really—lay dead on beaches and in jungles, leaving behind grieving mothers, fathers, brothers, sisters, and girlfriends. Who could blame them if they drank until their minds were dulled to the reality that they were on their way to foreign shores where life was cheap—and short? He should thank his lucky stars he had been relegated to the safe confines of Hotel Street, courtesy of his injuries at Pearl Harbor, instead of marching through swamps and dodging bullets.

The radio crackled to life. Rob tried to ignore it, but the staticky voice was intrusive. The call was obviously not meant for him, but was directed to Honolulu Police. Still, he had developed a sixth sense of being able to absorb police calls almost in his sleep. That night was no different.

A sailor stumbled into the street and fell against the passenger door of the Jeep. The impact jolted Rob to full alertness.

"Watch out there, son," Rob said. He felt foolish for calling the man "son." He knew that he was scarcely a few years older than the drunken ensign, but rank and authority seemed to age a person, at least in the eyes of the enlisted men. Particularly enlisted men who knew you were all that stood between them and the stockade.

"Sorry, sir," the sailor said. Then he giggled and promptly vomited onto the front tire.

"Back away," Rob barked.

The sailor giggled again. He tried to step back, but his heel caught the curb. Down he went. He rolled onto his side in the vomitus and threw up again, but Rob wasn't watching him now. His attention had been riveted to the voice on the radio. Random words grabbed his attention, barely decipherable but nevertheless clear as a bell in his mind.

"Bodies...armed and dangerous...Mooney...APB."

Then "Sadie MacKenzie."

He put the Jeep into first gear and sped away, barely missing the drunken sailor wallowing in his own disgorged fluids.

By the time Rob reached Sadie's house, it seemed as if every cop in Honolulu was already there. Radio cars lined the street on both sides and uniformed officers stood in clumps of three and four on the sidewalk and in the front yard. Residents of the community had also come out, dressed in their bedclothes, to see what drama was occurring at their infamous neighbor's house.

Tongues were wagging, he was sure. "See, I knew no good would come of having a whore in our midst." He wondered which one would be the first to carry it to its illogical conclusion: "First you let whores into the neighborhood and next thing you know, you have murderers in your midst."

Rob slammed on the brakes, shifted into park, and jumped out of the Jeep. He rushed across the yard to the front door, where a burly cop with mutton-chop sideburns blocked his way.

"Hold on there, soldier boy," the cop said. "Where do you think you're going?"

"I know the woman who lives here. She's a friend of mine."

"Well, that might be well and good at Schofield, but it don't earn you no merit here."

Rob bit his tongue. He figured it would do no good to argue the merits of martial law with this thick-headed knuckle-dragger.

"Who's in charge?" Rob asked.

"That would be Detective Harbaugh."

"Let me speak to him."

"I don't take my orders from you."

"Shall I raise Major Steer on the radio?"

The cop blinked. Everyone knew Frank Steer, at least by reputation. And no one wanted to get on his bad side.

"What shall I tell him, Officer..." Rob studied the cop's nametag. "Smithson? Shall I refer to you by name when I tell him how uncooperative the Honolulu Police are being?"

"You wait here," the cop said. "I'll fetch Detective Harbaugh."

Rob heard voices inside the house, then a dapper man, at least in his fifties if not older, approached. He wore a derby hat over a brown herringbone suit that would have better fit in a silent film from the 1920s than in Hawaii in the mid-1940s.

"I'm Harbaugh," the man said. "You're a little out of your element here, aren't you, soldier?"

"I'm sure you're familiar with a little something called martial law, Detective." Rob said it with conviction, relying on the detective to be unfamiliar with the actual nuances of the law and who was in charge of what. He saw uncertainty on Harbaugh's face. Some police officers actually knew what it meant and understood the limits of authority of both the military and the police, but others—particularly those who might be more concerned with appearances than substance—could be snowed by the mere words "martial law."

Then Rob played his hole card. "The woman who lives in this house works on Hotel Street. Major Steer has taken a personal interest."

Harbaugh stepped aside and allowed Rob to enter. "Suit yourself," he said, "but don't touch anything."

Rob had never been in Sadie's house before. In fact, he had never been in any prostitute's house, but he had his own expectations of what one might look like. Sadie's residence shattered any expectations he might have had. This was the home of a sophisticated, educated person who could fit in with the best that Honolulu society had to offer.

"The mother of one of our vice officers was murdered tonight," Harbaugh said. "A neighbor saw a woman at the house and found the body after she left."

"How do you know it was Sadie?"

"The woman left in a Zephyr, and officers found black pearls from a necklace that belongs to her."

Rob knew that necklace. It cost him more than he should have spent, even on the black market, but he had given it to Sadie last Christmas—an anonymous package he left on her *lanai*. She had never said anything about it to him, and he was convinced she didn't know its source. He now felt guilty at being responsible for having provided the clue that might link her to a crime he was sure she had not committed.

"So you know who Sadie is," Rob said.

"We all know who Sadie is. And we also know of her vendetta against Mooney."

"I suppose, then, you also know that Mooney has beaten her. And raped her."

"Can you really rape a whore?" Harbaugh asked. "And as for the beatings, well, we call that motive."

"Motive to kill Mooney's mother?"

"To hurt Mooney's mother is to hurt Mooney."

"Mooney doesn't strike me as one who's close to his mother," Rob said. "And if you're looking for people with a motive to hurt him, there's a far longer list than just Sadie MacKenzie. I'm on that list. Hell, half of Honolulu is."

"That's a fair point," Harbaugh said, "but none of the others on that list showed up on Mooney's doorstep tonight."

"Detective," a gravelly voice called from a hallway. "I think you need to see this."

Rob and Harbaugh joined the speaker, a uniformed officer, at the doorway to Sadie's boudoir. As with the living room, Rob was again surprised at the secrets Sadie had to offer. The bedroom was almost childlike, with stuffed animals and light colors. Rob was no psychiatrist, but it didn't take a genius to understand that this was the domain of a person who was trying to recapture, and re-characterize, a stolen youth—and Sadie's had, indeed, been stolen from her, along with her innocence. By Mooney. Harbaugh was right; Sadie had motive.

The bedroom overflowed with police officers, pawing through Sadie's personal things. Two of them stood at a dresser and fondled her lingerie. It clearly was not a search for clues but mere voyeurism as they held up articles of clothing, then exchanged lewd remarks and laughter.

"Over there," the gravelly-voiced officer said. In front of a closet, a cop held a white dress on a hangar. Rob followed Harbaugh, and they both examined the swath of red on the dress.

"If I was a betting man, soldier boy, I'd wager that's the blood of Mooney's mother," Harbaugh said.

"For all you know, it might be Sadie's own blood, from an encounter with Mooney."

Harbaugh turned to the gravelly-voiced officer. "Did you find a black pearl necklace?"

"No, sir. We found plenty of necklaces in her jewelry box, even some pearl necklaces, but no black pearls."

A loud guffaw drew their attention to the two cops playing with Sadie's lingerie. One of them held a pair of sheer black panties in front of his crotch as he wiggled his hips, to the amusement of two other Neanderthals who watched and whistled.

Rob crossed the room in two strides. He thrust his hand upward and caught the officer at the throat, driving his head back. He bent the man backward over the bureau and his fingers clutched his neck. The cop's eyes bulged; his face turned red. The panties dropped to the floor.

The other cops had frozen at Rob's assault, but now sprang to life. One hooked his arm around Rob's neck and pulled back, while another squeezed Rob's wrist in a vise-like grip and tried to pry it away. A third cop pulled a leaden sap from his belt and raised his arm.

"Enough!" Harbaugh barked.

The sap remained poised in the air. Everyone turned and looked at Harbaugh.

"Let him go," Harbaugh said.

Rob shook himself loose as the arm around his neck eased its pressure. He realized that he was walking on dangerous ground. There was no love lost between the military and the police, and he had now gone into the lion's den and pissed on the lion. He looked at the officer he had assaulted. He knew that the next words out of his mouth should be an apology, but instead he said, "Leave her personal things alone."

"Just how well do you know this Sadie MacKenzie?" Harbaugh asked.

"She's a friend."

"I'll just bet," someone said from the rear of the semi-circle of cops facing him.

"She's not like that," Rob said, realizing instantly how foolish the words sounded.

"I thought you said she worked in Hotel Street," Harbaugh said.

Rob nodded.

"Then she's like that."

Rob bent and gently picked up the panties. As he turned to put them back in the drawer, something on them caught his eye. It apparently caught Harbaugh's, as well.

"What's that?" Harbaugh pointed at faint smears of fluid that glistened in the lamplight.

But they both knew: semen.

"And that," Harbaugh said, pointing to another spot of fluid. He took the underwear from Rob and held it to the light. "It's hard to tell on the black material, but if I was a betting man," he added, "I'd make my second wager tonight. I'd bet that's blood."

Chapter Thirty-Six

MORE FRIGHTENED THAN she had ever been in her life, Sadie retraced her route back down Ala Moana Boulevard to John Ena Road, then turned southeast on Kalakaua Avenue, toward Diamond Head. Soon she was moving along the Kalaniana'ole Highway, retracing the infamous route that Grace Fortescue and Tommie Massie had taken one January morning in 1932 with the body of Joseph Kahahawai in the backseat of a blue Buick sedan, headed for the Halona Blowhole.

She swung past the dormant volcano Koko Head, curved around the popular pre-war tourist destination of Hanauma Bay, and on toward the Blowhole, which had been formed thousands of years ago by an underwater lava tube that funneled crashing waves through its aperture then rifled them dozens of feet into the air in explosions of white foam. As the waves receded after each assault, they sucked into the ocean anything that might find its way into the opening in the lava rock. That had been the goal of Massie and Fortescue, to dispose of Kahahawai's body in a manner so as to ensure it was never found, but they had been caught. Would she be, as well? Not if God was smiling, as her mother would have said.

But it had been a long time since God had smiled on her. Although she cherished the thought deep in her heart that God had a plan for her life beyond Hotel Street, she was unable to fathom what that plan might be. She didn't know why God would allow Dust Bowls and poverty and death and orphaned and abandoned brothers and war and suffering and Mooney, but she held to her faith that God had a better day in store for her. Without that faith, she would be left with nothing, and so she had clung tightly to it for the past two-and-a-half years, and she would continue to cling to it. She thought how Joshua had once said that his favorite verse in the *Bible* was "And it came to pass."

"Because," he said, "it comforts me to know that when bad times come, they don't come to stay; they come to pass." Sadie had adopted that philosophy as her own. Each night, as she lay alone in her bed after servicing dozens of men during the day, she prayed that Hotel Street and Mooney would pass.

She slowed as she approached the turnoff to the Blowhole. White foam spewed skyward, illuminated by the moon's glow. She pulled off the road and drew as near to the hole as she dared take her automobile. Droplets spattered on her windshield as she got out. She walked to the trunk, almost reveling in the mist that sparkled in her hair and moistened her face. She stood immobile at the rear of the Zephyr for a few moments, her face raised skyward and her mouth open, and tasted the brine on her tongue. Then she raised the trunk lid.

Mooney stared up at her, his eyes open but lifeless, his torso and throat awash in his own blood. She set her heels flush against the rough lava and grabbed Mooney by the arms. She leaned backward, using her full body weight to tug him upward from the floor of the trunk. Both arms slipped from her hands at the same time, and she staggered backward then tumbled to the hard ground. Mooney's upper body sprawled over the lip of the trunk. His head and arms hung downward, fingers touching the rock. Sadie saw blood stream down his hands and drip into a pool directly below his head. Part of her said that she should feel sorrow at his death, but then she thought of the blood that spread beneath the dinner table at Mooney's house and that painted his mother's body. She thought of the fist that crashed into Ricky's cheek. And she thought of the terror of that day when Mooney nearly ripped her apart with his swollen phallus. Sympathy for Mooney would be a sadly misplaced emotion.

She regained her feet, grabbed Mooney's arms, and pulled again. Though he outweighed her by a good hundred pounds, fear fueled by adrenaline filled her with almost superhuman strength. As she tugged backward, the lower half of his body slid over the metal bumper and crashed earthward. Scarcely breathing, and afraid to pause lest she lose all momentum, she dragged the body around the Zephyr and toward the

Blowhole.

It seemed as if time slowed to a halt as she pulled, each hard-gained foot agonizingly won. Her heels slipped in the rocks more than once, as did her hands in the slick blood that coated Mooney's wrists and hands. She felt pinpricks of pain in her buttocks and back when she fell onto the sharp lava rock, but she got up each time and continued pulling as if she had never fallen. As wave after wave funneled its way up the tube and high overhead, the light mist turned into a driving rainstorm. Salt water matted her hair and soaked her dress.

When she was within ten feet of the opening, she looked up at a sound that reached her ears even through the roar of the geyser. Headlights turned off of the highway and crunched over lava toward her. She squinted into the darkness, but could only faintly make out the shape of the vehicle.

She continued tugging toward the Blowhole. Five feet away now.

She heard a vehicle door open.

Three feet.

Then footsteps on crunchy lava.

One foot, then she was at the lip of the Blowhole. She dropped Mooney's arms, rushed around, and knelt by his side.

Heavy footsteps approached. Loud enough that she could clearly hear them.

She braced herself and pushed against Mooney's torso. He flipped over onto his side, and then rolled into the hole just as she heard a man's voice call out.

"Sadie, no!"

She stood and spun around. "Robert? How did you find me?"

"You once told me that, if you ever disappeared, Mooney would be the culprit and this is where he would dispose of your body." Rob's eyes took in her wet and matted hair then focused on the bloody dress. "Sadie, what have you done?"

"I need your help."

"Not until I know what you've done."

"Robert, promise you'll help me."

"I want to, but I may not be able to unless you tell me what happened."

"In the trunk of the car," she said.

"What?"

"The knife. In the trunk of the car."

He watched her for a moment, then went to the back of her car and returned carrying the bloodied weapon.

"Did you kill Mooney's mother?" Rob asked. He held up the knife. "Did you use this on her?"

"How can you ask that of me?"

"I can't just ignore things. Now tell me: did you kill Mooney's mother?"

"No."

"Who did you push into the Blowhole?"

Sadie remained mute.

"Was it Mooney?"

"Please give that to me," she said.

He looked at the knife then back at Sadie. "This is evidence."

"Robert, I need you to trust me."

In the near distance, sounds of sirens cut through the night air. Rob looked over his shoulder, then back at Sadie. "I called for the MPs to help look for you. They'll be here soon," he said. "Tell me what happened tonight."

"Robert, no matter what anyone says, you have to believe in me."

"Of course I do, Sadie, but how can I help you if you won't confide in me?"

"It's better that you don't know. It's for your own good."

"But you're asking me to destroy evidence. To get rid of this knife."

"No, I'm asking you to give it me."

"So you can get rid of it."

She said nothing.

Concentration distorted Rob's face as he struggled with the request. The sirens were hard upon them now. He looked over his shoulder, expecting to see his military brethren as tires crunched on lava rock and engines roared. Instead, a host of police cars descended. There were no

MPs in sight. Rob faced Sadie again.

"They must have followed me from your house. I would never have led them here had I known."

"I know, Robert. Now, you must give me the knife, and then please go tell Joshua that I'll need his lawyerly skills tonight. My life may depend upon it."

Rob stepped forward to hand the knife to Sadie. Just as she reached for it, a billy club landed on the backside of his neck. He pitched forward on his face. The knife flew from his hand and skittered across the lava. Sadie reached for the knife. Another billy club met its mark, this one on the top of her head as she slapped the blade toward the Blowhole, where it stopped at the edge.

Sadie fell to the ground beside Rob. Belts, boots, and billy clubs rained down on both of them.

Vice officer Akahi "Skip" Mahelona oversaw the brutal beating without a hint of conscience. He glanced into the open trunk of the Zephyr. If in fact that was Delbert Mooney's bloody brown-and-white shoe, then they were likely too late to salvage either Mooney's life or his body. Mooney had been a mentor to him when he started with vice, training him in the ways of graft and corruption that had lined his pockets and bought for him a comfortable lifestyle even in this time of war. More than that, Mooney had been his friend—at least as much a friend as Mooney was capable of having. Aloof and churlish, even on his best of days, Mooney didn't seem to want friends. There were even rumors, carefully spoken, about Mooney and his "predilections." Skip didn't know if those rumors had any truth but, if so, perhaps Mooney was better off dead before they saw the light of day.

Turning, he saw three military Jeeps pulling up, each occupied by a single driver. He stepped aside as the MPs dashed into the melee, clubs swinging, and tried to extricate their man, who was curled up in the fetal position, hands clutched over his head to protect himself. He folded his arms across his chest and watched as the MPs pulled their man to his feet, who, in turn, lifted a dazed and bleeding Sadie MacKenzie. And there, by the edge of the Blowhole, lay the likely murder weapon.

Chapter Thirty-Seven

JOSHUA ROLLED ONTO his back and opened his eyes. A soft breeze whispered through the room from the louvered window by his bed. He looked at the clock on the bedside table, but the hands were blurred. He grabbed it and held it close to his face. He squinted to make out the time, which slowly crystallized into view: 1:53 in the morning. He heard again the banging noise that had awakened him. Then the buzzer.

He threw off the covers and sat on the edge of the bed. He worked his feet into slippers and grabbed his glasses. He snatched his robe from a bench at the end of the bed and slipped it on as he felt his way through the darkened house to the front door. As he neared, he heard a man's voice over the banging.

"Mr. Sinclair! Please open the door. Mr. Sinclair, Sadie needs you."

Joshua quickened his step at the pronouncement of her name. He unlocked and opened the door to confront a disheveled soldier on the *lanai*. Blood covered the blouse of his uniform. Both eyes were blackened and his lower lip was split with a gash nearly a quarter-inch wide. A black armband with white lettering—MP—grabbed his attention more so than his injuries. He hadn't seen the boy in two years and, but for the armband and his skin color, might not have recognized him due to his injuries.

"Mr. Sinclair, Sadie sent me," the soldier said. "She needs you."

"You're Robert."

He nodded. "She's in trouble, Mr. Sinclair. She needs you."

Having left Robert at his house in the care of Nani, Joshua strode into the police station on Merchant Street and rapped his knuckles on the front counter to attract the attention of the duty officer.

"Can I help you, sir?" the desk sergeant asked. He rolled his chair back and stood.

"I demand to see my client. Sadie MacKenzie."

The desk sergeant approached the counter and leaned on his elbows. He was a heavyset *haole* with a florid complexion and a wheezy style of breathing. "Well, now, when you say client, you mean she's the whore who services you?"

Joshua's lip quivered as he fought back rage. He spoke in an even voice that belied his true emotion. "I'm her attorney."

"So *you* service *her*."

Joshua took a business card from his vest pocket and laid it on the counter. "I demand to see my client right now."

"Or else what?"

"As we speak, Major Steer is being summoned. He won't be happy rousted from his bed. Perhaps you'd like to take it up with him."

"You seem to be unaware of your surroundings. This is the Honolulu Police Department, and we've regained control of the building from the Army."

"I dare say neither Major Steer nor the legion of officers under his command will make such a fine distinction. Are you prepared for that?"

The sergeant pushed off of his elbows and straightened. "I'll check with the jailer and see if your client is up to receiving visitors." He smirked. "I understand she's feeling poorly."

Then he disappeared through a swinging door at the rear of the duty room. A few minutes later, a dapper man in a derby hat appeared. He wore a smile on his face that, from the right angle, might also be interpreted as a sneer. Joshua had seen that look before, on the faces of men who held four aces while sitting across the table from him. Joshua didn't share the man's confidence. He didn't know if his own befuddlement was the result of having been awakened from a deep slumber or merely the addle-mindedness of approaching age, but if ever there was time to keep his mental footing firmly beneath himself, this was that moment.

"I'm Detective Harbaugh," the derby wearer said. "And who might you be?"

"I am Joshua Sinclair, esquire, and I demand to see my client."

"Well, now, counselor, who is your client? We have a number of miscreants and malfeasors enjoying our hospitality tonight."

"Sadie MacKenzie."

"Ahh, the killer of mothers." He paused, then leaned forward and whispered conspiratorially. "And of police officers."

"You have proof?"

"Well, counselor, I'm not a highly educated man such as yourself, but—"

"You."

"I beg your pardon?"

"The proper grammatical usage would be 'such as you,' not 'such as yourself.'" It was petty, Joshua knew, but at moments such as this, the fingers of one's mind sought purchase wherever they might find it.

"Like I said," Harbaugh continued, "I'm not a highly educated man such as *you*, but I have seen a court case or two in my day. It's no secret that Sadie feuded with Mooney." He held up a finger. "Motive. We also found her in possession of a knife." He held up a second finger. "Means. And she was seen at the Mooney residence just moments before discovery of the body of Mrs. Mooney." A third finger went up. "And that would be opportunity. We have a trifecta."

Harbaugh pushed his derby hat back on his head and winked when he said the word "trifecta." It was time to shift gears, from Joshua Sinclair, the importer/exporter, to Joshua Sinclair, the criminal defense attorney.

"Let me see if I've got this straight, detective. Sadie feuded publicly with Officer Mooney, not Mrs. Mooney. To your knowledge, has she ever met Mrs. Mooney, much less said a cross word to her?"

Harbaugh remained silent.

"I'll take your silence as a no. Whose blood is on the knife?"

For the first time, Joshua saw uncertainty on Harbaugh's face. He took a shot.

"Was there, in fact, any blood at all on the knife? I understand that it was perched on the edge of the Blowhole. Might the geyser have cleared the blade of any traces of blood? Assuming, of course, that there was blood in the first place."

Joshua saw that his shot had struck home.

"And you said she was seen moments before the body was found," he added, "yet I understand the blood on Mrs. Mooney's clothing was not so fresh and that the body had, perhaps, smoldered a bit. So the question is not whether Miss MacKenzie was seen moments before the body was found, but whether she was seen moments before the murder occurred. I suspect the answer to the latter is also in the negative."

Besides, Sadie had been at his house earlier in the evening, which, assuming the time of Mrs. Mooney's death could be accurately established, might provide an alibi.

"There is still the matter of Mooney," Harbaugh said.

"Yes, let's pursue that line. Was Mooney in fact killed tonight?"

"We believe he was."

"If Miss MacKenzie is to be charged, then I shall demand to examine his body."

Then Harbaugh did something unexpected: He smiled again.

"If you'd like to see your client, counselor, follow me and keep your mouth shut until we get there."

Harbaugh turned abruptly and led Joshua through the door he had entered moments before. Joshua followed silently, his mind awhirl with thoughts. From what Robert had told him about what was found at Sadie's house, she had been set up, most likely by Mooney. Just as it was true that Sadie despised the man, so, too, did Mooney hate Sadie. What better way to have his revenge than to implicate Sadie in a murder? And if he had done so, then Mooney was the probable killer of Mrs. Mooney.

Of more immediate concern was the fate of Delbert Mooney. Joshua had no doubt that he could make a convincing case for justifiable homicide. In fact, he was aware of many with a motive to kill the man, starting with the entire roster of sporting girls in Hotel Street. And Robert had said that Mooney was missing. Lack of a corpse would certainly undermine any prosecution effort, but something troubled Joshua as he followed Harbaugh. At the end of their conversation, Harbaugh had smiled. Not the sneer he started with. No, this one was genuine, and it could mean but one thing.

The police knew something that Joshua did not.

Sadie lay perfectly still on her side on a wafer-thin mattress with a tiny pillow wadded up beneath her head. Barely more than a thick blanket, the mattress provided no padding between her bruised body and the hard wooden planks that supported her. She had started on her back rather than balanced on her side, but even the slight pressure of her body weight seemed like hundreds of pounds pressing her down. She felt each individual bruise, the result of hard-toed boots and billy clubs of outraged police officers as she had curled into a fetal position and covered her head with her arms on the wet lava rock.

Blood crusted in her eyelashes, nearly sealing her eyes shut. At least one tooth was loose, and she believed at first that one or both jaws might be broken. When she regained her senses earlier, she tried to call out for help but pain silenced her. She was determined not to cry. She had done what she had to do, and now she would be strong and bear up to whatever consequences she must face.

Footsteps sounded outside her solitary cell. She had neither seen nor heard anyone since she had been there. Perhaps medical help was finally on its way. She shifted her weight and tried to sit up, but even the slightest movement sent waves of pain riding through her body, starting with her head and rolling to her toes, then back again. A dull ache from the bruises reached her head and pounded at her temples.

The footsteps were right outside her cell when she heard a voice she recognized.

"Good God, man, get a doctor over here immediately or I'll see you hauled off in chains."

For the first time since finding Mooney's false clues planted in her house, she smiled. If there was one person in these islands who would sacrifice his very life for her, it was Joshua Sinclair. Sadie turned her head and forced her eyelids apart. She watched as the jailer opened the cell and Joshua, clad in one of his patented white linen suits, but looking as if he had dressed hurriedly, entered and rushed to her side. He knelt by her cot and looked down at her.

"I knew you would come," she said. Her jaws still hurt, though the pain had lessened, and her voice was weak and soft. Joshua had to lean close to hear.

"Help me to sit up," she said,

After Joshua aided her to shift to a sitting position, he looked toward the cell door, where the jailer stood as if expecting something. When Joshua spoke this time, there was steel in his voice.

"Get a doctor. Now!"

Sadie smiled again. She knew she was hearing the Joshua of old. The young man who had once been renowned as a criminal defense lawyer.

"Robert found you," Sadie said.

"Yes."

"Is he okay?"

"He has injuries, but he seems to be fine. I left him with Nani."

"Did he tell you what happened?"

"He said the police thought you killed Mooney's mother." He paused. "And Mooney."

"I didn't hurt Mrs. Mooney. I would never do that."

"I know you didn't. But the police say they have evidence."

"It's evidence that Mooney ensured they would find. At my house and at his mother's house. I assure you, Joshua, I did not harm Mrs. Mooney."

"And Mooney?" he asked.

"Mooney is an evil man. I believe that he killed his own mother."

"Why would he do that?"

"I can only answer by my initial statement: Mooney is an evil man."

"They say that you killed him."

Sadie stood. It took some effort, and each movement jarred the nerve endings throughout her body, but she felt an urge to walk. She took a first unsteady step, then another. When she reached the opposite wall of the tiny cell, she turned to face Joshua.

"You must defend me," she said.

"It's been many years since I was last in a courtroom. But I'll find you the finest criminal lawyer Hawaii has to offer." He paused, then added, "No, not Hawaii; the entire United States of America."

"Joshua, you and I both know that you have to do this. It has to be you."

"Don't you want someone with more experience?"

"No one believes in me the way you do. No one."

Joshua sighed. She could see that the decision weighed heavily on him, and she hated to put this kind of pressure on him. But she had to. The words she had spoken were true; no one believed in her the way he did. And that would be important in ways he likely could not understand unless he knew exactly what had happened. But he must never know. And so she was asking him to defend her on blind faith and nothing more.

It was as if Joshua could read her mind. "There are things you're not telling me," he said.

"Things I can't tell you."

"Why not?"

"Because you'll be compelled, as my attorney, to use what I tell you in my defense."

"Of course," he said. "That's what a criminal lawyer does."

"But there are things I cannot let you use in my defense. And I know that if you know those things, even if you promise you won't use them, you ultimately will."

"How can you be so sure?"

"Because you love me, you'll use them. So it's critical that you not know."

Joshua opened his mouth as if to argue a counterpoint, but he quickly shut it. She could see from his face that he knew she was right. Whatever it took to prove her innocence, he would do. And she would not force him to make a promise to her that he could not keep.

He nodded. "Okay, Sadie, I'll be your lawyer."

"On my terms?"

"On your terms."

"Good. Now, let's discuss my defense."

Chapter Thirty-Eight

ROB PACED THE floor, ignoring Nani's ministrations to sit down and be still, when Joshua entered the house.

"Are you all right?" Joshua asked.

"I'm fine. What about Sadie?"

"She's been badly beaten, but she's now being treated by a physician."

Joshua brushed past Rob and sat at the dining table. "Nani, do you have any of that good Kona brewing?"

"I'll bring it to you," she said and disappeared into the kitchen.

"Come, sit," Joshua said.

"I don't want to sit." Rob continued to pace, limping badly on his right leg.

"I need your assistance with Sadie's case, and I need you to sit, listen, and think clearly," Joshua said.

"Case? What do you mean 'case'?"

"I believe that she'll be charged with two counts of murder—those of Officer Mooney and of his mother."

"That's ridiculous. Sadie wouldn't have hurt Mrs. Mooney. She doesn't have it in her."

Nani returned and placed a tray of coffee on the table. Its aroma filled the room, ordinarily a comforting smell, but that night merely a reminder that things were not as they should be. Joshua helped himself to two lumps of sugar as Nani poured, and then she retreated to the kitchen. Joshua stirred to dissolve the sugar and took a sip. He regarded Rob carefully as he set the cup on the table.

"That's the same denial Sadie made," Joshua said.

"You say that like it's a bad thing."

"What I mean is that she denied killing Mooney's mother, but she didn't deny killing Mooney, himself. That troubles me. Did you know that, under the rules of evidence, silence can be deemed an admission?"

The words brought the limping to a halt. Rob pulled out a chair and joined Joshua at the table. Joshua slid an empty cup toward him, then lifted the carafe and filled it with coffee, which Rob promptly ignored.

"There's something that Sadie isn't telling me," Joshua said. "And something you're also not telling me."

Rob remained silent.

"I'm Sadie's lawyer," Joshua said. "She may face the death penalty, and if I'm to help her, I must know everything there is to know. Do you understand? Everything."

Rob nodded.

"Whatever you tell me, I'll keep confidential," Joshua said. "But I can't operate in the dark. I'm confident that Sadie had nothing to do with Mrs. Mooney's demise, but her silence concerning Mooney troubles me. As does yours." He sipped coffee. "As does that of the police."

"What do you mean?"

"I sense that the authorities realize their case for Mrs. Mooney is weak. However, they are strangely, albeit silently, confident in the case of Mooney. Which means they, too, know something that I don't. If I'm to operate effectively as Sadie's counsel, I must know what she knows. I must know what you know. And I must know what the authorities know. But right now, I know nothing."

Rob stood and paced again. Now he seemed to walk with ease, as if worry and concentration had pushed away the pain. Joshua sat silently and waited. He knew, based on things Sadie had said, that this man cared very deeply for her. He also knew that, in the end, Rob would tell what he knew, because doing so would be to Sadie's benefit. So he waited.

At last Rob spoke. "There was a body."

"A body?"

"At the Halona Blowhole. Just as I arrived, I saw Sadie push it into the hole."

"Was it Mooney?"

Rob shook his head. "I don't know."

"But you suspect that it was."

"Who else could it be? Mooney's missing."

"Yes, who else could it be." Joshua thought a moment then asked, "So the body was gone by the time the police arrived?"

"Unless they were lurking and watching, then yes. It was a few moments later that they arrived. There was a knife—"

"But no body?"

"No body."

"Does anybody know what you saw?" Joshua asked.

"Just Sadie. No one else."

"If Mooney went into the Blowhole, he's long gone by now. So that raises the question of what evidence the police have that he's dead. It's difficult to prosecute a case for murder if there's no corpse." He paused. "Not impossible, but certainly difficult."

"Couldn't the knife tie Sadie to Mrs. Mooney's murder?"

"Maybe, if it came from Mrs. Mooney's house or if her blood is found on it."

"I think that the water from the Blowhole washed it clean."

"Even so, it would merely be circumstantial anyway."

"Why won't Sadie tell you anything?" Rob asked. "If she tells you that she killed Mooney, isn't that a privileged communication to her lawyer?"

"That's why her silence puzzles me."

"What exactly did she say?"

"As you just said, her communications with me are privileged."

"And you understand, don't you, that I don't give a damn about your privilege? All I care about is seeing that Sadie is set free."

"Point taken," Joshua said. He refilled his cup with coffee and blew on it to cool, then sipped. "She simply said that if she told me everything, it would be knowledge that I would use to defend her, but that she couldn't permit me to use it. It's as if she's protecting someone."

Rob stopped pacing and stiffened. "Protecting someone?"

"Yes."

"Mr. Sinclair, I appreciate your kindness, but I have to go."

Rob turned for the door, but Joshua stood and grabbed his arm. "You know who it is, don't you?"

"I can't say."

"MP-client privilege?"

In spite of himself, Rob smiled.

"Do you understand that my goal, my single-minded purpose, is to protect Sadie?" Joshua asked. "Just as, I suspect, is yours."

"And just as hers is to protect someone else."

Joshua hadn't thought about it that way before, but suddenly everything made perfect sense. "It's the boy, isn't it?" he said. "Ricky."

After the MP left, Joshua went to his desk, pulled out a note pad, and began jotting down his thoughts. The prospect of combat in a courtroom once sent adrenaline coursing through his body. As a young lawyer, he quickly discovered that reputations forged in delivering winning verdicts brought accolades, honors, respect, and even financial reward. But it took no more than a lost motion or two, or the odd negative verdict, to expose chinks in the foundation of that reputation. The scrutiny of high profile criminal cases shone a harsh light on poor preparation and inattention to detail that often resulted from sleepless nights worrying about an ill and dying child.

Worse yet, while courtroom failures lessened the esteem in which he was held by others, the real damage was that, when it happened, innocent people went to prison; sometimes they even died. When that happened, Joshua might still walk away with a fee in his pocket, but he left behind ruined lives and shattered families. It was a hard way to learn the lesson that court cases were not about the lawyers; they were about the clients. And when people's lives and liberties were at stake, there was no margin for error.

That was when Joshua shifted away from courtrooms and into boardrooms. Business deals were far more lucrative than criminal case fees, and when they fell apart, all that was lost were a few dollars and opportunities—but no one died, no one was locked up, and no one lost their husband or father. Ultimately, Joshua went into business for himself, rather than serve as counsel for others, leading to a very successful enterprise, a nice home in an exclusive area of Honolulu, and, after the death of his beloved Juanita, desperate loneliness.

It was into this prosperous but solitary existence that Sadie MacKenzie sailed just a few years earlier. He had done what he could for her, but he had been unable to remove her from Hotel Street. Through careful planning and investment of her money, though, he had helped to position her to break free, as they had discussed that night at dinner. But now, her freedom and her very life might be in the balance, and she had pinned her hopes on Joshua. It was bad enough that his trial skills were rusty and his courtroom mind long since dulled by non-use, but she had also tied one of his hands behind his back. Although she had not directly denied killing Mooney, she had implied that full knowledge of the events of that night would prove her innocence, yet she would not allow him to have the very knowledge he needed to succeed. To have a chance, he had to know what the prosecution knew.

In February of 1943, military governor General Emmons had returned control over criminal cases to the civilian courts, with the exception of cases involving members of the military or orders of military authorities. Joshua had even heard talk recently that reinstatement of *habeas corpus* might be imminent. As soon as daylight approached and the courts building was open, he would be first in line to file such a petition and demand that Sadie be brought from her cell and produced in open court to face her charges and the evidence against her. Although it was unlikely to be granted, an unfiled petition was guaranteed not to be granted.

And so he began handwriting his pleadings.

Rob didn't know where to start his search. He wasn't even sure that he knew for whom he was searching. He knew the boy only by the name Ricky, but didn't know a last name, an address, or even that Ricky was, in fact, the person Sadie was protecting. He would be searching for the unknown based on sheer speculation, a seemingly hopeless task under the best of circumstances.

He had another problem, as well. By now, his failure to return to

Schofield Barracks for treatment of his injuries had surely been noted by his superiors. Although MPs were given flexibility because of the nature of their duties, it was not an unbridled flexibility. Even they had places where they had to be at certain times, particularly when they were ordered to report for medical care, and the failure to be there placed you in AWOL status—away without leave. If he was hauled off to the stockade, he would be unable to assist Sinclair in Sadie's defense.

So, first things first.

Steer lay on his back and blinked his eyes as his senses slowly returned. Had he heard a pounding in the night? He cocked his head and listened.

There it was again. A distant *boom boom boom*.

His pulse quickened. The last time he had heard sounds like that had been in the early morning hours of December 7, 1941. But the Nazis were on the run in Europe, and even the Japs, stubborn little bastards that they were, had withdrawn to a perimeter around their island nation, girding themselves for a fight to the death on the soil of their homeland. Another surprise attack at Pearl was virtually impossible.

Then he heard it again, this time a steady pounding. Tootsie roused next to him.

"Who's at the door, Frank?"

Of course, the pounding was at the front door. Whoever it was, and whatever news they delivered, it couldn't be good. Good news always waited until daybreak; bad news never waited at all.

He sat up and threw the thin blanket aside. "I'll go see."

He grabbed his robe from the foot of the bed and slipped it on as the banging at the door continued. Barefoot, he headed toward the front of the house, tying his robe as he went.

"Hold your horses," he growled.

The banging increased its tempo and its volume. "Major Steer," a male voice called.

"Wait just a goddamn minute!" Steer yelled.

The knocking ceased abruptly. "Yes, sir," the voice said. Intrusive, but at least respectful.

Steer opened the door to greet a disheveled MP with a battered face and bloody blouse. It took a moment for Steer to recognize exactly who stood before him.

"Sergeant Sandford, is that you?"

"I'm sorry to disturb you, sir," Rob said, "but it couldn't wait."

"What in God's name happened to you, son?"

"Frank, who is it?" Tootsie asked as she came into the room behind him. Her raven hair cascaded across her shoulders. One of Hawaii's premier hula dancers, she was exotically beautiful even just awakened in the middle of the night.

"I'm sorry to wake you, ma'am," Rob said.

Her mouth opened in astonishment when she saw him. "Frank, bring the young man inside. He's hurt."

Steer stepped aside and opened the way across the threshold. "Better do as she says, son. When she makes her mind up, it's hell to cross her."

Sandford entered, but stood at attention, his hands behind his back.

"At ease, soldier," Steer said. Tootsie swept over, grabbed Rob's right arm, and led him to the divan.

"Frank, go make some tea," she said.

"That's not necessary, ma'am," Rob said. "I just need to talk to the major for a moment, and then I'll be out of your way."

"Go back to bed, honey," Steer said. "I'll be along directly."

"But the boy is hurt."

"It's nothing, ma'am."

"He's a big boy, honey," Steer said. "Now go on back to bed."

Tootsie looked over Rob's injuries then clucked her tongue disapprovingly, as if shaming him for a barroom brawl. After she returned to the bedroom, Steer sat in a rigid chair across from the divan and fixed his gaze on Rob.

"Now, son, you want to tell me what happened to you and why you're banging on my door at such a God-awful hour?"

Rob took a deep breath then recited the events that led him first to Sadie's house and then to the Blowhole, including the beating at the hands of the police but excluding the body that Sadie pushed into the Blowhole.

Throughout the telling, Steer sat impassively, his face a closed book. When Rob finished, Steer leaned back in his chair and clasped his hands together in his lap.

"Sadie MacKenzie is the young woman who spoke so eloquently during the strike," Steer said.

"Yes, sir."

"And you believe she's innocent?"

"I know it in my heart, sir."

Steer nodded. "Are you one of her customers?"

"No, sir."

"Never?"

"Never."

"Not even once?"

"Not even once."

Steer exhaled deeply. "I'm not sure I understand your interest here, son. The woman is a whore, is she not?"

"She works in Hotel Street, but she's not a whore."

"I'm afraid I don't see the distinction."

"I'm not sure I do either, sir. But Sadie is my friend, and I believe her to be innocent in all respects."

"I see." Steer stood and, with his hands clasped behind his back, paced in front of the divan. He followed a well-worn path on the thin rug, a trail he had obviously traveled many times before.

"I assume you have a request to make of me," Steer said. "Otherwise you wouldn't be sitting in my parlor, and I'd be lying in bed next to my wife."

"I'd like for you to have her transferred from the jail to the stockade."

"And have her tried in a military court?"

"Yes, sir."

"You know I can't do that, son. Jurisdiction for crimes like this has gone back to the civilian courts. Been that way for over a year now."

"Yes, sir. But the military courts still maintain jurisdiction over crimes involving military personnel or military orders or proclamations."

"That, in itself, seems an insurmountable burden. But even if there is a way, what benefit is there to Miss MacKenzie in being tried by a military tribunal?"

"Mooney had it in for Sadie since the day she first arrived. No doubt he has poisoned all those around him in the Honolulu Police Department. She won't be able to get a fair trial in a civilian court."

"From what I hear, this girl seems to have thumbed Mooney in the eye every chance she got. Maybe he had a good reason to have it in for her."

"No, sir. I was physically present the day Mooney first brought her to Francis O'Brian. There is no doubt in my mind that she was brought there against her will. And she was brought inside the Polynesian Rooms barely conscious, courtesy of Mooney's iron fist. I personally witnessed that."

Steer nodded. Although he didn't know those facts to be true, he had no reason to doubt Sandford's words; they were certainly consistent with Mooney's reputation. He also remembered the young woman having spoken vaguely of those events.

"Assume you're correct and that she can't get a fair trial in a civilian court," Steer said. "That brings us back to my first question: How do I deal with General Order Number Two?"

"The exception for military personnel."

"How does that come into play here?"

Sandford looked at the floor. He appeared to be gathering courage to say something, but the words seemed to be caught in his throat.

"Speak up, soldier," Steer said.

Rob got to his feet and stood at attention. "Sir, I was aiding and abetting Sadie in the commission of whatever crime the police have arrested her for."

Steer abruptly ceased his pacing. "Are you saying you helped her kill Officer Mooney?"

"No, sir. I believe she is innocent of that act. But the police believe she did. And I was there with her at the Blowhole. Whatever she did, whatever she was trying to cover up, I aided and abetted in that action, or so they surely think. So whatever they want to charge her with, I was involved. A co-conspirator, if you will. And that puts jurisdiction squarely back in front of the military courts."

"Do you think you can make that logic fly?"

"They beat me just like they beat Sadie, so the police are guilty of a crime against military personnel, namely assault and battery of a military policeman. The whole affair involves Sadie and it involves me, and the two are inextricably intertwined." He paused for a moment. "A civilian trial could light a powder keg under the whole Hotel Street issue. Is this really the time to pour kerosene on the fire?"

Steer stared at Rob for a long moment. At last he broke into a smile. "Son, I think you missed your calling. You would have made a fine lawyer."

"Thank you, sir."

"You realize, of course, that if you voluntarily insinuate yourself into a crime, whatever it might be, you put yourself at risk. You might be found guilty."

"That leads me to my second request."

"And what might that be?"

"I need authority to conduct a search for someone."

"Search for who?"

"Someone who can prove that Sadie is innocent."

"And, by extension, you?"

"That's correct, sir."

"So you want permission to insert yourself into a criminal case, as a criminal defendant, then you want permission to search for proof of your own innocence, and you want the Army to bless that?"

"Yes, sir."

Steer took a deep breath and held it. There was obviously more to this young man's relationship with Sadie MacKenzie than he was letting on. Otherwise, why would he put himself at risk, particularly when there were no guarantees that a military court would treat the girl more benignly than a civilian court? Yet there was no doubting his passion and his earnestness, and Sandford obviously believed in the woman's innocence.

Steer nodded. "Permission granted, son. You have twenty-four hours, and no more. In the meantime, I'll have Miss MacKenzie transferred to the stockade."

"Thank you, sir."

And then the young MP was gone, leaving Steer to wonder what had just happened.

Chapter Thirty-Nine

JOSHUA STOOD PATIENTLY outside the doors of the territorial courthouse, sweaty hands clutching a hastily-drawn, but well thought out, petition for writ of *habeas corpus*. If granted, whatever it was that prompted the devious smile from Detective Harbaugh would be brought into the light of day. It seemed like hours passed while he waited. A breeze mussed his hair that he had washed and carefully combed. Appearances were important, and he had bathed and groomed himself meticulously, then dressed in his finest linen suit. As he presented his petition to the judge, he did not want to appear as a wild-eyed, hysterical shyster, but rather as an articulate, polished advocate.

As soon as the front doors were unlocked, Joshua went in search of Albert Cristy, the Senior Judge for the First Judicial Circuit of the Territory of Hawaii. Son of a Congregational minister and Harvard Law-educated, Judge Cristy presided over the grand jury after the hung jury mistrial of the Ala Moana Boys in 1931, and was later accused of intimidation for supposedly forcing it to indict Grace Fortescue, Tommie Massie, Edward Lord, and Albert Jones for the murder of Joseph Kahahawai. More recently, Cristy had weighed in on the issue of martial law in the Islands. If there was any sympathetic ear in Hawaii to the cause of *habeas corpus*, surely it was that of Albert Cristy.

Joshua located the jurist as he was entering the private entrance to his courtroom.

"Your Honor," Joshua said.

The fifty-five-year-old Cristy turned. Thin-faced, with brown hair and mustache showing the gray of winter, he looked at Joshua.

"Can I help you, counselor?"

"I need a writ," Joshua said.

"*Ex parte?*"

Joshua hesitated and cleared his throat. "*Habeas corpus.*"

Cristy's eyes narrowed. "Surely you know that I'm forbidden to issue such a writ."

"I know that good arguments exist that suspension of the writ, and the reasons therefor, are no longer justified. I know that good arguments exist that suspension of the writ under the current state of the war, with no imminent danger of invasion, is unconstitutional and also that it violates the Organic Act."

He paused and locked eyes in an unwavering gaze with the judge. "I'm not a trial lawyer, Your Honor, nor am I a constitutional scholar, but I know these arguments exist because they've been made before. I have read them in the press before." Another pause, then, "They are your arguments, Your Honor."

Cristy's face seemed to harden for a moment, then his jaw eased and the ends of his lips curled slightly upward. "Perhaps we should converse in my chambers, Mr...?"

"Sinclair. Joshua Sinclair."

Cristy pushed the door open and gestured inside. "Please step inside, Mr. Sinclair. I always enjoy a lively intellectual discussion."

As Joshua entered, the judge added, "And I trust you have brought your papers with you."

Rob went, on foot, from saloon to saloon, whorehouse to whorehouse, and opium den to opium den in neighborhoods where sin knew no clock. He even went door-to-door among densely-packed hovels and shacks where people lived in misery. In most instances, his uniform allowed him access as he roused folks from their beds, but at the same time, it sealed many lips. Prostitution might be regulated on Hotel Street, and a blind eye turned across the river, but male prostitution—with boys—occurred only in the shadows. No one was inclined to discuss it with an individual in law enforcement. No one was inclined to admit it even existed.

As he reached the end of a narrow street in Blood Town, he prepared to cross over and work his way back down the other side toward his Jeep. A noise drew his attention to an alley. It sounded like the kick of a bottle on concrete, followed by the scuffle of footsteps.

He peered into the narrow alley, which was cloaked in darkness. Though it was mid-morning, given the width and the overhang of roofs, he doubted that the sun ever made its way to its deepest recesses. He stepped into the mouth of the opening and stood for a moment to allow his pupils to adjust to the dimness.

He heard more scuffling sounds, then a rhythmic slapping, each impact punctuated by a deep-voiced grunt and a higher-pitched exhale of breath. He eased his way forward, his senses on full alert. He unsnapped his holster and placed his right hand on the butt of his weapon. It sounded to his trained ears as if an assault was being perpetrated, but strangely, there seemed to be no resistance offered. Either a consensual act was occurring or a weapon was involved that eliminated resistance.

As he moved closer, the sounds grew louder, yet still subdued. The rhythm of the slapping accelerated; the high-pitched exhales transformed into whimpers; the grunts became more pronounced. Rob could make out shadows behind a row of trash cans, against a brick wall. A large figure behind a much smaller figure, faces toward the wall. Rob squinted to absorb details. No weapon that he could see. Pants around ankles of the large figure, a man with a beard. Rob looked for the hiked-up skirt of his partner.

But saw pants around ankles. Another man.

He stepped closer, still quiet, still unseen. The features on the smaller figure were more visible. A boy, probably no more than twelve or thirteen years old.

Rob fought nausea as he withdrew his weapon from its holster.

Desk Sergeant Albert Kekoa fought to keep his eyes open. He had not slept well the night before as he and his wife had been up for hours with a colicky newborn. When he arrived for his morning shift, he got a brief report on the overnight goings-on—something about a missing vice officer, but he had, frankly, been inattentive and couldn't recall any of the details. He knew of the missing officer, though. Everyone knew Mooney, but Kekoa had problems of his own, with the new baby and all.

He started at the sound of a throat clearing. He realized that he had been dozing and quickly came to attention. At the desk stood two military policemen, both young, both *haole*, and both unsmiling. Through the fog, he seemed to also recall something in the morning briefing about an MP and a whore. He wished he had paid more attention.

"Howzit, bruddahs. What can I do fo' you?"

"We're here to pick up a prisoner named Sadie MacKenzie," the taller of the two MPs said.

Kekoa slid the booking report over, put his finger on a column, and drew it down until it landed on the name of the prisoner.

"She was brought in last night."

"Yes, sir," the MP said. "We have orders to transfer her to the stockade at Schofield."

"Why? What she do?"

"I don't know, sir. I'm simply following orders."

Kekoa stood and approached the counter. "I can't just turn a prisoner over to you. She's in my custody."

The MP placed a folded page on the counter. "My orders are signed by Major Steer, sir. He is provost marshal for the Territory."

Kekoa unfolded the page and read the document. Sure enough, it ordered the release of Sadie MacKenzie into the custody of the U.S. Army for criminal prosecution under Section 1(j)(1) and (3) of the February 8, 1943 U.S. Army Proclamation signed by Lt. General Delos C. Emmons, Military Governor of Hawaii.

"I have orders, too," Kekoa said. "My job is not to allow prisoners to just walk out of here."

"Sir, are you familiar with General Order Thirty-One issued by General Richardson?"

"Sure, bruddah, evahbody knows about Thirty-One. Evahbody also knows it got pulled back by Order Thirty-Eight."

"Section three point oh one survived the rescission." The MP went into recitation-from-rote-memory mode, as if he ran into this problem often. "No public officer, deputy of such public officer, public employee, or any other person shall, for any cause, in any manner, way or form impede, oppose, or interfere with any member of the armed forces of the United States in his performance of his military functions, military duties, or military orders."

Kekoa tried to comprehend what the MP was reciting, but it sounded like military jargon or legal gobblydegook to his untrained ear. He did understand the intent of what he was being told, though. In layman's terms, the MP was saying, "Don't fuck with the United States Army."

"Are you impeding, opposing, or interfering with our performance of military orders?" the MP asked.

"I wouldn't do that, brah."

"Then take us to Sadie MacKenzie."

It was with a sense of euphoria that Joshua returned to the police station with a signed writ of *habeas corpus* in hand. *Ex parte* victories were a little unfair, of course, obtained in unopposed presentations to the court, but the highs were still just as high. Joshua knew that if this writ were challenged, it would likely be overturned, but for now, it should be enough to at least temporarily bring Sadie out of a solitary cell and to shine light on the evidence the police had against her. With that knowledge, he would then have a starting point to assemble her defense.

He passed an Army Jeep heading in the opposite direction as he arrived at the station and entered. He walked boldly to the counter and slapped the writ down, drawing the attention of a slack-faced *kanaka* officer sitting at the duty desk.

"I have an order from Judge Cristy ordering the Honolulu Police Department to immediately produce Sadie MacKenzie in his courtroom."

The desk sergeant stood, almost as if he were in a daze, and approached. He picked up the writ and scanned it slowly, then looked at Joshua.

"Dis one popular *wahine*. What she do?"

"What do you mean by that?" Joshua asked. "Popular, how?"

"Evahbody's got orders for her. You too late, bruddah. Army boys jus' left here with her. MPs."

The words slammed into Joshua with tsunami force. "I have a writ from Judge Cristy."

"I see dat, brah, but dat *wahine* already gone. You probably passed dem when you came in."

"But I have a writ." Joshua was aware that the words came out in a whine.

"Dey had an order from Major Steer. Das a higher trump card."

Chapter Forty

"WHEN'S THE LAST time you ate?" Rob asked.

He and the boy from the alley sat in a small diner on the fringes of Blood Town, empty except for the two of them, a short order cook, and an obese waitress. The boy shoveled another forkful of scrambled eggs into his mouth and washed it down with chocolate milk.

"Day befo yestahday."

His voice was high-pitched, nearly a soprano. His Hawaiian features were smooth, his almond eyes large. He had jet black hair that swept across his forehead and covered his ears. Small particles of snot had crusted around one nostril. Rob also thought he detected a narrow streak down one cheek that resembled the trail a snail might leave in its wake. Rob had seen such a thing before: the tracks of a tear.

"Still not going to tell me your name?"

The boy shook his head.

"My best friend from back home was named Jimmy. You remind me of him. You look like a James. That your name? James?"

The boy shook his head again.

"How about I call you that, anyway? I'll call you Jim. Is that okay?"

The boy nodded.

"Okay, Jim it is, then."

Jim finished the last of his toast and polished off the chocolate milk. "What you want from me? You got money? I lost money because of you."

Rob shook his head. "No, nothing like that. I'm just looking for somebody. You know a boy like you named Ricky?"

Jim nodded as he said, "No." He probably had no idea that his knee-jerk reaction, reflected in the nod, was to tell the truth, while the words that came from his mouth were those of a practiced liar.

"He's not in any trouble," Rob said. "But a friend of mine is. And Ricky can help her."

Jim sat silently for a long moment. Rob resisted the urge to prompt him for fear it would merely push him away. He sensed that Jim wanted to tell him the truth, but he had to arrive at that conclusion on his own.

At last, Jim said, "You *maka'i?*"

"I don't know what that means."

"Police."

"Yes. I'm a military policeman. But I'm not here as a policeman. I'm here as a friend. What's the Hawaiian word for friend?"

"*Hoaloha.*"

"Like *aloha?*"

Jim nodded.

"Well, that's why I'm here. I'm trying to help my *hoaloha*. Did I say it right?"

Jim nodded again. "Who's your friend das in *pilikia?*"

Rob knew that word. He'd been dealing with *pilikia* his whole life: trouble.

"Her name is Sadie."

Jim smiled at the name. "Miss Sadie is *hoaloha* to Ricky."

"Sadie is in *pilikia,* and she needs all the *hoalohas* she can find right now." He paused then added, "Will you help me find Ricky?"

Jim sat for a long time without speaking. At last he said, "You got money?"

Joshua arrived at the front gate of Schofield Barracks, where he was stopped at the security checkpoint. He looked out the window at a young MP who approached, clipboard in hand.

"Can I help you, sir?" the MP asked.

Joshua was struck by how interchangeable this young black man could have been with the injured MP who had been in his house last night, apparently cut from the same cloth.

"I'm here to see Major Steer."

"Do you have an appointment?"

"No, but I'm sure he'll see me."

"Yes, sir. What is your name, sir?"

Unfailingly polite, as was the young man last night, even through his cracked lips and bruised jaw.

"Joshua Sinclair, esquire. I should like to speak with him about a legal matter."

"Just one minute, sir." The MP stepped back into the booth and picked up a telephone. Joshua watched as he spoke, then hung up and stepped back outside.

"I'm sorry, sir, but Major Steer has a full schedule today. If you'd like to make an appointment—"

"It's a matter of some urgency," Joshua said. He held the legal papers out the window. "I have a writ from Judge Cristy."

"Yes, sir. But Major Steer has a full schedule today. As I said, if you'd like to make an appointment—"

"I've been led to believe that Major Steer might be of some assistance in this matter."

"Who led you to believe that, sir?"

"A military policeman named Robert Sandford."

The MP stiffened. He obviously knew Robert. Joshua probed deeper. "This matter involves a young lady named Sadie MacKenzie. Perhaps you know of her."

"Just a moment, sir." The MP returned to the booth, spoke into the telephone again, more animated this time, then stepped back outside. "Major Steer will see you, sir. I'll give you directions to his office."

Steer looked up from his desk as Joshua was ushered in. Steer stood and offered his hand.

"Mr. Sinclair, good to see you again," Steer said.

"Thank you for seeing me, Major." Joshua extended the legal papers and placed them in Steer's outstretched hand. "I understand that you have Sadie MacKenzie in custody in your stockade."

"Indeed we do." Steer drew his hand back and unfolded the papers.

"That's a writ of *habeas corpus*, signed by Judge Cristy," Joshua said. "It requires you to produce Miss MacKenzie in his courtroom forthwith."

Steer examined the document. "You understand, do you not, counselor, that the writ of *habeas corpus* has been suspended in the Territory of Hawaii."

"I know that General Order Thirty-one did just that, but that General Order Thirty-eight rescinded Thirty-one."

"Well, now, that's a common mistake."

"I beg your pardon?" Joshua asked. But he knew exactly what Steer would say next; he just hadn't expected Steer to know the minutiae of the legal arguments.

"Allow me to take you through the chronology," Steer said. He turned and looked out his window at the base. "On December 7, 1941, the Japanese attacked Pearl Harbor." He paused for a moment. When he spoke again, his voice took on a wistful tone. "I watched the beginning of the attack out this very window."

"I know my history, Major."

"I don't mean to insult you, Mr. Sinclair. I'm just trying to establish the context. Following the attack, Governor Poindexter issued a proclamation that, among other things, declared martial law and suspended the writ of *habeas corpus*. General Short then assumed the role of Military Governor of Hawaii and confirmed that the writ had been suspended."

Steer turned back around and sat in his desk chair. "Which brings us to the confusion caused by General Orders Thirty-one and Thirty-eight. Not to be critical of my superiors, but when General Richardson issued Thirty-one, which suspended the writ of *habeas corpus*, it was a case of belt and suspenders."

"I don't understand what you mean by that," Joshua said.

"Please, Mr. Sinclair, have a seat."

"I prefer to stand, if it's all the same to you."

"As you wish. Look at it this way, Mr. Sinclair. A belt holds up your trousers. So do suspenders. If you have one, you don't need the other. And if you have the other, you don't need the one. So when Governor

Poindexter issued his proclamation suspending the writ on December 7, he put a belt on the trousers. And when General Richardson issued Thirty-one, also suspending the writ, he added suspenders. But the trousers didn't need both, so when General Order Thirty-eight rescinded Thirty-one, it merely removed the suspenders from the trousers. But the belt is still there. There are no writs of *habeas corpus* in Hawaii."

"So you say." Joshua pointed to the document in Steer's hand. "And yet, there one is, duly signed by a judge of the Territory of Hawaii. The pants have fallen down."

"Notwithstanding the writ, Miss Sadie MacKenzie sits in my stockade, under my jurisdiction as Provost Marshal under a state of martial law in the Territory of Hawaii, which even you don't dispute exists." Steer paused then asked, "Or do you?"

"My argument, sir, is that the circumstances that justify its imposition under the Organic Act, those being either actual invasion or the imminent danger of invasion of the Islands, no longer exist."

"I hope to God that's true."

"But even if not, I fail to see how these charges implicate military orders or military personnel. Because if they don't, the military has no jurisdiction over them."

"Let me ask you a more practical question, counselor." Steer leaned back in his chair, propped his feet on his desk, and locked his hands behind his head. "My understanding is that Miss MacKenzie is a whore."

Joshua bristled. "She's no whore."

Steer sighed. "My point is this: There's a move afoot by so-called decent society to round up all the whores in Honolulu, shuttle them back into Hotel Street, pour gasoline on it, and set it afire. If I turn custody over Miss MacKenzie to the civil courts, that same so-called decent society will then sit in judgment of her. Whether she's a whore or not, she does, in fact, work on Hotel Street. She'll be tried in a civilian court that will determine whether a Hotel Street sporting girl is guilty of murdering, in her bed, one of the fine citizens of Honolulu and one of its most highly respected law enforcement officers. Is that really what you want?"

Joshua stared blank-faced at Steer as the import of the question sank in. He slowly melted into a chair across the desk from the Provost Marshal.

Steer removed his feet from his desk and leaned forward. "You care for Miss MacKenzie, do you not?"

"Like she was my own daughter."

"What is it about this young woman that inspires such loyalty?"

"I don't understand your question."

"One of my men has personally interceded on her behalf."

Joshua nodded. "Robert Sandford."

"One of my best men, and yet he has willingly imperiled his own safety as well as his career in appealing for my intervention."

"So what are your plans?"

"My intent is to convene a military tribunal tomorrow to inquire into the circumstances of the disappearance of Officer Mooney and the death of his mother. I'll require the civil authorities to appear and present their evidence, whatever it may be. And Miss MacKenzie will then be allowed to offer her defense."

"Will she be permitted counsel of her choosing?"

"Of her choosing?" Steer asked. "Or of yours?"

"I'm her attorney. That's of both our choosing."

"In that case, I'll permit your appearance as her attorney."

"And in that case, I would like to see my client."

"I haven't seen Ricky fo' six months."

The words were spoken by a sad *kanaka* woman, sheathed in an oversized *mu'umu'u* that draped her corpulent frame like a tent. Rob regarded her with a pity he hoped he was able to successfully hide. Even back home, he had not seen comparable poverty to the hovel in which he and Jim sat as they talked with the woman who identified herself only as Emma. Although she had welcomed Jim warmly, she put up a defensive shield as soon as she laid eyes on Rob's uniform.

"I give him birth, and he does not see me in all dis time," Emma said.

"Who are his friends?" Rob asked.

"He has no friends. Only men who have money." She sniffled as she added, "He does bad things for money. He dishonors his *ohana*."

"Family," Jim said without prompting, but Rob already knew that one.

"I need to find him," Rob said.

"You soldier-boy," Emma said. "Make *pilikia* fo' Ricky. Make *pilikia* fo' me."

"No, ma'am. I need his help."

She screwed up her face.

"*Kokua*," Jim said. "He needs help—*kokua*—for Miss Sadie. Tutu, this man is good to me. No *pilikia*."

Emma cut her eyes back from Jim to Rob. "You know Miss Sadie?"

"She's my friend, and she needs help."

Emma sat silently. It appeared to Rob that she was engaged in some sort of inner debate. He sensed that, even if she told the truth about not having seen Ricky in six months, she nonetheless knew where he might be. The question was whether she would lower her defenses long enough to trust a soldier. A black soldier.

Chapter Forty-One

THOUGH THE CELL was clean and, unlike that in the police station, was well-lit, Sadie still felt as if she were in the dark. Her future, particularly her immediate future, was more uncertain than ever. With her virginity already a distant memory, she had accepted her lot and determined to make the most of it. If she had to service fifty men a day, then why not fifty-five? Or on those days when the lines stretched longer, the days she spread for 100, then why not 105? Every extra dollar represented hours that she could buy from the back end of her sentence and effect an early release. With the drumbeats of reform sweeping the city, the time was nigh for her to make her move.

Then Mooney reared his ugly head again. It had now been put down, never to surface again, but the damage had been done. It appeared as if Mooney was going to get the last word, condemning her to prison if not the death chamber. The only faint glimmer of hope was the fact that she was now under the control of Rob's friends in the United States Army, and not Mooney's at the Honolulu Police Department. She had no regrets over her actions the night before; her only regret was that what had happened had been made necessary by Mooney, himself.

Now she braced herself for the consequences.

She looked up as her cell door opened and Joshua stepped inside. So lost was she in her thoughts that she hadn't heard his approach.

"I was afraid you wouldn't be able to find me," she said as she stood. "Tell me what's happening."

"Please, have a seat."

Sadie perched on the edge of the cot, her hands primly folded in her lap. "Did Robert have me brought here?"

"I believe he was behind it, yes."

"Then this is a good thing."

"Yes."

"How is Robert?"

"Your young man is fine. He's out now searching for the boy you call Ricky."

Sadie stiffened and bolted to her feet. "No, he mustn't."

She saw instantly by Joshua's reaction that she had confirmed what he suspected—that she was protecting someone, and she had now confirmed who that someone was. She knew, also, that the confirmation would strengthen his resolve to find Ricky. It was ironic, she thought. She had failed to protect Billy back in California by being passive, and now she had failed to protect Ricky by being too aggressive.

"Sadie, please sit," Joshua said.

She sat again.

"This is very important," Joshua said, "and I ask that you please heed what I have to say. You trust me, don't you?"

"Of course I do, Joshua."

"And you believe that I would never do anything that was not in your best interest, don't you?"

"I do believe that."

"I know that you feel you must protect Ricky from the consequences of last night. And I know that you have suggested to me that a true account of last night's events will prove your innocence. The only conclusion I can draw from those two facts is that this young man is responsible for the death of Officer Mooney, whom I do believe to be dead, even though there's no body to be found."

Sadie remained silent.

"There are several ways to approach your defense. We can start by challenging any assertion that Mooney has been killed. However, the police can present circumstantial evidence to establish that he's dead. I don't know what evidence they possess, but they obviously have something. The detective with whom I spoke is far too confident for me to believe that they don't."

"What if there is no body to be found?"

"Robert confessed to me that he saw you dispose of a body at the Blowhole."

She fell silent again.

"Unless you discovered that body at the Blowhole, or confronted the person there, then it must have been transported by some means. That raises the question of whether there might be evidence in your automobile. Blood, articles of clothing, other personal items belonging to Mooney, something of that nature."

Sadie kept her silence. Yes, there was blood on the rear bumper of the car, likely in the trunk, and certainly pooled on the ground at the back of the vehicle. Were there other telltale signs? She racked her brain, trying to picture the events as they transpired, but all was hazy, as if viewed through a fog. She squeezed her eyes shut and tried to sharpen the image as she removed Mooney's body from the trunk, then grasped his hands and pulled him to the Blowhole.

Something nagged at her. She squeezed her eyes tighter. Something was out of place, but what was it?

A socked foot. One shoe was missing.

She opened her eyes and looked at Joshua. "What do the police say?"

"They say absolutely nothing."

She nodded. "You said there are several ways to approach my defense. What else?"

"I gather from your response that the police are likely in possession of some evidence to establish that Officer Mooney, either alive or dead, was in the trunk of your automobile."

"What other ways, Joshua?"

"The second way is the truth, that Ricky, and not you, was responsible for Mooney's demise. That Mooney likely had done something, or was about to do something, that justified taking his life. In short, self defense."

He watched Sadie carefully, as if searching for giveaways that he had hit on the truth, but Sadie kept her countenance stoic.

"Is that what happened, Sadie? Did Mooney assault the boy and he defended himself?"

"Let me ask you something, Joshua."

"Certainly."

"What is the likelihood that a jury—"

"There will be no jury. Only a military tribunal."

"Fine. What is the likelihood that a military tribunal will believe that a man of Mooney's stature would engage in perverted acts with a boy."

"Perverted?" Joshua's face registered surprise.

"Sodomy."

"I—I don't know."

"Your own disbelief gives me the answer I seek," Sadie said.

"Is that what happened, Sadie? Was Mooney sodomizing this boy and he defended himself?" He paused as a realization hit him. "Did *you* defend him from sodomy?"

"Would that be a valid defense?"

Joshua stumbled to the end of the cot and sank down. "Good God, Sadie. Is that what happened?"

"Answer my question, Joshua. Would that be a valid defense?"

"Yes, I believe it would. If it was forcible sodomy, Ricky would be justified in defending himself. And if a person is justified in using deadly force to defend himself, then homicide committed by a third party coming to his aid would, likewise, be justified."

"And if it wasn't forcible sodomy? What then?"

Joshua stared at her blankly. She felt a pang of conscience at inflicting this confusion on him, but he was clearly having difficulty making sense of the implications of her questions.

"Answer me, Joshua. If the sodomy was consensual, if it was for money, would homicide be justified?"

He blinked rapidly, then removed his glasses and cleaned them, as if they were responsible for the fog that clouded his perception.

"I suppose that, if the third party was under the impression that the sodomy was forcible, even if it was not, then homicide might be justified."

"And if the third party knew the sodomy was consensual, then what?"

Now it was Joshua's turn to remain silent.

"Joshua, justified or not?"

"I suppose—not."

Sadie took a moment to digest the answer, which she had anticipated, then asked, "Is there a third option for my defense?"

Joshua put his glasses back on, stood, and paced. He seemed to be deep in thought as he struggled to regain his composure. She knew she had given him much to think about, and much to suspect.

"Joshua, a third option?"

At length he stopped pacing and faced her. "I suppose a third option would be conflicting stories, both equally viable, that would confuse the trier-of-fact. Unless the tribunal can decide on one version of events, beyond a reasonable doubt, then there should be no conviction. Assuming, of course, that the tribunal takes its duties seriously."

"Of course," Sadie said. "That's always the catch, isn't it?"

Chapter Forty-Two

WHAT LITTLE SADIE knew about courtrooms and trials, she had gleaned from the rare occasions she had gone to the movies while still living on the mainland. To make matters worse, neither she nor Joshua had ever been exposed to the concept of a military tribunal. Joshua had spent the better part of the previous day learning the rules of procedure, which he tried to explain to her.

Military tribunals in World War II Hawaii were often convened on no more than one or two days' notice, and they were not courts of record. That meant, Joshua said, that there would be no court reporter and no transcription of the proceedings to preserve errors for appeal—but since no appeals were permitted anyway, it wouldn't matter. Her case would be presided over by an officer with little or no training in the law. As a result, the rules of evidence and the presumption of innocence would have little, if any, application. What it ultimately would come down to was simply whether the presiding officer believed the defendant or the prosecution.

"And I'm a whore," Sadie said, "whose credibility is suspect by virtue of my profession."

"To the contrary," Joshua had protested. "You are a delightful and brilliant young lady who has been mistreated by the police."

She appreciated his loyalty, but she knew the odds were against her as she was escorted in chains into the meeting room that would serve as a courtroom. Nani had sent down a simple white cotton sheath for her to wear, one that covered her elbows and ankles. Though everyone in the room would know she was a whore, she still dressed like a schoolgirl.

Joshua waited at one of two tables set up to face a dais with a third table, behind which sat a single chair for the presiding officer. A baby-faced soldier with lieutenant's bars on his collar sat next to Joshua. They both stood at her entry.

"Please remove the chains," Joshua said to her guards. She anticipated resistance, but they silently obliged his request.

"Sadie, this is Lieutenant Childress. He's your Army lawyer."

The baby-faced lieutenant dipped his head in a cross between a bow and a nod. "Ma'am."

"Joshua," she said, "I thought you were going to be my lawyer."

"Lieutenant Childress has been appointed by Major Steer to defend you. I'll take the lead in defense strategy, but Lieutenant Childress will make the oral presentation of our case."

"Are you comfortable with that?" she asked.

"It's the only thing that I *am* comfortable with."

"Very well, then. Lieutenant Childress, I appreciate your help."

"Yes, ma'am."

He spoke the words like a man who was already defeated. And, Sadie supposed, he most likely was. She had not told Joshua that she overheard her jailers discussing her case, and actually placing bets on the outcome. She heard one of them say that, statistically, over ninety-nine percent of the cases that had been tried by military courts had resulted in convictions. She hoped to be a one-percenter, but she knew that her defenders faced an uphill battle.

A more seasoned officer, with sprinkles of gray in the bristles of his close-cropped hair, entered and sat at the companion table. She wasn't surprised that she had been assigned a junior attorney while the prosecution was more experienced. To result in a ninety-nine percent conviction rate, every deck was clearly stacked in favor of the prosecution.

She watched as the prosecutor opened a duffle bag, took out a blood-stained man's shoe—a brown-and-white oxford wingtip Brogue—and set it on the table. She turned her head slightly and saw Joshua also looking at the shoe.

Almost as if on cue, the rear door opened and Detective Harbaugh entered the room. He again wore a tailored suit and derby hat. Hair oil glistened at his temples, and he reeked of sickly sweet, cheap cologne.

There was no one else in the room, a troubling thought to Sadie. Justice done in secret was rarely justice done. She wondered if Robert had miscalculated in pulling strings to enlist the assistance of the military for her trial.

And where was Robert? Had he been successful in locating Ricky? She was hoping, deep inside, that he had. She even had to fight the impulse to tell Joshua exactly where Ricky was, so that he might be summoned. Though she felt guilty for thinking that way, terror had a way of making a person do the unthinkable. Her life on Hotel Street was living proof of that.

The prosecutor approached Lieutenant Childress; his nameplate identified him as "Hoskins" and the bars on his collar touted him as a captain. Hoskins handed Childress two sheets of paper, then he approached Harbaugh and said something. Harbaugh followed him out of the room, obviously to confer about his testimony.

Lieutenant Childress scanned the pages, then looked around Joshua at Sadie. He spoke in a whisper.

"I understand you don't wish to testify."

"No, sir. I don't."

"Will you reconsider?"

"Do you think I should?"

He slid one of the typewritten sheets of paper toward her. At the top was the word "Exhibits." He pointed at the second item on the page: "Delbert Mooney's shoe."

"I suspected as much when I saw it on the table," she said.

"Found in the trunk of your automobile. With what appears to be Mooney's blood on it." He consulted the second page. "They also found blood in the trunk, on the bumper, and a trail leading to the Blowhole."

"But no body," Joshua said. "No body, no murder."

"A myth perpetuated in pulp novels," Childress said. "This is very damning circumstantial evidence of murder. And, might I remind you, no second-guessing appellate court will ever consider what is done here."

"What does this mean?" Sadie asked.

"It means we'll need to offer some explanation for the shoe in your trunk and the blood trail from your car."

"I have no explanation that will put a smile on your face."

At those words, Childress froze, his mouth slightly open. Then he leaned back and focused his attention on the sheet of paper again.

"Son of a bitch," he muttered under his breath.

Sadie knew she had angered Lieutenant Childress, and for that she was sorry, but she had her own rules she had to live by. She glanced at Joshua, who seemed intent on studying the shoe on the prosecutor's table, almost as if entranced by it. He glanced at the door at the back of the room. Seemingly satisfied that Hoskins and Harbaugh would not re-enter, he stood and approached the neighboring table. He took off his glasses and held them behind his back with both hands, then leaned over until his face was scant inches from the footwear. He straightened, put his glasses back on, and held his hands at the heel and toe, as if measuring the length.

"Sinclair, what are you doing?" Childress asked. "If they catch you tampering with evidence, they'll—"

"I haven't touched it, and I won't." He turned toward Childress. "Do you have any kind of aide or assistant as part of your duties as defense counsel?"

"No. Why? What are you thinking?"

"Just an idea," Joshua said. He withdrew his billfold from his inside coat pocket, opened it, and counted out a large number of bills. "Yes, that's sufficient," he said softly, as if to himself. Then, out loud, "How long will the trial last?"

"A couple of hours, maybe more if I'm actually given a defense by my client to work with."

"I have an errand to run. I should be back within two hours. Sadie, I'll leave you in Lieutenant Childress's good hands."

"Where are you going?" Sadie asked. "I thought you were going to assist the lieutenant."

"That's exactly what I'm going to do. Lieutenant, attack the physical evidence with all you've got. Without a body, it's the key. If the sponsoring witness takes the stand before my return, keep him there as long as you can."

Before Sadie or Childress could ask anything else, Joshua bolted from the room. Sadie looked at Childress, who said, "He's as crazy as you are."

Sadie left him alone to study his notes and devise a plan out of nothing. A few minutes later, the rear door opened and Hoskins re-entered, along with Harbaugh and a Hawaiian vice officer she knew only as Mahelona. Harbaugh and Mahelona sat on the front row of the tiny gallery area, while Hoskins returned to his place at the prosecutor's table.

Almost as if on cue, a loud rap sounded on the side door. It opened and a solemn-faced, balding Army officer, with a colonel's insignia on his collar, entered and took his place behind the table on the dais. Hoskins and Childress stood as he entered, but the civilians remained seated. Sadie assumed Harbaugh and Mahelona did so out of ignorance; she did so out of defiance.

"Be seated," the colonel said. He was tall and thin-faced, with an undertaker's countenance. Fitting, she thought, for a man who might well pronounce her death sentence.

"This tribunal will now come to order. I'm Colonel Barker, presiding officer. Captain Hoskins, do you wish to make an opening statement?"

Hoskins stood and recited his statement as if from rote memory. "Thank you, sir. My statement is simple. The defendant, Sadie MacKenzie, is a sporting girl from Hotel Street who decided that the rules didn't apply to her. She decided to take money from servicemen for sex, then to flaunt it in the face of the authorities and of polite society. She took her ill-gotten gains and used them to buy real estate and businesses, dragging the sordidness of Hotel Street throughout Honolulu. But Officer Delbert Mooney of the Honolulu Police Department stood in her way. He tried to ensure that she stayed where she belonged, and she didn't like that. And so she decided to play God. She took Officer Mooney's life so that she could continue hers unhindered. That's what we're here for today. To pass judgment on a woman for whom sex-for-money trumped decency."

With that, he sat back down.

Yes, Sadie thought, the statement was, indeed, simple. Simple-minded was more like it. And strangely effective. She wondered, though, why there had been no mention of Mrs. Mooney's death.

She shifted her attention to the young Lieutenant Childress as he stood and cleared his throat.

"Miss MacKenzie, will you please stand?" he asked.

Uncertain of his plan, she hesitantly slid back her chair and rose. Childress stepped over until he stood side-by-side with her. She barely came to his shoulder.

"Please step back," he said.

Still uncertain, she took a step back, and Childress stepped directly in front of her. She had to lean to the side to look around him and see Colonel Barker, who also leaned around to see her past Childress.

Childress moved back to his place. "Thank you, Miss MacKenzie. You may be seated."

As she sat, Childress commenced his statement. "Sir, I am not a big man. I stand five feet ten inches tall and I weigh a tad more than one hundred sixty pounds, yet my frame blocks her from your view."

He paused. Sadie could see that he had Barker's full attention. She also thought she could see where he was going. She had misjudged Childress. Sometimes youth and inexperience were outshone by clear thinking.

"I have it on good authority that Officer Mooney, the alleged victim of a crime, stands two inches taller than I and outweighs me by as much as fifty pounds. Yet the prosecution would have you believe that Miss MacKenzie somehow overpowered Officer Mooney, snuffed out his life, and then disposed of his body."

He approached the prosecution table and picked up the bloodied shoe. He held it high for all to see.

"This appears to be the sum and substance of the prosecution's case: a shoe. But where is the body? How do we even know that Mooney is deceased?"

He paused dramatically for his audience of one to mentally frame his answer to the rhetorical question.

"Here are the facts that you will hear in this trial," he continued. "Miss MacKenzie arrived at Mooney's house in search of him. Within a few minutes, maybe as few as two or three, she left the premises. A neighbor will testify to this. Scant seconds thereafter, the bodies of Mooney's mother and father were discovered by this neighbor. Mooney's mother had been brutally stabbed to death and was laid out in a bed next to her husband, who was apparently deceased from natural causes. But insufficient time had elapsed for Miss MacKenzie to have accomplished this murder of Mooney's mother. That is not in dispute, and that is why the prosecution has opted not to pursue charges against Miss MacKenzie on this matter."

So that explained it, Sadie thought.

"Mrs. Mooney was murdered in her home by someone, but surely not by Sadie MacKenzie. And Officer Mooney has now conveniently disappeared. Are the two events connected? Do not they raise questions about the certainty of Captain Hoskins's statement? I ask you to draw your own conclusion."

"How do you explain the bloody shoe?" Colonel Barker asked.

The interruption seemed to startle Childress, but he quickly recovered. "The shoe is not in evidence yet, sir."

"No doubt it will be soon enough. So how do you explain it?"

"I trust the prosecution can establish, beyond a reasonable doubt, that the shoe belongs to Officer Mooney?"

He looked to Hoskins as if expecting an answer, but continued before Hoskins could do anything other than stare blankly back. The silence in response to the question appeared to have an impact on Barker.

"And I trust the prosecution can establish, beyond a reasonable doubt, that the blood on the shoe belongs to Officer Mooney?"

More blank staring from Hoskins.

"Or is it the blood of Mrs. Mooney on the shoe? If so, will the prosecution continue to claim it as Mooney's shoe?"

Now Sadie thought she sensed panic on the face of Captain Hoskins, as if realizing his once indomitable case actually had holes in it. Nicely played, Lieutenant Childress.

Chapter Forty-Three

JOSHUA ENTERED HOUSE of Mitsukoshi Department Store at King and Bethel Streets and sought out men's clothing. He was on a desperate mission that, as far as he knew, would accomplish nothing. It wouldn't be the first time in his life that he had undertaken such a mission. His missions years earlier to save the lives of both his wife and daughter had also been fruitless; would his current mission result in the same fate for Sadie as that of Juanita and Angela? Possibly, but failure was only guaranteed by inaction, success only made possible by effort.

He completed his business as quickly as possible then moved on to Kramer's Department Store on Fort Street, in search of the same item. He quickly glanced at his pocket watch as he entered the menswear department. How much time before he had to return to Schofield?

Sadie kept her eyes lasered on vice officer Akahi "Skip" Mahelona, who leaned back in the witness chair and awaited Captain Hoskins's next question. She knew Mahelona from past experience to be glib, loose with the truth, and driven by greed. From her perspective, it made him mercurial and far more dangerous than Mooney. At least Mooney was predictable. There was rarely any thought to his actions; just impulsive, almost uncontrollable, brutality that you could see coming from a mile away. Mahelona, on the other hand, was always trying to weigh the percentages and figure out what action in any given circumstance would enhance his status and his bank account. As a result, it was often difficult to predict what his move would be.

Captain Hoskins approached Mahelona and set the bloody shoe on the railing in front of him.

"Officer Mahelona, please examine the article I have placed before you," Hoskins said.

Mahelona leaned forward and studied it closely. Sadie could almost see the gears turning in his mind as he did. After a few seconds, he leaned back.

"That is Delbert Mooney's shoe," he said.

Lieutenant Childress stood swiftly. "Objection. No foundation has been laid."

"Sustained," Barker said.

Hoskins tried another tack. "Officer Mahelona, have you ever seen that shoe before?"

"Yes. I found it in the trunk of Sadie MacKenzie's car at the Blowhole."

"Was there blood on it at the time?"

"Yes. And there was blood on the floor of the trunk, too."

"What did you think when you saw that shoe in the defendant's trunk?"

"I thought Sadie had done away with Delbert, just like she did his mother."

Childress sprang to his feet as if shot from a catapult. "Objection. Assumes facts not in evidence. Move to strike the last portion of the witness's answer."

"Lieutenant Childress," Barker said, "there is no jury here. I'll consider all the evidence in making my decision. Objection overruled."

"But sir—"

"Please sit down, Lieutenant."

Childress melted back into his seat. Sadie reached over and patted his hand.

Hoskins continued, now with a smug smile on his face. Sadie saw that this simple ruling had bolstered his confidence. "Officer, what makes you think that's Delbert Mooney's shoe?"

A scuffling noise at the rear of the room drew everyone's attention. Turning, Sadie saw Joshua enter, carrying a cardboard box. He made his way to the defendant's table and set the box on the floor between her and

Childress. They looked into the box then at each other. They both smiled.

"I apologize for the interruption," Joshua said to Colonel Barker.

"And just who are you, sir?" Barker asked.

"Joshua Sinclair. I'm part of Miss MacKenzie's defense team."

"Then please sit down. There will be no further interruptions."

"Yes, sir."

Joshua sat next to Sadie. She took his hand and gave it a squeeze.

"Officer Mahelona," Hoskins said. "I believe there was a question pending on the table. What made you think, when you saw this shoe in the trunk of the defendant's car, that it was Delbert Mooney's?"

"Because I've seen him wear those shoes many times."

"Thank you, Officer Mahelona. I have no more questions at this time."

"Officer Mahelona," Childress said before the witness could take a breath, "did you find a body at the Blowhole?"

"Sadie had already disposed of it."

"And you know this how?"

"We found Delbert's bloody shoe and no Delbert."

"Do you always assume Mooney is dead when you can't find him?"

"I do when I find his bloody shoe."

"You're sure the shoe before you belongs to Delbert Mooney?"

"I am quite certain, sir."

"I see." Childress reached into the cardboard box and extracted a brown-and-white oxford Brogue with wingtips. "What size shoe does Mooney wear?"

"Size ten."

Childress stood and approached the witness stand, then set the new shoe on the railing next to the bloody one. "What size shoe is that?"

Mahelona looked inside. "Ten."

"Is that Delbert Mooney's shoe?"

Mahelona sat silently. Sadie could see that he was calculating, as he always did. What answer would suit him best? If he said no, and it turned out the shoe had been delivered from Mooney's house, it would make him a liar. But if he said yes, and the shoe had come from some other source, his identification of the bloody shoe would be in question.

While Mahelona connived, Childress returned to the cardboard box. He picked it up and carried it to the witness stand. He took another identical brown-and-white oxford Brogue and placed it on the railing next to the first two.

"Is that Delbert Mooney's shoe?" Childress asked.

Mahelona stared at the shoes.

Childress pulled out another and set it on the railing. "Or that?" He reached into the box and produced yet another, and another, and another. "Or that? Or that? Or that?"

Mahelona remained mute.

"The truth is, Officer," Childress said, "you don't know if any or all of those shoes belong to Delbert Mooney, do you?"

"No, I don't," Mahelona said at last, and obviously with some pain.

Childress grabbed the bloody shoe and held it under Mahelona's nose. "Nor do you know if this shoe belongs to Mooney, do you?"

"No."

"Or if that is Mooney's blood? Or if Mooney is even dead, do you?"

Silence.

"Officer Mahelona, I have asked you a question, and I remind you that you're under oath. So I ask you again, is that Mooney's shoe?"

Mahelona tore his eyes away from the shoe, looked at Sadie, then at Childress. "I don't know."

Sadie exchanged a glance with Joshua, who nodded, but his face remained grim. Sadie knew this was likely a hollow victory. Although Childress had scored what would have been a strong point in a jury trial in a civilian courtroom, she understood that in this tribunal, the issue of Mooney's demise was really not an issue at all, but a foregone conclusion. Everybody believed the bloody shoe to be Mooney's, and its presence in the trunk of her car was damning. Whether there was legal proof beyond a reasonable doubt was irrelevant. It would be hard to fault Colonel Barker if he had such an attitude. After all, Mooney was in fact dead and, by now, his pulverized body was shark bait. Still, Childress and Joshua were putting up a sterling fight. She would not begrudge them the inevitable verdict.

The sound of voices interrupted the proceedings. Mahelona was just leaving the witness stand, dismissed after his inept testimony, when the door behind them burst open. Sadie spun, as did Joshua and Childress, to see the source of the interruption. Rob Sandford strode confidently into the courtroom, his hand firmly clenched on the arm of Ricky, whom he dragged into the room. Ricky's face was contorted by pain from the firmness of Rob's grasp of his elbow.

Colonel Barker snapped, "Sergeant, you're disrupting these proceedings."

"I apologize, Colonel, but I have an eyewitness," Rob said.

"We already have eyewitnesses, soldier."

"To Mooney's death?"

Barker's face went slack. "You mean this boy actually witnessed Mooney's murder?"

"No, sir. I mean he witnessed Mooney's death by self-defense."

Hoskins leaped to his feet. "Objection. The defendant has not claimed that she killed Mooney in self-defense."

"No," Barker said. "The defense appears to be that there is no evidence that Mooney is even dead, but apparently this witness can establish that for you. That's a big hurdle overcome for you, isn't it?"

"But self-defense is a surprise. I'll need time to prepare."

"How do you know you'll need time until you hear what this witness has to say?"

While Barker and Hoskins debated, Childress and Joshua seemed stunned by the new events. Sadie leaned toward them and whispered, "You mustn't let Ricky testify."

"Why not?" Childress asked.

"You simply can't. He's a child."

"He can prove your innocence, can't he?" Joshua asked. "By establishing his own guilt."

"Is that true?" Childress asked.

Sadie said nothing in response, thereby giving Childress his answer.

"Miss MacKenzie, I'm your attorney, and I must make my decisions based upon my judgment as to what is best for your defense," Childress said.

"Some things are so horrible that they must never see the light of day," Sadie said. "Ricky is a boy, with no one to look after him."

"Sadie, my dear," Joshua said, "he's not your responsibility."

"I have made him my responsibility, just as you have made me yours. And I'm telling you that you cannot let him testify."

"Miss MacKenzie," Childress said, "I'm afraid it may not be my decision to make."

"Lieutenant Childress!" Barker said. There was a harsh edge to his tone.

Childress stood at attention. "Yes, sir?"

"I hate to break up your little tea party, but I asked you a question. Do you have any objection to putting this witness on the stand? I assume that you don't."

"I don't know what this witness has to say, sir."

"None of us do. But the sergeant here seems convinced that he has relevant testimony to give, and I think we all need to hear it. So, to repeat, do you have any objection?"

Childress looked at Sadie, who pled with her eyes. Childress heaved his shoulders in a sigh. "I have no objection, sir."

Sadie sprang to her feet. "Then I want to testify."

Joshua grabbed her arm and tugged. "Sadie, please sit."

She yanked her arm away from him. "Colonel Barker, I want to testify."

"Does your counsel concur?"

Childress and Joshua answered in unison. "We do not."

"Well, then, that sort of puts us in a pickle, doesn't it?"

"Don't I have a right to speak in my own defense?" she asked.

"You do, but I urge you to exercise caution. Your counsel, who are both trained in the law, don't seem to think that's such a good idea."

"I thought a trial was supposed to be about the search for the truth."

"That's why I think we should hear what this young man has to say."

"But you don't need to hear what he has to say if you hear what I have to say."

"Oh?" Barker said. "And just why is that?"

"Because I killed Mooney."

Chapter Forty-Four

IT SEEMED FOR a moment as if all the air had been drained from the room. Hoskins was at a loss, his victory having just been handed to him on a silver platter. Childress seemed resigned to his fate. Joshua and Rob were both crestfallen, their desperate efforts to save Sadie apparently having come to naught. Even Colonel Barker appeared shocked at this turn of events. This was clearly out of the ordinary in the military's courts, where guilty verdicts were routine, albeit usually with more effort required than Sadie's spontaneous confession.

Ricky met eyes with Sadie. She smiled at him, as if to say "everything's okay; I'll take care of you."

"I killed the son of a bitch," Ricky blurted out. "And I'm glad."

Barker leaned forward on his elbows, his hands clasped on the table. He looked from Sadie to Ricky and back to Sadie again.

"Here's what we're going to do," he said at last. "We'll hear from this new witness and then we'll hear from Miss MacKenzie. Then I'll make my decision."

"Sir, I object," Childress said. "Miss MacKenzie has Fifth Amendment rights that she has—"

"Just waived," Barker said. "And now that she has, it seems that your best legal strategy would be to let her explain her confession." Childress remained standing, prepared to press his objection. Barker added, "Son, sometimes a lawyer has to just step aside and let the truth come out."

Childress nodded. "Sir, yes sir." He sat, stunned.

"Co-counsel?" Barker asked Joshua.

Joshua turned to Sadie and took her hand in his. He searched her eyes as if searching her heart.

"Are you sure you want to testify?" he asked.

"It's something I must do, Joshua."

"Then I'm here beside you." He turned back to Barker. "We withdraw our objection."

"All right," Barker said, "Sergeant, please escort this young man to the witness stand."

As Rob led Ricky forward, Sadie willed him to be strong. He had spent his life struggling to survive, pretty much on his own from a young age, on the streets, offering himself up to deviants for a quarter here and a dollar there, all with the goal merely of feeding himself day to day, but long since having given up on love, comfort, and security. A life spent much as Sadie's had been for the past few years—full of exploitation and degradation, devoid of self-respect and, most importantly, devoid of hope.

Ricky settled into the hard-backed witness chair, seeming much smaller than he actually was. His frail frame was dwarfed by the high back of the chair and the raised dais next to him, and was virtually squashed by the full weight of military authority in the room. He placed his hand on an offered *Bible* and agreed to an oath to tell the truth, the whole truth, and nothing but the truth, so help him God.

Colonel Barker took over the questioning. "Tell us your whole name, son," he said in a kindly, almost grandfatherly tone.

"Ricky Kahike." His voice came out in a soft whisper, accompanied by a tremble. He turned his head and looked squarely at Barker as he answered each question.

"Do you know Officer Delbert Mooney?"

"I do."

"How do you know Officer Mooney?"

"He gives me money sometimes."

"Gives you money for what?"

Ricky paused. He looked at Sadie, tears in his eyes. Tears in her eyes, as well.

"Son," Barker said, "what does he give you money for?"

Sadie nodded at him.

"Money to let him do things," Ricky said. "Sex things."

"Were you a pimp? Did you find girls for him?"

"If he wanted girls, he could go to Hotel Street."

"Then what kind of sex things?" Barker asked.

Ricky dropped his head. His shoulders shook and a steady rat-a-tat of tears dropped into his lap. "Sex things to me."

"You mean homosexual things?"

"Yes."

A visible wave of revulsion passed across Barker's face. For a moment, Sadie was heartened that Barker would come to believe what she had believed since the day she first arrived in Honolulu: Mooney deserved to die.

When Barker spoke again, there was a tremble in his voice that fairly matched that in Ricky's. "Son, why don't you tell us what happened the other night with Officer Mooney?"

Ricky raised his head and looked at Barker again, then returned his sights to Sadie. She again willed him to be strong. He nodded a silent acknowledgement of her support.

"Mooney picked me up in his mama's car. He said he had money."

"Come on Ricky," Mooney said. He waved a handful of bills in Ricky's face as the boy leaned over the open passenger window of the Buick Roadmaster.

"That's a lot of money," Ricky said.

"It's all yours if you want it. Get in."

Ricky opened the door and slid into the passenger seat. The first thing he noticed was what looked like blood spatters on Mooney's pants and shirt.

"Did you hurt yourself, Mooney?"

"What?"

"Is that blood?"

Mooney looked at himself, as if seeing the blood for the first time. He remained silent, but Ricky noticed the knot in his jaw as Mooney clenched his teeth.

"What did you do, Mooney? Beat a whore again?"

"Yeah, I took care of a whore tonight. I took care of her real good."

"Did you take that money from her?"

Mooney didn't answer.

"Mooney, did you take that money from her?"

"Shut up."

"But Mooney—"

Mooney's right hand snapped off the steering wheel, fingers curled. His knuckles slammed into Ricky's cheek just below his left eye. Ricky rocketed back against the door; his head bounced off the window glass.

"I said shut up," Mooney said.

"Come on, brah, what you did that for?"

Tears filled Ricky's eyes and blurred his vision. It wasn't the first time Mooney, or some other son of a bitch, had struck him, and it wouldn't be the last. Sometimes they got excited when they beat him. Ricky knew that it was just their way of being able to convince themselves they weren't really deviant. As shame erupted within them, they would lash out at Ricky, as if he were somehow responsible for their urges. Or so they thought. Funny how the shame never changed what they were going to do; it would merely smolder inside them until the next time it erupted in knuckles and kicking feet.

Ricky did what he always did to soothe the beast. He put his hand on Mooney's crotch and rubbed, but stayed quiet. Just a silent reminder of what was to come.

On Ala Moana Boulevard, the road narrowed and roughened as they drew nearer to the old animal quarantine station. Mooney stared hard at the rearview mirror of the car. Ricky noticed a tightening of his jaw.

"What's the matter, Mooney?"

"I thought I saw a car back there."

Ricky turned and looked out the back at nothing but blackness.

"There's nobody there."

"I thought I saw headlights, but they're gone now."

"Like I said, nobody there. Just you and me out here, brah. And I'm gonna take care of you good."

Mooney pulled the Roadmaster to the side of the dirt road. He sat for a moment, his eyes glued to the rearview mirror. Ricky opened his door and got out. A few seconds later, Mooney got out. He looked down the road behind them, squinting in the darkness. He twisted his head, like a dog listening to its master.

"Do you hear something?" Mooney asked.

"I don't hear nothing."

Ricky ducked into the trees, and Mooney followed. Ricky had been here before, with Mooney as well as others. It was far from the crowds of Waikiki or the teeming throngs in Chinatown. Isolated and, for the men who brought him here, safe. They reached the clearing that had served as a bedroom for so many trysts over the past few years that Ricky was almost surprised it didn't have maid service. He took Mooney by the hand and led him to the center of the clearing, then turned to face him.

He ran his hand across Mooney's cheek. The stubble of Mooney's whiskers scratched at his flesh. Mooney put his hand on Ricky's cheek and held it there.

Mooney seemed odd tonight, Ricky thought, more distant than usual. Something told him that more than a simple beating was in store for him, but what, he didn't know. He removed his hand from Mooney's cheek and tucked both hands into the back pockets of his tight shorts, as if adopting a casual stance. With his right hand, he made sure it was still there, tucked deep in the pocket.

"Show me your money," Ricky said.

Mooney kept silent as he reached into his pocket and removed a fold of bills. Ricky reached for it, but Mooney snatched it away and tucked it back into his pocket.

"You know the rules," Mooney said. He bared his teeth. "Play first; pay later."

"You don't trust me?"

"I don't trust anybody."

An absolute truth, Ricky knew. He dropped to his knees, opened Mooney's fly, and extracted his rigid member. There was something on it. Difficult to see in the darkness, just shadowy splotches. Wet and sticky. Had Mooney already come? Ricky tilted his head to allow in moonlight from over his shoulder so he could see better.

"Mooney, there's blood on it!"

Ricky let go, stood, and stepped back, wiping his hands on his shirt. Mooney had said he took care of a whore. Had he killed her? Was it Sadie?

Mooney grabbed him by the shoulders and forced him back to his knees. He put one hand behind Ricky's head and pulled it toward his bloody penis. Ricky leaned back with his whole body, pressing hard against Mooney's hand.

"Just do it," Mooney said.

"You gotta disease?"

Mooney kept pulling. "Do it."

"I nevah saw blood on one before."

Mooney let go of Ricky's head and took the money from his pocket again. He held it over Ricky's head. Ricky snatched at it, but Mooney dropped it on the ground beside him.

"It's all yours," Mooney said. "Just forget about the blood."

Ricky grabbed the money and slid it close. He took Mooney in his mouth. It tasted coppery, the blood lubricating his lips. He closed his eyes and earned his pay.

When Mooney started the humming sound that always preceded his orgasm, Ricky increased the tempo of his efforts. He was ready to get this over with, take his money, and go. The hum grew louder, then higher in pitch. Ricky opened his eyes and rolled them upward to catch a peek. Mooney's arms were raised over his head, his hands clenched, his face aimed skyward. The hum became a screech, like an animal in a zoo. Mooney exploded into Ricky's mouth with more force than he had ever felt. Ricky let go, rocked back on his heels, and looked up at Mooney.

Mooney's right fist slammed down onto his face. Ricky pitched over to the ground and lay still. Still, except for his hand working its way to his back pocket for the switchblade. Ricky knew only one of them would walk from this clearing tonight—either Mooney or Ricky.

Mooney straddled Ricky's body, fists raised again.

Sadie's voice came out of nowhere. "Mooney!"

Mooney turned his head in the direction of her voice.

Ricky pulled out the switchblade and exposed the blade. Then he drove it into Mooney's throat.

Chapter Forty-Five

"THAT'S NOT WHAT happened," Sadie said as she rose to her feet.

Ricky stopped speaking and dropped his head. Tears streamed down his cheeks.

Barker addressed Rob. "Sergeant, escort this young man from the stand, but stay close."

"Yes, sir." Rob approached the stand, where Ricky still sat head down, sobbing. He spoke gently. "Come on, Ricky. Let's go."

Ricky looked up. When he spoke, his voice was barely audible to any except Rob and Barker. "I told the truth."

"I know you did," Rob said.

He took Ricky by the arm and led him out of the courtroom. After the door closed behind them, Barker said, "Miss MacKenzie, please take the stand."

Sadie, who had felt so bold just moments before, suddenly realized her legs were barely capable of supporting her to merely stand, much less to walk those ten steps to the witness chair. Joshua placed his arm around her, and she leaned on him as they walked, confident that she would fall if he were to move. Once she was seated, a uniformed officer approached with a *Bible* in hand and extended it toward her.

"Place your right hand on the *Bible*," the officer said.

She complied and closed her eyes as he spoke again. "Do you swear to tell the truth, the whole truth, and nothing but the truth, so help you God?"

God? The same God who had brought her to Hotel Street and sold her into bondage? The same God who had permitted her to daily degrade herself, body and spirit, with strangers? Who had taken her mother and father and brother from her? And who had now deposited her on the witness stand to implicate herself in the death of Mooney? Did she even believe in such a God anymore?

But then she remembered that even the Israelites—the Children of God—had been taken into bondage in Egypt, then wandered in the Wilderness for forty years before reaching the Promised Land. And by so doing, God had tested their faith. Was that what was happening to her? Was Hotel Street her Egypt and her spiritual despair her Wilderness? Was God merely testing her faith as he had the Israelites? If so, she determined that she would not be found wanting.

"I do."

She sat and looked at Joshua, who had returned to the defendant's table. She read compassion in his eyes, as she had for the entire time she had known him. Her guardian angel. No, God had not abandoned her.

"Miss MacKenzie," Barker said. "I admonish you that you are under oath. You heard Ricky Kahike's testimony, which was also under oath. Now, think long and hard about what you're going to say. Just tell us what happened that night with Officer Mooney."

Sadie took a deep breath. "It started when I realized someone had been in my house. I knew it had to be Mooney."

Sadie watched from her hiding place as Mooney delivered a heavy blow with his knuckles to Ricky's face. When Ricky collapsed, Mooney straddled his body and raised his fist again.

"Mooney!" Sadie yelled.

She charged across the clearing. Startled, Mooney turned his head at the sound of her voice.

"You!" he said. He stood, ignoring Ricky, who scrambled away on his hands and knees. He faced off with Sadie. "I've always dreamed of this," Mooney said. "The chance to deal with you once and for all."

"You killed your mother," Sadie said.

"She was a whore."

"As am I."

"And you'll die, too."

"Not at your hands." She held up the knife, and moonlight glinted off its blade. "Is this your mother's blood?"

Mooney laughed. "Am I supposed to be scared by a skinny waif like you, just because you're armed with a knife?"

She reached into her pocket for the derringer, but it seemed to elude her grasp. Just as she pulled it from her pocket, Mooney stepped closer, and his fist suddenly shot forward. Knuckles slammed into Sadie's chin. She staggered backward a step. The derringer flew from her hand into nearby brush. Fireworks shot across her vision and a haze moved in on her consciousness, but she kept her feet.

"Come on, girl. You still have the knife. Use it." He opened his coat. "See, no gun. You have me at a disadvantage."

"You're never at a disadvantage."

He growled his laugh again. "That's something you ought to keep in mind when you wake up a grizzly bear."

"And you're the bear, I suppose?"

"Aye. I'm the bear."

With a scream, Ricky launched himself onto Mooney's back. He wrapped his arms around Mooney's head and clawed his fingernails at Mooney's face. Mooney reached behind him, grabbed Ricky by the back of the neck, and, with one move, swung him up and over, flat on his back onto the ground. Just as he pulled back his foot to swing a heavy shoe into Ricky's face, Sadie lunged forward with the knife and drove it into his back up to the hilt.

Chapter Forty-Six

THERE WAS SILENCE in the courtroom as Colonel Barker re-entered and somberly took his seat on the dais. Sadie sat next to Joshua and fought back tears, not wanting to break down as Ricky had done earlier. Joshua's face was ashen, a color she was sure was reflected in her own countenance.

Colonel Barker sat silently for a moment. He cleared his throat and began to speak. "As I said before, we've got ourselves quite an interesting situation. We have two witnesses who have both confessed to the killing of Delbert Mooney. Their stories are identical up to a point, and then they diverge. Some people might call that reasonable doubt. But I call it perjury. By someone. Both witnesses can't be telling the truth. One of them is lying, and if I can figure out who that is, I should throw them in jail."

Joshua grabbed Sadie's hand and clutched it tightly.

"But there is one overriding factor," Barker continued, "one consistency in both testimonies. And that is the conduct of Officer Mooney. Two things are clear to me: One, Officer Mooney engaged in deviant sexual behavior with a minor, and two, he was killed in self-defense. Either by Ricky Kahike in defense of himself or by Sadie MacKenzie in the defense of Ricky Kahike. Regardless of who delivered the knife assault, the motivation was clear and, under the law, justified."

Sadie sat stunned, unsure what she was hearing. She looked at Joshua, who smiled broadly.

"Miss MacKenzie," Barker said, "I find you not guilty of the charges against you. You are free to go."

Chapter Forty-Seven

SADIE STOOD ON the pier with Joshua. Next to her sat the same battered valise that she had carried when she disembarked from the *Lurline* just days before the Pearl Harbor attack. She gazed up at the Navy transport ship *U.S. Grant*, which had originally been built for the transatlantic passenger trade after the turn of the century. It had served as a troop ship during the war and, in early 1942, carried Japanese residents of Hawaii to the west coast to be delivered to internment camps. Putting that sordid bit of history behind, it now traveled between the Islands and the west coast on missions of mercy, carrying hospital patients and wounded soldiers from Hawaii to facilities on the mainland. That summer day in 1944, it would carry Sadie to California.

"I hoped Robert would be here," she said. She had not seen him since the end of the so-called trial three days earlier. The intervening time had been filled with activity as she, with Joshua's help, got her financial affairs in order and prepared to leave. Now that moment was at hand.

"I'm sure he has duties at Schofield," Joshua said. "I have no doubt he would be here if he could."

"You'll take care of Ricky?" she asked.

"Nani is taking him shopping for clothes, as we speak."

She turned to face Joshua, who smiled at her. Throughout her ordeal, the love of this man had helped to carry her. She knew, but would not say aloud, that she would never see him again, and the thought broke her heart.

He pulled his pocket watch from his vest and glanced at it. "I'm afraid it's time for you to board the ship."

Suddenly overcome with emotion, she threw her arms around him and wept on his shoulder. He squeezed her tightly, and his tears tickled her cheek. When they broke their embrace, she grabbed her valise and hurried up the gangplank.

As the *U.S. Grant* broke its moorings and moved to sea, she stood on the port side and watched as Joshua faded from sight. In two-and-a-half short years, he had filled a gap in her heart left by the loss of her parents. She knew, too, that she had filled a gap in his, though he had never spoken of it. They were two lost souls brought together by fate, and each had saved the other. She had saved him from loneliness, and he had saved her from the moral abyss. Even after the things she had done, Joshua had loved her unconditionally and he had believed in her. He had seen something in her worth saving. She owed it to him to put this chapter of her life behind her and to do something with the next chapter. Something big. Something good. Something worthy of him.

As Waikiki passed by, she remembered the first time she had walked in the cool white sand and felt the foam of the surf around her ankles. When she first arrived, she had been forbidden to do that very thing, but the war in the Pacific had brought changes to Hawaii that no one would have dreamed possible. And so she had walked that beach.

Soon Diamond Head passed and the *U.S. Grant* moved into the open Pacific. Sadie strolled to the bow of the ship, where she faced the future and turned her back forevermore on the isle of broken dreams.

Epilogue

BY THE END of the summer of 1944, with the desperate Japanese on their last legs in the Pacific, the police had regained control of Hotel Street from the military. On September 21, Territorial Governor Ingram Stainback issued an order shutting down the regulated brothels in the Territory and, on September 22, members of the vice squad went door to door to ensure that business was at an end. The heyday of Hotel Street was over by the close of business that day.

In the spring of 1946, a jazz nightclub opened on the eastern fringes of downtown Dallas, Texas, in a part of town known as Deep Ellum, an area eerily similar in some respects to Hotel Street. Filled with tattoo parlors, nightclubs, saloons, and pawn shops, it was the breeding ground for the careers of musicians such as Blind Lemon Jefferson, Robert Johnson, and Leadbelly Ledbetter.

The new nightclub, called *Joshua*, was managed by a young man named Billy, and its owner was also its star performer, a young singer with a scar on her forehead, known simply as Sadie. A woman of mystery, she was reputed to be one of the richest women in Dallas, but also to have dark secrets in her past. Her repertoire included hits by Dinah Shore and Billie Holiday, but she soon branched out to include originals she wrote for herself. Many of the new numbers included references to tropical breezes and exotic locales, and she often mixed into her shows traditional music from the Hawaiian Islands. Her signature song, though, was a rendition of a Billie Holiday favorite with which she ended every show, and it never failed to bring tears to the eyes of her audience.

One night in the early fall of 1946, a young soldier in uniform entered *Joshua* and took a table alone at the back. He was not the usual sort of customer, and very few seemed to notice him. That night, as Sadie concluded her show, the young soldier stood from his table in the shadows and added his harmony to her song. It was the first time that most of the customers realized a man of color was in their midst, but his mellow baritone voice quickly soothed any concerns. Tears flowed in *Joshua* as the two sang together.

Tears from the customers.

Tears from Sadie.

And tears from Robert Sandford, whose long search had finally come to an end.

> *Them that's got shall get,*
> *Them that's not shall lose,*
> *So the Bible said and it still is news.*
> *Mama may have, Papa may have,*
> *But God bless the child that's got his own,*
> *That's got his own.*

Source Notes: Hotel Street

WHEN I FIRST started researching Hotel Street and its history for *Isle of Broken Dreams*, I knew virtually nothing about it. Other than mentions in James Jones's *From Here to Eternity* and the occasional reference in episodes of *Magnum, P.I.*, Hotel Street was a blank slate for me. What I soon learned helped direct the story of Sadie MacKenzie as she struggled to fight her way out of Hotel Street, which proved to be as fascinating as it was bizarre.

Many of the events, people, and things depicted in the novel are real, including the "rules"—the "you-may-nots"—that governed the sporting girls of Hotel Street; Major Steer's proclamation following the Pearl Harbor attack that "The price of meat is still three dollars;" the struggle between the police and the military as to who would be responsible for regulating Hotel Street; and the prostitute strike in the summer of 1942. Some things you just can't make up; only Sadie's story is fiction.

After a quick bit of research, I turned up two great resources to start my education on the backdrop for the story, both of which sent me scurrying to other sources. The first was a wonderful study written in 1992 by Professors Beth Bailey and David Farber for the *Radical History Review*, called "Hotel Street: Prostitution and the Politics of War." According to a footnote, the article was drawn from their upcoming book called *The First Strange Place: Race and Sex in World War II Hawaii*, published that same year by Free Press.

Later in 1992, another excerpt from the book was published in *MARHO: The Radical Historian's Organization, Inc.*, under the title "Prostitutes on Strike: The Women of Hotel Street During World War II." I quickly located and obtained a copy of the book, which had been re-

released by The Johns Hopkins University Press, and which filled in more of the details, not only of Hotel Street, but of the entire culture of sex and race during the war.

The second resource was a documentary produced by Rhys Thomas called *Sex in World War II: The Pacific Front*, which aired on The History Channel in 2002. It was the perfect complement to the work of professors Bailey and Farber, and broadened my research even further.

In my research, I was first introduced to a woman who was probably the most well-known, or notorious, prostitute in Hotel Street, Jean O'Hara, who flaunted her profession by moving her trade outside of Hotel Street and cavorting around town in a fancy automobile. O'Hara scandalized Honolulu when, after being indicted on criminal charges of assault and battery against a police officer (who had actually, it appears, beaten her instead of vice versa), she published her story and released it on the streets of Honolulu, under the title *My Life as a Honolulu Prostitute*, later republished as *Honolulu Harlot*. Arguably what she had really been indicted for was being too brazen a whore. O'Hara responded by filing suit against the police department, which capitulated and dropped the charges.

Ms. O'Hara may or may not have been the inspiration for the heroine in the only novel I am aware of that fully captured life on Hotel Street, *The Revolt of Mamie Stover* (Signet Books 1951), by William Bradford Huie, a novel which, itself, scandalized America.

Other great sources for filling in the historical gaps about Hotel Street include Richard Greer's article in *The Hawaiian Journal of History* called "Dousing Honolulu's Red Lights" and Ted Chernin's article, also in *The Hawaiian Journal of History*, called "My Experiences in the Honolulu Chinatown Red-Light District," based upon his time in Honolulu during World War II. Other more scholarly articles, in the vein of professors Bailey and Farber, include "Prostitution: Protected in Paradise?" (*University of Hawaii Law Review*) and Marilyn Elizabeth Hegarty's doctoral dissertation at The Ohio State University in 1998, entitled *Patriots, Prostitutes, Patriotutes: The Mobilization and Control of Female Sexuality in the United States During World War II*.

For information on martial law in World War II Hawaii, nothing could top two wonderful law review articles written by Garner Anthony during the early and mid-points of the war and published in the *California Law Review*. The first, published in May of 1942, is called "Martial Law in Hawaii," and the second, published in December of 1943, is called "Martial Law, Military Government and the Writ of Habeas Corpus in Hawaii." Interestingly, the author, Garner Anthony, is identified in a footnote to the first article as "Practicing attorney, Honolulu, Hawaii," while in the second he is identified as "Attorney General, Territory of Hawaii." He also argued several court cases involving the legality of martial law; his credentials for the topic seem solid to me.

To learn more about the suspension of the writ of habeas corpus, and being a lawyer myself, I dug into case law, relying heavily upon two cases that were argued by Garner Anthony, author of the two *California Law Review* articles. One of those cases, *Duncan v. Kahanomoku*, 327 U.S. 304 (1946) originated in 1944 as *Ex Parte Duncan*, 66 F. Supp. 976 (D. Hawaii 1944) and reached the United States Supreme Court shortly after the end of the war.

The other case, *Ex Parte White*, 66 F. Supp. 982 (D. Hawaii 1944), includes language that states: "It was stipulated that if Albert Cristy, Senior Judge of the Circuit Court, First Judicial District, Territory of Hawaii, were called he would testify to the same effect as he did in *Ex Parte Duncan*, D.C., 66 F. Supp. 976, to wit, that he knew of no reason why the civil courts of the Territory could not have functioned normally in August 1942 and they would have done so except for military orders to the contrary." Is it any wonder, then, that the fictional lawyer Joshua Sinclair sought out the real-life Judge Albert Cristy in his efforts to obtain a writ of habeas corpus on Sadie's behalf?

I relied on numerous sources for a study of life in Honolulu, both before and after the Pearl Harbor attack. One particularly helpful book, primarily because of the photographic record it presents, is *Hawaii Goes to War: Life in Hawaii from Pearl Harbor to Peace*, by DeSoto Brown (Editions Limited 1989). Others include *At Dawn We Slept: The Untold Story of Pearl Harbor*, by Gordon W. Prange (McGraw-Hill 1981), *Target: Pearl Harbor*, by Michael Slackman (University of Hawaii Press 1990), and a compilation of articles edited by Bob Dye called *Hawaii Chronicles III: World War Two in Hawaii, from the pages of Paradise of the Pacific* (University of Hawaii Press 2000).

And for the description of Sadie's passage to Hawaii from San Francisco, I am indebted to Lynn Blocker Krantz, Nick Krantz, and Mary Thiele Fobian for their wonderful photographic essay and text in *To Honolulu in Five Days: Cruising Aboard Matson's S.S. Lurline* (Ten Speed Press 2001).

I hope you were intrigued by this strange world I found in World War II Honolulu, and I hope my presentation of the backdrop against which Sadie's story played out was delivered as accurately as possible. Obviously I took literary license in some respects, but throughout I tried to remain as true as possible to the actual historical facts and to the spirit of the time and, quite frankly, to the spirit of the sporting girls of Hotel Street who served key, although controversial, roles in American history.